GONE

GONE

A SHADOW SLAYERS STORY

NELLIE H. STEELE

A Novel Idea Publishing

*For my Dad, Paul
Happy Birthday!*

ACKNOWLEDGMENTS

A HUGE thank you to everyone who helped get this book published! Special shout outs to: Stephanie Sovak, Paul Sovak, Michelle Cheplic, Mark D'Angelo and Lori D'Angelo.

Finally, a HUGE thank you to you, the reader!

CHAPTER 1

*D*amien's heart thudded in his chest as he stared at Gray and Alexander. "What do you mean she's gone?"

Having just returned triumphant with Michael after retrieving Celine's portrait from 1791, he stood stunned by the news that Celine was missing.

"I told you," Gray answered. "No one has seen or heard from Celine in almost a week. Since the night she sent you back to 1791. She hasn't called, texted, or come home. We can't find her. She's gone."

Damien stalked a few steps away, disbelief on his face. Michael approached him, putting a steadying hand on his shoulder.

"I realize this is difficult to hear, Damien," Alexander began, his British accent still strong despite the centuries of life in America.

"Difficult to hear?" Damien interrupted, incredulous at the comment. "Difficult to hear? No, difficult to hear is 'you lost your job' or 'I'm leaving you for your brother.' No, this isn't difficult to hear this is… this is… incomprehensible!" Damien raked a shaky hand through his brown hair.

"Damien, please," Alexander replied. "You've been through quite a bit. You're tired and upset. Why don't we…"

Damien spun to face him. "Upset? You're damn right I'm upset!"

"Hey, Damien," Michael said, squeezing his shoulder. "We'll find her, man. Let's go grab a drink and discuss this."

"Grab a drink? Are you serious? This isn't a case of a lost set of keys or a misplaced article of clothing! Celine is gone! For a week! We need to be out there searching for her, finding her!"

"Don't you think we've tried that?" Gray questioned.

"I have no idea what you've done!" Damien snapped. "When was the last time she was seen? By whom? Where could she have gone? And why?"

"I agree with Michael," Alexander stated. "Why don't we reconvene in the sitting room. We can discuss the details there."

Damien threw his arms in the air in frustration.

"There is nothing to do right now, Damien. Michael is correct, we will find her, but it will not be tonight. And it will not be by executing an ill-conceived plan."

Damien sighed, nodding his head. "All right," he assented, his voice just above a whisper as he stared at nothing.

"Come on, man," Michael prompted him. "Let's head down for that drink. We both can use one."

"Damien," Alexander said before they departed.

Damien twisted to look at him.

"We will find her."

Damien nodded as Michael led him from the room.

Alexander followed, turning back to find Gray still standing in the room. "Coming, cousin?"

"Yes," Gray answered, "but I want to re-hang this picture first. We need it, now more than ever."

"Let me help," Alexander replied, picking up one side of the painting while Gray grabbed the other. Together, they carried the portrait of Celine downstairs and hung it above the fireplace in the foyer. "It's good to see it back in its rightful place."

"I agree. Now if we could only retrieve Celine. At least the portrait can protect us until she is back."

"Shall we join Michael and Damien?" Alexander questioned.

"Yes. As much as I don't want to relive the last few days, they have a right to receive answers to their questions."

"He's just as upset as you are, Gray. Please try to remember that."

"I realize that. And Celine would want me to remember that, too."

Gray and Alexander entered the sitting room. An orange glow lit the room, emanating from the fireplace. Michael and Damien both nursed brandies. Michael paced the room while Damien sat near the fireplace. He hunched over his drink, staring into it as though it held the answers to all his questions.

Gray poured a brandy for Alexander and himself. "Listen, Damien," he began, "I realize what a shock this is. It was to me, too. We all want to find Celine and we will."

Damien's leg bobbed up and down. "I don't understand. How could she just disappear? Could this have something to do with our visit to the adjudicator? Was this my fault?"

"For not being related by blood, you are just like her," Gray murmured, shaking his head as he sipped his brandy.

"What?" Damien questioned.

"It isn't your fault, Damien," Alexander reassured him.

"The last time she visited the adjudicator she disappeared for twenty-five years," Damien replied.

"I'm well aware of what happened the last time. I don't need to be reminded," Gray answered. He paused for a moment. "But Alexander is correct. This has nothing to do with the adjudicator."

"How can you be so sure?" Michael chimed in.

"Adjudicators do not revisit prior decisions or conversations," Alexander explained. "If the adjudicator planned to do something to Celine, it would have done it at your meeting. Not after."

Damien let the information sink in. "You say she disappeared the night we left for 1791?"

"Yes," Gray answered. "I found a note in our bedroom. She wrote she was going to meet Celeste. She didn't say where. That was the last correspondence any of us had with her."

Damien leapt from his seat, pacing the room as he digested the information. "And you spoke with Celeste?"

Gray glared at him. "Yes, of course I spoke with Celeste. When she didn't come home, that's the first person I talked to."

"And she said what?" Damien questioned.

"She said she spoke with Celine around ten. They spoke for about fifteen minutes before they parted ways. It appeared Celine was returning home when she left. That was the last Celeste saw of her," Gray explained.

Damien pondered it a moment. "And the note was in Celine's handwriting?"

"Yes," Gray answered, wrinkling his brow.

"What did she speak with Celeste about?" Michael queried.

"According to Celeste, she asked to meet Celine to discuss the physical symptoms Celine was experiencing. The painful memories. Celeste was concerned Celine's involvement in creating her vampiric condition led to Celine's symptoms. Celeste felt compelled to tell Celine she did not hold her responsible. She was concerned the stress would harm Celine," Gray responded.

"I want to talk to Celeste," Damien requested.

"No!" Gray barked.

"What? Why?" Damien asked.

"You're not going anywhere near Celeste in her condition. Either of you."

"She is the last one to have seen Celine. She may have information we need!" Damien entreated.

"We've already spoken to her. Both of us," Gray said, pointing between himself and Alexander.

"But you may have missed something. Something I can pick up on!" Damien insisted.

"The answer is no," Gray answered.

"Perhaps it should be arranged," Alexander suggested.

"Are you crazy, Alex? If something happens to either of them, Celine will never forgive us."

"We should keep Michael away, I agree. But Celeste wouldn't be foolish enough to attack Damien. I will go with him. It should be safe," Alexander suggested.

Gray considered it for a moment. "Fine. Speak with her again. Just be sure she keeps her distance from him."

"Great!" Damien exclaimed. "Let's go."

"Just a moment, Damien. We should postpone this discussion until you've both had some proper rest."

"Proper rest? Are you kidding? I can't rest!"

"Damien, your conversation with Celeste is useless if you are too tired to process the information," Alexander stated.

"Okay, okay, fine. Tomorrow night then," Damien agreed. "So, what else can you tell us?"

"There isn't much else," Gray admitted. "Celeste was the

last to see her. There has been no trace of her. We've checked buildings on the estate, checked in town. There's nothing."

"I realize you said this had nothing to do with the adjudicator," Damien said, "but 'disappeared without a trace' sounds supernatural, doesn't it?"

"We were aware the last time she disappeared because of the adjudicator," Alexander answered. He paused, glancing to Gray. "We… were given the chance to say goodbye."

Damien swallowed hard, realizing how horrific that must have been for them. "But it's not like a normal person could have taken her, right? She'd just blast them with one her fireballs and come home."

Gray nodded. "You're right, it's not a normal person. She wasn't abducted. I'm not sure that knowledge helps us."

Damien collapsed onto the couch. "What a mess."

"Perhaps you and Michael should get some rest," Alexander suggested. "We'll start fresh in the morning."

"Or evening. Celeste will be unavailable in the morning," Damien answered.

Alexander chuckled at the statement. "Yes, but we can review other things."

"I couldn't sleep if I tried. Where is Celine and her special touch that puts people to sleep when you need her?" Damien jumped from the couch, pacing the room.

"I'm sure Millie can help you with that," Alexander suggested.

"A nice sedative, the doctor's favorite drug of choice," Michael lamented. He did not have fond memories of Millie's rounds of sedation as he recovered from his vampire bite, courtesy of Celeste.

"It's a good idea. You need your rest," Gray agreed.

Damien shook his head. "No, thanks. I'll go attempt to rest. I won't rest, but I don't want to be drugged. I need to keep a clear mind. What time should we reconvene?"

"Whenever you both feel up to it. We'll be here," Alexander assured him.

"Shoot for 7 a.m.?" Damien suggested.

"That's fine," Alexander answered.

"Great, see you tomorrow morning," Damien replied. Damien and Michael headed to the foyer, leaving Alexander and Gray remaining in the sitting room.

"Poor Damien. This is a lot for a human to bear," Alexander noted.

"Yes, the sedative will do him good."

"Too bad he refused it."

Gray sipped at his brandy. "Refused or not, he's getting it. They both are. I may need your help."

"Bold move, Gray. Is it necessary?"

"If we don't, he'll worry himself sick. And if anything happens to him while Celine is gone, she'll never forgive me. Come on, we've got our work cut out for us."

Gray set his glass down, striding from the room. He tracked down Millie, having her fill two syringes with a sedative.

* * *

Damien and Michael climbed the stairs and navigated the halls to their rooms.

"I'll see you in the morning," Michael said before ducking into his room. "I hope you sleep."

"You, too."

Damien entered his room. He glanced around, sighing. Tears formed in his eyes. Before going to 1791 to retrieve Celine's painting, he had spent several nights here with Celine. He recalled eating ice cream and discussing the mystery of her painful memories before falling asleep. She hadn't been concerned, spending her time worrying about

Michael's recovery and her sister's condition more than herself.

Celine's painful memories: another mystery they hadn't solved. When did it end? After centuries of being tormented by archenemy Duke Marcus Northcott, Celine had finally banished him to the netherworlds. With the torments from that evil man behind her, they had hoped to live a peaceful life. Instead, a variety of physical symptoms ranging from nausea to pain accompanied by memories shooting across her brain, plagued Celine. When hypnotized, Celine had admitted a presumption of danger caused these symptoms. They had never ascertained what the danger was because Damien and Michael were transported to 1791 to find Celine's missing portrait.

With that problem solved, they had returned home to find that Celine's problems had only worsened. Damien paced the floor.

"Where are you, Celine?" he asked to an empty room.

He changed his clothes, slipping into pajama pants and a t-shirt. He continued his pacing barefoot. His mind reeled. The incredulousness of the situation weighed on him. A dozen questions rattled through his mind. Why had they insisted he rest? He'd never be able to!

A knock sounded on his door. He glanced at it. Michael, he surmised. He must not be able to sleep either. A late-night planning session was just what they needed.

Damien plodded to the barrier, pulling it open. "Couldn't sleep either, huh? Oh, ah, sorry," he said as Gray entered the room. "Thought you were Michael."

"Sorry to disappoint," Gray replied. "Mind if I come in?"

"Well, you're already in, so I guess not," Damien answered.

"You're supposed to be asleep," Gray chided.

"I'll be all right," Damien replied.

"Let's make sure of that," Gray countered.

"Listen, Gray, I get that you want to do right by Celine but..." Damien began before Gray jabbed him with the needle. "Hey! What the hell? What are you... what're you doing?" Damien slurred as the fast-acting sedative took effect.

"We'll find Celine. Get some rest, Damien," Gray answered, walking him to the bed.

Gray let Damien fall onto the mattress, covering him with a blanket. He turned off the lights and exited the bedroom. He repeated the same maneuver with Michael, leaving him to rest as well. With Michael and Damien asleep, Gray returned to his suite for a long night of pacing.

* * *

CELINE STARED out of the small window into the night sky. The moon waned. Days had passed since Celine wandered into the mill's cellar, becoming trapped by Marcus Northcott. Celeste requested a meeting with her, luring her to the mill's basement. Celeste had not acted out of malice. She had been forced to do Marcus' bidding. Her vampiric condition costing her freedom of choice in the matter.

Celine heaved a sigh. No amount of supernatural force on her part had freed her from her prison. Marcus's enchantment of her cell held her fast, making escape impossible. It also made rescue impossible.

She had awoken earlier when a flood of new memories entered her mind. They provided evidence that her cousin, Damien, and friend, Michael, returned from their time traveling journey. They had retrieved the painting. Marcus confirmed that fact. Despite his loss of the painting, Marcus had joined her earlier to gloat. He lost the portrait but maintained his control of Celine herself.

Celine stood and shuffled to the window. She breathed in the cool night air. She longed to reunite with her family. She yearned to witness the excitement on Damien's face as he presented them with the painting. She craved observing Michael's cool demeanor as he let Damien shine. She desired to gaze into Gray's stormy blue eyes.

She shook her head, a tear rolling down her cheek as she imagined the shock on Damien's face when Gray informed him she was missing. Damien would take this the hardest. Guilt would ricochet through him. He'd insisted on solving the problem, even if it cost him his health. Damien wouldn't sleep, wouldn't eat until she was found. Yet, according to Marcus, no one would ever find her.

Celine imagined the world without her. Everyone would move on. They would be forced to. What would become of her? Would she spend eternity in this cell? No, she promised herself, she would rally. She would find a way. She had returned to Gray after a twenty-five-year absence. She would return to him again, she vowed.

"Admiring the stars, Celine?" a voice asked behind her.

She squeezed her eyes closed, annoyance filling her. "Haven't we spoken enough today, Marcus?"

"I assumed you'd be in a better mood. Your friends have returned triumphant! You should be overjoyed."

Celine stalked from the window to the door. "I'd love the chance to celebrate with them. Perhaps you'd be inclined to open the door and allow me a night out."

Marcus roared with laughter. "Oh, Celine, when did you become such a comedienne?"

"I wasn't joking," Celine countered.

"Then I am sorry to disappoint you, my dear. Any celebrations must be put on hold. Unless you'd care to celebrate with me."

Celine rolled her eyes, a grimace on her lips. "I wouldn't care to do anything with you."

"Oh, why do you insist on being so stubborn, Celine? Do you not realize the potential that exists by joining me?"

"Marcus, we have entertained this conversation many times already. My answer has and will always be 'no.'"

Marcus sighed. "Then I leave you alone to reconsider."

"There is nothing to reconsider, Marcus. We are at a stalemate!" Celine shouted as he walked away from her.

"No, my dear," he answered, turning to face her. "Stalemates exist when there is no way forward for either party. While I agree there is no way forward for you except to join me, I have multiple avenues yet to be pursued." He turned on his heel, stalking away.

Silence settled over the room as his footsteps receded. Celine returned to staring at the night's sky. Turmoil ruled her mind. Marcus was correct, he held the upper hand. Centuries of warring between them had gotten them nowhere. She left a wake of destruction and collateral damage wherever she traveled. How much more would she cost her family?

CHAPTER 2

*D*amien awoke to sunlight streaming through his window. He squinted against it as he checked the time. His eyes grew wide as he read it.

"Nine-thirty?!" he exclaimed, leaping from his bed. He opted for a quick shower before dressing, hoping it helped him become more alert. A haze clouded his mind.

As the hot water ran over him, Damien recalled the events of last night. Gray had administered a sedative against his wishes. Frustrated, he climbed from the shower. After wiping steam from the mirror, he stared at himself. A myriad of thoughts crowded his mind. He focused on all of them and none of them at the same time.

He stared at the mirror without seeing himself after a while. The room seemed to melt away as his mind drowned out everything except the buzz of his own thoughts. His eyes stared but did not see. Colors faded. Noises dampened.

A loud knock pulled him from his meditation. He swallowed hard, reviving himself. He pulled on his clothes before unlocking the door leading to Michael's bedroom.

"Morning," he greeted Michael.

"Morning," Michael answered. "Do you feel as bad as I do? I assume you got the royal treatment, too? A nice, unexpected needle shoved into your arm?"

"Yep," Damien admitted. "I haven't recovered yet. My head is a mess. I'm barely stringing thoughts together."

"What the hell was in that? It was like an industrial strength sedative. I've been asleep for ten hours!"

"Better question is why does Gray hate us so much? We just want to help find Celine!"

"No idea. Did the shower help at all?"

"Not much," Damien admitted. "I'll leave you to it. See you after for breakfast?"

"Yeah. I'll be quick, don't worry. We won't miss much more of the day."

Damien nodded, returning to his room to wait for Michael. He grabbed his laptop, pulling up his phone tracking app. He activated the tracker on Celine's phone. He and Michael used it before to track Celine here. Perhaps it would work again. He waited as it loaded. After a moment, the screen read NOT LOCATED. He sighed, slamming the laptop shut. He couldn't track her cell phone. Although being gone a week, her cell phone might be off or dead. He'd try again later, but this route appeared fruitless.

Michael appeared in fifteen minutes, showered, and dressed. "All right, let's get a start on finding Celine!"

Damien perched on the edge of the bed. He nodded without moving from his spot.

"You okay, buddy?"

Damien nodded his answer again.

"Hey, we will find her, Damien. We will. This is Celine. She's indestructible, right? You told me that."

"What if she's not?" Damien asked, his voice wavering.

"You can't think like that. Okay? We've got to think positive. We will find her."

Damien nodded again.

"We won't find her if we stay in this room all day."

This comment earned a chuckle from Damien. "Good point."

He stood, heaving a sigh.

Michael clapped him on the back, squeezing his shoulder. "Thanks, man."

"You were there for me when I went haywire with Celeste. My turn."

"Speaking of Celeste, you aren't experiencing any… effects again, are you?"

"Not one. Like it never happened," Michael assured him.

"And you'd tell me if you were?"

"Man, I hope so. I never want to live through that again."

They navigated downstairs to the kitchen, intent on making a light breakfast before seeking out Gray and Alexander. They made a large pot of strong coffee, hoping it lifted any remaining haze from their brains.

Bolstered by two cups, they set off to find the others. They began their search in the sitting room, finding only Millie. "Good morning, gentlemen! How did you sleep?"

Michael rolled his eyes at her. "Are you joking?"

"No, I am not," she countered. "I am curious to understand if the sedative had its intended effect and if it produced any ill side effects."

"The ill side effect was that I slept until mid-morning," Damien lamented.

"How are you feeling now?" Millie inquired.

"Sluggish," Damien admitted.

"Would you mind if I checked a few vitals?" Millie asked.

"I would," Damien contended. "I'm too busy. We've got to find Gray and Alexander."

"It will only take a few moments," Millie assured him. "Please sit."

"No!" Damien shouted. "There is no time! Celine is missing and I've got to start searching for her!"

"Celine would not want your health to suffer while doing so. You are no use to her if you are too ill to continue searching."

"I am not ill!"

"Perhaps it's best to just give in," Michael suggested. "It's taking longer battling with her than to just let her take your pulse."

Millie cocked her head, grinning at him. "Thank you, Michael. And you are not ill now, we'd like to keep it that way. Damien, you are under a tremendous strain. The pressure of time travel coupled with the stress and worry over Celine can conjure negative effects. We must be vigilant concerning your health."

"Fine," Damien acquiesced, collapsing onto the couch. Millie checked his pupils, took his pulse, and listened to his heart. "Do I pass?"

"You do. Your pulse is elevated, and your pupils are sluggish. The latter is from the sedative. The dose may have been a bit too strong. Please be mindful of your stress levels, Damien. I realize the worry you carry, but you must temper this with proper rest and relaxation."

"Relaxation, ha!" Damien retorted.

"To the best of your ability."

"I'll keep an eye on him," Michael assured Millie.

"It appears your trip to the past has done wonders for you, Michael," Millie assessed.

"I am much better, yes. No ill effects from Celeste," Michael answered.

"Wonderful to hear. You should get adequate rest, too."

"I will. And I'll make sure he does, too."

"Good enough. And now that I am satisfied, I will tell you Gray is at Alexander's house. You can meet them there."

"Thanks, let's go," Damien said, standing and racing to the door.

"Rest, Damien! Rest!" Millie shouted as he and Michael disappeared from the room.

They donned their jackets, Damien pulling his on as he rushed out the door. "

Wait up," Michael called as Damien scurried down the path to Alexander's. "Millie made a few good points. You need to take it down a notch, buddy."

"Are you kidding me?" Damien asked.

"No, I'm not. No sense running yourself into the ground. What good will you be to Celine if you're too exhausted or stressed out to help?"

"I'm fine. I just feel behind. She's been missing for a week. The longer someone is missing, the less likely it is they are found. You know that, right? We need to get up to speed. And I need to start working on this. *Then* I'll settle."

"Okay, okay. Lecture over," Michael agreed.

They traveled through the woods. Damien recalled walking here only a week ago with Celine. She'd experienced one of her painful memories. The incident had crippled her, dropping her to her knees, unable to move. Did these memories have anything to do with her disappearance? Were they connected? Did she become ill walking back to the house? Did she collapse before reaching it? Was she prey to an animal or person in her weakened state? Questions darted across his mind faster than he could process them.

Alexander's house came into view. He sped toward it with Michael following close behind. Damien pounded on the door, yelling for Gray and Alexander. Alexander opened the door, ushering them into the foyer.

"Hello, gentlemen. We are in the sitting room," Alexander greeted them, motioning toward the room.

Damien and Michael entered, finding Gray staring out the window.

"I trust you were able to rest," Alexander stated, following them.

"Rest isn't the word," Damien answered. "Never do that again!" he threatened, waving a finger at Gray.

Gray chuckled. "Or what?"

Damien was at a loss. Michael chimed in, "Do you really think Celine would have been happy with that type of behavior?"

"Celine wouldn't have been happy if you'd gotten yourselves killed running around half-cocked searching for her."

"We're not idiots," Damien countered.

"Debatable," Gray retorted.

"Enough bickering," Alexander demanded.

"Fine," Gray agreed. "But understand this. While Celine is missing, I am responsible for your well-being. I will not compromise your safety because it makes you feel better."

Damien rolled his eyes, sinking onto the couch. "He makes a point, Damien. There are supernatural forces at work here that you do not even understand," Alexander added.

"Forces that are powerful enough to have done something to Celine," Gray interjected.

"Yes, and you both are only human. You must remember this," Alexander chided.

"We'll be fine," Michael assured them.

"I'll be better when we find Celine," Damien stated.

"We all will be," Alexander agreed.

"Okay, get us up to speed," Michael prompted. "You told us the long and short of it last night. Now repeat it. This time in detail."

Gray and Alexander relayed the information again, along

with any steps they had taken thus far. Damien paced the room as he listened to the information.

"So, you've checked with Celeste. You searched the path from Celeste's hideaway to the house. You've tried calling and texting her. She has her phone, right?"

Gray nodded. "To my knowledge, yes."

"You've searched the grounds, the buildings nearby, and nothing?"

"Right."

"Didn't you use Celeste to find her when she was Josie? Can she do it again?"

"We did. She hasn't been able to help," Gray confirmed.

Damien ceased his pacing, standing in silence for a moment. "We're missing something."

"Obviously," Gray answered.

"I'd like to speak with Celeste," Damien requested.

"Fine," Gray answered. "But as we said last night, you can't go alone."

"Agreed," Damien replied.

"We'll go as soon as the sun sets," Alexander promised. "I'll accompany you."

"Great. Until then, we'll have a look around the property. Meet you back here at sunset," Damien said. "Come on, Michael."

"Be careful!" Gray called after them as they exited.

Damien and Michael pulled on their jackets, returning to the wooded path. "What's the plan?" Michael asked.

Damien shrugged, his hands shoved deep in his pockets. "I'm not sure, but I couldn't just sit there. Even if we just wander the paths and search for clues, that's better than nothing."

"Clues?" Michael inquired.

"Yeah, clues. Like her phone laying in a clump of leaves or her ponytail holder wrapped in a pine branch."

Michael scrunched his face up. "Ah, Damien…" he began.

"Don't say it. It's a long shot, I realize that. But at least we've covered the grounds. We would have done it anyway when she went missing."

"True. Okay, any particular place you want to start?"

"No. Perhaps we should try the places she had those painful memories. I'm not sure why, but I just feel those are connected to her disappearance."

"All right. You were with her for one of them, right? Lead the way."

Damien and Michael began at the cliffs, where Celine experienced her first sense of foreboding. They spent over an hour searching the area but found nothing. They proceeded to the area just outside of Celeste's daytime hideaway. Before searching, Damien ensured Michael exhibited no ill effects from being within a close proximity of Celeste despite it being daylight.

After Damien was satisfied Celeste posed no threat to Michael, they searched the area. Celine had experienced two episodes here, one of them severe. No evidence of Celine existed in the area.

They moved to the opening in the woods, the sight of another severe episode. After another careful search, they turned up nothing. Damien lingered here despite the absence of any traces of Celine.

Michael allowed him some time before speaking. "Sorry we didn't find anything," he stated, hands on his hips.

Damien shook his head.

"Should we head back to Alexander's? Grab some dinner before you meet with Celeste?"

Damien didn't move.

"Damien?"

Damien shook his head again. "Something's here," he murmured, staring at the ground.

"What?" Michael questioned.

"I… I feel something. Like something's here."

Michael glanced around. "We've already searched the entire area. We came up with nothing."

"Yeah, I realize we've searched, but…" His voice trailed off. "But I can't shake this sensation."

Michael humored him. "Okay, let's take another look around. Hey, try calling her phone, see if we hear it ringing."

"Good idea." Damien dialed Celine's number. The line rang a few times, but they heard no ringtone. "Nope, nothing."

They spent another hour searching every inch of the space, kicking leaves around, examining branches and searching under limbs.

"Nothing's here, man," Michael finally said. "And it's almost dark."

Damien sighed, shaking his head. He stared at the area. What was he missing? Why was he plagued by this sense? What was it about this space that called to him?

He stared at the trees. A slight breeze rustled the branches. The needles on the pine tree danced. The scent of white pine overwhelmed him. Colors faded from vivid to gray scale. His eyes lost their ability to focus.

Without warning, his body jolted. He blinked several times.

"Damien!" Michael yelled.

"What?" he responded.

"You okay?"

"Yeah, why?"

Michael stared at him, confusion written on his face. "You were standing there, staring ahead. I was talking to you, and you were totally unresponsive. Like you couldn't hear me."

"Must have been lost in thought."

Michael stared at him another moment.

He sucked in breath. "Should we go?"

"Sure," Michael agreed.

They hiked the path to Alexander's. Alexander and Gray insisted they eat before visiting Celeste. Damien gulped his food, wanting to meet with Celeste as quickly as possible. He set off with Alexander after dinner.

"Hey," Damien inquired, as they walked to the abandoned house Celeste's coffin lay in, "did you find anything at the clearing in the woods? The spot where Celine had that severe painful memory?"

"No," Alexander informed him. "Why?"

"We searched there earlier. We didn't find anything either. But I had a strange sensation there. Like something was calling to me."

"Hmm," Alexander answered.

"I'm not crazy," Damien countered.

"I didn't say you were. But I'm not sure what to make of it."

Damien shrugged as they approached the abandoned house. "Hope Celeste is home," he said as they climbed the stairs.

They entered the structure. "Celeste? Celeste!" Alexander called.

Celeste emerged from behind a bookcase, closing it behind her to hide the secret room where her coffin lay hidden. "Good evening, Alexander. What brings you by? Oh, Damien, hello."

Damien refused to acknowledge Celeste, his dislike of her still fresh from his encounters with her in the past. "We told Michael and Damien the unfortunate news about Celine when they returned last night. He desired to hear the story about your meeting with her firsthand."

"I see," Celeste replied, stalking toward them. She focused

her crystal blue eyes on Damien. "There isn't much to tell, I'm afraid. I met with Celine around ten."

"Where?" Damien questioned.

"Here," Celeste answered. "We spoke for about fifteen minutes. She took the path back to the main house when she left. That's the last I saw of her."

"What did you discuss?"

"My condition. Her desire to reverse it. I told her I didn't hold her responsible. That we would work together to resolve the situation. I hoped the conversation helped to ease her nerves."

"And that was it?"

"Yes."

Damien stared at Celeste.

"Something wrong, Damien?" Celeste inquired.

"I find it suspicious you were the last person to see her."

"If you plan to accuse me of something, you'd better have proof. I don't take accusations lightly. She is my sister…"

"Your sister who you almost sold to the devil. Who you were complicit in tormenting for years!" Damien shouted.

"Careful, Damien. I love my sister. I always have. Whatever problems existed between us are in the past."

"Yeah, right," Damien accused. "Your love for your sister is beyond questionable."

"I will let that slide, given your distress. But this conversation is finished. You may want to control your lunatic friend before he finds himself in trouble," Celeste advised Alexander before stalking out of the house.

"I don't trust her," Damien stated, staring after Celeste.

"I agree with you. But in this case, I do not understand what benefit Celeste gains from Celine's disappearance."

"Payback?" Damien suggested with a shrug.

"For her vampiric condition? Doubtful."

"Why?"

"Celine is the most invested in restoring Celeste. Other than Teddy, no one else cares. With Celine gone, Gray and I aren't chomping at the bit to help her."

"Perhaps Teddy has found a solution for her. And she doesn't need Celine, so she got rid of her."

"If Teddy has found a solution, Celeste wouldn't still be in her coffin."

"Good point," Damien admitted, stalking away, sighing.

"I understand your distrust of Celeste. And I don't disagree. But I am not sure it helps us in any way. I doubt Celeste harmed her sister for revenge or any other selfish purpose." Damien didn't respond. "I don't care for her either, Damien, but she does have half a heart when it comes to Celine, particularly now that the Duke is gone.

"Yeah, I guess you have a point. I just can't trust her. Every time we've been around her, she's been siding with that monster. I guess she can't side with him if he's not here though."

"Shall we return to the house? You and Michael should rest."

"I guess," Damien sighed. "Rest. Yeah, right!"

"I understand how difficult this is, nevertheless, you must try. Celine will have our heads if she returns, and you are ill."

Alexander's comment earned a chuckle from Damien. They exited the abandoned house and took the path to Alexander's house. Gray and Michael waited there.

"Well?" Michael inquired as they entered the sitting room.

"Nothing," Damien answered. "Just like Gray said. Celeste spoke with Celine. Celine left, and no one has seen her since." Damien collapsed onto the couch.

"I don't trust her," Michael said.

"Same thing I said," Damien confessed.

"Neither of us trust Celeste either," Gray replied. "But this time she isn't lying."

"We should follow her! Perhaps she'll lead us right to Celine!" Damien offered.

"Do you honestly think we haven't tried that?" Gray questioned.

Damien shrugged his shoulders in response.

Gray rolled his eyes. "Of course we followed Celeste. She led us nowhere."

"Perhaps she realized you were following her and did that on purpose," Michael conjectured.

"You two really deem us amateurs, don't you?" Gray asked. "We've been dealing with these problems for centuries. Don't presume that anything we do is ineptly done."

"Okay, okay!" Michael answered, holding his hands up in defeat. "Just trying to offer suggestions."

"We're all tired and anxious. Perhaps everyone should rest," Alexander suggested.

"You mean perhaps you should drug us and force us to rest?" Michael snapped.

"No, I mean rest," Alexander corrected.

"Assuming you can be trusted to rest," Gray added.

"We're not children," Michael contested.

"No, you're not. But you are human. You're vulnerable. The last thing we need is one of you to disappear, become hurt or distract us from the search for Celine."

"He makes a good point," Damien admitted. "We can't waste resources or be distracted from Celine's disappearance. The longer she's gone, the less chance we have to..." His voice trailed off, unable to finish the sentence.

"We'll find her. But we need to be smart and sharp to do it," Gray replied. "Let's head back to the house."

Damien and Michael agreed. Alexander suggested he accompany them and stay while they searched for Celine. The quartet traveled the path to the main house, disbanding in the foyer. Michael and Damien navigated upstairs to their rooms. Michael expressed his wish that Damien have a restful night, admitting he was exhausted and would likely sleep.

Damien pulled his door shut behind him. He stared at his bed. He would never sleep. Instead, he paced his room, stopping to stare out the window every few minutes. He searched for any sign of Celine as though she may appear wandering through the woods. He laid in bed, attempting sleep. Within minutes, he popped his eyes open. It was no use. He could not rest. He felt trapped, smothered, as though the walls were closing in on him. He had promised to rest, but he would go mad in this room.

CHAPTER 3

$\mathcal{D}$amien chewed his lower lip as he fretted over his cousin. Perhaps fresh air would ease his nerves. He snuck from his room and down the stairs, pulling on his jacket and entering the night air.

He meandered to the cliffs, drawn to the sound of the waves crashing against the rocks below. He stood for several moments, staring out over the dark ocean. His thoughts were a jumble. Upset over Celine clouded his reasoning. He failed to understand how they would find her. Perhaps it was his tiredness overcoming him, but he was panicked. He saw no way forward.

Movement on the path drew his attention. Gray emerged from the trees. "You're supposed to be sleeping," he chided as he approached Damien.

Damien returned his gaze to the darkened horizon. "Yeah, yeah, I know," he admitted. "Couldn't sleep, so I figured I'd try some fresh air."

He slid his eyes sideways, eyeing Gray. He'd never gotten comfortable with Gray. Gray intimidated him, though he never had given him any reason to dislike him. Other than the jab to the arm last night. "You're not going to sedate me again, are you?"

Gray chuckled. "No. But I am going to insist you return to the house and rest."

They stood for a few moments in silence, each staring at the ocean.

Gray spoke again. "Celine would hate you running around the property at night alone."

Damien smirked as he crossed his arms. "Yeah, I bet. She told me that once before."

Gray turned to face Damien. "I realize this is a shock to you, Damien. Celine's disappearance is a shock to all of us. I'm only doing my best to ensure when she comes home, and she will come home, nothing has changed."

"So, it's not because you hate me?"

Gray laughed, turning back to stare at the horizon. "I don't hate you, Damien."

A moment of silence passed. "Do you hate me?"

"No," Damien answered. "No, I don't hate you."

"Perhaps our problem is each of us reminds the other that Celine was someone else for a time," Gray reflected.

Damien nodded. "Yeah, perhaps that's it. I don't hate you. But it is weird to think she lived for centuries before she ever lived as Josie." Damien paused, then added, "I'm sure it's equally strange to realize she lived twenty-five years as Josie without you."

Gray faced him again. "Yes, it is. Well, now that we've identified it, what say we agree to be friends." He extended his hand for Damien to shake.

Twisting toward him, Damien accepted it. "Deal."

"Now, shall we return to the house? It's growing cold out here. Celine will have my head if you catch cold while she's away."

Damien nodded. "Sure."

* * *

"Good evening, my dear," Marcus voiced as he approached Celine's prison.

Celine rolled her eyes, standing from her seat on the floor. She did not respond.

"You're quiet this evening," Marcus said, peering in through the barred window.

"I grow weary of these games, Marcus."

"As do I," Marcus admitted.

"I will never join you. Why do you insist on pursuing me?"

"You are worth it, my dear."

Celine approached the door. "Do you really expect your new technique to work?"

"Isolation can prove an effective method, Celine. It provides one plenty of time for reflection."

Celine crossed her arms over her chest. "It still surprises me you cannot accept you've lost even after centuries."

"Ah, but I have not lost, Celine."

Celine barked out a harsh laugh. "How do you figure that?"

"You are amused. I would not be. I may not have won… yet. But neither have you. Which implies I have not yet lost."

Celine set her face in a scowl.

"I can never understand what it is about Buckley that draws your interest.'

"I love him," Celine admitted.

"I do not believe that," Marcus retorted.

"I don't care what you believe."

"Don't you? We shall have to change that."

"You cannot, Marcus."

"We shall see. While I admire your strength, it can be one

of your most loathsome qualities when used in the wrong instances."

Marcus paced the room. "If you cannot come to your own realization, Celine, I will force you. I have provided you with ample time to consider your choices. Now I shall inflict more stringent measures."

"You are a monster!" Celine shouted at him.

"No, Celine, I…" his voice cut off abruptly. He cocked his head as though listening. His gaze fell upon the stairway across the room. He waved his arm left to right in front of him. Celine approached the bars, curious about what he was doing.

"Celine? Marcus?" Celeste's voice called. She descended the wooden stairs, searching the room.

Marcus sighed, waving his arm in the opposite direction.

Celeste raised her eyebrows as she spotted them. "Ah, there you are."

"What are you doing here, Celeste?" Marcus questioned.

"I would like to speak with my sister."

"No," Marcus stated.

"I have information that may help your cause," Celeste entreated.

Marcus considered her statement. "While I doubt your sincerity, I am curious. Proceed."

"Alone," Celeste requested.

"No," Marcus replied, narrowing his eyes. "Whatever you must say shall be said in my presence. Celine has not earned the privilege of visitors. Particularly those who may be sympathetic to her cause."

"Really, Marcus," Celeste spat, "I've never known you to be so… apprehensive."

"Careful, Celeste. I still hold your life in my hands."

Celeste ignored him, approaching Celine's cell, peering in through the small window. "Hello, Celine."

"Hello, Celeste," Celine answered, gazing at her through the bars.

"I hope you are holding up under the strain."

"Oh, get to the point, Celeste," Marcus groaned.

"I had a visit earlier from Damien," Celeste began.

Celine clutched the bars, pulling herself closer to the opening. "Damien? How is he?" she demanded, breathless.

"Quite distressed," Celeste admitted. "He is aware of your absence. He has taken it very badly."

A tear rolled down Celine's cheek.

Celeste continued, "It is clear he is desperate to find you, Celine. A desperation that I fear may lead to difficulty for him when you are not found."

Celine backed away from the door, pacing her cell as another tear fell.

"And Gray? How is he?" Celine questioned.

"Holding up, but it's wearing on him." With no response from Celine, Celeste again continued. "Celine, I realize this is not the solution you want to hear, but perhaps it is time to concede. Please understand, I do not say this to harm you, but to help you."

Fury burned in Celine. "I will not submit to that man!" she yelled, pointing to Marcus.

"Even if it costs Damien his life?"

"Is that a threat, sister?"

"No, a warning. Celine, Damien is human. He cannot withstand the pressures of this world, especially without your help. He will break, Celine. He teeters on the edge now. Please consider the consequences."

Tears rolled down Celine's cheeks as she considered the effect on Damien.

"Celine, please. I love you. I want only the best for you. But if Damien suffers ill-effects, you will take this upon yourself. It will eat you up. It will destroy you, Celine. I am only considering your welfare and the welfare of your family. Celine, please," Celeste begged. "I do not wish to see you like this. No one does."

Celine sighed, but offered no response.

"Consider it, sister," Celeste breathed, peering into the cell. "I love you, Celine."

Celeste turned to depart.

"I love you, too, Celeste. Be safe," Celine replied.

A tear fell onto Celeste's cheek. She whirled around to face Celine and hurried back to the door. "Oh, I love you, baby sister," she said, reaching for Celine. "I do not wish you to hurt like this. Please understand that."

Celine met her on the opposite side of the door. "I realize that, Celeste," Celine cried. "Take care of my family, please."

"How touching," Marcus chimed in. "Now, you may leave, Celeste. Celine and I have much to discuss."

Celeste glared at Marcus. "Despite my advice, I hope my sister never yields to your demands!"

Marcus jerked her away from the cell door. "You have worn out your welcome, Celeste."

"Don't touch her!" Celine screamed from the cell.

Celeste yanked her arm from him. "No reason to get hot under the collar, Marcus. Your temper is so short these days. I am leaving." Celeste stalked away from him. "Goodbye, Celine. And good luck," she called as she reached the stairs.

Celine stalked away from the door as Celeste disappeared up the stairs.

"I hope you listened attentively, Celine. I did not command that performance from your sister," Marcus interjected. "She advised you of her own free will."

"Haven't you? You hold her life in your hands. Do you expect me to assume she has any free will?"

"I did not threaten or require her to speak to you, Celine. You have my word."

"Your word means nothing to me. You are a cruel and intolerable man."

"You misjudge me, Celine. You find me cruel only because we disagree."

"I find you cruel because you are cruel. Leave me, Marcus, I have nothing further to say to you." Celine crossed her arms, turning away from him.

"Fine. I will grant your request and leave you alone. But consider what your sister advises, Celine."

Marcus strode away, leaving Celine alone. His footsteps receded, replaced by silence.

Celine sank to sit on the floor, weeping. Celeste spoke the truth. Damien would take her disappearance on himself. It would weigh on him until it drove him crazy. With each day that passed, he would grow more desperate. As she received updates from Celeste or Marcus, guilt would burden her soul, too. Misery would prevail. What would she do then? Would she give in? Would she continue to fight despite having lost the battle?

Celine collapsed to the floor, curled in a ball. Tears clouded her vision, and she laid on the cold, stone floor.

"Damien," she cried. "I'm sorry." Her eyes closed as she drifted away.

* * *

GRAY AND DAMIEN walked in silence to the house.

"Can you sleep?" Gray queried as they stood outside Damien's door.

"Uh, I'll try." He paused a moment, his hand on the doorknob. "Celine used to sit with me. That helped a lot."

Gray knit his brow. "Well, I won't hold your hand as you fall asleep, but if you want some company, I can stay. How about a drink?"

Damien considered the idea. Strange as Gray's presence might be, he hated to be alone. "I mean, I don't want to impose so…" he began.

"Why don't I just grab those drinks," Gray suggested. "I could use the company, too."

Damien smiled at him. "Okay, thanks!"

Gray returned with two glasses of brandy. They entered the bedroom. Gray chose the chair, settling into it as Damien climbed onto the bed. Damien sighed, glancing around the room, drumming his fingers on the bed. He pondered if being alone would have been as uncomfortable as he felt right now.

"You should try to sleep." Gray chided.

"Easier said than done," Damien admitted before sipping his brandy.

"Celine is much better at this than I am, I'm sure," Gray replied.

Damien chuckled as he tapped his glass. "Yeah, she is. Sorry."

"Don't apologize. I realize my shortcomings. Celine is… an extraordinary woman."

"She is," Damien agreed. After a moment, he added, "But you're pretty cool, too. I mean, you have extraordinary talents, too, right?"

"My dear Damien, my talents are nowhere close to Celine's."

"What do you mean? Can't you all do the same supernatural stuff?"

Gray chuckled, balancing his glass on the chair's arm. "No. No, we can't. Celine can do far more than I can."

Confusion crossed Damien's face.

Gray glanced at him. "The supernatural world is structured by echelons."

"You mean, some of you are more powerful than others?"

"Yes, correct."

"And Celine is more powerful than you?" Damien questioned.

"Infinitely," Gray admitted.

Damien nodded, inquiring, "What about Alexander?"

"He's a bit better than me. But Celine is leaps and bounds above both of us. Her power is… impressive."

"Hmm," Damien mumbled, pondering the information.

"I've only seen her abilities matched by one other person," Gray stated. Damien cocked his head to the side. "Marcus Northcott."

"The Duke? Hmm. I'd rather not talk about him. At least we are rid of him. We ran into him in the past. He was as charming then as he was in our time."

"Yes. He was a vile man." Silence fell between them. "Now, you should try to sleep."

Damien yawned, slouching down the bed and pulling a blanket over him. "Yeah. I'm sleepy. Hope that's a good sign!" He switched off the light. "Good night!" he called into the darkness.

"Good night, Damien," Gray answered him.

He shook his head in the darkness. It wasn't the same as Celine. He missed her. He stared at the ceiling, wishing she were here.

"Celine," he whispered. He closed his eyes, imagining her return. They would find her, he assured himself. We'll find you, Celine, he promised as he drifted to sleep.

* * *

DAMIEN AWOKE TO DARKNESS. The blackness surrounded him, blinding him. Something was wrong. It was cold, damp. He shivered in the darkness. He reached out with his fingers, searching the area near him. They touched cold earth underneath him. Where was his bed, he wondered? Had he sleep-walked somewhere? Had Gray dozed off and missed him exiting the room?

Damien's eyes began adjusting. He still could not see much. The details remained hazy, as though a shroud veiled them. A musty scent filled the air.

He raised himself to sitting. "Hello?"

A muffled noise responded. His pulse quickened.

"Hello?" he called louder into the darkness.

A garbled sound answered him. He reached out in front of him.

"Is someone there?" he called.

He crawled forward on his hands and knees. "Who's there?"

Noises continued, none of them comprehensible. As he moved forward, something approached. His vision was too blurred to make it out. Light in color, it stood out, glaring against the dark backdrop. He recoiled, fearing what it may be, unable to identify it.

"Hello?" he called again.

The object moved toward him in slow motion. He backed away until he hit something behind him. His breathing quickened.

"Stop!" he shouted.

The blurry figure continued toward him. Hushed noises persisted. He held his hand in front of him, a last attempt to stave off the approaching entity.

CHAPTER 4

amien's heart thudded in his chest as the blurry figure approached him. He scrambled back, his limbs feeling sluggish.

Warm flesh touched his hand. Fingers wrapped around his and squeezed. Damien blinked, trying to clear the haze from the scene. An arm encircled his shoulders. Warm breath floated past his ear.

"Damien," Celine's voice whispered.

Damien shot up to sitting, gasping for breath. "Celine!" he called, reaching into the air.

Gray raced to his side. "What is it? What's wrong?"

"Celine! I saw her! She was with me!" Damien gasped.

"What? Where? When?" Gray glanced around the room.

"Just now!" Damien exclaimed. Damien raced from his bed into the hallway. "Celine!" he called. "Celine!"

"Damien, you were dreaming," Gray replied, following him.

"No, I…" Damien paused, pondering for a moment. He shook his head. "No."

"Yes, Damien," Gray assured him. "It was a dream, you were asleep."

"But it was so real! She held my hand, she called to me." He returned to his room, sinking onto his bed.

Moments later, Michael raced in along with Alexander and Millie. "We heard a commotion, what's wrong?" Alexander inquired.

"He was dreaming of Celine," Gray answered.

"No!" Damien insisted. "She was with me."

"Here?" Alexander questioned, his brow furrowing.

"No," Damien answered. "No, we were... I'm not sure where we were. It was damp and cold. There was dirt, like outside. Celine came toward me and grabbed my hand. Well, I assume it was Celine, I couldn't make the figure out. Everything was hazy. Then she whispered my name."

"It was a dream" Gray insisted.

"No! It was real!" Damien countered.

"Dreams can be very vivid, particularly when we are under tremendous stress," Millie interjected.

"No, I..." Damien began, his voice trailing off.

"I believe you," Michael stated.

Damien smiled at Michael. "Thanks."

"She probably came to make sure you were asleep though, so you may want to get some more rest," Michael said with a grin.

"She'd do that," Damien agreed, chuckling. "I'll try to go to sleep. Thanks for checking on me, everyone."

Everyone except Gray filed from the room. Damien slid under the covers again. He felt foolish for having woken the household. Yet, he still couldn't believe what he experienced was a vivid dream. There must be more. He sensed it. It was a clue or a warning. What did it mean? Damien fell asleep pondering the value of the clue.

* * *

CELINE STARTLED FROM HER REST. She hadn't been asleep. After her confrontation with Marcus and Celeste's visit, she had wept for an hour before drifting away. Her mind focused on Damien.

Celeste's warning concerning his ability to handle her disappearance disturbed her. She dwelled on his well-being. Instead of falling asleep, she had fallen into a trance. In the trance, she had found her way to Damien, their special connection opening the path. She called to him, but he could not see her. Approaching him, she grasped his hand, pulling him close to her.

"Damien," she whispered before he vanished.

Celine recalled each detail, pulling herself up to sitting. A plan formed in her mind. A slight smile crossed her lips. Marcus's enchantment prevented her from escaping or anyone from finding her. But she had found a way out. A difficult, dangerous way, but a way. She could communicate with the outside world. Therefore, she could be rescued, she reflected.

Celine glanced out her tiny window toward the sky. Dark clouds sailed past the waning crescent moon. Despite the heavy clouds that rolled through the night sky, the moon remained visible, veiled behind the mist. Celine, hidden behind Marcus' spell, was like the moon behind the black clouds. Visible yet obscured. And like the moon, she could be found.

* * *

MICHAEL HELPED himself to the eggs on the sideboard. Damien wasn't down yet. He wanted to check on him earlier but didn't want to disturb him if he was asleep. Instead, he opted to eat, and hoped Damien appeared for breakfast. So far, he sat alone in the dining room.

Avery joined him within five minutes, pouring herself a cup of coffee. "Good morning."

"Good morning," he answered.

"It's good to have you back," Avery replied, joining him at the table.

Michael pushed the eggs around on his plate. "Thanks. It's good to be back. I'm not as fond of time travel as Damien."

"I've never done it. But I'm with you. I'm not sure I'd want to."

Michael chuckled as he scooped up the scrambled eggs. "It's not all it's cracked up to be."

Avery traced the rim of her coffee cup with her finger. "Terrible shame about Aunt Celine. I hope we find her soon. He doesn't show it, but Uncle Gray is dreadfully upset."

Michael nodded his head. "So is Damien. We all are, really."

"I'm sure."

Michael blew out a long breath. "We had a few issues before we went to 1791. But to come back and she's not here… I wish she was here."

"You are very close with her. Damien, too."

"Yeah," Michael admitted, pausing. "Hey, do you mind if I ask you a strange question?"

"Not at all!"

"When Damien and I were in the past, we came across a cottage on the property, near the cliffs. Is it still there?"

Avery sipped her coffee. "The caretaker's cottage? Yes, it is. The cottage hasn't been used in years, but it's still standing. Why?"

"Ah, no special reason."

"Oh, come on," Avery prodded. "You didn't ask for nothing."

"No, I didn't. You're on to me," he chuckled, holding his hands up. "Damien and I had an idea about my moving there since I hadn't found anything else. It's no big deal though, just idle chatter while we passed the time."

"Sounds like a wonderful idea," Avery admitted. "I'm sure Mother would approve."

Michael bit into a slice of bacon. "Well, I'm in no rush. With Celine gone, Damien will hate the idea of me moving, even if it's that close."

"I don't blame him. We'll all miss you, especially Max and Maddy."

"Like I said, I'm in no rush, but it's something to consider."

As Michael finished his statement, Max and Maddy, Avery's children, raced into the room. "Uncle Michael!" they shouted.

"Hey, guys!" Michael greeted them.

Maddy threw her arms around Michael's neck. "We missed you, Uncle Michael!"

"I missed you both, too," Michael expressed. "What have you been up to while Uncle Damien and I were gone?"

Max shrugged. "Stuff."

"Stuff? Care to elaborate?" Michael asked.

"Nope," Max replied, plopping onto the chair next to Michael.

"Max, that's no way to speak to an adult," Avery corrected.

"It's okay," Michael answered, placing a hand on the boy's shoulder. "Something wrong, buddy?"

Max let his chin rest in his palms, not responding. "We've been searching for Aunt Celine," Maddy admitted. "But we haven't had any luck."

"Ah," Michael answered, realization dawning on him. He gave Avery a knowing glance. The two children, in an effort to help, tried to find Celine. Besides the upset they sensed in the household from Celine's disappearance, having not found her added to Max's dejection.

"Max, you're just a child," Avery replied. "You don't have to solve adult problems."

"I'm not a child!" Max argued. "I'm going to be eleven in a few months!"

Michael wrapped his arm around Max. "Wow! You're getting old!"

"It's not funny. I'm being serious! I want to help find Aunt Celine."

"I'm sure you do," Michael answered. "We all do. But we have to work together because it's a big project. There are lots of things to investigate."

"I've been trying to investigate, but I can't find any clues!"

"Oh? What have you investigated so far?"

"Well," Max pondered a moment, then began naming places, ticking them off on his fingers as he went. "We tried the closed off wing, the basement, and a few of the sheds on the property."

"Nothing in any of them?"

"No! No sign of her!"

"Hmm," Michael mumbled. "I have an idea."

"What is it?" Maddy asked.

"Well, you may not find Aunt Celine this way, but it would be a real big help for everyone. I'm only going to tell you if you really, truly want to help."

"We do want to help!" Max exclaimed.

"You mean it? Pinky swear?" Michael asked.

"Pinky swear!" Maddy promised, locking pinkies with Michael.

"How about you, Max?" Michael asked.

"Scouts honor!" he replied, holding up three fingers, a trick he had learned from Uncle Damien.

"Okay. It would really help if you both spent some time finding pictures of Aunt Celine."

"Pictures of Aunt Celine? Why?" Max questioned.

"Because everyone misses Aunt Celine. And everyone would like to be reminded of her. So, it would help if you found some pictures. Perhaps made a card saying how much we miss her. Then everyone can remember her until she's back. Do you think you can do that?"

"We can do that!" Maddy answered.

"Yeah! And we'll even make cards to welcome her home, too! We'll start today," Max promised.

"That sounds like a great idea," Michael agreed. "Take your time, look through all the pictures. Make sure you pick the best ones, okay?"

"We will!" Max replied, standing from the chair. "Come on, Maddy. We have a lot of work to do!"

"They missed you. You're so good with them," Avery mentioned after they left.

"I missed them, too. They're good kids," Michael admitted. "They miss Celine, too. They need to express that. It must be hard for them to process, not fully understanding the circumstances. Hell, I fully understand the circumstances and it's hard for me."

"You get used to it," Avery responded, taking Michael's hand in hers.

"Thanks," he answered. "You make it look effortless."

Michael smiled at Avery as Damien entered the room. "Hey, good morning," Michael greeted him.

"Morning," Damien mumbled, helping himself to breakfast.

"I'll let you two talk," Avery said, excusing herself.

"Get any sleep?" Michael asked, sipping his coffee.

"Some," Damien replied. "Not much after that…"

"Experience?" Michael filled in.

"Yeah." Damien paused, stifling a yawn. "Hey, thanks for not calling it a dream. It didn't feel like a dream."

"No problem. What do you think it was?"

Damien shrugged, rolling his eyes. "Probably a stupid dream, like Gray said. He never believes me."

"I don't understand why," Michael answered. "We live in a world with witches, warlocks, vampires, doppelgängers from the mirror world, time travel, adjudicators and at least a half a dozen more things we don't know about yet and he can't believe you saw Celine last night?"

Damien chuckled as he sipped his coffee. "Nope. That's where he draws the line, apparently."

"Well, his loss. What's our plan?"

Damien shook his head. "I have no idea. For once, I have no plan. Not even an inkling of a plan."

"That's okay. We'll come up with something."

"What? Where do we even start? Wander around the estate and continue to find nothing? Pester Celeste when the sun sets?"

Michael didn't respond. "Let's check around some of the other buildings nearby. The houses on the outskirts of the estate. Oh, hey, that reminds me. I asked Avery about the caretaker's cottage. She said it's still there. Want to check it out with me?"

"Sure. Then you can leave, too, and I'll be alone here," Damien complained.

"I'm not going anywhere while Celine is gone," Michael promised. "But we still can look."

"Okay. Sorry, I'm just… tired."

"Yeah, I know," Michael answered, clapping Damien on the back. "It's fine. We'll take it slow."

Damien finished his breakfast, downing a second cup of

coffee before they began their journey. They spent the morning hours searching the properties on the fringes of the estate. Their last stop before lunch was the caretaker's cottage. They found it in decent shape. With a good cleaning and some minor maintenance, Michael and Damien surmised it would be a functional house for Michael. Again, Michael assured him he would not move until Celine was found.

They returned to the house for lunch. After lunch, Damien opted to lie down, stating exhaustion from his sleepless night was catching up to him. He strolled through the foyer. His eyes slid upwards to the portrait above the massive fireplace. Celine's portrait. He stopped, staring up at it. The lifelike portrait seemed to stare back, her bright blue eyes captivating even on canvas.

Damien smiled at the painting, recalling it held a piece of Celine's soul. A part of Celine guarded him. It made him feel safer. If he could have, he would have laid down in the foyer near the painting and slept. He stared at it for another few moments.

"Where are you, Celine?" he asked aloud.

"Part of her is there," Millie answered him, strolling across the foyer to meet him.

"I know," Damien answered. "It helps to realize that."

Millie eyed him for a moment before returning her gaze to the portrait. "Have you decided against the nap?"

"No," he sighed. "Just didn't make it there yet."

"Will you be able to sleep?"

"I hope so. I am exhausted. I ache all over."

"Tension can do strange things to the body, Damien," Millie noted. "You must try to get proper rest. If you need a sleep aid, just ask."

"I don't. At least, I hope I don't. Let me try the nap. If I can't sleep, I'll let you know."

"All right. I hope you sleep. Pleasant dreams," Millie wished him as he trudged up the stairs.

Damien crawled into bed. Dreams, he scoffed as he considered Millie's last statement. Yes, perhaps he could have another dream of Celine for everyone to ignore. Their rebuke of his dream as meaningful annoyed him. Michael believed him. At least that's what he said. His musings turned from his annoyance with his housemates to brooding over Celine's disappearance. He had no ideas, no clues on proceeding. It frustrated him. He always had a plan. This time, when Celine needed him the most, he had nothing.

He tossed and turned, frustrated with himself and his situation. He stared out of the window. Bright sunlight shone in. The light dimmed. A cloud must be passing over the sun, he surmised. He closed his eyes for a moment, drifting away.

Damien glanced around, rubbing his eyes. He failed to recognize his surroundings. Had he sleepwalked? He pushed up to sitting. Where was he? Trees soared overhead, standing motionless. Their leaves, normally bright with color this time of year, were colorless. Even the pine trees were gray. Eerie silence surrounded him. He stood, glancing around. He shrugged his hoodie closer around him. A shiver shot through his body. He rubbed his hands together, blowing on them to warm them. Why was it so cold, he wondered?

A strange reverberating sound drew his attention. He swiveled his head in its direction. "Hello?" He received no answer. "Hello? Is someone there?"

The noise sounded again. Damien inched toward it. "Hel-lo?" he called again, shivering. He crossed his arms, trying to keep warm. The noise rang out again.

Damien shivered again, his heart thudding as he tried to discern what was happening to him.

CHAPTER 5

 amien strained to make out the sound. It resounded again. This time it was discernible. "Damien," Celine's voice echoed.

"Celine?" Damien responded, his heart racing. "Celine, where are you?"

"Here," her voice answered, echoing all around him. "Focus, Damien, focus on my voice."

"Celine?" he cried, panic filling him as he gawked around in search of her.

"Focus, Damien. Deep breaths."

Damien swallowed hard. He fought to steady his breath. Closing his eyes, he focused on her voice. When his breath was steady, he opened his eyes. Celine stood in front of him, a few feet away.

She smiled at him. "You found me."

His eyes grew wide, and he reached for her. "Celine!" he exclaimed, his heart skipping a beat. Then the world melted away. His body jolted. "No!" he cried as the scene faded.

Damien opened his eyes. "No! No!" he shouted.

"Damien, Damien!" Michael said, shaking him. "Are you all right?"

Millie rushed into the room along with Alexander.

"Huh? What?" Damien asked, his forehead wrinkling.

"I overheard a noise when I passed your door," Michael replied. "I popped my head in to check. Your breathing was erratic, and you were shaking. I called for Millie. I assumed something was wrong."

Damien caught his breath. "I was dreaming, I guess."

"About Celine?" Alexander inquired.

Damien nodded. "Yes, about Celine."

"Would you mind if I checked your vitals?" Millie asked.

Damien shook his head.

"Tell us about the dream," Millie prodded as she checked Damien's pulse.

Damien furrowed his brow, recalling the details. "I was in a place I didn't recognize. It was a strange place. I remember being cold. Freezing, in fact. Then I heard Celine's voice calling to me. At first, I couldn't recognize or understand it. But then it became clearer. I couldn't see her. She told me to focus. So, I did and then she was there. She said, 'You found me' and I reached for her. But then everything faded away, and I woke up. It didn't seem like a dream. It was so real. It was like she was with me."

"I have no doubt it was," Millie admitted. "Your pulse is elevated a bit. Nothing to be concerned about. I'm glad you slept."

Damien scoffed. "I'm still exhausted. In fact, I feel worse."

"I'm sorry to hear that," Millie answered. "You should retire early this evening. The stress is undoubtedly over-whelming."

Damien nodded and ran his fingers through his hair. "I doubt I'll make it far past dinner, to be honest."

Alexander chimed in, "How about a chess game to pass the time until dinner, Damien? It may relax your mind."

"Sure. I am not sure how great of an opponent I'll be. I am not sure I can concentrate."

"I'll go easy on you," Alexander promised.

"Thanks," Damien answered as he stood.

"You sure you don't want to try another nap?" Michael asked.

"I'm sure. I'm exhausted, but I'm afraid I won't sleep tonight." He chuckled for a moment.

"What's funny?" Michael inquired.

"I was just remembering Celine used to say that all the time when she was Josie. Remember?"

Michael grinned at him. "Yep, I remember. She'd get so mad at us for suggesting she nap."

"Yep," Damien answered, returning the grin. "Life's weird, huh?"

"We have no shortage of weird," Michael agreed.

CELINE OPENED HER EYES, smiling to herself. She attempted a second contact with Damien. This time, he had spotted her. His mind, jumbled with stress and panic, had focused enough to find her. The result of the latest contact pleased her. Perhaps soon she could speak with him and pass along information. She must be careful. Too long of an exposure to the environment could prove fatal. Particularly for a human. Still, progress was being made.

Noise drew her attention to the area outside of her cell. Celine stood and approached the door. The familiar form of Marcus Northcott approached. She stalked away from the door, uninterested in the upcoming conversation.

"Good evening, Celine," Marcus said.

"I'm finding it difficult to agree there is anything good about this evening," Celine admitted.

"My, we are in a sour mood this evening!"

"If my dreary mood bothers you, you can leave. I wouldn't mind," Celine suggested.

"No bother at all, Celine. Besides, we have another important discussion to engage in."

Celine did not respond.

"Cat got your tongue, dear?"

"Whatever you're dying to say, Marcus, say it."

"You never appreciate my dramatic flair, Celine."

Celine rolled her eyes, crossing her arms and staring at him. "

Fine. You have been here over one week."

"And?"

"Have you reconsidered my offer?"

Celine flicked her eyebrows up. "No."

"It would be prudent for you do so."

"Okay, let me consider it." Celine paused, tapping a finger against her lips. "No."

"I am not amused, Celine."

"You never appreciate my dramatic flair," Celine mocked.

"Don't push me, Celine."

"I shouldn't be able to. You have the upper hand, as you informed me."

Marcus paced the floor in front of the cell. "You are correct, my dear. I do. And I plan to use it to my advantage."

"Oh?"

"Yes," Marcus informed her. "With you here, unable to protect your family, they shall be easy prey for me."

Celine balled her hands into fists and raced to the door. "Do not harm my family."

"Or what, my dear?" Marcus hissed, bringing his face close to the window. "What will you do to stop me?"

Celine set her jaw, anger burning through her.

Marcus stepped away from the door, pacing the floor outside the cell again. "You can do nothing to stop me, Celine. But I am a patient and forgiving man. I shall give you one more night to consider my offer. If you have not changed your mind by tomorrow evening, I shall begin my assault."

"Patient and forgiving? You are a vile creature, Marcus."

He ceased his pacing, smirking at her. "Do you recall what I told you in the wee hours of the morning following your sixteenth birthday? I'm certain you do. Heed those words, Celine. Consider carefully your predicament and choose wisely. Good evening, my dear."

He nodded to her and sauntered away.

Silence fell over the room as his footsteps receded. Celine stalked to the small window, peering outside at the night sky. She considered Marcus's last statement. She, indeed, recalled the conversation the morning after her sixteenth birthday. She recalled it in vivid detail, as though it happened only yesterday.

The night of her sixteenth birthday had changed her life forever. Marcus requested her to become a member of his cult, to join him in his quest to rule the world. After revealing her father's dead body to her, he asked her to kill the man responsible for his death to prove her loyalty. She refused, stealing his prized *Book of the Dead* and running from him. In the end, she had drawn his blood, sealing her fate as a supernatural being, in a desperate attempt to escape him.

Michael and Damien assisted her that night, relieving her of the book and returning to this time with it. After that evening, she would wait for over two centuries for them to return the book to her. Her life would not be pleasant. Marcus would torture her.

Her torment would begin the morning after that fated night. Celine recalled storming to her sister's house from the beach where she had opened the time portal for Michael and Damien. She burst through the doors, intent on leaving to return to her father's home.

Her brother-in-law, Teddy, her sister, Celeste, and Marcus followed her there. She recalled the massive argument that ensued.

"Where do you presume you are going, Celine?" Teddy bellowed at her.

"To my father's. I shall leave tonight. I will not spend another night in this house," she insisted.

"Celine! You shall do no such thing!"

"Do not presume to tell me what to do!" Celine shouted.

"Celine, calm yourself, you speak out of turn!" Celeste insisted.

"How dare you suggest that I calm myself," Celine screamed. "Papa is dead! You are complicit. All of you! I shall not subject myself to this madness any longer."

Celine whipped around, climbing the steps.

She made it three steps up when Teddy roared, "Yes, Celine. You are correct. Your father is dead!"

Celine ground to a halt at hearing the words. They echoed in her head as her eyes filled with tears.

Teddy continued, "And as such, your father's home is no more. Your father resided in the Governor's mansion, which will soon house the new governor. You, my dear sister-in-law, will reside with your new guardians until such time as you are to marry."

Celine set her jaw, realizing the meaning of his words.

"If I am not being clear, Celine, you shall live with us."

"I must deal with my father's things."

"Oh, they will be dealt with. I shall see to it," Teddy

assured her. "You will not leave this house. Not unless you are accompanied by me or your fiancé."

Celine cocked her head. "My fiancé?"

"Never fear, Celine," Marcus chimed in, his voice steady, unemotional. "We shall observe an appropriate grieving period before we wed."

Celine flew down the stairs. "I will never marry this man."

"Celine, you will listen and obey me as your guardian. Now go to your room."

Celine's eyes burned with fury. Anger prevented her from responding. She fled up the steps to her room, hot tears spilling down her cheeks. She slammed the door behind her, flinging herself onto her bed, weeping.

Moments later, her door opened. She glanced over her shoulder.

Marcus entered the room.

She leapt from the bed. "How dare you enter this room!" she spat. "Get out!"

"Calm yourself, Celine. There are things we must discuss." He offered her his handkerchief. "Dry your eyes, my dear."

Celine refused the offer. "There is nothing we must discuss."

"But there is. I admire your strength, Celine. I admire that fiery spirit. But make no mistake, as your husband, I will not tolerate outbursts such as the one displayed moments ago in the foyer."

"You will never be my husband! I shall never marry you!" Celine shouted through tears.

"You are distraught so I shall be lenient. But I warn you, Celine, I will not permit this behavior to continue."

Celine stalked away from him, wiping at her cheeks.

Marcus approached her, putting his hands on her arms. "Now, my dear, I suggest we begin anew. Tonight did not turn out the way I desired, but we shall move forward together."

Celine shuddered as his hands gripped her. She pulled away from his touch. "I shall move nowhere with you."

"Celine, do not be rash in your judgement. You have little choice in the matter. I shall soon become your husband."

"Never! Get out!"

"I will not be spoken to in this manner! With the life I shall provide you, you should be on your knees thanking me."

Celine raised her hand to slap him. He grabbed her arm as she swung. "Don't do anything you may regret, Celine," he hissed at her.

"I would not regret striking you," she countered.

He released her arm, throwing her onto the bed. "I shall ignore your comments. You are hysterical. You may thank me later. For now, you should sleep."

He stalked to the door, opening it and stepping out. Before pulling it shut, he said, "Resign yourself, Celine. We are bonded, you and I. Bonded as one for eternity. We are destined. There is no use in fighting. I shall have you, Celine. You shall be mine."

Celine's mind snapped back to the present. Marcus's words echoed in her mind. She lived in misery that night and for many nights after. She now lived in misery again. Two centuries later, her life continued to be disrupted by Marcus. With his latest threat, she'd have to move her timetable up. Despite the danger, she would appeal to Damien again tonight. She prayed he could withstand it. She wouldn't put his life in danger, but she had to try.

Celine settled on the floor of her cell. She took a deep breath before relaxing. She laid back, breathing deep. "Let's try this again, Damien," she whispered.

* * *

Everyone settled in the sitting room. Michael reviewed his work. Millie read and Alexander and Damien engaged in a game of chess. Damien struggled to stay awake, but as time passed, his exhaustion waned a bit. By dinner, he was tired but not exhausted.

Conversation was kept light during dinner. Still, the dark pall of Celine's absence hung over the meal. After dinner, Damien excused himself to turn in for the night. Millie offered him a sedative, but Damien refused. Given the ill effects the sedative had on him, he preferred to try natural sleep.

He stretched out as he slid under the covers. Celine entered his mind. No, he refused. He couldn't dwell on her disappearance now. It would prevent his sleep. And he desperately needed sleep. He considered changing his mind, asking Millie for the sedative. He reasoned he'd feel worse with it. He closed his eyes, counting sheep. He drifted off in the mid-seventies.

Damien opened his eyes, glancing around. He recognized his surroundings despite not being in his room. He had been here before, during his nap. The same trees loomed over him. The same eerie silence pervaded the space. His mind sensed more details of the space this time. The features were not as hazy. He noted the lack of color in the place, the strange musty smell. The cold bothered him. He shivered against it.

Noise reverberated around him. He couldn't understand it, it was indiscernible. "Hello?" he called.

"Damien," Celine answered, her voice echoing. "Focus, Damien."

Damien concentrated on the sound of Celine's voice. He closed his eyes, deepening his breath, focusing his energy.

After opening his eyes, he saw Celine standing in front of him.

She smiled at him. "You're getting better at this."

"Celine, is it really you?"

"Yes, D. It's me." Celine approached him.

He reached for her. Her warm hand grabbed his.

"You're freezing." She pulled him close.

"Celine, I miss you."

"Damien, you..." Celine snapped her head to the side, searching behind her. "You must go," she urged, her eyes wide. "I shall come to you again."

"No, Celine," Damien argued. "Celine, please. Don't go! No!"

"Go, Damien," Celine replied, backing away. "Go!"

The vision faded away, the world closing in on him.

Damien shot up to sitting, gasping for breath. "Celine! No!" he called. "Wait!"

His body trembled, his hands like ice. He pulled the blankets around him, still too stunned to move. The vivid dream felt real again. The sudden departure of Celine left him troubled. He glanced to the clock, it read 11:03 p.m. He should try to go back to sleep, but he realized sleep would escape him. Still, exhaustion coursed through him, as though he had been steamrolled.

Damien laid back, his heart rate returning to normal. He shut his eyes, searching for Celine. He could not find her, only blackness. He pushed it from his mind, determined to sleep. After twenty minutes, he gave up. He could not sleep despite the weariness he experienced.

Damien climbed from his bed, pulling on his shoes and a hoodie. He emerged from his room, padding down the hall to the foyer. He descended the steps, heading for the front door. Perhaps some fresh air would calm his frayed nerves and soothe him into sleep.

He placed his hand on the doorknob, about to turn it when a voice sounded behind him. "Aren't you supposed to be asleep?"

Damien jumped, startled. He spun to find Gray staring at him, his arms across his chest.

He swallowed hard before responding. "Couldn't sleep, had another one of those dreams."

"You look like hell," Gray replied. "Come in and have a brandy. You shouldn't be wandering around in the middle of the night."

Damien acquiesced, abandoning his plan for a walk. Perhaps the brandy and company would soothe his nerves enough to sleep. He followed Gray into the sitting room, finding Alexander there with another guest.

"What the hell is she doing here?" he demanded.

CHAPTER 6

eleste rolled her eyes as Gray responded, "Trying to help."

Gray poured Damien a drink.

"Good evening, Damien. Couldn't sleep?" Alexander greeted him.

"No, I couldn't. No wonder! I probably sensed the Wicked Witch of the West was here!"

"Calm yourself, Damien," Gray said, handing him a brandy. "She won't harm anyone."

"She is the enemy! She ruined Celine's life. And she bit Michael! How can you stand there and say that?" Damien shouted.

"Things change," Gray replied.

Celeste heaved a sigh. "I am on your side, Damien."

"Yeah, right!"

"You have a lot to learn about the supernatural world, Damien," Celeste added. "Gray is correct. Allegiances change, alliances vary. Things are not as black and white as you'd like them to be."

Damien frowned at her.

Alexander added, "She's correct, Damien. It seems foreign to you, but we have dealt with this for centuries. Trust us."

Damien collapsed onto the couch with his brandy, nodding.

Alexander narrowed his eyes at him. "What has interrupted your sleep? You look unwell."

"Same thing I said," Gray added.

"Another one of those dreams," Damien answered, rubbing his face. "I wake up from them exhausted. More exhausted than before I slept!"

"Dreams?" Celeste prodded.

"He's been having dreams about Celine," Gray informed her.

"I talked to her this time. I wanted her to stay, but she told me she had to go. She left," Damien added, staring straight ahead. He ran his fingers through his hair. "Every time I close my eyes, this happens. Every time. I don't know how Celine handled this."

"How Celine handled this?" Celeste echoed.

Damien nodded as he sipped his drink. "When she was Josie, she had dreams like this. Same type of thing. She'd wake up with her heart racing, gasping for breath, couldn't sleep after. I don't understand how she survived being this exhausted all the time."

"Perhaps you should discuss this with Millie," Gray suggested.

"I agree. This seems to be troublesome," Alexander added.

Damien shook his head. "No. I don't want a sedative or any drugs."

"Millie may be able to relieve the source of these nightmares," Gray responded.

"Why not speak with her tomorrow? It couldn't hurt," Alexander added.

"I guess it couldn't," Damien agreed. "But I won't take any

drugs! I can't afford to have my senses dulled while Celine is missing."

Gray smiled at him. "I appreciate your stubbornness, Damien. It reminds me of Celine."

Damien appreciated the comment. He finished his brandy. "So, any new leads you're working on in the middle of the night?"

Gray chuckled. "Nothing that needs your immediate attention. Do you think you can sleep after the brandy?"

"I'd rather hear your theories," Damien countered.

"How about a game or two of chess," Alexander suggested. "It may soothe your mind."

"Why does no one ever want to share information in this house?" Damien threw his hands in the air.

"There's nothing to share, I'm afraid," Celeste answered. "We haven't any real theories. Just discussing possibilities, all of which are rather improbable."

Damien considered her statement for a moment. "Try me."

"Damien, we're not holding anything back," Alexander assured him. "We had a brief discussion about any misgivings Celine may have had about returning to her life with us. The possibility that she left on her own came up. We dismissed it almost as soon as it was mentioned."

"She wouldn't leave," Damien insisted.

"I agree, which is why we dismissed the idea," Gray answered. "But..." He paused. "Is it possible she went to Josie's home? To your aunt's?"

Damien pondered the questions. "Why wouldn't she tell us?"

"Perhaps she doesn't realize."

"Huh?" Damien questioned.

"Those painful memories she experienced, perhaps they

harmed her in some way. Perhaps she's developed amnesia or reverted to Josie."

"Ohhhh," Damien answered, understanding dawning on him. "Oh, I never thought of that! Maybe! I could text Aunt Monica and ask her. Wait," he paused. "I'll have to be careful how I word it. If she hasn't seen or spoken with Celine, I don't want to panic her."

"It's more important to find out if she has seen or heard from Celine than beat around the bush."

"If Aunt Monica concludes Celine is missing, she will come up here. I love Aunt Monica, but the last thing we need is Josie's mom running around asking questions while we search for Celine."

"Good point," Gray conceded. "Okay, word it however you want, but try to find out."

"As far as her being at our old place. I don't know a good way to check that…" Damien paused again. "Oh, wait, I do!"

"Short of traveling there, which I am happy to do," Alexander chimed in, "there is no other way."

"There is," Damien answered. "I can do it right now. Just a second!" He dashed from the room.

"My, he does get a bit overzealous at times, doesn't he?" Celeste asked.

"Celine says you get used to it," Gray answered, pouring himself another brandy.

Damien rushed back into the room, his laptop in hand. He opened it and began clattering on the keys.

"What are you doing?" Gray queried.

"Well, we have several cameras in the house for security, smart thermostat, lights and so on. I can check our account to see if there has been any movement or changes in temperature. I can also check Celine's accounts to determine if she has accessed them. I tried to track her cell phone already. I can't locate it, so we're out of luck there. It makes sense, her phone is probably dead if she has it."

Damien continued clacking on the keyboard. He brought up a series of windows displaying various views of their old home. Gray, Alexander, and Celeste peered over his shoulders at his screen.

"Okay, front door shows no cars in the driveway." He clicked to another display. "No one in the living room, no movement in the upstairs hall, nothing in the office."

Damien clicked to another screen. "No history of lights being used, no calls for heat, thermostat is and has been in away mode since before Celine disappeared. So, she's not at home."

Gray sighed. "It was worth a shot, I guess."

Damien continued typing. "

What are you doing now?" Alexander inquired.

"Logging in to a few of her accounts, email, social media, that kind of stuff."

"You can do that?" Gray questioned.

"Yep, I can do it. For being a cybersecurity expert, she picks the most ridiculous passwords. Okay, nothing on social media, emails have been unread for over a week. She hasn't checked anything."

"What does this prove?" Celeste queried.

"If Celine reverted to Josie, she'd be checking her email," Damien assured them. "Josie was always connected. The only time she wasn't was when she started having the issues with the dreams and… well, became Celine."

"The lack of access on Josie's accounts seems to suggest she has not reverted to Josie," Alexander surmised.

"Correct," Damien concurred. "Last piece of evidence for that theory will come from Aunt Monica tomorrow. I'll text her in the morning. If there is no sign of Celine with Aunt

Monica, I'd say it's safe to assume Celine did not revert to Josie."

Damien closed his laptop. "If you don't mind, could we play that game of chess now?"

"Of course," Alexander replied.

Damien and Alexander spent the next two hours engaged in a few games of chess. Damien excused himself in the wee hours of the morning, supposing he could sleep. He fell asleep just before sunrise. Despite having no answers, he felt as though he had accomplished something by ruling out one possibility.

CELINE PULLED herself from her communication with Damien. She wanted to speak with him, but something warned her to leave. She opened her eyes, allowing her senses to return to her cell. She sensed danger. After climbing to her feet, she glanced out the window into the basement. Marcus must be nearby. The danger she sensed must be his presence. Within seconds, the sound of footsteps reached her ears. A figure descended the stairs, approaching her cell.

"Ah, Celine, you are still awake. How fortunate," Marcus said.

Celine wrinkled her nose at him. "What do you want now?"

"I wanted to impart one last important detail from our conversation."

"It could have waited," Celine assured him.

"Ah, but it may influence your decision, my dear. There-fore, I made the effort to return." He dangled a small crystal vial on a string. It sparkled, glowing from within.

Celine's brow furrowed and her curiosity overcame her. "What is that?" Celine inquired.

"Remember when Benjamin Abbott painted your portrait and captured a piece of your soul?" Marcus questioned.

"Yes," Celine answered.

"While I was… away, I learned how to transfer soul shards from one object to another."

Celine cocked her head as understanding set in. Her jaw dropped open in disbelief.

"While it proved difficult, I retrieved your soul shard from your portrait, Celine." He dangled the container in front of her. "So, if you are expecting your portrait to preserve the Buckley household when I begin my assault, it will do you no good. I have rendered it useless."

"You are lying!" Celine screeched.

"Oh, come, Celine. Have I ever lied to you?"

"Give it to me," Celine demanded.

"Oh, no, mon chérie!" He stared at the sparkling vial. "I couldn't bear to part with it. It is my most prized possession. For now."

Celine set her jaw, furious and frustrated.

"Well, I shall allow you to return to your contemplation. Au revoir, Celine."

He strolled away, disappearing up the stairs.

Celine held back tears. The situation was becoming more dangerous by the moment. She hoped she could force a solution soon. Yet she still had to proceed with caution. She couldn't endanger Damien's life to save hers. She wanted to reach out to him again, but she stopped herself. Patience, Celine, she chided herself, patience.

* * *

Damien awoke mid-morning. He yawned and stretched. A glance at the clock sent him leaping from his bed. He raced around his room, dressing for the day. He admonished himself for sleeping so long. He should have set the alarm. How foolish he had been. The few hours of sleep helped, but he hated to get such a late start on the day.

He hurried from his room down to the dining room. Coffee should still be available on the sideboard. He'd grab a cup before searching for everyone. As he entered the dining room, he found a note on the table. *Gone to Alexander's. Meet us there when you wake up. ~ Gray*

Damien gulped down a cup of coffee, impatient to get to Alexander's. While he drank it, he pulled his phone from his pocket. He opened his text app and sent a text to his aunt, Josie's mom: *Good morning Aunt Monica... just checking in... how are you?*

He finished his coffee and zipped his hoodie as he made his way across the foyer. He stepped into the crisp air outside. Already autumn was fading, giving way to winter. Soon it would snow here. His phone chimed as he set off on the path to Alexander's. He pulled it from his pocket, swiping it open. He received a return text from Aunt Monica: *Hi sweetie! I'm doing just fine! It's great to hear from you. How is the move going? I miss both of you!*

Damien read it, pondering it as he formulated a response. Aunt Monica missed both of them. Did she mean in general, or did she mean because she hadn't heard from Celine? Damien devised a response to find out: *We miss you, too! Speaking of... has Josie called or texted you? She said she was planning on calling and I didn't get to ask her if she did.*

Alexander's house came into view. He hurried toward it, impatient to continue searching for Celine and to get out of the cold. As he approached the door, his phone chimed again. He considered checking the message before knocking, but the cold drove him to seek entrance. He knocked at the door.

Alexander greeted him in moments. "Come in, Damien," he invited him.

Damien entered the foyer, pulling his phone from his pocket. "Good morning. I got Gray's note. Sorry I wasn't here earlier. I slept in."

"No problem at all," Alexander assured him. "We're in the sitting room."

They entered the sitting room, joining Gray, Millie, and Michael.

"Hey, good morning, buddy. Finally got some sleep, huh?" Michael asked.

"Yeah, a little," Damien admitted. He swiped open his phone. "I'm talking to Aunt Monica. Following up on the Celine flipped back to Josie theory. She just answered."

Damien read the message: *I haven't heard from her. I assumed she was busy with the move and new contracts. The last time I heard from Josie was about two weeks ago.*

Damien typed back: *I'll remind her to call, she's been really busy with those new contracts.*

Monica responded in seconds: *Thanks, sweetie, although I realize how busy you both are. Don't be too hard on Josie when you remind her ;)... She hates that!*

Damien answered: *Haha, I know!*

He pocketed his phone. "Okay, she hasn't heard from Josie in two weeks. So, she is not with Aunt Monica, nor has she contacted Aunt Monica."

"Well, that's that then," Gray said. "Back to square one."

"Back to square zero is more like it. We have nothing to go on! This is so frustrating," Damien fumed, collapsing on the couch. "How can we ever find her?"

"We found her after twenty-five years. We'll find her now," Gray assured him.

Damien sighed and ran his fingers through his hair. "I guess."

"Let's work on these troubling dreams you're having, Damien," Millie suggested.

"They aren't troubling," Damien countered. "It's nice to be with Celine again. If it wasn't for the ill-effects, I'd almost want to have them."

Millie smiled at him and rubbed his arm. "Tell us again about them. What has been the same in each? What has been different?"

"Uh, well," Damien began. "They all occur in the same place. And they all include Celine."

"Those are the similarities, what are the differences?" Millie prodded.

"The amount I can see or hear."

"What do you mean?" Millie questioned.

"The first one, I could barely make out anything. I realized I was outside, but everything was blurry. Like a haze covered my eyes. And I couldn't hear anything. It all sounded muffled, like I was underwater. The second one, I could see things around me, but my hearing was still muffled. After a few seconds, I could hear Celine's voice and then after I concentrated, I could see her. In the third episode, I could see Celine almost right away."

"So, this is a recurring dream. Each time you have it, you progress a little further."

"That seems like a fair assessment," Damien agreed.

"The obvious answer is this is related to Celine's disappearance. Your subconscious mind is struggling to process the anxiety and worry you are experiencing. It's manifesting in your sleep by allowing you to see Celine."

"That makes sense, too."

"Can you alleviate them?" Gray queried. "The negative

physical effects are taking a toll already and he's only experienced three dreams."

"We can try hypnosis. Let his subconscious tell us why things are manifesting this way."

Damien gulped and grimaced. "Hypnosis?"

"Yes," Millie replied with a chuckle. "It doesn't hurt."

"Yeah, I realize that. But it seems… weird. Letting you probe around in my subconscious mind."

Millie chuckled again. "Celine does it. There is nothing to be afraid of."

"I guess," Damien conceded.

"Good," Millie answered, removing a pendant from her pocket.

"Oh, wait, here? Now?" Damien questioned.

"Why not?"

Damien ran his sweaty palms down his pant legs and shrugged. "Feels weird with an audience."

"We could leave," Michael suggested.

"I'd prefer to stay," Gray countered. "In case there is anything we can use to find Celine. Some idea stuck in his subconscious."

"Good point," Damien answered. "Okay, okay, let's just do this."

Millie stood and perched on the edge of the coffee table. "Sit back and relax."

"Wait!" Damien shouted.

"What is it now?" Gray inquired.

"You don't suppose there's another person lurking around in my head like Celine was in Josie's, do you?"

"Heaven help us if there is," Gray murmured to Alexander. Alexander snickered at the statement.

"No, I don't imagine there is. Now, sit back and relax, Damien," Millie answered.

Damien leaned back into the couch cushions, fidgeting a

bit. He swallowed hard, adjusting himself. He blew out a long breath.

"Okay, I'm ready." Michael perched on the edge of his armchair, across from Damien.

Alexander and Gray remained standing, watching from across the room.

Millie dangled the shiny pendant. "Since this is your first time under hypnosis, I'll explain the process, then begin. I want you to concentrate on the pendant and my voice. Listen to my instructions and try to relax. All right?"

Damien nodded, swallowing again. "Okay."

"There's no reason to be nervous, Damien. Just relax," Millie urged, spinning the pendant in front of him. "Concentrate on the pendant, note how it catches the light. Listen to my voice and focus on the pendant. You can feel your body relaxing. Your limbs are getting heavy, your tension is easing. You feel sleepy, your eyes are getting heavy. Close your eyes when you feel relaxed, Damien."

Damien's eyes blinked a few times before closing.

"You are feeling more and more relaxed," Millie said, pocketing the pendant. "I'm going to count backward from ten to one and when I reach one, you will be completely relaxed." Millie began her slow, methodic countdown.

When she reached one, she asked, "Are you relaxed, Damien?"

"Yes," Damien murmured.

"You've been experiencing a recurring dream of late," Millie began. "Are you aware of the dream to which I refer?"

"Yes."

"Describe the dream. What do you see?"

"Trees. But not normal trees." Damien's brow pinched in concentration. "They are gray, there is no color. It's so quiet here. No birds, no insects, no sounds."

"Trees? So, you are outside. Have you seen this place before?"

"No. Never. It's so cold here. So…" Damien's voice trailed off.

"Continue, Damien. What else?"

Damien's brow furrowed again.

"What is it, Damien? What do you see? Is it Celine?"

His breathing increased. His body shook.

"What's wrong with him?" Michael asked, leaping from his chair.

"I'm not sure. Damien," Millie said, "Damien, you are safe. There is nothing to fear. Relax."

Damien continued to gasp for air, shivering.

"Damien, relax," Millie urged.

"What's happening, Millie?" Gray inquired.

"I'm not sure." Millie approached Damien, feeling his pulse. "His pulse is elevated along with his breathing. He's shivering as though he's cold."

"He complained about the cold before," Gray recalled.

"Damien," Millie called again, "Damien, can you hear us?"

There was no response.

"Pull him out of it," Gray insisted.

"Damien, I'm going to count backward from ten. When I reach one, you will awaken." Millie began her count, speeding through this time. She reached one but Damien did not respond.

She paused a moment, staring at him before turning to everyone else. "He's non-responsive."

"What does that mean?" Michael queried.

"Can you get him out of this or not?" Gray questioned as he approached them.

Millie shook her head, her forehead creasing. "I'm not sure. I cannot get through to him. We've lost the connection to him."

"Is there anything we should do?" Alexander asked.

"We must keep him warm. Perhaps this is some kind of shock." Millie pulled a blanket over him, tucking it in around him.

"Help him!" Michael demanded.

"I don't think I can," Millie conceded. "He must find his own way back."

CHAPTER 7

*D*amien searched the surrounding landscape. Silence surrounded him as he scoured it. Everything was gray. Trees, ground, sky, all shades of gray. Where was Celine?

"Celine?" he called. "Celine, are you there?"

He shivered against the icy cold. The bitterness penetrated him. A screech pierced the environment. It deafened him. He clapped his hands over his ears. The sound was sickening and terrifying. He dropped to his knees, still clutching his ears as the gut-wrenching sound continued. He grew colder, his teeth chattering as he knelt on the ground. He squeezed his eyes shut.

A warm arm wrapped around him, pulling him close. He opened his eyes, uncovering his ears.

"Celine!" he exclaimed.

"Damien," she said, her voice reverberating. "What are you doing here?"

"Looking for you. Why did you leave last time?"

"Damien... mustn't... here alone... cannot stay... too dangerous."

Damien furrowed his brow, shaking his head as he shivered. "I can't understand."

"Focus, Damien," Celine instructed, grabbing his chin and staring into his eyes. "You must focus."

Damien nodded.

"You must tell the others, Damien. Shadow World. Tell them, Shadow World."

Damien tried to form the words, but his lips barely moved from the cold.

"Shadow World, focus, Damien, you must focus. Shadow World. Remember, Damien, Shadow World."

Damien blinked a few times, the world narrowing around him. He fought to stay but found he was unable.

Celine's voice faded to a whisper. "Shadow World, Shadow World, Shadow World," she repeated as it faded away.

Damien's vision darkened, the world blacking out around him.

* * *

MICHAEL PACED as Damien's breathing continued to be labored. Damien shivered uncontrollably.

"I can't believe this, I just can't believe it," he fumed. "I am here with two warlocks and a medical doctor, and none of you can do anything to help him. This is unbelievable."

"Calm down," Gray advised. "You aren't helping."

"Neither are you!" Michael shouted.

"Quiet, both of you! He's trying to speak!" Millie shouted.

Damien's lips moved, but no words came out. He continued moving his lips, the same motion over and over, yet no sound emerged.

Michael rushed to his side. "Damien? Can you hear us? Say something, buddy."

"Sh… Sh… Sh…" Damien whispered.

"Sh? What's he trying to say?" Michael voiced. "Come on, Damien, you can do it. What are you trying to say?"

"Sha… Sha…" Damien struggled. He groaned, pinching his forehead, his eyes squeezed shut. "Shadow… Shadow World!" he managed, his voice at a fever pitch. After conveying the message, he slumped, motionless.

"Did he just say…" Alexander asked, turning to Gray, aghast.

"Sounded like it," Gray answered.

"But that's…" Alexander began.

"Impossible," Gray finished for him.

"Damien? Damien?" Michael called.

Millie felt his pulse.

"Well?" Michael demanded.

"He's alive, but unconscious. He's passed out from hyper-ventilating. He's still quite cold."

Michael pulled his hoodie from the back of the armchair, laying it across Damien's chest. "Come on, buddy, warm up! And wake up!"

"His breathing is regulating, and his pulse is slowing," Millie reported. She retrieved a vial from her medical bag. She waved it under his nose.

His face contorted as he smelled the putrid scent. He startled awake, blinking his eyes a few times.

"Wha-What happened?" he questioned, his voice hoarse. His eyes struggled to stay open, as though he was exhausted.

Michael rubbed his arm. "You passed out, buddy. How do you feel? Are you warm enough?"

"Passed out? What?"

"You slipped away from us," Millie informed him, again checking his pulse. "You displayed some concerning physical symptoms. Your breathing was elevated and erratic, your pulse was racing, and you were shivering. You passed out after a while."

Damien shook his head, trying to understand.

"Do you remember anything from the session?" Gray asked.

"Gray, please!" Millie implored.

"Uh," Damien pondered, "I was in that place again. I was alone. I was so cold, and a loud screeching pierced my ears. Then Celine came. She was so warm. She told me to come back and tell you something. What was it?"

"Shadow something?" Michael recalled. "You said something about a shadow."

"Shadow…" Damien began. "Shadow… Shadow… Shadow World, she said tell them Shadow World!"

Alexander and Gray exchanged a glance, shock apparent on their faces.

"Are you sure?" Gray asked, his eyes wide.

Damien reflected for a moment. "Yes, she said, 'Tell them Shadow World.'" Damien offered a sharp nod. "I'm sure."

Gray and Alexander shared another glance.

Michael noted the exchange. "Does that mean something to you?"

"I'm not sure. Is it even possible?" Gray asked Alexander.

Alexander flicked his eyebrows up. "Normally, I'd say no, but this is Celine we're dealing with. Impossible is not in her vocabulary. If anyone has found a way, it would be Celine."

Michael flung his hands out. "Would someone mind telling me what the hell is happening? What are you two talking about?"

Alexander strode to a bookcase across the room. He selected a book and paged through it. He found the entry and handed it to Michael.

Michael glanced at the page, reading aloud. "Shadow World… A non-earthly realm existing in the void. Shadow

World is a harsh, unforgiving environment: colorless, silent and cold. The realm is rarely visited except by adjudicators, who enjoy its neutrality. What does this even mean?" He glanced to Alexander and Gray, his forehead scrunched.

"Many spaces exist beyond the earth. Shadow World is one of them," Alexander explained.

"I still don't…" Michael began.

"He's saying Damien was in Shadow World. That Celine was there with him. His description fits, but it's impossible," Gray contended.

"Why?" Michael asked.

"For many reasons," Alexander expounded. "First, as the book mentions, Shadow World is harsh. A human could not survive there for long. Second, one does not simply slip into Shadow World. It is difficult, perhaps impossible for a human."

"It's difficult even for us. I doubt either of us could enter that place if we tried," Gray added, sinking into a leather armchair.

"Yes, but could Celine?" Alexander posed.

Gray rubbed his chin as he considered the question. "Perhaps. But even if she's found a way, how is he getting there?"

"So, Celine is trapped in Shadow World?" Damien croaked, his voice still hoarse.

Millie poured him a glass of water to sip, checking his pulse again.

"No, I doubt it. I'm not sure even she could survive there for weeks. She must be coming and going. But from where and how?" Gray pondered for a moment. "You say she's not there at first when you arrive?"

"This time she wasn't," Damien answered. "The other times she's there, but I can't see her at first. And her voice is all distorted. But I can feel her. She can touch me."

"This time she wasn't there when you arrived, though?" Gray repeated.

"No, she came and asked what I was doing there. She said I couldn't stay but to tell you Shadow World and then everything went black."

"Amazing," Alexander remarked as he collapsed into the armchair next to Gray. "She has found a way to slip in and out of Shadow World *and* to call a human there, too."

"More importantly," Gray said, shooting his cousin a pointed glance. "She's found a way to communicate."

Alexander fluttered his eyelids. "I am… astounded. This is quite a revelation."

"I agree. It's… almost beyond belief," Gray answered. "I am also, however, concerned."

"Concerned?" Michael inquired.

"Yes," Gray replied. "We have a way to communicate with Celine, but it's dangerous. These physical symptoms will continue to wear on Damien each time he enters Shadow World."

"Perhaps that's why she only makes contact for minutes at a time," Alexander suggested.

Gray jumped from his seat, pacing the floor. "Yes, it seems she's being cautious. She's well aware of the toll this would take on him. Still, we must be cautious on our end, too. We must keep an eye on him, monitor him day and night. He should never be left alone."

"I agree," Alexander replied.

"He's slipping into this every time he tries to sleep. It's exhausting him," Gray added.

"Sedatives may help with that," Millie chimed in.

Gray chewed his lower lip. "Yes. A sedative will likely stop him from being able to slip into Shadow World. But we must be careful not to block Celine's ability to communicate."

"It will be a delicate balance to strike," Alexander admitted.

Michael screwed up his face, snapping the book closed and tossing it on a nearby table. "Wait, you guys are proposing he continue to go there?"

Gray spun to face Damien. "Do you think you can communicate to Celine to contact you during the day? So, you can rest with a sedative at night?"

Damien considered it for a moment before he nodded his head. "I can try. I am learning to navigate this place. If I stay focused on Celine, it's much easier."

"No, no, no, wait!" Michael insisted. "This is dangerous. Are you serious?"

Gray screwed up his face. "Yes, I'm serious. Why do you two never believe I'm serious?"

"I can do it," Damien affirmed. "I'm okay. I can do it. I want to do it."

"All right," Gray said. "Then we move forward with this plan. The next time she contacts you, tell her the plan. And ask where she is. Once we have that information, we'll determine what to do next."

Michael sank onto the couch next to Damien. "How are you holding up?"

Damien collapsed back into the cushions. "I'm okay. Exhausted, but okay."

"You should remain here tonight. You've taken quite a physical toll," Alexander suggested. "You shouldn't waste energy returning to the main house. I'll have a room prepared."

"And I'd recommend a sedative," Millie added.

Damien pushed himself straighter. "No. We haven't told Celine the plan yet! She may try to contact me!"

"We can't risk it," Gray countered. "You'll take the sedative. We can't afford for you to slip off to Shadow World and become too ill to return."

"But…" Damien began.

Gray wagged a finger at him. "No buts. Besides, Celine knows not to draw you back too soon. And if she tries and can't reach you, she'll try again."

"One more night. I can withstand it," Damien argued.

"Damien," Gray lectured, "I want her back as much as you do. We have to do it smart and safe. We're making progress. We have a lead. We're one thousand times better off than we were hours ago. Take the win."

"He's right," Michael agreed, clapping his hand on Damien's shoulder. "You've got to rest up for the next time Celine contacts you. You have to stay focused so you can tell her the plan."

Damien sighed, frustrated but resigned. "Okay."

Millie snapped her bag shut, a smile on her lips. "Wonderful. We'll administer the sedative following dinner. You'll have a good, long sleep. You'll be more than ready the next time Celine contacts you."

"One more thing," Gray added. "Let's keep this development to ourselves. It doesn't leave this room, understood? Shifting alliances or not."

Everyone agreed to play things close to the vest. Damien spent the hours until dinner teaching Michael how to play chess. The activity kept him quiet and resting while allowing his mind to relax. Alexander and Gray searched for information among Alexander's reference collection about Shadow World. They hoped to learn as much as possible, including a way to enter the realm themselves. If they could enter the world and speak with Celine, it would ease the burden on Damien.

When dinner rolled around, they had learned nothing to allow them to enter the realm. For the time being, the responsibility to communicate with Celine laid solely with Damien. After dinner, Millie administered the sedative, despite Damien's protestation. With temporary misgivings, he bucked against the previously agreed upon plan until everyone convinced him it was for the best. He assented, agreeing only after the promise of one final game of chess as the sedative kicked in.

As they finished the game, Damien yawned.

"Tired?" Michael asked.

"Very," Damien admitted.

"Get some sleep, buddy. See you in the morning!"

Alexander walked Damien to his room, planning to stay with him as he slept. "What you're doing is very brave, Damien."

"Thanks. But I'd do anything for Celine."

"I realize that. But Shadow World must be frightening, especially now that you know the dangers."

"I'll be okay. Celine will protect me."

Alexander smiled at him, nodding his head. "She will."

Damien shook his head as they entered the bedroom. "I'm concerned about her more than myself. She'll protect me, at the cost of herself."

"She can take care of herself very well, Damien. She's smart. She won't risk either of your lives."

"But if something happens, she'll sacrifice herself. If Shadow World is dangerous for her, too, I worry she'll..." Damien's voice trailed off.

"We'll find her, Damien, before that happens," Alexander assured him.

Damien yawned as he climbed into bed. "Let's hope. I am so tired."

"Have a good rest, Damien," Alexander said as he settled into the armchair across the room. "See you tomorrow."

Damien relaxed into the pillows behind him. He fought

sleep for a few more moments, allowing his mind to go over the day's events. They had a channel to communicate with Celine. That pleased him. He wanted to meet her again, though he realized he wouldn't with the sedative in his system. He was frightened to close his eyes. What if Celine needed him and couldn't contact him? Had he made a mistake? He stared at the ceiling as worry coursed through him. If Celine was willing to sacrifice so much, to use such a dangerous method to make contact, what kind of danger did she face wherever she was?

"Celine," he whispered into the darkness, "please be okay." He closed his eyes, drifting off to sleep.

* * *

CELESTE ENTERED the sitting room around midnight. Gray and Alexander poured over a series of books.

She arched an eyebrow. "Working a new angle?"

"No," Gray lied, "searching for any information about Celine's situation after being human again."

"Did Damien contact his aunt?" she asked as she settled onto the sofa.

"He did. She hasn't heard from Celine."

Celeste's brow furrowed. "Yet you're still pursuing this?"

Gray tossed the book down and strode across the room. "There's nothing else to pursue, Celeste. At least I feel as though we're doing something."

"How is Damien holding up? I'm surprised he's not here monitoring something or another on his laptop."

"Damien is exhausted," Gray answered. "The toll on him is overwhelming. He's paying the price for his lack of sleep last night."

Celeste's gaze fell to her lap. "Poor Damien. He is so close to Celine. I can imagine how devastating this is for him."

"Yes. The poor boy is beside himself," Alexander chimed in. "We gave him a sedative to sleep. I hope it helps him."

Celeste heaved a sigh. "Humans should not involve themselves in our affairs. Perhaps he should visit his Aunt Monica until the situation is resolved."

Gray crossed his arms, staring into the black night outside the window. "He'll never leave with Celine missing."

"Then force him," Celeste replied.

Gray rolled his eyes at the suggestion, returning to the books spread across the desk. "No. Besides, Celine wouldn't want that."

"We can concern ourselves with Celine's wants when she has returned. Until then, Damien should be removed from the situation for his own good. Michael, too."

Gray narrowed his eyes at her. "Why are you so insistent, Celeste? Do you have information you'd like to share?"

Celeste rose from her seat and stalked to the window. "No. I am not aware of anything specific. I only believe they would be better off away from the overwhelming circumstances. For their own safety. It could take a toll on their health. Celine wouldn't want that."

Gray shared a glance with Alexander.

"We'll take it under consideration," he promised. "For now, they stay."

* * *

CELINE PACED the floor of her cell. Why had Damien been in Shadow World without her? She hadn't summoned him there. Had she not sensed him calling to her, he may have died there. Mere seconds too long in the harsh environment could kill him. The chance she took bringing him to the world for moments at a time was a huge gamble. Still, it was her only way to communicate with her family.

It would be slow-going, but she would inform them of her situation. Extreme caution on her part must be exercised. She would not take too many chances with Damien's life.

She stared out the window as the sky darkened. Her musing turned toward the instructions she passed to Damien during their last encounter. Had he passed the information along? Did Gray and the others receive the message? She wasn't sure. Perhaps she'd gather more information the next time she met with Damien.

Celine longed to try tonight, but she was unsure it was a good idea. Damien's excursion earlier would leave him exhausted. Another trip may prove too much for him. Could she chance it? She'd make a determination later.

As darkness crept over the sky, she prepared herself for the inevitable confrontation with Marcus. He had given her until this evening. She could not join him. Yet, she must stall until her family could locate her. It would be a delicate balance to strike, a fine line to walk. But she had no choice.

The last streaks of light faded as footsteps sounded above her. Celine swallowed hard as they continued down the stairs behind her.

"Good evening, Celine," Marcus greeted her.

"Hello, Marcus," she answered as she climbed to her feet.

"A greeting! How fortunate I am this evening! Might I assume good news is forthcoming?"

Celine faced him, considering her response. "Marcus, I'd like to speak honestly for a moment."

He waved a hand in the air to encourage her. "By all means, my dear."

"We have been locked in this battle with each other for over two centuries," Celine began. "It must end."

"I couldn't agree more," Marcus replied. "This conflict between us is never what I desired."

"I realize this is not the ending you expected."

Marcus clasped his hands behind his back. "It is not."

"When I met Gray…"

"Celine," Marcus interrupted her, "let us not speak of him tonight."

"Oh, Marcus," Celine said, hurrying to the door and grasping the bars, "he has been my husband for over two centuries."

"I realize that, Celine."

Her shoulders slumped. "Then you must realize what you ask of me is impossible!"

Displeasure shown on Marcus's face as he wrinkled his nose. "Righting your mistake, while unpleasant for you, is not impossible, Celine."

"I do not consider my marriage to Grayson a mistake!"

"Damn it, Celine, I have had enough of these games!" he shouted.

"As have I, Marcus! Constant battles, collateral damage, no peace. We must stop!" she screamed back.

"I disagree!"

"Surely, I do not hold this much interest for you after centuries, Marcus. It's time to move on."

Marcus did not respond, his jaw set in frustration.

"It isn't about me, though, is it? It's about winning, it always has been. Fine! You've won! You've bested me, Marcus. Now, let's end this." She flung her arms out.

"I plan to end this, Celine," he replied. "The question is with whom do I start with?"

Celine gripped the bars of the window again, pulling herself closer to it. "What do you mean?"

"I mean which member of your family do I destroy first?"

"Marcus…" Celine began.

"No, Celine. You are correct, enough of the games. For centuries I have allowed you chance after chance, hoping you would realize your mistakes on your own. You have squandered your opportunities at every turn. You have run out of opportunities. Now you must be left with no other choices."

"No, Marcus, do not do this!"

Marcus turned from her, pacing the floor. "Whom do I start with, Celine? Celeste? No, your dear sister isn't punishment enough for your behavior. Besides, she may still prove useful to me." He spun, stalking in the opposite direction. Celine set her jaw, seething inside. "Perhaps Grayson. Hmmm, no, he should suffer watching his family being destroyed one by one. Perhaps an easier target. A human one. Oh!" He smiled to himself and twisted to eye her. "What about dear Damien?"

CHAPTER 8

Celine gasped, a tear rolling down her cheek. "Do not harm Damien, Marcus, I warn you."

Marcus chuckled. "Have I touched a nerve, my dear?"

Celine glared at him, her nostrils flaring.

"Never fear, Celine. I shall not begin with your precious Damien. No, I believe I'll begin with Avery and her children, again."

"Marcus, please," Celine cried. "This will not help the situation in any way."

"I disagree. I imagine it will be quite enlightening for you."

"Harming my family will not endear you to me, Marcus."

"No, I don't expect it will. I have no illusions about what this will achieve. The intent is not endearment, but rather surrender."

Celine swallowed hard. His threats were never idle. He had attacked her family many times before. This time she wouldn't be there to protect them. Gray and Alexander would be alone to attempt to deflect any attacks. Marcus, far more powerful than either, was capable of destroying them easily. He wouldn't destroy them outright. He would toy with them first, drag it out, make her and them suffer. A tear rolled down her cheek as she contemplated the dire circumstances.

"I will provide a report tomorrow evening. Good night, Celine." He spun on his heel, stalking across the room.

"Wait!" Celine called to him.

He stopped halfway across the room. "Unless you have changed your mind, Celine, I am finished with this conversation."

"I'd like to speak with Celeste," Celine requested.

Marcus ignored her, taking another two steps toward the stairs.

"Marcus, wait!" Celine called.

"Celine, I will not continue to play these games. I warned you. You refused to heed my warning. The only way any of your requests will be honored is when you've made a show of good faith on your part." He again spun away from her.

Celine swallowed hard, choking on the lump in her throat. "Fine. I am ready to concede." The words stuck in her throat, difficult to speak.

Marcus twisted to face her, his head cocked to the side. "I'm sorry? I'm not sure I heard you, Celine."

"You heard me, Marcus. Do not make me repeat it," Celine spat. "Now, I'd like to see my sister."

Marcus approached her cell. "While this is a positive first step, you are in no position to make demands, my dear."

Celine sighed, closing her eyes for a moment. "Marcus, this is not easy. Please, do not make it harder than it already is."

"I don't imagine it is," Marcus admitted. "All right, Celine. I shall arrange a meeting with Celeste."

"And you will not harm my family?"

"Your former family, Celine."

A tear rolled down Celine's cheek at the words.

"And no, I will not launch an attack on them. But I do require a show of good faith."

Celine gazed up at him, her brow crinkling.

"Your wedding ring."

Celine glanced to the gold band around her finger. "Marcus…"

"Celine, this is not negotiable. He is no longer your husband. Remove your ring."

"No," Celine defied him.

"Then we have nothing more to say." He turned away again.

"Wait," Celine cried. She rubbed the ring around her finger, closing her eyes. She memorized the weight of it on her finger, the cool feel of the metal on her fingertips. A whimper escaped her lips as she slid the ring off her finger. She held it in her fingers a moment longer, vowing to retrieve it one day. She stalked to the cell door and held the ring out.

Marcus accepted her wedding band. "You've made a wise choice, Celine. I shall arrange the meeting with Celeste."

Celine wiped another tear from her cheek, nodding. "Thank you."

Marcus reached through the cell door, offering her a handkerchief. He wiped a tear from her cheek. "Do not cry, Celine. It will become easier."

He pocketed the ring, leaving Celine alone as he crossed the basement and ascended the stairs.

Celine doubled over, her body wracked with sobs. She slid down the wall to a seated position. After a moment, she collapsed to the floor, weeping. Her mind replayed another moment when she had relinquished her wedding ring. Just over twenty-five years ago she had handed the ring back to Gray. Having been granted a new life by her adjudicator, she had given him her wedding ring while saying goodbye. She recalled the moment as though it were yesterday.

She stood with the adjudicator on the beach at midnight. She begged it for another life, a normal life. The adjudicator granted it to her: twenty-five years to live as a human. If she did not revert to her current state, she could live and die as a human. Relief coursed over her as she realized the second chance she was granted. Relief mixed with turmoil as Gray approached them on the beach.

"Celine," he called as he witnessed the scene. She had no words for him, but he needed none. The tears shining in her eyes told him all he needed to know. "Celine," he lamented again.

"Come, Celine Devereaux Buckley," the adjudicator stated. "We must go."

"Please," she begged it, "give me a moment to say goodbye."

The adjudicator glanced at her, its sideways eyelids blinking. "So be it."

Celine walked toward Gray, who was trailed by Alexander, both of them having run to the beach. "Gray, I…"

Tears formed in his eyes. "Celine," he murmured, cupping her face in his hands, "don't do this."

"I'm sorry, Gray. It is done."

"Undo it, Celine. We can fight him."

"It cannot be undone, Gray. We cannot continue like this. Marcus is too large a threat. I cannot allow his attacks on your family to endure."

"Celine, this isn't your fault…"

"Gray, it is. And it must stop. I must be the one to stop it."

"Celine, please," Gray answered, his voice quivering. "I love you."

"I love you, too. And that is why I must do this," Celine responded, tears spilling onto her cheeks as regret consumed her. She took his hand, kissing him as her tears continued to fall. She glanced to her hand, spinning the wedding ring on her finger. She slid it off, placing it in his hand.

"No, Celine," he cried.

She closed his hand around the ring, unable to speak. She turned away from him. Gray grabbed her arm, pulling her back. "Don't go, Celine, please."

"Please don't make this harder than it already is, Gray. I must do this. I must protect you."

"Promise me you'll come back."

Celine sniffled, choking out the words. "I can't."

Alexander approached. "Celine, no," he uttered.

Celine grasped his hand, squeezing it. "Look after him," she requested of Alexander.

"Of course, Celine. But I hope and pray we'll see you again."

Celine nodded to him, stepping backward. Gray clung to her hand in a desperate attempt to stop her from leaving. She tugged it away. He lunged toward her, but Alexander prevented him from reaching her. "Let me go!" Gray shouted at him.

"Gray, you must let her go. Believe she will come back," Alexander advised.

"Celine!" Gray called to her again as she reached the adjudicator. The creature wrapped its wing around Celine, launching skyward from the beach. "CELINE!" Gray shouted as they disappeared through the clouds.

His pained voice rang through Celine's mind as she laid on the cold, stone floor weeping. She elected to leave him for twenty-five years to keep him safe. She would not lose him again. She vowed the surrender of her wedding ring would only be temporary. This was not a goodbye. She would rejoin Gray and her family.

Her tears ceased. She dried her cheeks as she allowed the

emotion to pass. She would be home soon, she assured herself. She had a plan, a way to communicate. She closed her eyes, forming Damien's image in her mind. She called to him, allowing herself to slip away into Shadow World.

Celine stood with her arms wrapped around her, protection against the bitter chill of the harsh realm. She waited in the grove of trees. She called to Damien over and over, however he did not respond. She could not see him; he did not appear in the realm. Celine waited longer than she should have, the cold beginning to affect her. When she could wait no longer, she allowed herself to slip back to her world.

She awoke from her meditation, rising to pace the floor. She had not reached Damien. Where had he been? Had something happened to him following the last encounter he'd experienced in Shadow World? Had she been too late to save him from the ill effects of the realm? Worry consumed her. She would try again tomorrow. For now, she would be left to console herself with memories of her family in happier times.

* * *

DAMIEN AWOKE LATE the next morning, still groggy from the sedative. Gray sat in the armchair, gazing out the window. Damien's mind still felt numb. He cursed needing the medication. Without it, Gray and Alexander feared he may slip into Shadow World too often and wind up hurt or worse.

Damien understood their concern. He shared it, although he trusted Celine. However, one slight miscalculation on her part could lead to disaster, according to the Buckleys. If he became unable to travel to Shadow World, their connection with Celine would be lost. They could not afford to lose that connection. It provided their only means of finding her.

Damien laid in bed, allowing his mind to recover. The extreme exhaustion he experienced waned. He had recovered some of his energy from the long, restful sleep induced by the sedative. Good, he mused. He would be ready for another communication with Celine in the severe environment.

After twenty minutes, he climbed from bed. "

Good morning," Gray said. "How do you feel?"

"Good morning," Damien answered. "Pretty good, a little groggy. I slept, and I did not have any encounters with Celine."

"No," Gray confirmed, "you didn't slip into Shadow World over night. We monitored you all night."

"Mind if we head out for some coffee?" he asked, pulling on his shoes.

He and Gray navigated downstairs, finding Alexander, Michael, and Millie in the sitting room.

"Good morning!" Alexander greeted him. "Coffee?"

"Please," Damien groaned.

"Did you sleep?" Michael asked Damien.

"I did, yes. No encounters, just rest. Still a little groggy, but overall, I feel rested."

"Any side effects, Damien?" Millie asked, grasping his wrist to take his pulse. "Nightmares? Unsteadiness when you arose? Inability to fully awaken?"

"No. None of those," Damien answered.

"Good. This dosage should work well for now. We'll adjust if it becomes too much after multiple uses. Let me know if you experience even slight side effects so we can adjust it before they become a problem."

"I will."

"Can't afford to get off-track now, buddy," Michael said, clapping him on the back.

"Yeah, right," Damien admitted, sipping his coffee as he sank onto the couch.

"You okay?" Michael asked.

"Yeah. Just a little anxious about Celine contacting me again."

"I bet. That place sounds awful," Michael agreed.

"It's not the place. I just… what if she tried overnight, and I wasn't there? When will she try again? What if she can only contact me at night? And I keep taking the sedative and she tries and tries and I'm never there."

"If Celine doesn't make contact in the next day or so, we'll switch your sleeping schedule," Gray suggested. "Let your mind be receptive during the night and sleep during the day."

"Oh, good idea," Damien replied. "Okay, that makes me feel a little better."

"Only a little?" Michael inquired.

"Yeah, I'll be worried until she contacts me. What if she can't get to me for some reason? Or what if she needs me sooner? Ah, I hate this. I won't be unstressed until she's home."

"If she does contact you during the day today, don't forget to tell her the plan. Daytime contacts only," Gray reminded him.

"I won't forget," Damien assured him with a nod. "Although, that leads me to another worry."

"What's that?" Alexander questioned.

"All the other times she's contacted me, I've been asleep. Or hypnotized. What if she can't get through to me when I'm awake? And now she can't get through to me when I'm asleep because of the sedative. What if we can't make contact?"

"Perhaps you should nap a lot?" Michael suggested.

"I can only sleep so much!" Damien countered, leaping from his seat.

"All the research we've done suggests that perhaps you weren't asleep when she contacted you," Alexander informed them. "You may have assumed you were asleep, particularly because the incidents occurred when you were attempting to sleep. However, if we are correct, you were not asleep, merely relaxed."

"So, he'll just need to keep his mind relaxed and, in theory, Celine should be able to communicate with him, right?" Michael queried.

"Correct," Alexander responded.

"Oh, that's just great! Relaxation is such a specialty of mine!" Damien said, his voice thick with sarcasm as he stalked around the room.

"Never fear," Alexander assured him. "Plenty of games of chess…"

"Walks around the property," Gray added.

"Music," Millie chimed in.

"And we'll have your mind relaxed enough for Celine to communicate," Alexander assured him.

"See, they've got it all taken care of!" Michael agreed. "All that's left for you to do is relax!"

Damien nodded, unconvinced but unwilling to argue. He sipped at his coffee, his mind wandering to Celine. Celine, he mused, are you there? Can you hear me?

"Perhaps you should put me under hypnosis again," Damien suggested. "That worked before."

"No," Gray answered without hesitation. "That's far too dangerous."

"I agree," Millie concurred. "The last time you were under hypnosis, we lost contact with you. We cannot risk that again."

"You have no contact with me when I've been in Shadow World before, what's the difference?" Damien countered.

"The difference is Celine controlled your other visits there," Gray contended. "Hypnosis somehow forced you into the realm without her calling you there. If she doesn't realize you're there, you could die."

"And quickly," Alexander added.

"We can't take the chance of not getting you back before something happens if Celine isn't there," Gray finished.

Damien let his coffee mug clattered to the table as he heaved a sigh. "Then we wait."

"Yes, we wait. I don't like it either. I want Celine back, but I won't risk your life to do it," Gray informed him.

Damien enjoyed a quiet morning. He waited for Celine to contact him, but she did not. He played a few games of chess, passed the time with some reading, and listened to some music. His mind felt anything but relaxed. It stretched and contorted, searching for any sign of Celine contacting him. Every stray noise, every passing thought he wondered if it was Celine. He began to drive himself crazy.

After lunch, he suggested a walk outdoors. With the planned relaxation already driving him crazy, he needed an escape. Gray and Michael accompanied him. They wandered the pathways throughout the estate. He spent time peering over the cliffs to the ocean. They made their way to the beach. He watched the waves crashing against the rocks, hoping it lulled his mind into a state suitable for Celine to make contact.

As wave after wave rolled in, he allowed the sound to fill his ears, muting anything else. He called to Celine in his mind. She did not respond. He kicked a stone across the beach, frustrated with himself.

"Should we head back?" Gray questioned.

Damien shrugged as he checked his watch. "I guess."

It was nearly two in the afternoon. No contact from Celine in over twenty-four hours. Worry settled on him.

"Mind if we go back through that clearing in the trees?"

"Sure. Whatever you want, buddy," Michael answered.

They climbed back up to the cliff's top, selecting the path to Alexander's that passed through the clearing of trees. As they approached the spot, Damien slowed. He wasn't sure why, but he felt close to Celine here. Perhaps it was because she had experienced one of her painful memories here while walking with him, and that incident was emblazoned in his brain. Either way, he wanted to take a few moments, surrounded and hidden by the trees, to relax before returning to Alexander's.

They stepped into the clearing. Damien stopped, taking a deep breath. He glanced around, recalling Celine's attack. Now she was worse off than she had been then. Poor Celine, he mused. She never received a moment's rest. He focused his gaze on the trees around him. Pine needles scented the air. Birds chirped overhead.

Damien stared at the tree in front of him. His brow furrowed in bewilderment. Was the tree diseased? Something was amiss. He glanced to the sky, blinking a few times. White clouds rolled by, but their blue background appeared like water. It ran like a stream, melting to the horizon below. Damien lowered his eyes, focusing again on the tree. The green dripped from the needles onto the ground.

What was happening? Was this a side effect of the sedative? A shiver shook Damien's body, and he collapsed to the ground.

CHAPTER 9

"Damien!" Michael shouted as Damien pitched forward. He reached out, catching him mid-fall and easing him to the ground.

Gray rushed over.

Michael screwed up his face and flicked his gaze to Gray. "He's freezing, shaking all over. What's wrong with him?"

Gray removed his jacket, placing it over Damien. "It's Celine. She's called him into Shadow World. We need to keep him warm."

Michael pulled his hoodie off, using it to cover Damien. "Hang in there, buddy. We're right here waiting for you."

* * *

Damien blinked a few times as his eyes adjusted to the colorless world. The bitter cold struck him, and his teeth chattered. He focused his mind, realizing where he was.

"Celine?" he called out.

"I'm here," she answered. Damien followed her voice,

spotting her racing toward him. She wrapped him in her warm arms.

"Celine!"

"Did you tell them, Damien?" Celine inquired.

"Yes. I told them Shadow World. Celine, they are giving me a sedative at night, so I don't slip in here without you. You can only contact me during the day."

"I understand. I have another message then you must go. You cannot stay any longer."

"Okay. I'm ready," Damien replied, his teeth chattering from the cold.

"It's Marcus, Damien. Marcus has returned. You must tell them, Damien. And you must be safe. Now go."

"The Duke? No, wait, Celine!" Damien cried, desiring more information.

"Go, Damien, we'll talk tomorrow. GO!"

Celine shoved him away, and he tripped backwards, falling into a black pit. He fell for a moment before he hit the bottom. It knocked the wind out of him. He gasped for air, shooting up to a sitting position. He struggled to visualize anything near him.

"It's okay, buddy, you're okay," Michael assured him.

"It's all right, Damien, relax," Gray added. "You're back. You're safe."

Damien gasped for air, shivering all over. Exhaustion surged, and nausea passed over him in waves. He crawled onto his hands and knees, retching.

"This one took a toll," Gray noted. "We need to get him back to Alexander's."

"Can you walk, Damien?" Michael asked.

Damien collapsed onto the ground, still recovering from the nausea. "We'll have to carry him. Help me get him up to standing," Gray stated.

Michael nodded, pulling Damien up with Gray's assistance.

"Got him?" Gray asked.

"Yep."

"All right, let's go." They dragged Damien back to Alexander's house. Gray shouted for Millie as they entered. Alexander met them in the foyer, assisting them in getting Damien settled on the couch. They covered him with blankets as Millie entered the room.

"What's happened?" Millie inquired as she took Damien's pulse.

"Celine contacted him," Gray replied. "He collapsed, shivering, gasping for breath, same thing he did under hypnosis. When he came out of it, he was sick."

"Vomiting?" Millie asked.

"Yes. Just once."

Millie faced her patient. "I see. Damien, are you still nauseous?"

Damien shook his head. "No," he whispered. "Tired."

"Tired. I'll bet. You are still very cold. Let's get him some hot tea and dry toast. I'd like to make sure he can keep food down and bring his body temperature up faster."

"Here," Alexander offered, "let's move you closer to the fire."

He assisted Damien in approaching the fire, situating him in a nearby armchair. Within a few minutes, they plied him with hot tea and toast. He sipped at it, happy for the warmth it brought him.

"Has he said anything about what happened in Shadow World?" Alexander asked Gray as Damien sipped his tea.

"Not yet. He was incredibly weak when he awoke and sick. I didn't push him. I didn't want to overwhelm him."

"I understand. That's for the best," Alexander agreed. "His health is our priority."

"How are you feeling now?" Millie asked as Damien finished the cup of tea.

"A little better," Damien admitted. "Could I have another cup of tea?"

"Anything you want," Michael offered, collecting his teacup to retrieve another cup.

"Your pulse is normal. Your body is warming. How is the nausea?" Millie inquired.

"Seems to be passed. I'm still weak, but I feel better overall."

"Good," Millie answered.

"I saw Celine," Damien responded in a louder voice, craning his neck to find Gray and Alexander.

Gray joined him by the fire. "It's okay. Tell us when you're ready. Don't strain yourself."

"It's okay," Damien assured them. "I'm okay. I want to tell you while it's fresh in my mind, so I don't forget anything."

"Okay," Gray agreed.

"She asked if I told everyone about Shadow World. I told her I did. And I told her about our plan. Sedative at night, contact during the day only."

"Good," Gray replied. "Is your mind at ease now that she knows the plan and she can contact you when you're not asleep?"

Damien shook his head, worry creasing his features.

"Why not?" Alexander inquired.

"Because of what she told me next," Damien responded. His brow furrowed as he recalled her statement.

"What did she tell you?" Gray queried.

Damien glanced between Gray and Alexander, then made eye contact with Gray. "She said..." his voice trailed off as he gathered the strength to say the words. He swallowed hard. "She said the Duke is back."

"What!" Michael exclaimed at the door, just avoiding

spilling Damien's cup of hot tea. "The Duke is back? Are you serious?"

Gray and Alexander exchanged a glance, vexation clear on their faces.

"Yes, I'm serious. That's what Celine said. She didn't explain anything more. She said I had to go."

"Yes, you were there long enough," Gray admitted.

"Damn it!" Damien cursed. "Why can't I stay longer so we can get more information?"

Michael continued to question the new information. "Is this Duke thing possible? How can that be?"

Gray crossed his arms, staring into the blazing fire. "I'm not sure, but Celine wouldn't send that kind of message if it weren't true."

"Perhaps she assumes it's true but doesn't have any confirmation," Michael suggested.

"No," Gray argued with a shake of his head, "she wouldn't conjecture. She's sure."

"It fits with something else," Damien informed them.

"What?" Alexander inquired.

"I didn't remember until now, but when Celine and I met with the adjudicator, it mentioned him. The adjudicator thing told her to talk to Marcus Northcott. It must have slipped past us because she was so focused on saving me, we never followed up on it!"

"This is unbelievable," Michael replied, sinking into an armchair opposite Damien. He ran his hand through his sandy blonde hair.

"That man is like a bad penny," Alexander admitted.

"Damn it!" Gray shouted, slamming his hands against the mantle before stalking away.

"Gray…" Alexander began.

"He has her, Alex," Gray interrupted, his voice unsteady.

"Marcus Northcott has Celine. Trapped somewhere. She can't get away. My God, what has he done to her?"

They spent a moment in silence as the news sank in. Each of them reflected on their new reality and worry for Celine swelled.

Alexander was the first to speak. "Did she say anything else? Give any indication of where she may be?"

Damien shook his head. "No. She made me leave after she told me that. And warned me to be safe."

Gray sank onto the couch, resting his elbows on his thighs.

"We'll find her, Gray," Alexander assured him.

Gray's voice rose in pitch as he spoke. "Will we? Wherever he has her, you can bet it'll be damn hard to locate her. And how the hell did that bastard come back to begin with?"

"I can ask next time I communicate with Celine," Damien offered.

Gray nodded, remaining silent.

"In fact, Millie, can you hypnotize me? I'll go back now and ask her."

"No," Alexander argued. "It's too soon. You cannot go back now. You aren't even recovered yet from the last visit."

"Then I'll go back in an hour or two whenever I recover."

"Damien, you can't. This isn't a trip into the park. This is dangerous," Alexander commented.

"I went before twice in a few hours. I can do it again. I'm with Gray. We need to find Celine now! We can't leave her with that maniac!"

Gray stood, rubbing the back of his neck. "No. Alexander is correct. You cannot go back. The trips are becoming worse on you. We need you healthy. If it overwhelms you, we'll have no way of communicating with Celine. We can't risk it."

"But…" Damien protested.

"The answer is no. I'm as upset as you are about Celine's

whereabouts, but we have to be safe. We'll find her, it's just going to take time."

"Time she may not have," Damien surmised.

"She's Celine," Gray responded. "She'll survive. She'll find a way. She's smart, and she's tough."

"She survived three years with that man before she met Gray," Alexander informed them. "And while no one wishes her to spend even another moment with him, she is capable of surviving."

Silence fell over the group again as the afternoon wound down. Damien continued to recuperate. Despite improving, he remained tired. Dinner conversation was stilted, a heavy pall hanging over everyone as their concern for Celine eclipsed all else. Following dinner, Millie prepared the sedative for Damien.

"Perhaps we should skip it tonight," Damien suggested.

"No, you need it now more than ever. You need to recover from today's events," Gray advised.

"I'm fine. There's so much to discuss. I don't want to be sidelined."

"I went through the same thing after my… bite," Michael replied. "Sometimes you need to be sidelined. For your own good."

Damien groaned.

"We can't take the risk!" Gray shouted.

"Fine, fine," Damien answered, holding his hands up in defeat. "Go ahead, doc. Stick me."

Millie administered the sedative. "You should start to feel drowsy in about an hour."

"Then let's make that hour count. What's our plan for the next meeting with Celine? And everything in between."

"We must find out where Celine is being held. That is the next piece of information we should request from Celine," Alexander answered.

Damien nodded in agreement. "Okay. What else?"

Gray stood staring out the window, his arms crossed. "How the hell didn't we realize that bastard was back? Celine did."

"He's hiding himself well," Alexander replied.

"We need to find him," Gray answered. "Poke under every rock until we find that bastard's hiding spot."

"I'm all for that, flush him out," Michael agreed. "Let him know we're aware he's here. Strip away his element of surprise."

"As much as I'd like to strike out, this is not wise," Alexander countered.

"Why?" Michael questioned.

"If he realizes we are aware of his presence, it may jeopardize any chance we have of finding and rescuing Celine. He may retaliate. Or worse, he may realize Celine is communicating with us."

"Good point," Gray conceded.

"Why did you say Celine realized he was back?" Damien queried.

"Her painful memories. It all makes sense now," Gray explained. "The danger she sensed, the flood of memories, the overwhelming sense. It was him. Every time, it was him. She sensed him but never made the final connection."

"The adjudicator mentioned it. Perhaps we should contact it to determine if we can glean any information about his whereabouts," Alexander suggested.

"I doubt it would have any information, but it can't hurt to ask," Gray agreed. "We must be careful though. No one can realize we're summoning it if we want our knowledge of the Duke's presence to remain a secret."

"I agree," Alexander concurred.

"Not a word of this to anyone. Understood?" Gray asked Damien and Michael.

"Lips are sealed," Damien said.

Michael agreed.

"Not even to Celeste," Gray added. "I find it hard to believe she's not aware of the Duke's arrival."

"As do I," Alexander agreed. "Theodore and Celeste are the first people he'd have contacted upon his return."

"We'll summon the adjudicator tonight. I don't want to be away from Damien when Celine may be in contact. Millie, are you and Michael okay to watch him for a few hours?"

"Sure," Millie answered as Damien yawned.

"No problem, we've got it covered," Michael responded. "And it looks like you're about ready to hit the hay. Want to head up?"

Damien shrugged, standing and stretching as he yawned again. "Yeah, the sedative is taking effect. I hate to leave this conversation, but I'm ready. At least tomorrow's a new day and, with any luck, a new conversation with Celine."

"Good night, Damien," Gray said, pausing for a moment. "And thanks for what you're doing."

"Good night, Damien. See you in the morning. Sleep well," Alexander said.

Damien climbed the stairs with Michael in tow. Gray retrieved his clothes from the main house last night. Damien changed and climbed into bed as Michael settled into the armchair. "It's ridiculous that I have to be monitored like a kid," Damien complained as he settled under the sheets.

"Hey, at least you haven't been handcuffed to your bed… yet!" Michael joked, referencing his own experience after his vampire bite courtesy of Celeste.

Damien chuckled at the joke. He laid back, contemplating the strange new world they lived in. Between the brutal aftereffects of his Shadow World visit and the sedative, he fell asleep in minutes.

* * *

CELINE PACED the floor of her cell. The sun lowered in the sky. Marcus promised her a visit with Celeste. If she was correct, Celeste would visit this evening. Despite his affinity for the dark side, Marcus was a man of his word. He promised to arrange a visit with Celeste, and he would.

She had visited with Damien hours ago. They had spoken longer than she anticipated. He had imparted their plan to keep him from physical harm by sedating him at night. Celine would no longer be able to contact him except during daylight hours.

A slight smile crossed her face. Gray and Alexander seemed to have the situation well in hand. They appeared to be taking good care of Damien. However, it saddened her that she could not reach out to Damien more often. But she realized the risks of repeated contacts. This plan was in everyone's best interest. It kept communication lines open and protected Damien.

Celine glanced out the window at the darkening sky. She hoped Celeste had information about Damien's condition. She planned to use Celeste to provide information about Damien so she could make informed decisions about future contacts.

She continued pacing the floor, waiting. As the stars blinked into the sky, footsteps sounded on the floor above. Celine raced to the cell door, peering from the window. She stared at the staircase as a figure descended. She recognized Marcus. Celeste followed him. Celine's heart leapt at the sight of her.

"Celeste!" Celine cried out to her.

"As promised," Marcus stated. "Your sister."

"Celine! Please tell me you are all right. I'm worried for you."

Celine nodded. "How is Gray? Damien? Alexander? Michael? Please tell me they are all right."

"They are distraught but surviving. Damien is taking it the worst. Gray says they are sedating him to help with his worry."

Celine stepped away from the door, pacing the floor.

"Celine, I am more concerned with your wellbeing. You are under a tremendous amount of stress."

"I'm fine, Celeste. I just need to be sure my family is safe."

"Your former family, Celine," Marcus reminded her. "I am your family now."

"Please do not remind me," Celine snapped.

Celeste glared at him. "Must you agitate her? She has given in to your demands. Yet you continue to harass her."

"I have spent over two centuries allowing her to cling to her pretense of a family. It is over. She is mine. I will not tolerate the continued veneration of the Buckleys."

So, Celine reflected, he meant to strip her of any connection she had with her family. She would be censored, not allowed to mention them. He planned to force the transition quickly. A tear rolled down her cheek as she realized the fire with which she was playing.

CHAPTER 10

Celine flicked away the tear that had fallen as she considered her new life with Marcus.

"Now look what you've done," Celeste admonished Marcus. "The least you can do is allow me a moment to console my sister!"

"Console away, Celeste. I shall not interfere."

"Might I embrace her? Surely that is not asking too much!"

Marcus sighed, rolling his eyes. "Fine."

Marcus opened the door for Celeste. She rushed to Celine, throwing her arms around her. The two sisters embraced in a cloud of tears.

"Oh, Celine," Celeste cried through tears as she wiped Celine's cheeks, "how brave you are. How little credit I've given you through the years."

"It's in the past, Celeste. Are you safe? I worry about you, too."

Celeste pulled her into a tight embrace. "Yes, I am. I am being careful, and Teddy is making sure I am safe during the day."

"You shouldn't have to deal with this," Celine lamented.

"I shall be right as rain soon, darling. Do not trouble yourself."

"Yes, you will be," Celine agreed. Skirting around Celeste, she approached the cell door. "You shall correct her issue, Marcus."

"Yes, I shall. I have already agreed."

"Then restore her," Celine demanded.

Marcus chuckled. "Patience, my dear, Celine, patience."

"I have little patience when it comes to my family."

"You are in no position to make demands, Celine," Marcus chided.

Celine cocked her head. "Consider it a wedding present."

Marcus smirked at her. "A wonderful idea. You shall receive the gift when we wed." He winked at her.

She frowned at him, her jaw tightening. "Marcus, I…"

"It's fine, sister. It won't be much longer, I am fine," Celeste chimed in.

"Celeste, please do not interrupt my conversation with my dear future husband."

Celine crossed her arms, staring at Marcus. "I do not expect you to dismiss my requests of you out of hand, Marcus."

"I have already assured you, Celine. Your sister will be returned to her rightful state once you are my wife. I will not discuss it further."

Celine narrowed her eyes. "This marriage will not work with that attitude."

She stalked away from the door. "Perhaps it is not worth my time."

"An idle threat, Celine," Marcus answered, letting Celeste out of the cell. "You have little choice. If you want to free yourself and save your sister, you must submit to my demands."

Celine swiveled to face him. "Even you cannot keep me here forever, Marcus. And once I am free, I am certain I can find a way to restore Celeste on my own. I admit it would certainly be much faster if you did it. But impossible? No. I don't agree. It is in your best interest to help Celeste. It would go a long way in garnering my favor."

"Are you certain it is your favor I desire?"

She arched an eyebrow and cocked her head. "Is it not?"

He smirked at her. "I shall consider your request."

"Thank you," Celine said with a slight smile. She would not push further tonight. She had not yet won the war, but the battle went in her favor.

"Now, are you satisfied with the conversation with Celeste?"

"Yes," Celine admitted. "I have learned what I needed to."

"Good. Then, my dear Celeste, that is your cue. I'm sure you have… business to attend to."

"Good night, sister," Celeste said, peering through the door's window. "I love you. Take care."

"I love you, Celeste. Be safe. Will you return tomorrow?"

Celeste glanced at Marcus.

"If it is to discuss the wellbeing of Grayson Buckley and his family, no," he answered.

"Damien is *my* family, and his wellbeing is important to me."

Marcus rolled his eyes and shook his head. "He isn't, really."

"He is! And it is because of me he is here."

"We shall agree to disagree on that matter, my dear. But I will keep you informed as to Damien's wellbeing."

"I prefer to hear the news from Celeste. She can make direct contact with him."

Marcus sighed, shooing Celeste away with his hand. "Fine. Now run along, Celeste."

Celeste said her final good night to Celine and disappeared up the stairs, leaving them alone to finish their conversation.

"There are several things we need to discuss," Marcus said.

"Such as?"

"The arrangements of our next steps."

Celine stalked away from the door, turning her back on him. "I leave those arrangements to you, Marcus. I can do nothing in here. Unless you can be persuaded to allow me out."

Marcus smirked at her. "I admire your tenacity, Celine, but be careful not to push me too far."

"Then you wouldn't have to provide updates on my family. I could check for myself."

Marcus shook his head at her, his brow crinkling. "What is it that you find so alluring about Grayson Buckley? For centuries I have pondered this question and cannot conceive of a suitable answer."

Celine scoffed, a soft smile forming on her lips . "There are some things, Marcus, you will never understand even if I explained them to you."

"I suppose it no longer matters. He is no longer any concern of ours. Well, I shall leave you, my dear. I have many things to attend to."

"Good night, Marcus."

"Good night, dear Celine."

He strode off, disappearing up the stairs.

Celine was left alone with her musings again. She pondered his last question to her, recalling the first moments she met Grayson Buckley. She closed her eyes, immersing herself in that memory from over two hundred years ago. She attended a ball at the governor's mansion, a party given by the governor whom her father had preceded. Escorted by her fiancé of over two years, Marcus, and her sister and brother-in-law, she arrived expecting another tedious night. She had succeeded in postponing their marriage thus far, but the day she dreaded drew nearer and nearer. However, this night would change her life forever.

The governor's wife introduced her to Grayson and his cousin, Alexander, traveling from the states on business. She recalled the moment her eyes met Gray's. Stormy blue, his eyes gazed at her with great interest. The touch of their hands had brought such comfort to her.

They spent a large part of the evening stealing glances from across the room until he asked her to join him in a dance. To this point in her life, Celine had never entertained the idea of falling in love. But she had the moment she met Grayson Buckley. She smiled as she recalled twirling around the dance floor with him.

He used the dance to pass her a note, asking her to meet him outside. Celine had gone without hesitation. Much to her surprise, Grayson had not asked her to meet in the moonlight to whisper sweet nothings into her ear. Grayson, like her, was involved with the supernatural, a warlock. He assured her there was another side to their existence. One not born out of darkness but aligned with the light. He claimed together they could fight the darkness. The proposition intrigued Celine, who wished to escape her existence tied to Marcus Northcott and his evil desires.

After explaining his role in the supernatural realm, Grayson asked to see her again.

"I will consider what you have told me carefully, Mr. Buckley," Celine answered as moonlight cascaded around her.

"Please, Miss Devereaux," Grayson beseeched her, "our supernatural similarities aside, I must see you again."

"Oh?" Celine questioned.

"I have never met a woman like you, Celine Devereaux."

"I can't imagine there are many of us in existence, no," Celine admitted.

"It's beyond that, Celine. You are captivating. Please, I must see you again."

His interest in her was clear. As was hers in him. She agreed to a clandestine meeting with him before returning to the ballroom.

Her absence as well as Grayson's attentions did not escape Marcus's notice. They would argue about it when they returned to her sister's home. Marcus would forbid her from seeing Grayson Buckley again, not that it would do any good. Celine would go on to meet with Grayson multiple times under a shroud of secrecy, infuriating Marcus.

"I will not be played a fool, Celine," Marcus told her. "You will end your liaisons with Grayson Buckley, or I shall end them for you."

But Celine was not a woman easily contained. She had her own mind and a host of amazing skills that allowed her to abscond into the night to meet with Grayson. Their mutual love for each other grew and their bond became unbreakable.

She smiled as she recalled those moonlit nights in Martinique. She remembered their immediate connection, his affectionate glances, how his hand held hers, how tender he was caressing her face as they kissed. She longed to be with him again. She would be, she vowed. Their connection was unbreakable. They would be together again.

* * *

DAMIEN AWOKE the following morning feeling rested but groggy. Alexander read a book in the armchair across the room. "

Good morning," Damien said, yawning.

"Good morning!" Alexander answered, clapping his book shut. "How do you feel?"

"Okay. Groggy but rested."

"That's good."

"Did you and Gray make any headway with your adjudicator visit last night?" Damien inquired.

"Unfortunately not," Alexander answered. "It confirmed Marcus's return but had no other information to offer."

"Damn," Damien cursed.

"Not to worry, I'm not convinced that information helps us in any way."

"Still, it may have. If we can locate the Duke, perhaps he'll lead us to Celine."

"Doubtful. He's a careful man. However, if he doesn't realize he's been found out, he may have been less cautious."

"Can't anything go right for us?" Damien grumbled, throwing his arms in the air.

Alexander chuckled. "Often in these cases, they do not. But let's consider the bright side. We have a connection with Celine."

Damien nodded. "Perhaps Gray should have asked if the adjudicator spotted Celine in Shadow World."

"No. Alerting the adjudicators that you and Celine are using Shadow World as a conduit for conversations isn't wise. We don't need them lurking around in search of you in an already dangerous place, making it more dangerous for you."

"Good point." Damien climbed out of bed and stretched. "Man, I need some coffee."

Alexander and Damien made their way to the sitting room after Damien dressed for the day. Damien went through the usual barrage of physical tests by Millie, assuring her he had no side effects.

"I wonder when Celine will reach out today?" Damien questioned. "I'm anxious all over again."

"Try to relax," Gray said. "Celine will contact you when she can."

"Yeah, I realize that. But then my mind just spins out of control. What if she can't? What if she's hurt? A million what ifs… Plus, once she contacts me this time, I can ask where she is, and this can all be over with."

"I doubt that," Alexander corrected.

"Why?" Damien inquired.

"It won't be that simple or we would have found her already," Alexander stated.

"Well, at least we'll know where to start looking," Damien muttered.

He leapt from his seat on the couch, pacing the room.

Gray followed his stalking with his eyes. "That's not going to make her contact you any faster. All it'll do is wear you out, then you won't have the energy to ask her where she is when she does connect with you."

"I can't just sit here! I'm going crazy!" Damien exclaimed, flailing his arms.

"How about a walk?" Michael suggested.

"Yes, a walk!" Damien agreed. "A walk did it yesterday. Come on, let's go."

"I'll go with him," Michael offered.

"As will I," Alexander added.

The trio spent the rest of the morning hours walking the property. While providing a distraction, it did little to settle Damien's nerves. Celine did not reach out. They returned to Alexander's house.

"Well, you're still up and moving, so I'm guessing you've not heard from Celine yet," Gray stated as they entered the sitting room.

Damien collapsed in a heap on the couch. "Not a peep."

"We even went to the clearing in the woods… *five* times," Michael noted.

"She didn't call you into Shadow World until mid-afternoon yesterday," Alexander reminded him. "Perhaps that is when she has a moment to herself to communicate."

Damien checked his watch. "Ugh. Two hours to go before that."

"Sounds like it's time for a game of chess," Alexander challenged him.

Damien sighed, stalking to the chess board. "Okay, okay."

They spent the afternoon engaged in several games of chess. As afternoon turned to early evening, Damien's frustration reached its peak. He stared out the window, drumming his fingers on the table.

"Your move," Alexander prodded him.

Damien glanced to the board, moving a pawn from one space to another.

Alexander's brow furrowed. "Really?"

"What?" Damien asked.

"That's a surprising move given the state of the board," Alexander said.

"Ohhhh," Damien muttered, his nose wrinkling. "Well, I've lost."

"Distracted?"

"Very." Damien checked his watch before springing from his chair. He paced around the room. "This is hours after she contacted me yesterday!"

"Patience, Damien, patience," Gray said.

"Patience is not a virtue I possess. Ugh! We should have a set time for this every day."

"Don't waste your time discussing details like that," Gray warned. "You have minutes in Shadow World. Let Celine lead the conversation."

"Yeah, yeah, yeah," Damien griped. "I know. It's just that I…" He stopped pacing, staring straight ahead.

"You what?" Michael asked, glancing up from his laptop.

"Damien?" Alexander questioned.

Damien pitched forward, collapsing. "It's Celine, she's contacting him," Gray announced as Damien began to fall. He raced to Damien, catching him before he hit the ground. "Put him by the fireplace, keep him warm." Alexander assisted in carrying Damien to the fireplace. Michael rushed to cover him with blankets. Damien's lips were already blue from cold and he shook uncontrollably. His breathing was elevated, and his pulse raced.

"Get Millie, she can monitor his vitals," Gray suggested. Michael hurried from the room in search of the doctor.

CHAPTER 11

$\mathcal{D}$amien stopped speaking mid-sentence. Something looked odd on the wall in front of him. He stared at it as he tried to formulate his next words. His brow furrowed as he realized what appeared odd to him. The wallpaper, burgundy with gold diamonds, melted from the walls. It slid down like sludge, pooling on the hardwood floor below and running from the room at every opening. A chill passed over him. He shivered before the world in front of him turned colorless. He blinked a few times, adjusting his eyes.

The room disappeared. Colorless tress surrounded him. A gray sky yawned overhead. The cold penetrated him and he shivered, wrapping his arms around him for warmth. Celine called to him. He spotted her rushing toward him. She wrapped him in a warm embrace.

"Celine! I didn't think you were going to communicate with me. I've been so worried."

"I'm trying to give you time to recover. I realize how hard this is on you."

"I'm fine, Celine, don't worry about that."

"Hush, Damien, there is no time for that."

"No, I have to find out where you are."

"The basement of the old mill, but Marcus has an enchantment that will not allow me to be found. But I am near to you. Now you must go, Damien."

"Tell me more so we can find you," Damien requested.

"No, Damien. You must go. Go, Damien, GO!" she shouted, letting go of him.

He floated for a bit, trying to stay in the realm, but eventually he fell away. The gray landscape faded to blackness. He fell through the blackness until he struck bottom. He gasped for air. He opened his eyes to find a crowd grouped above him. The room spun and nausea turned his stomach upside down.

"Damien," Gray called. His voice sounded miles away.

"Damien," he said again, his voice garbled. "Are you sick?"

Damien nodded. Gray and Alexander sat him up, and Millie placed a vomit bag to his mouth. He threw up twice before collapsing backwards. Cold permeated him. Exhaustion made it impossible to keep his eyes open. He closed them, slipping away.

"Damien! Damien!" Gray called, shaking him.

"Is he okay?" Michael asked, throwing more logs on the fire.

"He's hypothermic," Mille responded. "We must monitor him closely. He's too exhausted to stay awake, but sleep is dangerous."

"Because Celine can call to him again?" Michael asked.

"No, because when you're hypothermic, you can die if you fall asleep."

"Is there anything we can do to help him?" Michael queried.

"Keep him as warm as possible," Millie answered. "Do you have a hot water bottle we can put on his head to help?"

"Yes," Alexander answered, rushing to retrieve and fill it. He returned in a few minutes, placing it on Damien's head. Millie rubbed Damien's arms through the blanket, trying to warm him. Michael did the same with his legs. They waited for him to awaken, hoping he had information about Celine's whereabouts.

* * *

CELINE OPENED HER EYES, slipping back from Shadow World. She sat up, wiping at her nose. Blood covered her hand. The latest trip gave her a nosebleed. She tilted her head back to stop the bleeding. The trips were taking a toll on her, too. She couldn't imagine the physical strain Damien was under. She would need to space her trips out more despite her ache to return home.

Celine still nursed her bloody nose when footsteps sounded above. Quickly, she wiped any traces of blood away with Marcus' handkerchief, hiding it in her pocket.

"Celine?" Marcus called into the cell.

Celine stood on unsteady legs. She swallowed hard, steadying herself. The energy she exerted pulling Damien into the world was enormous. Normally, she had several hours before Marcus arrived. She was ill-prepared this time; his arrival closer to her trip than she preferred. She forced herself to approach the door as Marcus stared at her.

His brow furrowed. "Celine, are you unwell?"

"No," she lied. "You woke me. I was asleep. Dreaming of a better time."

Marcus considered her statement. His eyes narrowed at her.

Celine met his gaze, refusing to break eye contact.

After a moment, he said, "I have something to discuss with you."

"What is it?"

"Now that you and I are aligned, I would like to make the allegiance permanent."

Celine raised an eyebrow.

Marcus furnished a book. "I have started a new book, my dear, after you stole my last one. I want you to sign it. Pledge your allegiance to me once and for all."

Celine seethed with anger. She would not sign any such book. Yet she had to ensure to feign compliance for the time being. Celine considered her response. "Have you cured Celeste?"

"Celine, we are not speaking of Celeste, we are speaking of you and declaring your allegiance."

Celine eyed the book, then returned her gaze to Marcus. "Have you declared yours?"

Marcus frowned at her. "You cannot be serious."

She crossed her arms and stared at him. "I am."

"I have spent centuries declaring my allegiance to you."

"No," Celine corrected, "you have spent centuries chasing me to win. That's quite a different thing to declaring allegiance."

Marcus stalked away a few steps. "I will not spend time arguing over this. Sign the book."

"No one is arguing. However, I will not sign before Celeste is cured."

Marcus approached the door again. "I will not tolerate this type of insolence!"

"And I will not tolerate this type of treatment. I have asked you for something and I expect to receive it. I shouldn't have to continue to ask."

Marcus was silent for a moment. "You are in no position to demand anything, Celine."

Celine rolled her eyes, letting her shoulders slump. "Oh,

Marcus, what is the harm? I have asked you for one thing and one thing only. Why do you object?"

"I'm not convinced you have earned any favors."

"Must one earn favors from their spouse? This sounds more like a business arrangement than a marriage."

"We aren't married yet, my dear."

She arched an eyebrow at him as she crossed her arms again. "We will never be if this trend continues."

"Resorting to idle threats, Celine?"

"Try me."

"Have you forgotten? I still hold the trump card."

"You're referring to my family."

He nodded to her.

"Then why not cure Celeste? If you're so confident in your trump card."

Marcus considered her statement. "Fine. I shall grant your request. Under the understanding that if you should… fail to follow through on your promises, the only recourse I shall have is destroying your former family."

Celine smiled at him. "Understood. And thank you."

"I suppose it is owed to you. I did promise you everything, didn't I?"

Celine smirked, recalling the promise made centuries ago.

"I shall return Celeste to her rightful state in the next few days."

"I want it done tonight," Celine countered.

"That's impossible, Celine. There is much to prepare. This is no small task."

"Tomorrow night, then."

Marcus scoffed. "My, you certainly have confidence in my abilities, don't you?"

"Of course, Marcus. I have every confidence in your abilities. One thing I have never lacked is the belief that you are a very powerful being."

"Now, about the book..." Marcus began before being interrupted.

"Hello, Marcus, Celine. I hope I'm not interrupting," Celeste said, crossing the basement toward them.

"You are," Marcus answered as Celine answered, "You're not."

"You're here now," Celine continued. "No sense in your leaving only to return later. Besides, we have wonderful news for you!"

"Oh?" Celeste asked.

"Yes. Marcus has promised to restore you from this... state to your normal one tomorrow evening!"

Celeste's face wore a shocked expression. She smiled, speechless.

"Isn't it wonderful news?" Celine prompted.

"Why, yes," Celeste answered. "I... I am so thankful... to both of you."

"No need to thank me, Celeste," Celine replied. "Although we do owe a debt of gratitude to Marcus. Would you mind giving us a moment to speak alone?"

"Anything you have to say can be said in my presence," Marcus responded.

"It is about my family which I assume you prefer not to hear."

"I'll manage," Marcus assured her, his lips crinkled.

"Suit yourself," Celine answered. "How is Damien?"

"I spoke with Gray earlier. He continues to search for you. The poor boy is beside himself with worry. I asked to speak to him myself, but Gray informed me he was asleep. Millie administered another sedative to keep him calm."

Celine turned from the door, stalking away. Sedated

already? Was Damien still ill following his visit to Shadow World? What physical toll was it costing him?

"I'm sorry, Celine. I had hoped to speak with him myself. To bring better news."

Celine held up her hand, returning to the door. "It's fine, Celeste. Thank you for the report."

"Of course, sister. Well, I shall leave you to continue your discussion."

"Just a moment, Celeste," Marcus interjected. "I shall accompany you on your way out. There is something we need to discuss regarding your transformation."

He turned to Celine. "Celine, I shall return tomorrow to visit you."

"Of course. I'm sure you have many things to attend to. Good night, Marcus."

"Good night, my dear," he said to Celine. Turning to Celeste, he bowed, "After you."

They left Celine behind as they crossed the room, ascending the stairs.

Once outside the mill, Marcus stopped, turning toward Celeste. "Enjoy your last night in your current state, Celeste."

"I enjoy nothing of this existence," Celeste lamented.

"You should enjoy your freedom," Marcus warned. "Before I return you to your previous state, I demand your unfettered loyalty. You shall, once again, pledge your soul to me, Celeste. You shall also swear your allegiance to me in the form of promising you will not assist Celine's former family in finding her."

"Is Celine aware of these… demands?"

"Celine will be pledging her loyalty as well. She will not object to anything I demand of you."

"Fine," Celeste answered. She stepped away from him.

"Oh, Celeste," he called. She turned back. "Inform Theodore. I shall require his loyalty, too."

Celeste turned without a word, stalking away.

* * *

MICHAEL PACED THE FLOOR, glancing at Damien every other second. "Is this normal? He's been like this for over an hour!"

"I'm not sure there is a 'normal' with this situation," Millie replied. "His body temperature is rising, though. That's a good sign."

"His lips aren't blue anymore. I guess that's good," Michael admitted, resuming his pacing.

A moment later, Damien began moaning.

"Damien?" Michael called, racing to his side.

Gray and Alexander joined him.

Damien's eyes opened. He stared at the ceiling for a moment before glancing around.

"Damien? Can you hear us?" Michael asked.

Damien's brows furrowed and a pained expression crossed his face. He groaned again. He opened his mouth, but no sound came out. He finally managed a word. "Sick."

"Sit him up," Millie instructed. She positioned the vomit bag near him. He retched once. "Better?"

Damien nodded, collapsing back.

Millie examined him. "Pulse and breathing are good. His temperature has almost returned to normal."

"Tired," Damien struggled.

"That's okay, buddy," Michael assured him, patting his arm through the blanket. "Just rest."

"Celine…" he whispered.

"It's all right. Wait until you're strong enough," Alexander told him.

Damien shook his head, disagreeing.

"Rest, Damien," Michael encouraged him. "When you're stronger, you can tell us."

Damien shook his head again. "Now! Celine… old mill." He sighed in relief, settling back into the pillow.

"Old mill?" Gray repeated, glancing at Alexander. "Let's go."

"No!" Damien exclaimed. "Wait!"

"Rest, Damien. We'll check it out," Gray imparted.

Damien tried to stop them, but he was too weak. There was more information he needed to impart.

"I'll come with you," Michael offered.

"I'll grab a few flashlights. Millie, stay with him," Gray said.

Damien groaned again.

"Sick again?" Millie asked him.

Damien shook his head. "Want to go," Damien murmured.

"I realize that, but you are far too weak," Millie replied. "With any luck, they'll bring Celine home with them. Now rest. I shall awaken you the moment they return."

Damien fought to stay awake, finding it impossible. He drifted off to sleep, worried about Celine.

* * *

Gray, Alexander and Michael approached the old mill. They stayed back for several moments, observing the building. "I don't see anything," Gray noted.

"No lights or anything," Michael agreed.

"No sign of the Duke either," Alexander chimed in.

"Still, we move carefully," Gray replied, standing from his crouched position and moving closer to the building. "Let me go first."

"Stay behind both of us," Alexander said to Michael.

Michael nodded, allowing both men to enter the mill

first. They swept the room with their flashlights. They spotted no one.

"Spread out, search for any signs of Celine," Gray instructed.

They separated, each of them searching in a different area. They found nothing. "There're steps leading downstairs over here!" Michael called as he searched.

"Don't go down!" Gray shouted. "Let us go first."

They rushed to the stairs. Alexander and Gray proceeded down the stairs first, inching down in case anyone waited below. They swept their beams around the room, finding no one.

"It's clear," Gray shouted to Michael. He rushed down the stairs.

"Anything?" he asked as he arrived in the basement.

"Nothing I see," Gray answered. "Let's look around."

They shined their lights around the room, searching every location. There was no sign of Celine. Across the basement was a door leading to a small room. The locked door wouldn't budge. They peered inside, finding the room empty.

Gray leaned against the door as frustration overcame him. "Damn it!"

"I'm sorry, Gray," Alexander said, placing his hand on Gray's shoulder.

"What the hell happened? Did he misunderstand her? Is it not Celine he's talking to?"

"I'm not sure. He was still exhausted, perhaps he misspoke," Alexander suggested. "He struggled to get the information out."

Gray shook his head, pacing the floor.

"Let's return to the house. Perhaps Damien has recovered and can share more information," Alexander suggested.

Gray glanced around a final time. He sighed. "Where are you, Celine?"

Alexander pulled his arm toward the stairs. The three men left the mill behind, dejected. They traveled back to Alexander's house, tossing their flashlights on the foyer table.

Millie met them at the door. "Anything?"

"Nothing," Gray griped. "Not a damn thing."

"Is Damien any better?" Michael inquired.

"He's asleep. I told him I'd wake him as soon as you returned."

"Do that," Gray encouraged. "I'd like to talk to him. Find out why the hell he sent us on a wild goose chase!"

"Gray, that's not fair," Alexander chided.

Gray shook his head, running his fingers through his hair. "I know, I know. I'm sorry. I'm just frustrated."

Michael stuck his hands on his hips. "Yeah, well, don't take it out on Damien. He's risking his life to find Celine. He's lying in there too sick to move while you gripe about him getting a message wrong and inconveniencing you."

"I wasn't wrong," a new voice entered the conversation. Everyone glanced in the direction of the voice. Damien stood in the sitting room doorway, wrapped in a blanket. "I wasn't wrong," he repeated.

"Damien!" Michael said, rushing toward him. "It's good to see you up! How are you feeling?"

"Better. Tired but not bad."

"You should still be resting," Millie chided. "Let's move this conversation into the sitting room where Damien can rest."

They traveled into the space and Millie situated Damien on the couch. "Are you sure you're warm enough?"

"I'm sure," Damien assured her.

"Now, what did you mean when you said you weren't

wrong, Damien? We searched the entire mill. We found nothing," Alexander informed him.

"Celine told me she was in the old mill. The Duke was keeping her there. But she said something about an enchantment. That he used an enchantment so no one could find her. Was there really nothing there? Not even a trace?"

"Nothing," Gray responded. "Tell us more about the enchantment. Why didn't you tell us that before?"

"I could barely get out what I did. You disappeared before I could tell you. And I don't know any more. Celine didn't tell me. I asked about it, but she said I couldn't stay."

Gray stood, pacing around the room. "An enchantment strong enough to hold Celine in and prevent anyone from seeing her or rescuing her? Have you ever heard of anything like that?" he asked Alexander.

"No. If Celine was human, I'd have said yes, but she's not."

"If she was human?" Michael questioned.

"Yes," Alexander responded. "There are a variety of standard enchantments that work well on humans. However, being powerful enough to hold off any assaults from Celine... well, that's another matter entirely."

"Perhaps it's a modification of one of those human spells," Damien suggested.

"We will start there with our research," Alexander agreed.

"Sounds like a good place to start," Damien agreed.

"You need to rest," Millie argued.

"I'm okay! I've been sleeping for an hour."

"She's right. You need rest," Gray agreed with Millie. "You've got to be ready for Celine's next contact. Give him the sedative."

"No! We have things to do!"

"You need rest! We told Celine the plan. She's using that information to determine when to contact you. If we change it and she's not aware, she could kill you summoning you. Go to sleep, get the rest you need," Gray lectured.

"He's right," Michael said. "I need sleep, too. I'm tired and I haven't even been through half of what you've been through. Come on, we'll both head to bed."

Damien grumbled. "Fine, fine."

Millie prepared the sedative, administering it before walking Damien to his room. She sat with him until Gray arrived, books in hand to research while Damien slept. Without the sedative, Damien would have tossed and turned, anxious to research the situation. With the sleeping aid, he was out in minutes, off to a dreamless sleep.

* * *

CELINE STARED at the sliver of moon visible from her window. She walked a fine line with Marcus. Her plan to save her sister seemed to be working. Celeste should be restored to her normal state soon. After that, she could be freer with her refusals of Marcus. But not too free. She still needed to protect her family. Pushing too hard before she could manage a way out of his trap could cost her family's lives. "One step at a time, Celine," she told herself.

Celine's brow creased. She snapped her head toward the cell's door. What was that sound? Was it footsteps? Had Marcus returned to continue their argument about her signature in his book? Celine braced herself for the confrontation.

CHAPTER 12

The noise continued overhead. Something was different. Marcus would have been down here already. Celine strained to listen. It sounded like multiple people walking above. Her heart skipped a beat. Someone was here. Damien must have passed the message along.

"Down here!" she called.

Lights appeared, shining down the stairway.

"Here, down here!" she called again.

Figures appeared on the stairs. The light glared in her eyes, making it impossible for her to identify the person holding it. The beam swung away, and she recognized Gray and Alexander.

Her heart leapt for joy at the sight of them. Gray called up the steps to someone else. Within moments, Michael joined them.

"Anything?" he asked.

"Gray! Alexander! Michael!" Celine shouted, waving from her cell. "I'm here!" The trio walked around the basement, searching the place. It became apparent to Celine they could neither see nor hear her.

Gray approached the cell. He jimmied the door, unable to open it. He shined his light inside, reporting to the others that he found nothing. Celine stood inches from him, unable to communicate. She reached out to him, unable to touch him.

He leaned against the door, his frustration clear. Celine stared at his face. She shared his pain. He slammed his hands against the door, upset, venting.

"He wasn't wrong, Gray," Celine answered him, despite his inability to hear her. A tear rolled down her cheek. "I'm here. I'm right here."

Alexander suggested they return to the house to seek more information. Celine watched them go. Tears continued to roll down her cheeks. They were so close, but she was unable to communicate with them. She hated to see them go. Her first glimpses of her family in over a week were bittersweet. But they were getting closer. Soon, she would reunite with them again. Soon, she promised herself, soon.

* * *

DAMIEN AWOKE after ten the next morning. The late-night administration of the sedative meant he slept until mid-morning. He cursed the late hour. He hated sleeping this long, particularly when there was a problem.

Across the room, Alexander read a book in the armchair.

"Find anything that may help?" Damien asked, stretching as he climbed from bed.

"A handful of notions that may prove to be useful. If we can pinpoint more information about the enchantment, we may have more luck. I wonder if Celine has any additional information."

"I'm not sure. I can ask her if she contacts me today."

Alexander nodded his head.

"Also, I'd like to visit the mill. I realize you didn't find anything there, but I would like to go."

"It can't hurt to have another look around. In the daylight, perhaps things will be clearer."

"I'm going to grab a quick shower," Damien said. "See you in a few."

Damien showered, changed clothes, and appeared in the bedroom, ready for his morning coffee despite the approaching of the noon hour.

As he ate breakfast, Damien discussed his request to visit the mill. Everyone agreed returning was a good idea. They set off for the mill after Damien finished his meal.

When they arrived, Gray and Alexander insisted Michael and Damien wait outside at a safe distance while they confirmed the location was empty. After they gave the all clear, everyone entered the building. They spent a few minutes checking the large room. No clues pointed to Celine being there.

After fifteen minutes, they descended the stairs to the lower level. Damien searched the area. He shook his head, finding nothing.

"Celine, where are you?" he asked, glancing around.

* * *

Footsteps sounded overhead. Celine glanced up. Someone was in the building again. She crossed the room to the door, peering out. Hushed voices floated down the stairs to her. She waited at the door. Within a few moments, figures descended the stairs. She smiled, recognizing Gray, Alexander, Michael, and Damien. Damien appeared fatigued but not unwell.

The four men searched the space.

"I'm here," Celine whispered.

"Celine, where are you? Damien asked.

"Here, D. I'm here," Celine answered, even though he could not hear her. An idea formed in Celine's mind. She strode across her cell, sitting against the wall. She breathed deeply, closing her eyes. She slipped into another realm.

* * *

"How can she be here, and we can't see her!" Damien exclaimed.

"That's rather the purpose of the enchantment," Alexander responded.

"It's so frustrating! Perhaps we should try some of those ideas you had for the..." Damien stopped speaking mid-sentence. He stared straight ahead at the cell door across the room. Within seconds, he collapsed to the floor, shivering with escalated breathing.

Gray raced to him, followed by Alexander and Michael.

"Is it Celine?" Michael inquired.

Gray glanced around. "Yes. I wonder if she realizes we're here."

"We must keep him warm. Cover him with your jackets," Alexander instructed.

They tossed the coats on top of him, doing their best to keep him warm while he remained in his trance.

* * *

The door across the room folded on itself in front of Damien's eyes. The stone walls melted around him, creating a river that flowed away from him. Gray trees stood behind the crumbling walls.

"Celine?" he called, searching the landscape for her.

"Damien!" Celine shouted, racing toward him. She

embraced him. "You found me. I can see you. All of you at the mill. I'm right there in the cell. I can see you. I can hear you. I'm right there with you."

"Perhaps if you call to us…"

"No. I tried last night. You can't see or hear me, but I can see and hear you."

"Do you know any details about the enchantment? We are working to break it, but Alexander said it would be easier if you provided details."

"I don't have any. I'm sorry. You must go, but there is one more thing."

"What is it?"

"If everything goes as planned, Marcus will cure Celeste's condition tonight. You mustn't try anything before then. Once she is cured, we'll work on getting me released from this prison."

"Okay. I'll tell them. When I can. Sometimes I'm sick after and it takes me a while to recover."

"I understand. Now you must go, Damien." Celine released him from her embrace. The gray world turned black as he returned to his own realm.

* * *

CELINE GASPED as she returned from Shadow World. She stood on weak legs, wiping the blood running from her nose, and raced to the cell door. Everyone huddled around Damien. She peered at the scene. He shivered uncontrollably, gasping for breath. She covered her mouth as a whimper escaped. The scene twisted her heart into a knot.

"Damien," she whispered through tears. "Please wake up."

"He's really cold," Michael stated, rubbing Damien's arms. Alexander rubbed his legs.

"Should I retrieve Mille?" Gray questioned.

Damien moaned.

"Wait, perhaps he is coming to," Alexander replied. "Damien? Damien!"

Damien's eyes remained closed, but he murmured, his head rocking back and forth. "... Celine... Celeste... see us..."

"He's out of it," Gray said, glancing to Alexander. "Should we get him back to the house?"

"Yes, he's terribly cold. He needs to be warmed while he recovers," Alexander answered.

"Okay. Lift him up," Gray said.

"I've got him," Michael said, shouldering Damien on one side. Alexander held up the opposite side. Together, they dragged him across the room, ascending the stairs.

Gray stood, glancing around. "If you're here, Celine, and you can hear me, we'll be back for you. Damien needs to recover, but we will be back after he's better. I love you, Celine."

"I love you, too, Gray," Celine cried.

Gray crossed the room, ascending the stairs.

Celine stepped away from the door as silence fell over the structure. Worse than her own imprisonment, she wept for Damien. The negative effects from the trips to Shadow World were clear. Witnessing how ill he was following a trip there disturbed Celine. Perhaps she should only communicate with him every other day. Perhaps daily was too much for him.

Celine pondered the situation. She would make one more trip tomorrow to inform him of Celeste's condition, then stop.

ALEXANDER AND MICHAEL carried Damien to the sitting room. They placed him near the fireplace, propping his head up with a pillow. They covered him with blankets.

Millie rushed from her spot on the sofa to take his vitals. "Another contact from Celine?"

"Yes. At least that's what we assume," Alexander answered.

"It must be," Gray replied. "It can't be a coincidence that she told him she is there and contacted him while he was there."

"We'll have to wait until he can speak to find out," Alexander answered.

"He spoke a little at the mill, but it was incoherent," Michael added.

"His vitals aren't too bad," Millie stated. "He's cold, but his heart rate is close to normal. His adrenaline must have been pumping while at the mill. It's helped him a bit."

"Will he wake sooner?" Michael asked.

"I can't say for sure. Let's hope so," Millie replied.

The group waited, tension building as each minute passed. Within thirty minutes, Damien groaned.

"Damien?" Millie asked.

Damien continued groaning, opening his eyes. A pained expression came over him. "Ugh. I'm sick."

"Sit him up," Millie instructed.

Gray began pulling him up to sitting.

"No, no. I don't need to throw up. I just feel nauseous. But I'm okay," Damien informed them.

"Millie thinks the adrenaline in your system may have helped your recovery," Michael said.

"I don't feel as bad as normal. Don't get me wrong, I feel awful overall. But I've been worse. Can someone help me to the couch?"

"Sure, buddy," Michael answered, easing him from the floor to standing.

"Easy," Millie advised. "Easy, don't push too fast."

Damien stood on shaky legs, grasping at Michael to stay upright.

"You okay?" Michael asked.

Damien nodded, holding the blanket tight around him. "Yes."

"I'll retrieve a cup of hot tea for you," Alexander informed him.

"Thanks, that would be great," Damien answered. "Then I'll tell everyone what Celine told me."

They situated Damien on the couch, keeping him covered in blankets. Millie monitored his vitals, ensuring the movement did not prove too much for him. Alexander returned with a cup of steaming hot tea. Damien sipped at it before launching into the details of his meeting with Celine.

"So, Celine is at the mill. She can see and hear us," he began.

"She can?" Gray exclaimed. "So, we could communicate with her that way? At least one-way?"

"Easy, let him finish," Michael chided.

Damien nodded as he sipped his tea. "It's okay and yes. She can hear everything we say. She said she's in that little cell. And yes, we can ask her things, then she could respond via Shadow World conversations with me."

"Except she's got to be careful. If she can see us, undoubtedly, she's upset witnessing your reaction to the visit with her," Alexander surmised.

"But I'm fine!" Damien answered.

"Someone needs to tell her that," Gray answered. "Did she say anything else? I'll go talk to her as soon as we're finished with this conversation."

"No!" Damien exclaimed. "You can't. She said the Duke is

curing Celeste tonight. She warned me not to do anything before that. I guess she doesn't want to mess it up. She said we would work on freeing her once Celeste is okay."

Gray smirked as he flicked his gaze into space. "She persuaded him to fix Celeste?"

"She is sly, isn't she?" Alexander said, glancing at Gray.

"That she is," Gray agreed. "Although I wish she'd worry about herself instead of Celeste."

"That's not Celine's style," Alexander replied.

"No, it's not," Gray answered. "I wonder if I could make it to the mill and back before Marcus arrives there. I'd like to tell her that Damien is okay. She's probably worried sick."

Alexander glanced at the clock on the mantle. "It's almost five. I wouldn't chance it."

"Damn," Gray cursed. "She needs to know Damien is all right."

"Tell her tomorrow," Michael suggested. "I mean, I realize you want her to know as soon as possible, but if you mess up the Celeste thing, she will not be happy with you."

Gray chuckled at the statement. "No, she would not be. Well, looks like we're on hold for the night."

"Time to hit the books. Find a way to disenchant the enchantment," Damien replied.

"Time for you to eat something and rest for the evening," Gray replied.

"I won't say no to the food, but I'd like to check out some of these books you're studying before you put me to sleep."

"I don't see the harm in it," Alexander answered. "But only an hour or so. You must rest. We're getting close to creating a solution that may break the enchantment. We need you to be healthy in the event that we need to contact Celine."

Damien agreed after a brief argument. They ate dinner and spent the early evening discussing information from the tomes in Alexander's collection. They formulated several disenchantment spells to test before Millie insisted Damien retire for the evening.

Damien spent the first thirty minutes after stretching out in bed worrying about Celine. Knowing Celine, she lay in her prison worrying over him, Celeste, Gray, Alexander, Michael, Millie, Charlotte, Avery, and the two children. He hoped it didn't stop her from contacting him again.

If Alexander was correct and Celine witnessed his reaction to the Shadow World visit, she'd be reluctant to contact him again. He sighed, his mind turning to other aspects of the issue. Would Celeste be cured tonight, he wondered? How had Celine accomplished that feat? What had she given up or promised to obtain that favor? Worry consumed him again. His mind rambled from thought to thought until the sedative kicked in, sending him to a dreamless sleep.

CELINE PACED HER CELL, apprehensive over Damien's condition. How was he, she wondered? Was he ill, unconscious, worse? Had he passed the message along to Gray? They must not act until Marcus cured Celeste.

Celine glanced out the window. The sun had set hours ago. Celeste would have risen from her daytime hiding spot. Had she met with Marcus? Had there been an issue? Celine groaned, resuming her pacing.

CHAPTER 13

Celine chewed her thumbnail as she paced the floor of her cell, worried over her sister's condition.

After another hour, footsteps fell above her. She rushed to the cell door, peering out. Figures descended the stairs, crossing the room. She recognized Marcus and Celeste. Was it done, she wondered? She received her answer as the duo approached the door.

"Good evening, my dear," Marcus greeted her. "May I present your newly restored sister?"

A smile crossed Celine's face. "It is finished?"

"It is. I have restored Celeste to her rightful state," Marcus assured her.

Celine glanced to Celeste, who nodded. "It is true, sister."

A tear escaped Celine's eye. She breathed a sigh of relief. One problem was solved. She hated to admit she owed Marcus Northcott for it, but she did. Although, she reflected, he caused the issue. It was only right that he should fix it.

"Are you sure?"

"I am positive," Celeste answered. "I have no more blood-lust, none of the effects I had even last night."

"You don't trust me, mon chérie?" Marcus inquired.

"I just want to be sure," Celine informed him. "Celeste, will you return in the morning? After the sunrise so I can be sure?"

Marcus puckered his lips, clasping his hands behind his back. "Your faith in me is concerning, my dear."

"If she is truly restored, it should be of no concern to you," Celine countered.

"I have no concerns other than your constant doubt of me. I pledged to cure Celeste, and I have done so. You should be pleased, Celine."

Celine forced a smile onto her lips. "I am pleased, Marcus. I only want to be sure that Celeste has sustained no side effects."

"Be assured there are no side effects. I am no amateur, Celine."

"I did not suggest you were. And I thank you for restoring Celeste."

"You are welcome, my dear. And now that you two have spoken, Celeste, might you leave us to discuss private matters?"

"Wait," Celine interrupted. "Celeste, have you spoken with Damien? Do you know if he is any better?"

"I have not, I'm sorry."

Celine stalked away from the door. She had no confirmation Damien was okay.

"Well, if you have no additional information, you may go, Celeste," Marcus informed her.

"I shall return tomorrow," Celeste promised. "I will inquire after Damien this evening for you."

"Thank you, Celeste."

"No, Celine," Celeste replied. "Thank *you*! Without you, sister dear, I would still be in that dreadful state."

Celine twisted to face her sister. "I was the one who put

you in that dreadful state."

"It was not your fault. We've discussed this, Celine. Stop blaming yourself."

"At least it is finished now," Celine responded. "See you tomorrow, Celeste. I love you."

"I love you, too, sister dear. Good night, Celine. Take care."

"Good night," Celine answered.

Celeste crossed the room, climbing the stairs.

"Are you pleased, Celine?" Marcus inquired when her sister left.

Celine crossed her arms and stared at him. "With Celeste's transformation, yes."

"But?"

Celine flicked her gaze to the stone floor. "I worry about Damien."

"And the others, I assume," Marcus grumbled.

"It is not something I can turn on and off with the flip of a switch," Celine admitted.

"I will never understand the draw of Grayson Buckley. But, no matter," Marcus replied with a wave of his hand, "that is behind you now. I shall soon have all the details handled for our impending nuptials. We shall soon be husband and wife, and you shall forget Grayson Buckley."

Celine stared at him, unimpressed. "And then will I be permitted out of my prison?"

"When I feel you have proven yourself, yes."

Celine's nostrils flared with irritation. "Always a question of loyalty, isn't there?"

"You've given me little to trust, Celine."

"I suppose I have," Celine admitted.

"You can begin proving yourself by signing my book," he said, waving the book in the cell window.

"Patience, Marcus," Celine stalled.

Marcus's jaw flexed. "I have had centuries worth of patience, Celine. And I have done what you asked. I have restored your sister."

"That remains to be seen tomorrow. Besides, I assumed I would sign when we married. It seems that is the best time. A finalizing of our union. A symbol of our bond, both material and ethereal."

Marcus smiled at her, his eyebrow arching. "I quite like that idea, my dear. Fine. I shall allow you to wait until then to sign. It will be a pleasure witnessing you pledge your soul to me as my wife."

"I imagined you would like that idea, Marcus," Celine replied with a slight smile.

He held her gaze for a moment. "Well, on that note, I should continue to make the arrangements. With the latest agreement, I find myself eager to conclude the preparations."

"As am I," Celine noted, allowing him to suppose she agreed. In reality, she only found herself anxious to conclude her stay with Marcus. With Celeste's condition corrected, she could work on freeing herself with her family's help.

"Really? How encouraging. Then I bid you good night, dearest Celine."

"Good night, Marcus."

He strode away from her, climbing the stairs to leave the mill. She sighed, letting her arms fall to her sides. His fury would know no bounds when he realized she had no intention on marrying him or signing his book. She hoped to be far away when he realized the depths of her betrayal.

Marcus's fury was something she was too familiar with. She remembered his anger when she informed him of her marriage to Gray. She recalled the moment he learned of their secret wedding.

"You shouldn't go back to that house, Celine," Gray warned her after the ceremony. "It's too dangerous."

"I must retrieve the music box from my father. It is the last thing he gave me before his murder. I must have it. Only that. I shan't be long. No one will be there. They will all still be at the ball."

"If you insist," Gray acquiesced. "But please, be careful."

"I promise," she added, kissing him before leaving.

She hurried to her sister's home, entering the darkened house. Emptiness and silence filled the space. Even so, she crept to her room and crossed to her dressing table to retrieve the music box."

"You haven't done anything foolish, have you, Celine?" a voice inquired from the darkness.

Startled, Celine spun around to face the noise. A lantern lit from near the corner, casting deep shadows across the face of the Duke.

"What are you doing here?" Celine questioned.

"Checking on you. Did you assume I wouldn't notice that you slipped away from the ball?"

Celine stood straighter, raising her chin and summoning all the courage she had. "I am leaving in the morning."

"You'll do no such thing, Celine. I will not allow it."

"You do not own me," Celine retorted.

"I may not, yet, but your brother-in-law is your guardian, and I'm certain he will agree with me."

"He is no longer my guardian," Celine countered.

"Oh?"

"No. That would now be Grayson Buckley, my husband."

His eyes grew wide and he sprang from his chair. "You foolish girl! You married him?"

"Yes, we are married," Celine answered, her chin raised.

He stalked closer to her, seething with anger, his fists balled at his sides. She braced herself, wondering if he may strike her. After a moment, he inhaled deeply, setting his jaw.

"No matter, we will simply have a small legal affair to clear up before our own wedding.

"Legal affair? We are married in the eyes of God."

"Oh, my dear Celine, the eyes of God no longer shine upon creatures like us. But if you mean in the eyes of the church, well, that, my dear, is what annulments are for."

Celine bristled. "Never. We are in love!"

He lunged at her, grasping her arms and pulling her toward him. "Love? You dare speak to me of love? I offered you the world, is that not love? Anything you desired I would provide for you. What more could you want?"

"Unhand me!" she cried, wriggling in his grasp. "Grayson and I are married, and tomorrow we will leave this place."

She freed herself, backing up a few steps, clutching her music box.

Marcus eyed her but allowed her to distance herself. "Yes, you do that. Leave this place with your new husband, with your love," he spat, disdain dripping from him. "But know this, my darling, wherever you go, I will be there. I will always be there, Celine. I will not rest until you are mine. And I will use whatever means necessary to persuade you. Let's see how far your love can take you."

Celine fled from the room, tears streaming from her face.

She swallowed hard as the memory slipped from her mind. His reaction would be no different now. His fury would know no bounds. She had to be prepared for the fallout from her decision. She considered giving in for a moment, wondering if the price she and her family would pay for this betrayal might be too steep. No, she resolved, she mustn't. She could not give in to his demands. They would manage. They would do what they must to fight against him. They had to.

* * *

DAMIEN AWOKE the following morning groggy. He yearned to roll over and sleep the day away, but his worry for Celine drove him from his bed.

Gray greeted him from the armchair. "Good morning."

"Good morning," Damien answered through a yawn. "Sorry, still a little groggy."

"It's fine. How are you? Recovered?"

"For the most part. Have you heard anything about Celeste?"

"She stopped by last night, asking about you. She didn't give anything away. My guess is she's indebted to the Duke."

Damien sighed, pondering for a moment. "Do you think she's always been? That she helped him abduct Celine?"

"If she did, I'm not sure it began willingly. Anyway, my concern is not Celeste's loyalties. Those have always been questionable at best. My concern is Celine."

"I hope she hasn't incurred any debts with that creep," Damien replied.

"Me too. Although she's smart. And she's savvy. We've dealt with him for a long time."

Damien nodded, staring at the floor. "I want to believe you, but I'm still worried."

"I understand, Damien. I've dealt with this for centuries and I'm worried, too. I just want her home."

"Me too."

"I hate waiting around for her to contact you, but I suppose we shouldn't go to the mill until we've got the all clear from her."

"Yeah, I hate it, too, but you're right. Another day of waiting."

Gray sighed as he flicked his gaze to the ocean outside the window. "Unfortunately."

"I'm going to take a quick shower to wake up," Damien said after a moment.

"All right," Gray said, returning to his book.

Damien closed himself in the bathroom. He stared in the mirror for a moment before turning the water on. He hoped Celeste was fixed. He couldn't stand this waiting. They needed to start trying their formulated incantations, testing them, learning from them. It was the only way they could rescue Celine. And they had to rescue her soon. The longer the Duke imprisoned her, the likelier things could go terribly wrong.

He stepped into the shower, letting the hot water and steam relax his tense muscles. Tiredness hung over him, although he wouldn't admit that to anyone. He couldn't. He couldn't risk them sedating him so Celine couldn't contact him. He turned off the water, toweling off. He wrapped the towel around his waist and pushed back the shower curtain, stepping out of the shower.

"You're a hard man to catch alone, Damien," a voice said.

"Oh, geez! Holy crap!" Damien shouted, almost falling into the tub. He gulped as he recognized Marcus Northcott across the room.

The man leaned against the wall casually, his arms crossed.

"How did you get back? And how did you get in here?"

"Carefully," Marcus replied.

Damien eyed the door, wondering if he could make a run for it.

"I wouldn't try for it," Marcus stated, noticing his gaze. "And in case you're wondering, they won't hear you if you call for help."

Damien gulped again. He squeezed his eyes shut, bracing himself for the inevitable attack he would sustain.

"What on earth are you doing?" Marcus questioned.

Damien popped one eye open. "Preparing?" he answered in question form.

"Whatever for?"

"Aren't you going to kill me?" Damien queried, opening both eyes.

Marcus rolled his eyes, striding toward him. "No. I am here to extend an invitation."

"An invitation?"

"Yes. If you wish to see Celine, meet me at 10 a.m. at the cave leading to the beach. Come alone, tell no one. I am trusting you, Damien. If you cannot abide by the rules, Celine will be the one who pays for your imprudence."

Damien's eyebrows rose toward his hairline. "You'll let me see her?"

"Yes."

"I'm not sure I can get away. As you mentioned, they're keeping a close eye on me. I've been… pretty distraught over Celine," he replied, dancing around an explanation.

"That, dear Damien, is not my problem. If you want to see Celine, meet me as instructed." He turned on his heel, stalking toward the wall.

"Okay," Damien answered, staring after him. "I'll be there!"

"I look forward to it, Damien," Marcus called behind him before disappearing through the wall as though it wasn't there.

Damien collapsed to a seated position on the edge of the tub. Sweat beaded on his forehead. He ran his fingers through his still-wet hair. His hands still shook from the encounter. He didn't know how he'd manage it, but he had to make it to that meeting. He considered telling everyone. No, he decided, he couldn't risk it. He wouldn't endanger Celine, and he was certain they'd never let him go alone to meet the Duke.

A knock at the door interrupted his musings. "Everything okay?"

"Yep," he called, trying to steady his voice. He pulled on his clothes, emerging from the bathroom. "Sorry, the warm water was really relaxing. Spent longer than I expected trying to clear my mind."

Gray nodded at him. "No problem. Hungry?"

"You bet! And dying for coffee! Oh boy, can't wait for breakfast. Eggs, toast, perhaps some bacon. Orange juice," he babbled.

"All right, let's head down then."

It relieved Damien that he was with Gray and not Celine. She'd have realized he was lying in a heartbeat and already have called him on it. Gray hadn't yet learned the telltale signs of Damien's fibbing.

After breakfast, Damien and Gray joined Michael and Alexander in the sitting room. Alexander explained the progress they made in their research. They had several avenues they planned to pursue. They awaited the green light from Celine to move forward.

Damien half-listened. His mind wandering to his encounter earlier this morning. He glanced at the clock every other second, drumming his fingers on his knee. He hoped his agitation didn't show. He determined he'd need fifteen minutes to get to the cave from here. He'd need a few minutes to sneak out.

"Game of chess?" Alexander asked as the time drew near for Damien to escape.

"Ah, sure!" Damien fibbed. "Oh, just a sec. I'd like to get a cup of tea. It really soothes my nerves."

"I'll get it," Gray offered.

"No, no, I'll get it," Damien insisted. "Stretch the old legs for a spell… eh… minute."

Gray gave him an odd glance. "I'll come with you then."

"No! I mean," Damien backpedaled, "it'll take me five minutes max. I'll be fine. Celine never contacts me this early.

Besides, if I'm not back in two minutes you can send out a search party."

Gray screwed up his face. "What's wrong with you?"

Damien poked a finger at his own chest. "Me? Nothing. Just tired of being waited on. I want to pull my weight. I feel decent for once, and I'd like to be somewhat autonomous. Do a little for myself."

"You're doing more than your share, Damien," Alexander asserted.

"Still. I'm capable of fetching my own cup of tea. So… I'll just go fetch it," Damien said, backing away toward the door. "Back in a minute!"

"He is odd," Gray admitted as Damien left the room.

"Judge much?" Michael retorted.

Gray waved a hand in the air. "I can't help it his behavior is odd."

"Let the poor guy alone. He's risking his life to communicate with Celine. If he wants a minute alone to get himself a cup of tea, let him have it," Michael argued.

Gray rolled his eyes. "Fine, fine." He paced the room, checking his watch often. "How long does it take to make a cup of tea?"

"While I doubt Celine would visit him this soon after her last visit, perhaps it's best to check," Alexander suggested.

"I agree," Gray answered, stalking from the room. Minutes later, he raced back in the room. "We've got a problem."

"What is it?" Alexander queried.

"Is it Damien? Did Celine call him to Shadow World? Is he sick?" Michael questioned, leaping from the couch.

"No," Gray replied. "He's gone."

CHAPTER 14

Celine awoke at dawn. Streaks of red, yellow and orange painted the morning sky as the sun rose. She paced her cell, waiting for Celeste's arrival. Each moment after the sun rose set Celine's nerves further on edge. Had something happened? Was Celeste not well? Did her transformation not go as expected?

An hour after sunlight banished night's darkness, footsteps sounded overhead. She gazed out the door's small window, hoping to see Celeste. Within seconds, Marcus and Celeste strode down the stairs.

"Good morning, Celine!" Marcus greeted her. "As promised, your sister, visiting you in broad daylight."

Celine smiled at Celeste.

"And how wonderful daylight feels upon me," Celeste admitted.

"Oh, one more piece of evidence for you, mon chérie," Marcus added, removing a cross from his jacket pocket. He waved it in front of Celeste. "No effect."

"None," Celeste agreed. "I am cured, Celine. And I have you to thank!"

"I am so pleased for you, Celeste."

"Are you quite satisfied, my dear?" Marcus inquired.

"Yes. I am," Celine admitted. Ample evidence proved Celeste's condition was restored. One issue could be eased from her mind.

"Celine," Celeste said, "I was unable to talk to Damien last night, however Gray assured me he was surviving. They are monitoring him carefully to ensure his anxiety over your disappearance does not overwhelm him."

"Thank you for the update," Celine answered has her mind spun. Celeste was unable to speak with Damien. Was he still ill from his visit to Shadow World? They were keeping him from Celeste. Why?

"Now, Celeste has many things to attend to, don't you, Celeste?" Marcus answered. Celeste nodded, averting her eyes from Celine.

"Run along."

"I love you, Celine," Celeste said, making eye contact with Celine.

"I love you, too, Celeste," Celine responded.

Celeste offered a weak smile before she crossed the room and climbed the creaky wooden stairs.

"I hope you are satisfied," Marcus said once Celeste departed. "And I have one more surprise for you, my dear."

"Oh?" Celine inquired.

He offered her a slight smile. "Yes. Consider it another early wedding present. I shall return later." Marcus strode away from the cell door toward the stairs.

"Wait," Celine called. "What is it?"

Marcus turned back. "Patience, Celine. I wouldn't want to ruin the surprise."

He disappeared up the stairs, leaving Celine to wonder what he meant. She hated surprises, particularly those from Marcus

Northcott. What did he mean? Should she try to contact Damien? Try to escape? No, she mused, it was too early. Too close to her last contact with him. It was too dangerous. She was left to wait, wonder, and worry what may be in store for her.

* * *

Damien cleared the door, backing into the foyer. He pretended to head to the kitchen, making his way out a side door along the way and racing into the woods. He ran along the path leading to the cliffs. As he emerged from the woods, he spotted the familiar form of Marcus Northcott standing near the cave. He slowed his pace, trying to slow his breathing as well. He swallowed hard, fear rising in his belly. He tried to push it down, hoping to generate an illusion of bravery.

"You made it," Marcus noted as he approached.

"Yep!" he said, his voice an octave higher than normal. He shut his eyes a moment, clearing his throat. "Yes, I did," he reiterated, forcing his voice lower.

"Celine will be pleased."

"I am too. I miss her," he admitted.

"Shall we?" Marcus asked, signaling to the path leading toward the mill.

"Sure," Damien said, feeling anything but certain.

Damien followed Marcus down the path. He side-eyed him much of the way. He'd met the Duke on a few previous occasions, but he'd never been alone with him. Nor did he know much about the man.

"You're quite brave, Damien. You didn't hesitate when given the opportunity to visit Celine," Marcus said as they descended a hill.

Damien wasn't sure how he felt about receiving a compliment from the Duke. "I would never hesitate when it came to Celine. She's my family and I love her."

"Such loyalty, particularly for someone who isn't really your family."

"She is my family," Damien insisted. "And I'd do anything for her."

"Including slipping away from the Buckleys to visit her," Marcus noted.

For the first time, Damien considered how foolish the decision was. No one realized what he was doing, no one could help him if the Duke was being disingenuous. He swallowed hard, realizing he may have just made the worst choice of his life. And possibly the last choice of his life.

Still, he convinced himself, he had to for Celine. He couldn't pass up the opportunity to see her in the flesh, to ensure she was all right. Visiting her in Shadow World was one thing but seeing her in person was another. Perhaps he could obtain additional information about how to free her. Damien eyed the Duke sideways. Then again, perhaps he was walking to his doom.

"I want to make sure Celine is unharmed," he answered.

"You'll find her quite well," Marcus replied.

"Ha! Do you expect me to believe that?" Damien retorted, almost immediately regretting being so bold.

Marcus ceased walking for a moment, turning to Damien. Damien flinched, bracing himself.

"Oh, stop that," Marcus said, noticing his stance. "Despite the lore the Buckleys have fed you, I am not a total monster. I would never harm Celine."

Damien raised his eyebrow. "I'm not sure anyone, including Celine, would agree with you."

"Celine has been under their influence for far too long. Now, come along," Marcus said, resuming his walk.

"How do I know you're taking me to her?"

"Why would I take you anywhere else?"

"To kill me?" Damien queried.

Marcus rolled his eyes, stopping again. "I wouldn't waste my time nor my energy killing you. You are insignificant to me."

Damien narrowed his eyes at the man. "Then why come to me at all?" Damien asked.

"Because you are not insignificant to Celine. Now, I don't have all day to spend with your ridiculous drivel, so if you are quite finished with your questions, please let us proceed."

Damien eyed him a moment as he walked ahead. Something struck him as odd in the last set of statements made by the Duke.

"Are you coming or not?" Marcus shouted back to him.

There was no time to consider it now. Damien hurried behind him, catching up. "Yeah."

"You're too inquisitive for your own good, Damien," Marcus chided. "It may get you into trouble one day."

"Sorry," Damien responded, "everyone says that."

"It was you who determined the location of the painting, was it not?"

"Celine's portrait? Yep, that was me," Damien boasted, again regretting his imprudence almost as soon as he uttered the words. Marcus could not be happy that Damien's investigative skills cost him Celine's painting. "Well, I mean..."

"You're too clever for your own good, too," Marcus interrupted him.

Damien swallowed hard, his heart thudding in his chest.

"Your talents are quite wasted as a human, you know."

Damien's brow furrowed. He was about to object, to tell Marcus he'd never consider any offers he may extend when the mill came into view.

"Here we are."

"She's at the mill?" Damien inquired, pretending to be unaware.

Marcus smirked at him. "

Aren't you concerned that someone will stumble upon her?"

"Never fear, dear Damien. I am not foolish enough to leave something like that up to chance. As you Americans say: this isn't my first rodeo."

They entered the building and Marcus motioned to follow him downstairs. Damien trailed behind him, curious to determine how he would reveal Celine. As they descended the stairs, he glanced around the room. Movement caught his attention, and he gazed toward the door across the room. A small face peered out of the bars.

"Celine!" Damien cried, running to the door.

"Damien? Damien!" Celine cried in greeting.

Marcus strode over to them. "Here is your surprise, Celine. Are you pleased?"

Celine grasped Damien's hand through the bars, smiling at him. "Yes, very."

"Would you care to go inside?" Marcus asked Damien.

"Yes!" Damien responded.

Celine stepped backward as Marcus opened the door. Damien rushed inside to her.

She wrapped him in her arms, tears rolling down her cheeks. "Damien!" she cried as she squeezed him.

"Celine, are you okay?" Damien asked.

"Yes, I'm fine. How are you? Celeste tells me you've been ill from the stress."

"I'm okay," Damien assured her. "I've been having… bouts of anxiety," he said, dancing around the truth, "but I am fine."

"Are you sure?"

"Yes, I'm sure. In a few hours after one of my… attacks, I am recovered."

Celine nodded, understanding his meaning. "Oh, Damien, it's so good to see you in person," she said, wrapping him in a bear hug again.

Damien squeezed her back. "You, too. I've been so worried."

"And now you can verify I haven't harmed Celine in any way," Marcus informed him.

"You're keeping her locked in a cell like a prisoner!" Damien cried.

"Damien, hush," Celine chided.

"I've done what is necessary to achieve the desired result," Marcus retorted.

"Which is?" Damien questioned.

"None of your business," Marcus countered.

"I beg to differ…" Damien began.

"Damien," Celine cautioned, "let's not spend what little time we have arguing."

"Yes, Celine is correct," Marcus agreed. "Particularly when there is such joyous news to share."

"Joyous news?" Damien questioned.

"Why don't you tell him, darling?" Marcus insisted. "I shouldn't like to take the opportunity from you."

"Tell me what?" Damien inquired.

Celine cast her eyes to the floor. She swallowed hard, searching for the words to inform Damien of the latest developments.

"Celine?" Damien asked again.

Celine's eyes rose to meet Damien's.

"Marcus and I are to be married," she admitted, her voice a hushed whisper.

"What?" Damien exclaimed. "Celine, you can't marry him! Besides, you're already married."

"Not anymore," Marcus informed him. "She has already renounced her marriage. All that remains is to formalize it."

"No," Damien argued, swiveling to face Celine. "No, you can't be serious."

"Damien, please. I realize what I am doing."

"Celine, no! Your choice is wrong. It's… it's just wrong! You can't! Did he threaten you? Us? We'll be okay, don't give in to him. You can't do this!"

"She has made her choice," Marcus retorted. "Your feeble protestations can do nothing now."

Celine stepped around Damien to the door. "Have you brought him here merely to torture him with this news?"

"Of course not, Celine. I've brought him here for something quite different."

"Oh?"

Marcus smiled at her. "Yes. I imagined you might enjoy having your favorite family member at our wedding. Perhaps, Damien, you could give the bride away."

"I'd never give her to you!" Damien shouted.

"Damien, please," Celine cautioned.

"Celine, I'm not going to let you throw away your life for… him!" he exclaimed, gesturing to Marcus.

Marcus narrowed his eyes at Damien. "Well, if that's your stance then I suppose it is time for you to go."

"No!" Damien responded, circling his arms around Celine.

Celine was torn. As much as she wanted Damien to stay, he was her only connection to the outside world. If he remained in this cell with her, she had no way of contacting anyone outside it. "Damien, I…" she began before noise interrupted her.

Marcus's brow furrowed, and he turned toward the stairs, waving his hand across the room. Footsteps sounded overhead. They approached the steps leading downward. Celine's eyes grew wide. Her perfect plan was about to be ruined.

* * *

"WHAT? GONE?" Michael asked, leaping from his seat. "Are you sure? Where?"

"Yes, I'm sure. And I have no idea where. If I had, I'd be there, bringing him back."

"Well, where could he have gone? Why would he leave?" Michael asked.

"Whatever caused him to leave must be serious," Alexander chimed in, standing from his seat at the chess table.

"Yeah, this is unlike Damien," Michael replied. "But in retrospect, he was acting weird. Nervous. I figured it was just the stress, but perhaps something happened."

"But what?" Alexander questioned.

"And where is the best place to begin searching?" Michael queried.

"It has to do with Celine. He wouldn't just disappear," Gray conjectured.

"Do you think he went to the mill?" Alexander inquired.

"Why would he do that? What could he do?" Michael questioned.

"Did she give him more information than he shared with us? Did he imagine he could help her? Test one of our theories?" Gray postulated.

"Only one way to find out," Alexander answered. "Let's go. We must find him."

"I agree. We'll start there," Gray replied.

Michael ran a hand through his hair. "I hope we find him soon. Perhaps we should take a blanket and Millie in case we find him sick."

"Good idea. I'll get Millie. You two go ahead, we'll catch up," Gray answered. He disappeared from the room.

Michael grabbed a blanket from the couch and followed Alexander out of the house.

Gray and Millie caught up with Alexander and Michael halfway to the mill. Millie puffed from exertion, trying to keep up with Gray's pace.

"I checked his room just to be sure when I called Millie. No trace of him," Gray informed them.

"Man, I hope he's at the mill," Michael said. "Perhaps we should split up. What if he isn't there? We're wasting time."

"Do you have a better place to begin?" Gray asked.

Michel considered it a moment, but nothing sprang to mind. He shook his head. "No. I don't. Sorry, I just hate pinning our hopes on one place. If we're wrong, it could cost Damien…" Michael stopped, unable to finish the sentence.

They arrived at the mill. "You two hang back, we'll check it out first," Gray stated, leaving Millie and Michael hidden behind a few nearby shrubs.

After a few moments, Alexander waved an all clear. Michael sprang from his hiding spot, racing toward the building. Millie followed at a slower pace.

"Anything?" Michael asked as he approached.

Alexander shook his head. "It appears not."

"Oh, no," Michael lamented. "Are you sure?"

"We'd like to have a more thorough check, but at first glance, it appears he is not here."

They entered the building. Michael glanced around, calling for Damien. "If he's anywhere, he'd be downstairs."

"I took a quick glance, I saw nothing, but let's check it out," Gray answered.

Michael hurried down the stairs, followed by the others. "Damien? Damien! Are you here, buddy?"

They searched the room, finding nothing.

"He's not here!" Michael declared. "Damn it! Now what?"

Gray shook his head, shrugging. "I'm not sure. Perhaps

that clearing in the trees? Maybe the beach? Where are his favorite spots?"

"Yeah, yeah, maybe the clearing," Michael spoke hurriedly, running a hand through his sandy locks. "He loves that spot."

"Let's split up," Alexander suggested. "Two of us to the beach, the other two to the clearing. Meet back at the house if we find nothing."

"I have my phone, text if you find anything. Okay, let's go," Michael stated, heading toward the stairs.

"Wait," Gray replied. He stood in the middle of the room, glancing around. "Celine! Damien said you can hear us. I hope you can. Damien's missing, we can't find him. Do not contact him until we find him. We don't want to take any chances with his life, and he gets very sick afterwards. We're taking good care of him, don't worry. But don't contact him until you hear from us."

He turned to the rest of the group. "Okay, let's go. Hopefully, she heard us."

* * *

As Michael appeared hurrying down the steps, Celine whispered to Damien, "Are they aware of where you are?"

"No," Damien whispered back. "He said not to tell anyone."

Michael called to Damien. The group had a discussion about other spots to check. They appeared ready to depart. Celine held her breath. So far, no damage had been done. She could explain away their appearance here with a bit of work. It wouldn't be easy, but she could do it.

Then Gray stopped, turning around in the room. He spoke directly to Celine. Celine's heart dropped. He revealed that he realized she could hear him and referenced contacting Damien. Celine closed her eyes as Gray finished his speech. There would be no explaining this. None.

She glanced to Marcus, noting the perplexed expression on his face. It was fleeting. Marcus's intelligence quickly pieced the puzzle together. Bewilderment turned to realization. He set his jaw; a gesture Celine recognized well. She prepared for the oncoming hurricane.

He turned to her, his posture stiff, his face set. He opened the cell door, joining Celine and Damien inside. Celine backed up a step, shoving Damien behind her. "You have betrayed me, Celine."

Celine did not speak. "I…" she began after a moment.

"YOU HAVE BETRAYED ME!" he bellowed at her.

CHAPTER 15

Celine shielded Damien behind her from Marcus's anger. "You left me little choice!" she shouted back.

Marcus lunged toward her, seizing hold of her roughly.

"Don't touch her!" Damien hollered, pushing between them.

Marcus growled, knocking Damien aside. He flew against the side wall like a rag doll, smacking into it and sliding to the floor.

"Damien!" Celine cried. She dove toward him, but Marcus pulled her back.

"No, Celine," Marcus argued. "We have much to discuss. But first, we must find a new venue for our discourse, as this one has been compromised."

"Wait! What about Damien?" Celine sobbed.

"Oh, do not worry, my dear, Damien will come with us. We wouldn't want your special contact to inform your former family of what happened here."

Marcus dragged her across the room toward Damien. He heaved Damien to standing, wrapping his arm around his limp body. Pulling Celine close to him, he uttered a few Latin words under his breath. The world around them faded to black.

They reappeared in a cave. "Welcome to your new home, Celine," Marcus snarked. "You will stay here indefinitely."

He released Damien, who collapsed to the ground, still unconscious. Celine knelt next to him, checking his pulse. It was weak, but there.

"Damien," she whimpered. "Wake up, please."

The injury he sustained could have killed him. Celine sniffled, thankful he was alive. She'd be more thankful when he awoke.

"Stop your sniveling, Celine," Marcus barked, yanking her away from Damien.

"He needs help," Celine pleaded.

"Later, perhaps. We have things to discuss. Such as your betrayal."

Celine's features twisted with worry. "Marcus, please! He's only human. He needs medical attention."

"You lost your privilege to request anything of me when you betrayed me."

Tears spilled onto Celine's cheeks. "What would you have me do? I love my family. I love my husband. I refuse to betray him. I will never marry you! I have told you time and again! You refuse to listen."

Marcus dropped her. She landed next to Damien. "We'll see about that, Celine." He strode to the mouth of the cave.

"Where are you going?"

"To do what I should have done centuries ago. To destroy your family!"

Celine's eyes grew wide. "Marcus! Wait!"

"No, Celine, this time I will not wait! You have betrayed me for the last time. I have given you more than enough chances. This time you shall be forced to face the consequences. The distraction of Grayson

Buckley shall be removed. Then, with nothing to divert your attention, you shall be more easily coerced into submission."

Celine rose, rushing toward him. "Marcus, please." She grabbed his arm, pleading with him.

He slipped loose from her grasp, shaking her off like a bug.

"Do not deign to beg me for any favors, Celine. I have none left to give." He stalked from the cave. Celine ran after him. She smacked into a force field at the mouth of the cave. She reached out, putting her hand toward the opening. An electric shock passed through her hand as she hit the invisible wall.

The enchantment that held her in her cell at the old mill surrounded her in this location, too. She was trapped, again. She turned back to the cave's interior. She hurried toward Damien's side. Still unconscious, she pulled him onto her lap, holding him in her arms. She willed him to awaken. He was all she would have left.

* * *

Marcus stormed toward the VanWoodsens' home. Anger seethed through him. However, he was shrewd enough to recognize the value in not reacting from pure anger. It was sloppy and left room for errors. He contemplated his plan. Celine would regret her betrayal. Once he left her with nothing, she would realize she had no alternate choices. She would have no reason to continue her irresponsible behavior.

He strode up the steps, thundering through the front door. Marcus found Celeste and Teddy in the sitting room.

"Marcus," Teddy greeted him. "Is everything all right?"

Marcus stepped to the drink cart, pouring himself a

brandy before speaking. He drank it, then hurled the glass across the room. It shattered into pieces against the wall.

"Marcus?" Celeste inquired. "Whatever is the matter?"

"Your sister has once again betrayed me, Celeste."

Celeste glanced at Teddy, unsure of her answer. "Perhaps…"

"No!" Marcus interrupted her, raising his voice. He tempered it before continuing. "No, no. I will entertain no excuses for Celine's behavior."

"Forgive me, Marcus," Teddy interjected. "But I assume Celeste hoped to discover the source of this betrayal. The girl has no contact with anyone. How has she betrayed you?"

"Hasn't she?" Marcus asked. "Think again, Theodore."

"I don't understand," Celeste responded.

"Somehow the very clever Celine has managed to contact her precious Damien even while in her enchanted cell."

"How is that possible?" Teddy asked.

"I do not know. I did not care to find out at the moment. But she has achieved it. She has been working against me even while she promised herself to me."

"How did you come to this knowledge?" Celeste asked.

"Does it matter?" Marcus retorted.

"Yes. Perhaps there is some misunderstanding that I may clear up on my sister's behalf."

"There is no misunderstanding. Grayson Buckley appeared at the mill earlier this morning. He spoke to Celine. He told her Damien was missing and she should not contact him until he has been found. Satisfied?"

"Damien is missing?" Celeste followed up.

"Damien is with Celine. An early wedding gift to her since she adores him so. It shall be the last kindness she receives from me."

Both VanWoodsens were silent.

"I'm sorry, Marcus," Celeste replied after a moment.

"Not as sorry as Celine will be when I am through with her. She has betrayed me for the last time."

Celeste rushed to Marcus. "You do not intend to harm her? Surely something can be done."

"Oh, something shall be done, my dear Celeste. Something indeed. And no harm will come to Celine herself. But the time has come for the Buckleys to be destroyed. I shall leave no one standing, not Grayson, not Alexander, not even those bloody humans she clings to so vehemently."

"Marcus," Celeste warned, "is this plan wise?"

Marcus grasped Celeste's arms, dragging her several steps. "Do you dare question me?"

"No! I only mean to ensure Celine's compliance."

"She will have no choice left but to comply when there is no one alive to help her."

Marcus released Celeste, who stumbled back several steps. She smoothed her dress, regaining her breath.

"We will do whatever you ask," Teddy assured Marcus.

"Good. I have many arrangements to make. We begin our siege tonight. By tomorrow morning, the Buckleys will be no more."

"You shall inform us of our part in the plan over dinner?" Teddy asked.

"Yes," Marcus answered. "Until then, Celeste, would you check on Damien? I have moved both Celine and Damien to the cave near the beach. Ensure he isn't dead. He could prove useful to us later." He instructed her on how to communicate with Celine through the enchanted barrier.

"Yes, of course," Celeste agreed as Marcus stalked from the room.

"I should go," Celeste said to Teddy.

She pulled on her jacket and left the house, heading to the cave. She arrived and used the instructions to view Celine inside. Tears streamed down Celine's face. She held Damien in her arms. His body appeared lifeless.

"Celine?" Celeste called.

"Celeste!" Celine answered.

"How is Damien?"

"Alive, no thanks to Marcus. How can you see me? Can you let me out?"

"No," Celeste responded. "Marcus only instructed me on how to speak with you, not how to break the enchantment that holds you inside. Celine, what happened?"

Celine sighed, she released Damien, letting him slide gently to the ground. Standing, she dusted herself off and joined Celeste at the mouth of the cave. "I found a way to slip into Shadow World. I was able to call Damien there, too. I used it as a conduit to communicate with him and hence Gray."

"What?" Celeste asked in shock. "Shadow World? How did… And Damien survived?"

"I only spoke with him for moments at a time. He became quite ill after each session, but I was desperate!"

"That is why he was always unavailable when I called," Celeste determined. "And why you were always so concerned about him."

Celine nodded. "Yes."

"Oh, Celine, darling. I am so sorry your plan failed."

Celine began to answer when Damien groaned. "Damien!" she exclaimed, rushing to his side. He writhed on the ground with his eyes still closed. "Damien, can you hear me?"

His eyes fluttered open. He blinked a few times, glancing around. "Celine?"

"Yes, D, I'm right here," she answered, taking his hand in hers. "Don't move. You're hurt. No, don't try to sit up, just lay back."

"I'm okay. I've got a killer headache though," Damien answered, groaning as he held a hand to his head. "Where are we?"

"Marcus moved us to another location. One where no one can find us. He realized that I betrayed him. I'm afraid his retribution will be swift and severe this time."

"Not if I can help it," Celeste promised. "Marcus once again owns my soul, but you, sister, risked your life to restore mine. I will not permit him to destroy your life."

"Celeste, you cannot risk betraying him. He will crush you."

"I do not intend to do it alone," Celeste added. "I shall tell Gray as soon as I leave here."

Celine's eyes widened with understanding. "Are you sure, Celeste? When Marcus discovers your betrayal, he…"

"Don't worry about that, it is my risk to take."

"Celeste! I…"

"Stop, Celine. I won't listen to it. I will tell Gray whether you approve or not. I haven't been a very good big sister. It's time I correct that."

"Oh, Celeste. Please don't do this out of guilt. I have forgiven you. We'll find another way."

"This is not out of guilt, Celine. It is something I must do. I will protect you as you have protected me."

"Please be careful, Celeste. And tell Gray I love him."

"I will on both counts. With any luck, we'll have you out of there before Marcus realizes we've betrayed him."

Celine smiled at Celeste. "If I wasn't stuck in here, I'd give you a huge hug, Celeste."

"When you're free, sister, I shall collect my payment," Celeste replied with a wink.

She departed from the cave's entrance, leaving Celine and Damien alone.

"Do you think we can trust her?" Damien asked.

"I'm not sure, but I lean to saying yes. She's never behaved this way before. Let's hope she follows through," Celine replied, staring after Celeste. She turned to Damien. "More importantly though, how do you really feel?"

Damien sat up despite Celine's protestations. "I'm fine. I feel like I've been run over by a truck who then proceeded to reverse and back over me again, but I'm okay."

"I wish we could get you medical attention now. You could have an internal injury we don't realize."

"We'll worry about that later. Despite my aches, I'm glad I'm here and you aren't alone."

Celine smiled at him. "I'm glad you're here too, D. I've missed you. Shadow World visits are no substitute for real world visits. And I am so sorry about how sick it made you!"

"I survived. And it didn't matter. I was ecstatic to be in contact with you." He paused for a moment. "Although, I'm happy to never return there. That place was weird."

Celine chuckled as she sank to a seated position on the cold floor. "Shadow World is a strange place."

"Alexander's book said adjudicators like it. How could anyone like that place?"

"They find it charming with its lack of color and noise. Relaxing, even. They find our world too loud and overwhelming."

"It was quiet there. Except that time I went there when Millie hypnotized me. You weren't there at first."

"Is that how you got there? I wondered. I sensed you calling me and came as soon as I could."

Damien wrapped his arms around his knees. "Before you got there, something was making an awful noise. Like a shrill scream."

"Oh, an adjudicator was near to you. They sometimes make those noises when relaxed."

"*That's* what it sounds like when it's relaxed?"

Celine laughed again. "Yes, D. Strange, I know, but true."

"This world just gets weirder and weirder."

"And you haven't seen the half of it!"

* * *

CELESTE BANGED on Alexander's door. It took a few moments for Alexander to answer.

His jaw dropped as he opened the door. "Celeste?"

Celeste strode into the house. "I must speak with you and Gray at once."

"Please, come into the sitting room," he instructed.

Celeste and Alexander entered the sitting room.

"Celeste?" Gray questioned, glancing up from the desk. He flicked his gaze to Michael. "You okay?"

Michael shrugged. "Yeah, I feel fine. No effect at all."

"There will be no ill effects from my visit," Celeste assured them. "I am cured."

"That explains the daytime visit," Alexander replied. "How?"

"I am not sure how much my sister was able to impart in her Shadow World visits, but Marcus Northcott is back. He cured me."

"And you decide to pay us a visit first?" Gray leapt from his seat. "Why?"

"I am here to warn you."

"Warn us of what?"

"All of you are in terrible danger. Marcus has discovered that Celine has been communicating with Damien. He is furious, determined to destroy all of you for her betrayal."

Gray closed his eyes, worry for Celine filling him.

Celeste continued. "He has moved her to a new location. I know where she is, but not how to free her. I can impart what Marcus has told me, then we should go at once to try to save her."

"We'll handle it, Celeste," Gray answered, dismissing her.

"Do not cast me off, this is no light matter! I am here to help!"

"Or lure us into a trap," Alexander suggested.

"It is no trap."

"And we should trust you why?" Gray prodded. "Marcus Northcott restored you why? Not out of the kindness of his heart."

"No. Celine orchestrated it. She risked her life for me, and I am repaying her."

"If this isn't a trap, tell us where she is and let us handle it."

"She is in the cave near the beach. Do not waste time, Marcus plans to strike your family tonight. Gray, you must rescue Celine and Damien before then."

"Damien?" Alexander queried.

"Yes, Damien is with her. Marcus took him to her earlier. It was while you searched for him that Marcus learned the truth."

"Marcus was there when we…" Gray began, realizing he had unknowingly revealed Celine's plan to the Duke. "But…"

"He masks himself," Celeste explained. "You'd never realize he was present."

"Is Damien all right?" Michael asked.

"Yes, he is fine. He was unconscious when I arrived. There was a scuffle when Marcus learned of Celine's visits. However, he's awake and seems recovered."

"How is Celine?" Gray inquired.

"Celine is Celine. Always worried for someone else. She misses you, Gray. She insisted I tell you she loves you."

Gray smiled to himself. "That's Celine."

"What can you tell us about the enchantment, Celeste?" Alexander asked.

Celeste imparted any knowledge she gleaned from Marcus about the spell. Gray and Alexander mulled over the information. They compared it to the materials they had amassed.

"Have you any idea how to reverse it?" Celeste questioned.

"We have some ideas, nothing we are sure of," Gray answered.

"We should try. At the very least, you can see and speak with Celine," Celeste replied.

"We should go now," Alexander suggested.

"Yes," Gray agreed. "Should we take Millie? In case Damien needs medical attention?"

"It's far too dangerous, but we should warn her so she can be prepared for our return," Alexander suggested.

"Do we need flashlights or anything?" Michael questioned.

"No, you stay here. It's far too dangerous," Gray argued.

"What? No! No way! Damien is out there and needs our help. I'm not going to sit here and do nothing!"

"Gray is correct. It is far too dangerous," Alexander agreed.

"I don't care how dangerous it is! I'm not leaving my friends out there!" Michael countered.

"Instead of arguing, perhaps we should be moving," Celeste insisted.

"Fine, whatever, let's just get going. I'll tell Millie," Gray replied.

He disappeared from the room. Alexander gathered a few reference books, and they met Gray in the foyer. They hurried to the beach cave.

"They are in here," Celeste said as they approached. She

unmasked the enchantment so they could see and hear inside the cave.

Gray approached the cave's entrance. "Celine," he raced toward her, bumping into the invisible barrier.

"Gray!" she exclaimed, approaching him but stopping short of running into the barrier.

"Celine, we'll get you out. Don't worry. We have a few ideas, hopefully one of them will work. Alexander and I…"

"Gray! Look out!" Celine shouted, interrupting him.

Marcus Northcott approached the cave with a determined stride. Alexander shoved Michael behind a nearby tree, hiding him from sight. Marcus threw his arms out, expelling an electric shock that radiated from him. It knocked everyone down in its path.

"Well," Marcus said, "I had expected to seek you out to destroy you. But you've saved me the trouble. And now your beloved Celine can watch you perish. Perhaps then the consequences of her betrayal will sink in."

The skies overhead darkened, thunder rumbled. Winds picked up, sweeping around them.

Gray shot a bolt of lightning at Marcus. It had little effect. "Pathetic as always, Buckley," Marcus retorted, continuing toward him. "I planned to save you for last. But I shall enjoy killing you first now."

"Marcus, no!" Celine shouted.

Marcus lifted Gray from the ground, tossing him away from the cave's entrance like a toy soldier. Alexander attempted to defend Gray, throwing a fireball at Marcus. It did little more than annoy the target.

"Patience, Alexander. I shall deal with you next," Marcus replied, lobbing a lightning bolt at him.

Alexander dodged it, diving to the ground.

"Alexander!" Celeste whispered. "Throw me the book!"

Celine watched helplessly as Marcus and Gray battled, exchanging supernatural assaults of various kinds. Marcus held the upper hand in the fight and realized it. He toyed with Gray, enjoying the game before moving in for the kill.

Celine approached the cave's entrance as Celeste paged through the book. "Hurry, Celeste. Gray can't last much longer."

"Yes, I'm trying. I don't even know if this will work." Celeste found the marked page, uttering the words on it.

"If this enchantment is broken," Celine said to Damien, "run. Take Michael and go to Alexander's as fast as you can. Stay there until we return."

"But Celine…" Damien began.

"No! Damien, no. I will have my hands full. I cannot worry about you and Michael."

"Okay," Damien acquiesced.

"Try now," Celeste said.

Celine pushed her hand toward the cave's entrance. A bolt of electricity shocked her back. "Nope."

"Try the one in this book," Alexander suggested, tossing another book over as he continued to attempt to help Gray.

"No, no, this one won't work," Celeste argued, shaking her head.

"Try anyway," Celine pressed.

"No, it won't work because…" Celeste began. She paused. "Wait. Perhaps if I…. Stand back."

Celine took several steps back, placing herself between the cave's entrance and Damien. Celeste uttered a few words from both books in front of her. She waved her arms around the entrance, grasping at the invisible barrier then pulling backward.

"Try again," she instructed.

Celine rushed forward, reaching out toward the entrance.

This time no barrier struck her. She reached through the mouth of the cave, grasping Celeste's hand.

"You've done it!" she exclaimed. She turned to Damien. "Run, Damien!"

She pushed Damien ahead of her, ensuring he ran toward Michael. Marcus had Gray pinned near the cliff's edge. He moved in for the kill. Celine took two steps toward them, drawing all her power into her. She screamed, launching an attack at Marcus.

CHAPTER 16

Startled by the strength of the attack, Marcus turned to discover the source. Celine flew through the air at him, knocking him down. They rolled, tangled together toward the woods. As they ground to a halt, Celine pressed Marcus's arms to the ground, pinning him.

"I shall show you the true meaning of betrayal, Marcus," she seethed through clenched teeth.

With a growl, he shoved her sideways, knocking her to the ground next to him. They both leapt to their feet within seconds. Celine lunged toward him, her fingers crackling with electricity. Marcus dodged her. Alexander and Gray each shot fireballs at him. He blasted back with another circular blast, flattening them both.

He turned to face Celine. They circled each other like wolves fighting over food.

"Retreat now, Marcus, and you may survive," she warned.

"Retreat? Whatever for, Celine? I am just warming up!" he retorted. He shoved his hands toward her, and she responded in kind. The power of their mutual attack was explosive. The two assaults collided, setting off a reaction. An electrical shock wave burst from between them, paralyzing everyone within a mile radius of them. Gray, Alexander, and Celeste were blown down, unable to move for a few moments. Damien and Michael, who were running through the woods, suffered a similar fate.

When the effect subsided, Gray sat up, glancing around. Alexander joined him along with Celeste. Gray stared at Alexander, aghast. "Where the hell is Celine?"

* * *

CELINE STOOD UP, glancing around. Her attack on Marcus had created a strange effect, like nothing she had seen before. She didn't see Gray or anyone else, only Marcus. He climbed to his feet, also glancing around.

Celine recognized her surroundings. Somehow their attack conjoined to create a shock wave, sending them to Shadow World. The colorless trees soared around them.

Marcus assessed their location. "What have you done, Celine?"

"I have done nothing! This is *your* fault!" Celine bellowed, lobbing a fireball at him.

He dodged it. "My fault? I did nothing!" he responded, throwing a lightning bolt her way.

She leapt to the side, and it sailed past her charring a tree behind her. "Nothing? You tried to kill my family! You call that nothing?" she queried, hurling another fireball his way.

He sidestepped, allowing it to blast the tree behind him. "You're so emotional, Celine. I simply attempted to remove the barriers that keep us apart."

She screamed, lunging at him. He grasped her arms, restraining her. "Stop, Celine. We have more pressing matters at hand."

"Such as what? What is more pressing than destroying you?" she shrieked, struggling against him.

Marcus nodded behind her. Celine ceased her struggle, gazing behind her.

Her adjudicator stood a few feet away, its eyes blazing red, wings flapping in agitation. "What is the meaning of this, Celine Devereaux Buckley?"

Celine pulled her arms from Marcus's grasp, spinning to face the adjudicator. "Apologies. We do not know how we came to be here."

"Impossible!" it screeched. "One does not slip into Shadow World, unbeknownst. What are the circumstances by which you came, Celine Devereaux Buckley?" it demanded.

"Ah, but Celine does… slip into Shadow World, that is. She's been using it as a conduit to communicate with a human on multiple occasions," Marcus chimed in.

"Explain yourself, Celine Devereaux Buckley!" the adjudicator demanded, its wings flapping furiously, eyes burning red with agitation.

"I… that is untrue. Marcus has left out several key facts, including that he imprisoned me, and I had no other choice! It was the only means by which I could communicate with my family to orchestrate a rescue."

"Is this true, Marcus Northcott?"

"Yes, however, it is none of your concern," he submitted.

"It is my concern when my peace is disturbed, Marcus Northcott!" the adjudicator shrieked, flying within inches of them.

"We apologize," Celine stated, "we did not mean to disturb your peace. We came to be here this time by accident."

"Explain, Celine Devereaux Buckley!" it demanded, its hot breath wafting across Celine's face.

"We were engaged in a… spirited argument. I'm not sure what happened, but there was some sort of melding of our supernatural powers and we both ended up here. We will depart from this realm without further controversy."

"Yet you choose to continue your battle after arriving here!" the adjudicator cried, pacing in front of them.

"Again, our apologies, if you would allow us to return…" Celine began.

"So that you might engage in another argument and return here to disturb my peace, Celine Devereaux Buckley?"

"We will not," Celine promised.

The adjudicator ceased pacing, staring at Celine. "What understanding have you and Marcus Northcott arrived at to ensure this?"

Celine glanced to Marcus, raising an eyebrow. "Well…" she began.

"As I suspected!" the adjudicator hollered. "You have fought for centuries. No more! I shall ensure your fighting ceases for the term of my repose! I will not be disturbed!"

It stalked back and forth in front of them. They awaited its decision. "I have decided," it stated after a moment. "Celine Devereaux Buckley, I shall return you to your realm. Since Marcus Northcott is the root cause of the issue, he shall remain in Shadow World for the duration of my repose."

"Now, just a moment…" Marcus objected.

"SILENCE, MARCUS NORTHCOTT!" it bellowed, its eyes returning to a fiery red.

Marcus appeared unimpressed. "I demand to see Bazios."

"I SAID SILENCE! Bazios cannot and will not help you! He is bound by my decision. Come, Celine Devereaux Buckley. I shall return you to the material realm."

Marcus grimaced. "Well, it appears you have won again, dear Celine. For now."

"Enjoy your stay, Marcus," Celine replied. "I know I shall." She stepped away, then turned back. "Oh, there is one more thing. You have something that belongs to me. I want it back."

"Oh?" Marcus questioned, playing coy.

"My soul shard. I want it."

"No. I believe I'll hang on to it. A reminder of you during my stay in Shadow World."

"I…" Celine began.

"Come, Celine Devereaux Buckley!" the adjudicator shouted at her.

"This isn't finished," Celine warned, before stalking away after the adjudicator.

It opened a portal in front of Celine. "Step through the portal. Goodbye, Celine Devereaux Buckley," the adjudicator concluded.

"Goodbye," Celine said. "And thank you."

Celine stepped through the portal, leaving behind Shadow World with Marcus Northcott in it. She stepped into the sky above the clouds in her world. She plummeted toward the earth, landing on her feet in a crouched position with a loud clap.

Gray raced toward her. "Celine!"

"Gray!" she answered, rising to stand.

He wrapped her in his arms, kissing the top of her head. "Thank God you're all right."

"I'm fine, Gray," she said, slipping her arms around his waist.

Alexander and Celeste joined them. Celine reached out to grab both of their hands.

"What happened?" Celeste asked. She glanced around. "Where is Marcus?"

"Gone," Celine answered. "For the moment, anyway."

"What happened? Where did you go?" Alexander asked.

"I'm not sure," Celine replied. "We ended up in Shadow World. How, I still don't understand."

"Shadow World?" Celeste questioned.

"Yes," Celine responded. "Our adjudicator was there. It was not pleased that we were disturbing its peace. In the end, it chose to keep Marcus there until it finished its repose. It returned me to earth and insisted Marcus stay."

"I can't imagine how that went over," Alexander answered.

"Not well, the adjudicator didn't give him much choice. Even Marcus wouldn't dare flout an adjudicator. Still, we must prepare. When he returns, I'm sure he'll want to pick up where we left off."

"I agree, but I'd like a moment to enjoy having you back," Gray answered, squeezing her in his arms again.

Celine returned his embrace. "And I owe you a hug as well," Celine said, stepping away from Gray and pulling Celeste into an embrace.

"I am so pleased you are free, sister. I apologize for my part in this."

"You had no part in this, Celeste. You had no choice due to your condition."

"What part?" Gray asked.

"Nothing, it's over," Celine answered.

"No," Celeste argued. "I was the one who lured her to the cell. When Marcus returned, he used my condition against me. I had no choice. If I wanted to survive, I had to do his bidding."

Gray shook his head at her.

"Stop, stop this. Celeste is no more responsible than I am. She had no choice. And it's over now. Thanks to all of you." Celine glanced among all of them. She reached out to embrace Alexander, thanking him for his help as well. "Now, I really need to find Damien. He deserves a hug, too."

"He was exceptionally brave," Alexander admitted.

"Yes, I agree," Gray added. "He went through hell, but he was determined to keep the communication lines open with you."

"He deserves a nice long rest," Celine replied. "Maybe some ice cream."

"Well, let's get back to the house and get him that ice cream," Gray answered, wrapping his arm around Celine's shoulders.

Celine grasped his hand as they set off down the path toward Alexander's home. They reached the edge of the woods, stepping under the canopy of white pines. Ahead, Celine spotted something laying on the ground. Within a moment, they were close enough to recognize Michael's and Damien's limp forms.

"Damien?" Celine shouted, racing toward him. Both he and Michael laid face down on the ground. Celine rolled him over. "Damien!" she cried again, shaking him.

Gray, Alexander, and Celeste joined her. They rolled Michael over.

"DAMIEN!" Celine shouted, feeling for his pulse.

"Is he breathing?" Gray asked.

"He has a pulse, he's breathing. Why won't he wake up?" Celine questioned, tears streaming down her face.

"Michael is the same. Perhaps the shock wave? We weren't affected, it knocked us down, but there were no other effects," Celeste answered.

"I'm not sure. We need to get them home, let Millie check them."

"Yes," Gray agreed. He lifted Damien.

"Careful," Celine warned. "Careful, in case he's hurt."

"I've got Michael," Alexander replied, lifting Michael.

They hurried back to Alexander's home. Bursting through the door, Celine raced to the sitting room.

"Millie!" she shouted. "Come quickly, it's Michael and Damien. Something is wrong with them."

Gray and Alexander carried them upstairs, placing them in the bedrooms they had been using. Millie followed Celine, checking first on Damien, then Michael. She did a full physical exam on each before discussing their conditions. Celine paced the floor of Damien's room.

"Try to relax, Celine," Gray advised. "You've been through a lot, too."

"I can't," Celine murmured. "Not now. What have we done to them?"

She crawled onto the bed, taking Damien's hands in hers. A tear fell onto her cheek. "Damien, please be okay."

Gray rubbed her shoulders. "It'll be okay, Celine."

"You don't know that!" Celine whimpered.

"Come on. He didn't survive Shadow World and multiple run-ins with the Duke to let a little electrical shock hurt him."

Celine wiped her tear away, smiling at Gray. "Thanks," she said as Millie entered the room.

Celine leapt from the bed. "Well?"

"First, welcome home. I have examined both Michael and Damien."

"And?" Celine demanded.

"They are suffering from the same symptoms. Both are non-responsive. Breathing is normal at this moment. Heart rate was slightly elevated but not significantly. Pupils are equal and reactive. There appear to be no signs of any trauma."

"What does that mean?" Celine asked.

"I'm not sure of the cause yet, but you said some sort of electric pulse may have hit them?" Millie asked.

"Yes. There was some reaction between one of the attacks Marcus and I launched against each other. It's never happened before, but it sent some kind of shock wave out. It didn't seem to affect Celeste, Gray, or Alexander, but it sent Marcus and me to Shadow World. I assume it was strong enough to affect a human."

"I see. Well, so far, there is no sign of anything serious. No breathing or heart trouble, no burns to the skin like you would see in a lightning strike, for example. Perhaps this is a reaction to the pulse. A sort of shock."

"What can we do? Will he come out of it?"

"I've never dealt with this before. Most of your attacks don't leave your victims this stunned, only a little maimed. But I will continue monitoring both of them. We'll note any changes, even small ones. In the meantime, we'll keep them warm to counteract the shock. Stay with them, talk to them."

"Do you suppose they will wake up?" Celine asked.

"There's no reason to believe otherwise, Celine," Millie assured her. "If their vital signs were any cause for concern, I wouldn't be saying this, but I am optimistic. Sometimes the body does this to protect itself, heal itself."

Celine wandered to Damien's bed, sinking onto the bed next to him.

"Thanks, Millie," Gray answered.

"You're welcome. Call me the moment anything changes. Are we planning on keeping them here?"

"Whatever you judge is best," Gray replied.

"Let's not move them for at least twenty-four hours. We'll reassess then."

"Fine. I'm sure Alexander won't mind."

"Alexander won't mind what?" Alexander asked, entering the room.

"Millie suggests we don't move Michael and Damien for at least twenty-four hours."

"No problem at all. And I assume you three will stay as well?"

Gray glanced to Celine, holding Damien's hand. "Yes, that would be best."

"I'll have the rooms prepared."

Celine gazed at Damien's sleeping form. She pulled his blanket a little higher around him. She squeezed his hand.

"Damien," she sniffled. "You'll be okay. You have to be. I'm so sorry for all of this. If I could take this from you, I would in a heartbeat. You just rest now, relax. Let your body heal itself and then you come back to me."

* * *

1812, LONDON

Damien rubbed his eyes and peered around again. Confusion clouded his face. He glanced toward Michael, curious to determine if Michael was experiencing the same phenomenon. The puzzled expression on Michael's face confirmed he was.

"Ah," Damien began, "are you seeing what I'm seeing?"

Michael cleared his throat before he answered. "Are you seeing horses and buggies, cobblestone streets, people in old-fashioned clothes?"

"Yep," Damien confirmed.

"Then I'm seeing what you're seeing."

Damien whirled toward him. "Okay, that's good, not great."

"What?" Michael asked, confused.

"Good that we're experiencing the same thing. Not great because I have no idea why we're experiencing this."

"Me either, how did we get here? Where did we get these clothes? Do you remember changing?" Michael asked, staring down at his nineteenth century garb.

"I don't. I have no idea how we got here or where we got

these clothes. I don't remember anything about being sent to London," Damien answered.

"How do you know it's London?" Michael asked.

Damien pointed to a structure dominating the landscape in the distance. "Buckingham Palace. Or at least part of it."

"Oh, right, good catch! It looks different. So, now what?"

"There's a wing missing, we must be in a time before it's built. It's not added until 1847. And no idea! I cannot remember what we're doing here, can you?"

"Nope. I don't even remember being sent here."

"Me either!" Damien exclaimed. "It's clear we've time traveled. But every other time we've time traveled, we've remembered doing it and what we were here to do. This time I've got nothing."

"I don't recall anything either. I don't remember Celine sending us here or what, if anything, she told us to do."

"Great! That's just perfect," Damien shouted, throwing his arms in the air. "Now what? We have no idea when we are or why we're in London in whatever year this is!"

"Perhaps I can find out from that kid on the corner. He's selling papers. They must have the date on them, right?"

"Yeah. Good luck. I doubt we have any money to buy the paper from him." Damien's face lit up. "Wait! Check your pockets!"

"Why?" Michael asked, already checking his pockets while he waited for a response.

"Celine usually gives us a letter of introduction and some money. If we can find it, perhaps we'll have a clue as to what we're doing here," Damien explained, checking his pockets, too.

"Nothing," Michael grumbled.

"Me either," Damien confirmed.

"No money either. So that's just great. Okay, let me try to

get the date at least. Perhaps that will jar something in our memories."

"Good luck," Damien called after him as he trotted to the child on the corner.

Damien eyed them as Michael approached the boy, speaking a few words to him. The child answered, Michael spoke again. After a moment, the child showed him the front of the paper. Michael stared at it, then spoke a few words before trotting back to where Damien waited.

"Well?" Damien asked.

"The date on the paper is December first, 1812," Michael answered.

Damien wrinkled his nose and scratched his head. What the hell were they doing in 1812 London?

CHAPTER 17

"1812?" Damien questioned. "1812... 1812... why 1812? Why London? What did you want us to do, Celine?"

"Was Celine in London in 1812?"

Damien shook his head, his lips pressed together in a thin line. "I'm not sure. This is so frustrating. We have no idea why we're here, where to go, what to do! Which begs the question: what the hell are we going to do?"

"I have no idea. We have no information, no letter of introduction, no directions on where to go. This is a nightmare," Michael said, running a hand through his hair.

Damien puffed out his cheeks. "We have to figure something out. Before we're sleeping on the streets of London in 1812."

Panic laced Damien's voice as the seriousness of their situation set in.

Michael noted the alarm entering Damien's voice. "All right, all right, just calm down. We need a place to sit down and think." Michael glanced around for a suitable location.

"The park," Damien said. "St. James Park. We can go there, find a place to sit down, regroup, come up with a plan."

"Sounds good," Michael agreed. "Do you know the way?"

"If we walk toward the river, we should get to it," Damien said, rubbing the back of his neck. "At least I think so."

Using the palace and river as their guide, Michael and Damien hurried along the sidewalk. Within moments, they came to the park. They spotted a bench, hastening to it.

"Okay, okay, okay. Think, Damien, think," Damien muttered to himself. After a few moments, he threw his hands in the air, frustration forming. "Nothing, I have nothing. Ugh!"

"Relax, we can figure this out," Michael assured him. "What's the last thing you remember?"

"Ummmm," Damien paused, his leg bouncing up and down. "Uh, I'm not sure. My memory is so hazy. It's like I can't remember. What about you?"

Michael furrowed his brow, concentrating. "Uh, yeah, mine is hazy too. Wait, wait. Being at Alexander's house? But I don't remember why."

Damien gave his memory another try. "Yeah, okay, yes, I can remember being at Alexander's. I think I can anyway. It may be a false memory because you said that. This is getting us nowhere!"

"Okay, that's fine. Like I said, calm down, we can figure this out."

"How do you propose we do that, Michael?" Damien shouted, leaping from his seat to pace. "I don't have a magical wand to wave."

"No, I realize that," Michael answered. "But we can talk through this and figure something out. We need a plan. It doesn't have to work, but we have to try something until it does."

Damien puffed out a deep exhale and sank onto the bench again, rubbing his hands on his thighs. "Okay."

"Okay, now," Michael said, "if Celine was in London,

where would she be? Do you know where she typically stayed when she was here?"

"Umm," Damien said, his voice trembling as he considered it. "No, I never discussed London with Celine. I don't..." His voice trailed off.

"What?" Michael prompted, realizing Damien was vetting an idea in his head.

"I never discussed London with Celine, but I did discuss it with Alexander. He mentioned it during one of our chess games. The Buckleys had an estate here before they moved to the States. They also had a house in London. Where did he say it was? I can't remember!" Damien exclaimed.

"Okay, okay, that's good. We just need to find the house. Just relax, think. What prompted the conversation between you? Try to remember what you were discussing, perhaps that will help you recall where the house is located."

Damien muttered, "Uh... we were talking about... uh... his house! We were talking about him building his house! He said he patterned it off the estate here. I asked him if he stayed there when he traveled, and he said not always. Many times, he'd stay in the London house. Which was on..." Damien paused, deep in thought. "Which was on... on... on Canterbury Way!"

Damien snapped his fingers, beaming and staring at Michael. "That's it! Canterbury Way!"

"Great job, buddy!" Michael exclaimed, wrapping his arm around his shoulders and shaking him. "New plan: we find Canterbury Way, figure out which house belongs to the Buckleys and hope somebody is home!"

"Wow, that is the worst plan ever, but okay, let's go!" They stood from the bench. "Do you know the way?"

Michael furrowed his brow and shook his head. "No! Why would I know the way?"

Damien shrugged. "You've been to London before, right?"

"Yeah. In the twenty-first century with a chauffeured car. I have no idea where Canterbury Way is or how to get there."

Damien frowned, his shoulders slumping as he glanced around. "Dang. Oh well, we'll ask for directions along the way and ask about the Buckleys when we get closer. Perhaps someone will be familiar with them."

As they exited the park, they stopped a well-dressed gentleman to inquire about Canterbury Way. They were fortunate to find he was familiar with the street, giving them directions to it. Twenty minutes later they arrived at their location.

"That wasn't too bad," Damien said when they spotted the Canterbury Way sign.

"Good thing. It's starting to get dark," Michael replied.

"You afraid of the dark?"

"No, but I don't want to be on the streets of London with Jack the Ripper."

Damian made a face at Michael.

"What?" Michael asked.

"Jack the Ripper isn't around now. He operated in the late 1800s. Plus, he killed prostitutes, so I think we're safe."

"Whatever," Michael answered as they strode down the street. "I don't care. I don't want to be sleeping on the streets of London."

"There are only a few houses on this street. Perhaps this will be easy."

"What do you suggest we do? Knock on every door?"

"No, but maybe if we hang around, we'll spot Alexander or Gray or Celine. Or we can ask someone if they come along."

"I hope someone comes along soon. It's getting cold!" Michael complained, rubbing his hands together.

They waited a few minutes, parading up and down the street, searching for any clues. They found none. Another few moments passed before Damien spotted a man walking down the street.

Not wanting to miss him, Damien hurried toward him, shouting, "Excuse me, sir? Sir?"

"Yes?" the man answered.

"Sorry to disturb you, but I was hoping you could help us. We're trying to find a friend's home. Perhaps you can help us. His name is Alexander Buckley. His home is on Canterbury Way, however, I've forgotten the address. Do you know it?"

"Ah, Buckley, yes. Alexander, did you say? Yes, Edgar and Abigail's son, if I recall. Their home is number four," he said, pointing down the street. "It's near the end."

"Number four, yes, that's right! Thank you so much, sir."

"Quite welcome, sir. I do hope you enjoy your visit to our country."

"Thank you!" Damien answered as they both said their good nights to the kind gentleman, allowing him to enter his home.

"Number four Canterbury Way, here we come," Michael said as the man disappeared from their earshot.

"I'm crossing my fingers Celine is here and we can get some perspective on what we're doing here," Damien said as they continued down the street.

"Yeah, me too," Michael agreed as they approached the steps leading to the house. "Especially since we don't have any letters of introduction. We're going to need someone to vouch for us. Perhaps we should ask for Alexander. The guy we talked to seemed to know his name."

"Good idea. That's probably the safest bet."

They climbed the steps, using the door knocker. Michael wiped a bead of sweat from his forehead. A white-haired gentleman opened the door, inquiring if he could help them.

"Hello. Michael and Damien Carlyle to see Alexander

Buckley," Michael answered, using their usual ruse for time travel of being brothers.

"Please come in, I shall inform him you have arrived. Are you expected?"

"Ah," Michael hesitated, as they entered the foyer "I am not sure if he received our correspondence. We did write."

He glanced to Damien, who gave him a slight nod, encouraging his ruse.

"If you'll wait here, gentlemen," the man said, signaling to a sitting room to the left, "I shall inform Mr. Buckley."

"Thank you," Michael answered as they entered the space.

They waited a few moments. Damien bounced his leg on the ground as he sat perched on the edge of the settee near the fireplace. "Is it hot in here or is it me?" Damien asked, pulling at his collar before the door opened.

Alexander appeared through the other side from where they had entered.

Damien leapt to his feet.

"Gentlemen," Alexander greeted them, "how may I help you?"

Relief coursed through Damien. "Oh, Alexander, are we glad to see you," he said, beaming at him. "We are in terrible trouble."

"I'm sorry to hear that," Alexander answered. "Although, I am not sure how I may be of help. I'm not quite sure why you've sought me out."

"Well," Damien began, "I remembered you telling me about the house in London. So, when we found ourselves here, we figured it was our best option. We don't remember why we're here or what we're doing here, but maybe Celine can help us."

"I told you about the house?" Alexander questioned, confusion entering his voice.

"Yes," Damien confirmed. "Is Celine here?"

"Gentlemen, my apologies, but I am baffled by your request and your statements."

Damien issued a confused look to Michael, who returned the expression. "Alexander, we're as confused as you are. I'm sorry we don't have more information to share. We're at a loss here."

Alexander continued to eye them with suspicion. "You stated I told you about the London house. Yet, I cannot understand how. Gentlemen, we've never met before."

Damien's jaw dropped. He furrowed his brow, glancing at Michael then back to Alexander. "Uh, you don't remember us?"

"I do not, and I am quite good with faces. Perhaps you might remind me of when and where we met?" he suggested.

"Uh," Damien murmured, collecting his thoughts. "1791," Damien stated, "Bucksville, Maine. Uh, no, Massachusetts then. At your family's estate. We were visiting Celine. She was calling herself Mina then."

"Odd," Alexander said, placing a finger on his chin in contemplation.

"What is?" Michael asked.

"I do not recall meeting you at my uncle's estate. And who is the woman you are referring to? You've mentioned her several times now."

"Celine," Damien said, expecting a response and receiving none. "Grayson's wife, Celine."

Alexander's face was a mask of confusion. "Grayson's wife? As in my cousin, Grayson?"

"Yes!" Damien exclaimed.

Alexander's posture stiffened. "Impossible! My cousin, Grayson, is not married."

Damien's jaw fell open. "What?"

He stared at Michael, shock on his face.

"No, no, no, no, no." Damien murmured as he ran his fingers through his hair.

"Sorry," Michael apologized, "my brother is flustered by your news. The last time we saw Celine, she was married to Gray. We were at the Buckley manor in Bucksville. What happened since then? I realize it's been years, but I was under the impression that Celine and Gray remained together."

Alexander's confusion grew. He shook his head. "Mr. Carlyle, my cousin has never been married. Not to a woman named Celine or anyone else. I'm sorry, I've little idea what you two are talking about. I wish I could be of more assistance, but I cannot make heads or tails out of your story."

Damien whipped around to face Alexander. "Do you know a woman named Celine Devereaux? She's from Martinique. Blonde hair, blue eyes, pretty."

Alexander studied him for a moment, then responded, "Yes, I am acquainted with a woman fitting that description. She no longer uses that name since her marriage."

"Her marriage?" Damien questioned.

"To someone other than Gray?" Michael inquired further.

"Yes," Alexander confirmed.

Michael and Damien shared a glance before Michael inquired, "Who is she married to?"

"Marcus Northcott," Alexander answered.

CHAPTER 18

*D*amien's jaw dropped at the bombshell admission. He stared at Michael, trying to make sense of it.

"Oh, no. I need to sit down," Damien said, plopping onto the couch.

"Are you all right? May I offer you a drink?" Alexander asked.

"Please," Damien breathed.

Alexander poured and offered him a brandy, doing the same for Michael. "Gentlemen, there seems to be some miscommunication. You are either very confused or something very strange is happening. Perhaps you should begin again, leaving nothing out."

Damien gulped his brandy, his hands shaking.

Michael began filling in the story. "It's complicated. We are friends of Celine's, at least I assume we are." He knit his brows, trying to explain the story in a way that made sense. "We…"

Damien interrupted him. "We're not from this century. We're from the future. We are aware of what you are, what Celine is, Gray, the Duke, all of you. We've traveled back several times to the past courtesy of Celine, who is Celine Devereaux Buckley where we're from, and her ability to open time portals. Once we traveled to Martinique, and we helped her steal a book from Marcus Northcott, the *Book of the Dead*. We used it to banish him from the earth. Another time we traveled to the year 1791. We helped Celine find her painting, the one Benjamin Abbott painted that captured a piece of her soul. Marcus Northcott stole it, and we helped her retrieve it. Now, every time we've time traveled before, we've remembered the events leading up to it, why we were there, and what we needed to do. This time we have no idea how we got here or why we're here. We have no memory of Celine sending us here. And now you're telling us Celine isn't even Celine. Celine is married to the Duke, which can't be true because we saved her from him back in Martinique. After that, she should have met and married Gray, traveled to America, had a portrait painted of her, left to go to Dunhaven, Scotland, et cetera, et cetera."

Alexander's eyes went wide. "That is a most interesting tale, Damien. Although, some of it may be factual, I don't believe Grayson has even met the Duchess Northcott. I can assure you Celine Northcott has never been to Bucksville. You and I have never met. And I don't believe anyone has ever gotten close to the *Book of the Dead,* other than when they've sold their souls to Duke Northcott. That covers all of it, if I'm correct. Now, gentlemen, I do not understand the reason for your tales but..."

"They aren't tales!" Damien shouted. "We need your help!"

"You mentioned being aware of what I am, what Celine is, what Gray is. What did you mean?"

"You guys have supernatural powers. You're a warlock."

Alexander arched an eyebrow. "And how did you come to this knowledge?"

"It's complicated."

"You ask for my assistance but refuse to give me any details?"

Damien tapped the side of his glass. "I'm related to Celine. Sort of. It's complicated. Where we come from, she's different. She knows us well. She introduced us to all of this supernatural stuff."

"I see."

"Look, Damien's right," Michael confirmed. "We really need help. We're floundering here. Everything we know you're telling us isn't true. We have no idea why we're here."

"And the only way we can get back to where we're from is with Celine's help. Oh, unless you can open a time portal?" Damien inquired, hope lingering in his voice.

"I'm sorry. I regret to inform you I do not have that ability. Few people do."

"So, we're stuck here," Damien moaned.

"Unless you can take us to Celine and convince her to help us," Michael proposed to Alexander.

"Take you to Celine? That's quite a tall order! I doubt the Duchess Northcott would entertain a call from me, let alone a request for help!"

"You said you were acquainted with her!" Michael insisted.

"I have met her on a few occasions. Acquainted, yes. However, we do not move in the same social circles. She sips tea with the Queen! Heavens, she'll likely be queen one day. Perhaps I could arrange for you to meet her, but that is as much as we could hope to achieve. A favor, likely not. Duke Northcott and my family are not on the best of terms. I doubt his wife would entertain the idea of helping me or anyone in my company."

"We have to try!" Damien cried.

"He's right," Michael agreed. "We can't stay here. We

aren't from this century, we have nowhere to go. We don't even have any money to get by until we figure out a plan. We need help and in order to return to where we're from. We need Celine."

Alexander considered the conversation, studying them both. "All right, I'll help you," he agreed. "There is something quite odd about all of this, yet I cannot help but feel as though you are being truthful."

Damien breathed a sigh of relief. "Thank you," he said, slumping onto the couch again.

"I cannot promise anything. But we shall try."

"That's all we can ask," Michael said. "Thank you."

"We'll call upon Duchess Northcott tomorrow. Let's determine how she reacts to your presence. For now, I shall have rooms made up for you to stay."

"Thank you," Damien answered.

"Yeah, we really appreciate this," Michael added.

Alexander exited the room. Michael collapsed onto the couch next to Damien. "Wow," he exclaimed. "This is..."

"Bad," Damien finished for him.

"Yep," Michael agreed.

"Perhaps once we meet Celine, it'll take a turn for the better."

"Man, I hope so," Michael added.

Within a few moments, Alexander returned to show them to their rooms. They agreed to get some sleep and hoped tomorrow brought better news. Neither of them could recall any additional details about why they were sent here, nor the events leading up to their visit.

Damien tossed and turned most of the night, sleeping off and on. He arose early the next morning, pacing the floor of his room. A light knock sounded at his door. He rushed to open it, finding Michael on the opposite side.

"Hey," Michael greeted him, stepping into the room. "Did I wake you? I couldn't sleep."

"No, I was awake. Couldn't sleep either. None of this makes sense. I keep replaying everything over and over in my head and nothing adds up."

"Yeah, same. And there's so many questions. Why 1812? Why London? How the hell did Celine marry the Duke? And what are we supposed to do here?"

"I'm not sure," Damien answered. "Was Celine aware this was going to happen and sent us back without instructions in some kind of rushed panic?"

"Do you remember anything like that?"

Damien reflected for a moment. He shook his head. "No, nope. Nothing."

"Okay, okay, let's start with what we do remember and try to work forward. Perhaps then we'll have an easier time remembering."

"Good idea. What's the last thing you remember clearly?" Damien inquired.

"You brought up going to 1791 to retrieve Celine's painting. I remember that, do you?"

Damien nodded, his eyes darting around as he called up the details of the experience. "Yes. Yes, I remember that. I remember that painter. The painting at the barn. The Duke broke Abbott's hand. Celine pulled a second Celine from a mirror, and we stole the painting from the Duke's bedroom. And we hid it in another painting."

"Right. *Ships in the Harbor!* That's how I remember it too. And then the Duke caught us, and we thought we were doomed. Or at least, I did. Then Celine hit him with a fireball, and we ran."

"Yeah, and she met us a few minutes later and sent us home." Damien nodded in agreement.

"Then what?" Damien paced the floor, deep in thought. "We told everyone we found the painting."

Michael considered it. "Yeah… no! Wait!"

"What is it?" Damien questioned.

"Was everyone there? We were in the unused wing. In that room the kids took us to when we first arrived at the house."

"I remember Gray," Damien paused. "And Alexander."

"Yes, I remember both of them too. But where was Celine? She wasn't there."

Damien rubbed his chin. "She wasn't?"

Michael reflected again. "No, I don't remember her being there."

"Where would she have been?" Damien questioned.

Michael paused before his eyes widened. "Gone. She was gone."

"Gone? Gone where?"

"No one knew. Gray said she went missing right after we left. That same night."

Damien shook his head. "No." He paused. "No… oh wait. Wait, yes. Yes, you're correct. Celine wasn't there. She was missing."

"Right. Then what?"

"I'm not sure," Damien admitted.

"Me either," Michael replied. "Umm."

A knock sounded at the door and Damien pulled it open.

"Good morning," Alexander greeted him. "I hope you slept well."

"Good morning," Damien answered, standing aside to allow him to enter the room. "The accommodations were most suitable, yes. Thank you."

"Ah, and Michael. Good morning."

"Good morning. Yes, we were just… brainstorming what happened, the best way to proceed."

"Ah," Alexander responded. "I hope I am able to assist you. However, I must admit I am quite at a loss."

"So are we," Damien informed him.

"My cousin, Grayson, arrived in the wee hours of the morning. It may help if you recount your tale to him. Perhaps we can solve something that way."

"Gray's here?" Damien asked.

"It's not a tale," Michael added before Alexander responded.

"Yes, Gray is here. If you'd like to join us for breakfast, you can relay the information to him."

"We'd be happy to," Damien answered. "Lead the way."

Alexander showed them to the dining room downstairs. Gray sat at the dining table. He rose as they entered the room.

"Gray, may I present Michael and Damien Carlyle? These are the men I told you about earlier."

"Grayson Buckley," Gray introduced himself, extending his hand. "A pleasure." Michael and Damien each shook his hand. "My cousin tells me you have quite a unique story."

"Please help yourselves to breakfast," Alexander said, signaling to food on the sideboard. "We can discuss this over our meal."

Michael and Damien filled their plates, sitting at the table across from Alexander and Gray.

"So, what is this story?" Gray inquired.

"Ah, well," Michael began, glancing around the table. "We don't come from this era. Where we come from, we know you, all of you. But things are different there."

"That sounds sufficiently vague. Care to give any details?"

Damien chimed in, "We're from the future. I realize how crazy that might sound, but it's true. We're very good friends with Celine. She's sent us into the past twice already. Both times we've remembered why we were there and had a clear goal to achieve. This time we don't remember the events leading up to this or what we're supposed to do here."

"Tell Gray about the scenario you explained to me regarding Celine," Alexander requested.

"About who she's married to?" Damien inquired.

Alexander raised his teacup to his lips. "Yes."

"Where we come from Celine is married to you, Gray. She's been married to you for a long while," Damien explained.

Gray scoffed, his eyes wide. "Me?"

"Yes," Damien answered.

Gray roared with laughter. "I've never even met the woman. Nor do I imagine I would care for her at all if I did."

"But…" Damien began.

"Any woman who can marry a man like Marcus North-cott would not be my cup of tea."

"I don't understand how that happened either, but it's plausible. That night she became…" Damien paused, searching for the words, "a witch was horrible for her."

Gray stared at him, unimpressed with the explanation. "Regardless, as is obvious, we are not married and never will be. This fantasy you have created, while you may find it amusing, is pointless."

"It's not a fantasy," Michael countered as he stabbed at a piece of egg with his fork.

"It is not reality," Gray argued.

"In either case," Alexander chimed in, "something must be done to assist you gentlemen to return to your proper place."

"Thanks," Damien said. "We appreciate your help. When do we leave to visit Celine?"

Gray snapped his gaze to Alexander. "You're taking them to meet her?"

"Yes. I promised to pay a call, allowing them to meet her."

"That is unwise," Gray counseled.

"I couldn't see how it could hurt," Alexander argued. "If my sources are correct, she accepts visits today between one and three in the afternoon. We shall try at half-past one."

"Great," Damien answered, finishing his breakfast. "We'll work on trying to remember more in the meantime. Perhaps it will help when we speak with Celine."

"Please feel free to use the sitting room. It should be available for the better part of the morning," Alexander informed them.

"Thanks," Damien answered. He and Michael stood and left the room, making their way to the sitting room where they met Alexander the night before.

"Interesting pair," Gray remarked as they departed.

"Their story is fascinating," Alexander answered.

"And untrue."

Alexander sipped at his tea. "They disagree."

"I don't doubt it. Insane people tend to believe their stories are true," Gray said, leaping from his seat to pace the floor.

"They don't seem insane."

"Could have fooled me," Gray replied.

"There is something about them that intrigues me. Something that draws me to believe them."

Gray rolled his eyes. "You are too kind, Alexander. You aren't serious about calling on Duchess Northcott, are you?"

"I am."

"Alexander, this is madness. You cannot set foot in that house."

"I realize the danger. However, Duke Northcott should not be at home."

"This is foolish," Gray warned.

Alexander stared into the remains of his tea. "That may be, but as I said, something about them draws me to want to help."

"Be careful, cousin. Those two may draw you further into trouble than you'd prefer."

"I will, Gray. Thank you."

* * *

MICHAEL COLLAPSED on the couch in the sitting room. "That went well. Why, no matter what happens, does that guy dislike us?"

Damien took a seat across from him in an armchair, shaking his head. "Gray? No idea."

"Yeah, Gray. 'Your fantasy is pointless.'" Michael imitated.

"What could have happened? How were we not there to help Celine?" Damien questioned.

"I'm not sure," Michael admitted. "Did the Duke change history again?"

Damien considered it for a moment. "How? Did he stop us from meeting her at all when she was sixteen? Why don't we remember it?"

Michael shot him a glance as he tapped his fingers on the couch's arm. "Our memories aren't too good these days."

"Good point," Damien conceded. "Let's try to work on that again."

"Okay," Michael agreed. "Where did we leave off?"

"We established that Celine was missing."

"Right. Gray said she had been missing for days. No one had seen her or heard from her."

Damien pushed his mind to recall the moment. "Yes, right! She left a note that she was going to see Celeste."

"Yes, that's right!" Michael exclaimed, sitting straighter. "They said they talked to Celeste, and she didn't know anything. She thought Celine went home right after speaking with her. You didn't believe her, and you and Alexander went to speak with Celeste."

Damien nodded, waving a finger in the air. "That's right. That's right. I went to talk to Celeste. She told me the same story. So, what happened? Did we find Celine? We must have, otherwise, how are we here?"

Michael pondered it a few moments, rising from the couch to pace around the room. "We were at Alexander's a lot. Something was wrong with you."

"With me?" Damien questioned.

"Yeah. I can't remember what, but everyone was always fussing over your health. Why?"

They spent the remainder of the morning trying to piece together the mysterious illness that plagued Damien as they searched for Celine. They were unable to do so even after hours of discussion. Their memories continued to be hazy and seemed to be returning in bits and pieces. They gave up as Alexander entered, inviting them to lunch. They planned to leave for the Northcotts' following the meal.

Damien picked at his food, finding it difficult to eat. Nervous butterflies filled his stomach. What would they find when they arrived at Celine's new home? Would Celine remember them? Would the entire nightmare end? While it was unlikely things would change in an instant, Damien hoped against hope seeing Celine somehow magically helped their situation.

Using borrowed cloaks, Michael and Damien followed Alexander as they wound through the streets of London on foot. Damien kept quiet, anxiety holding his tongue captive. Michael, too, remained untalkative, also nervous about the upcoming visit.

As they neared the Northcott residence, Alexander informed them they may not even be granted an audience. "Duchess Northcott may recognize my name and find herself too busy to entertain."

"I hope not," Damien mustered.

"As do I, for your sakes," Alexander answered. "Here we are."

They approached a stately home with several steps leading to the front door. Alexander climbed them, followed by Michael and Damien. He knocked at the door, giving his name to the butler who answered it. The butler showed them into a parlor off the foyer and asked them to wait. A large clock ticked away the time. Had it not been for the noise, Damien might have assumed time stopped. His leg bounced up and down with agitation. He placed his sweaty palms on his thighs, taking deep breaths to steady his nerves.

Within fifteen minutes, Celine entered the room. Something seemed different about her, Damien noted. She carried herself rigidly, and the friendly countenance he was accustomed to seemed absent.

"Mr. Buckley," she stated in a crisp British accent, "this is a surprise."

"Duchess Northcott," Alexander greeted her with a bow. "How kind of you to take the time for my request."

She offered him the briefest of smiles before perching on the couch across from Michael and Damien. "May I offer you tea?"

"No, thank you, Duchess."

"Then may I ask the nature of your visit?"

Damien watched the exchange with great interest. Celine was not acting like Celine. The accent alone was odd. When they first met Celine as a young woman in Martinique, she possessed a heavy French accent. When they visited her again in 1791, her accent had waned, replaced by an American one following her marriage to Gray. Damien had never heard her with a British accent. Moreover, she was formal and stiff, nothing like the Celine he knew.

"I desired for you to make the acquaintance of my cousins, Mr. Michael Carlyle, and his younger brother, Mr.

Damien Carlyle. They have traveled from the States with my other cousin, Grayson."

Celine glanced to the two men, holding her hand out, palm down. Damien stood to accept it, bowing to her. Michael followed his example.

"How pleased I am to make your acquaintance," Celine responded, her voice emotionless.

"As we are to make yours," Damien answered.

"What business brings you to London, Mr. Carlyle?" Celine asked politely.

Butterflies fluttered in Damien's stomach again as he uttered the only words he could muster. "We need your help."

CHAPTER 19

Celine arched an eyebrow at him, her expression emotionless. "I beg your pardon, sir?"

"If I may, Duchess," Alexander interjected. "What my less than eloquent cousin means is we had hoped to ask a favor of you."

She set her icy blue eyes on Alexander. "A favor, Mr. Buckley?"

"Yes. I understand how awkward this may appear. However, my cousins have a great desire to attend a formal London event. There is no one better than yourself to orchestrate an appropriate invitation."

Celine gave no indication of what crossed her mind, her face remaining expressionless. "You wish me to arrange an invitation for them to an upcoming social?"

"Yes. As I said, I understand this request to be odd, however, you are undeniably the best person in London to speak with."

"It is odd, yes. However, as you stated, I am the best person in London to coordinate such an invitation."

"Then you'll do it?" Damien asked, perching on the edge of his seat.

Celine arched an eyebrow at him. "Are all Americans as forward as you, Mr. Carlyle?"

"He means no harm, Duchess," Alexander explained. "He is merely overzealous."

"I see. Despite the odd nature of your request, I shall be happy to arrange an invitation." She rose from the couch, stepping to a desk in front of a nearby window. She glanced through a small book there. "It appears Lord Blackburn is hosting a ball in honor of his now-eligible daughter. Will this suffice?"

"Without doubt. It would be a most generous invitation," Alexander stated.

"I shall make the request of Lady Blackburn tomorrow. I will send word as soon as I've secured the invitation," she said, snapping the book shut.

"How gracious, Duchess Northcott. I am truly indebted to you," Alexander said with a bow.

"Think nothing of it," Celine answered. "If there is nothing else, I have much correspondence to finish."

"There is not. We have taken enough of your time. Thank you for the honor of your gracious hospitality," Alexander replied, bowing again.

"Good day, Mr. Buckley," she responded.

"Good day, Duchess Northcott," he answered as she departed.

Michael and Damien leapt to their feet, bowing as she left.

"Come," Alexander directed them, "we should return home."

They retrieved their overcoats from the butler before departing the house. As they strolled down the street away from the Northcotts' residence, Damien began the conversation. "Okay, if no one else is going to say it, that was weird."

"Yeah, I agree," Michael concurred.

"She acted like a different person. I hardly recognized her. And what was with the accent?"

"Right?" Michael asked. "That's new."

"Are you saying she is not, in fact, the woman you believed her to be?" Alexander questioned.

"No, no," Damien corrected. "That's definitely Celine. But her behavior was unlike her."

"I found nothing unusual," Alexander commented. "Although, as I said, we're not well acquainted."

"Not just her accent, her posture and everything. So stiff and formal, so unlike our Celine," Damien continued.

"Yeah, even when we've seen her in the 1700s, she hasn't acted like that," Michael agreed.

Damien pondered over it for another moment, before changing the subject. "Why did you divert the conversation when I asked for her help?"

"Because it was wise to do so," Alexander replied.

"Wise?" Michael questioned. "We're stuck in 1812 for some unbeknownst reason and you figured it was wise to have the one person who could help us take us to a ball with her instead of just help us?"

"It was imprudent to explain to her the circumstances at this time," Alexander insisted.

"Imprudent?" Michael queried. "I find it imprudent to continue to play around in a time period we shouldn't be in."

Alexander ceased walking. "You cannot tell her what you told me."

"Why?" Damien cried.

"For many reasons, not the least of which is the first thing she will do is inform her husband. He will then wonder who you are, what you know, and how you've come to this knowledge. The scrutiny of Marcus Northcott is not something you want to invite upon yourselves."

"If we can't tell Celine anything, how can we expect her to help us?" Damien argued.

"I didn't say you could never tell her, but it is quite foolish to impart such information the first time you meet the woman. She has no reason to be sympathetic nor to be trusted to keep it secret."

"I just don't like the idea of staying back here longer than we need to, especially when we have no idea why we're here," Michael countered.

"We shall tell her when the time is appropriate. No sooner. I'm not even sure I believe this incredible story. I can't imagine how Duchess Northcott may react to the news. There will be no returning for you if Duke Northcott deems it best to question you himself about your story."

"All right, all right," Damien conceded as they resumed their walk. "You make a valid point. We'll follow your timeline."

"Our next opportunity to converse with Duchess Northcott will be at the ball we hopefully secured an invitation to. We'll make our next carefully crafted move then. However, we must be careful. Duke Northcott will be in attendance. Too much attention shown unto his wife will surely not go unnoticed."

"Yeah, we've got to stay off his radar," Michael agreed.

"His what?" Alexander questioned.

"His radar," Michael answered.

Damien shook his head. "Radar hasn't been invented yet."

"Ohhhhh," Michael answered.

"He means we don't want to be noticed by Duke Northcott," Damien explained.

"Interesting turn of phrase. I quite agree with the sentiment. With that settled, we should return home and discuss the next phase of our plan."

* * *

CELINE RETURNED to the desk in her bedroom, intending to continue her correspondence for the day. She found herself unable to focus. Something disturbed her about the encounter with Alexander Buckley and his cousins. While it was a surprising visit to begin with, since she had little to do with the Buckley family, there was something more that unsettled her.

Celine had a gut feeling about these men, and her premonitions tended to be correct. What was her sixth sense trying to tell her? She dismissed the questions, determined to focus on the task at hand. After half an hour, she found herself unable to concentrate.

She left the task in favor of playing the piano. However, she also found this task to be a tedious exercise, and again, was unable to concentrate. Instead, she paced the floor of the sitting room, settling on the window seat in front of the large bay window. She remained there, lost in thought until Marcus returned home.

He interrupted her musings as he entered the sitting room, pouring himself a brandy. "Good evening, my dear."

"Good evening, Marcus. Back already from the House of Lords?" Celine inquired.

"Already? It is not that early."

"Oh," Celine answered, glancing at the clock, "my apologies. I must have lost track of the time and did not realize the lateness of the hour."

Marcus approached her, pushing a lock of hair behind her ear. "And what has you in such a pensive mood, my darling?"

Celine hesitated before responding. "It is nothing you need concern yourself with, husband."

He narrowed his eyes at her. "Hmm. Something is on your mind. Tell me what it is?"

"Alexander Buckley paid me a call this afternoon."

"Buckley? Whatever did he want?" Marcus inquired.

"To request an invitation to an upcoming social event for his American cousins who are visiting."

He sipped at his brandy. "That's rather odd."

Celine nodded in agreement. "Yes, I found it so."

"Did you agree?"

"I did. I shall call upon Lady Blackburn tomorrow to discuss the possibility of an invitation to her ball."

"Hmm," Marcus muttered.

"Do you object?" Celine questioned.

"No. No, I do not object. But I find it rather odd."

"I quite agree. However, I did not see the harm in it."

Marcus flicked his gaze from his brandy to Celine's eyes. "These cousins, what are their names?"

"Michael and Damien Carlyle. They paid the call with Alexander earlier."

"I've never heard the name," Marcus responded. "I shall inquire after them tomorrow."

"Please let me know what you find?" Celine requested.

"I shall. We should dress for dinner, dear."

"Yes," Celine agreed, kissing his cheek before leaving the room. "I shall go at once."

* * *

PRESENT DAY, **Bucksville**

Celine sat on the edge of Damien's bed, his hand in hers. She had hoped to find him awake earlier this morning. Neither Michael nor Damien's condition had changed overnight, both of them still unresponsive. Millie checked their conditions first thing in the morning, noting no major changes.

Celine fussed with his covers, rubbed his forearm, and murmured a few encouraging words. She found the situation impossible. She had faced tough circumstances before, but this one was gut wrenching. She had never faced an unknown illness of a human in the past. She felt helpless.

By lunchtime, Damien showed no signs of waking. Celine chose to eat a light lunch in Damien's room, refusing to leave him alone. After her meal, she rejoined him on his bed, lying next to him as he slept. Celine watched his chest rise and fall rhythmically. It brought her a sense of peace to count his breaths.

Her fixation on his breathing aided in her ability to notice a slight change. Around 1:30 p.m., Celine perceived a change in his breathing pattern. His breathing quickened. His pulse raced. His brow crinkled as though something confused him. Celine rose from the bed, racing to the hallway. She called to Millie, who hurried down the hall from her room toward Damien's bedroom.

"What is it?" the doctor asked.

"It's Damien. His breathing has changed, and his pulse is racing."

Millie began a physical exam. Celine slipped to Michael's room, noting he suffered from the same acute physical changes. She returned to Damien's room as Millie finished her exam. "Michael is exhibiting a similar set of symptoms."

"His breathing is elevated, as is his pulse," Millie agreed. "He made a few minor vocalizations while I examined him as well. Nothing major, just a few groans. There is something else rather odd, though."

"What is it?" Celine asked.

"His body temperature seems to have dropped. It's only

by a slight amount. It's no cause for concern at this moment, but I'd like to determine if Michael exhibits this symptom as well."

Celine nodded and Millie exited to perform an exam on Michael. She returned ten minutes later. "He is exhibiting the exact same symptoms."

"What do you suppose it means?" Celine questioned.

"I'm not sure. However, I am hopeful this is their bodies' way of trying to restart and come out of the coma they are in."

"Did you notice the expression on his face? Is he in pain?"

Millie shook her head. "He doesn't appear to be. He may be dreaming."

"Dreaming? That's a good sign, right?"

"Yes. It means his brain is active, which is a very good thing. Will you stay with him for the afternoon? Notify me of any changes. I'll return before dinner for another exam. I'd like to monitor his temperature."

"Yes, I'll stay."

"I'll ask Gray to sit with Michael."

"Thanks," Celine replied, climbing onto the bed with Damien. She slipped her hand under the covers, grabbing his. She didn't want to remove his arm from under the covers with his lowered body temperature. She stroked his hair with her other hand.

"Damien," she murmured, "are you trying to come back to us?"

1812, LONDON

"I'm still surprised she granted you an audience," Gray replied, wandering around the sitting room following dinner.

"She was most gracious," Alexander admitted from his armchair. "She agreed to solicit an invitation to Lord Blackburn's upcoming ball."

Damien screwed up his face. "Gracious? You call that gracious?"

Alexander pressed his fingertips together. "Michael and Damien found her behavior odd."

"Odd?" Gray inquired.

"She was nothing like the Celine we know," Michael admitted.

"Perhaps because she is *not* the Celine you believe you know," Gray countered. "That Celine is a figment of your collective imaginations."

"It's not!" Damien exclaimed, leaping from his seat to pace the room.

"I cannot fathom why you are continuing with this madness, cousin," Gray said to Alexander.

Michael tapped his finger against the arm of his chair. "It isn't madness. Something is very wrong here."

Gray glared at him, his arms crossed. "According to you, who can't remember how you got here or what you're supposed to do here but who claim to be time travelers from the future. You're mad. You belong in an institution!"

"It's far from implausible. And they do know what we are," Alexander pointed out.

"There's a simple explanation for that," Gray answered.

"Which is?" Michael questioned.

"You discovered the existence of the supernatural and it drove you mad!"

Damien slouched his shoulders. "For the hundredth time, we're not crazy. And even if we are, I'd like to go home and in order to do that we need Celine's help."

"And to secure Duchess Northcott's help, we must create a plan," Alexander reminded them. "We have made no progress on that front."

"Short of just asking her for her help, what else can we do?" Damien questioned.

Alexander pondered for a moment. "You claim to be well acquainted with Duchess Northcott."

Damien sank onto the couch, balancing his elbows on his knees. "Very well acquainted."

"Yes, they are very well acquainted with a woman who does not exist," Gray added.

Alexander ignored him. "Is there something you know about her that might be used to gain her trust? Some little-known information that could signify a connection with her?"

Damien and Michael exchanged a glance. "Uh," Damien began, rubbing his chin.

"We know about her parents," Michael answered. "Uh, Marquis Gaspard Devereaux was her father. Her mother died giving birth to Celine. She has an older sister, Celeste, who is also a witch. She's the one who introduced Celine to the Duke."

"Well, that should prove helpful," Gray mocked.

Michael crinkled his brow. "What?"

"Ignore him, he's being unhelpful," Alexander advised.

"I'm being truthful. Everyone knows that information. I've never met the woman and I know that information," Gray responded.

Michael flung a hand in the air. "She spoke English before her father realized it. He hired her an English tutor, but she didn't need it, she already spoke English. Does that help?"

Alexander considered it, rubbing his lips. "Interesting, but I'm not certain it's substantial enough to make any impression on the Duchess."

Michael banged his head against the back of the chair.

Damien snapped his fingers. "Wait a minute," he began. "Her father, Celine's father, is he alive?"

"No," Alexander answered. "He is not. He died quite some time ago."

"When she was sixteen?" Damien questioned.

"I'm not certain, but it sounds correct."

Damien slid to the edge of his seat. "How?"

"The poor man was murdered," Alexander recounted.

"Days before her sixteenth birthday. He was murdered on his way to return to France, right?"

"Yes, I believe that was the account. What does this have to do with gaining her trust?"

"I'd like to know the same," Gray added. "I'm not sure bringing up the painful memory of her father's demise is going to win you any favor with the Duchess."

"It's not his death, it's who is responsible."

"Some wretched seaman who robbed him for a few pieces of gold if memory serves," Alexander answered.

"No, no, no, no," Michael corrected, a smile playing on his lips. "That might be the man who actually committed the murder, who wielded the knife, but he's not the man responsible."

"What are you getting at?" Gray inquired.

"The man responsible for the murder of Marquis Devereaux is none other than Duchess Northcott's loving husband, Duke Marcus Northcott."

Alexander's jaw dropped open. "What?"

Gray scoffed and shook his head. "I find that hard to fathom."

"It's true. Marcus Northcott had her father killed so she would have no one and she'd turn to him," Michael explained.

"But she had a married sister. Theodore VanWoodsen became her legal guardian following her father's death," Alexander said.

"Celeste and Teddy were up to their eyeballs in the Duke's dealings. They more than happily allowed him to do whatever he wanted with her," Damien explained.

Silence fell over them for a few moments.

"This is incredible," Alexander replied.

"Incredible or not, can you prove any of it?" Gray questioned.

Michael and Damien glanced to each other.

"No," Damien admitted.

"So, the information is useless," Gray replied.

"How did you come by this information?" Alexander queried.

"We were there the night Celine became… what she is," Damien answered. "That ceremony… he… the Duke tossed her father's dead body in front of her and told her he was her new family. The Celine we know realized very quickly his involvement in her father's murder.

"Obviously, this Celine did not. She married the man," Gray countered.

"By choice or because she had no other options? Does this Celine not realize it, or has she suppressed it?" Damien asked rhetorically.

"She seems quite content with him," Gray argued. "She parades about high society as though she owns everyone."

"That's a gross overstatement. Besides, she'll likely be queen of this country one day. I suppose she knows that," Alexander added.

"I assume the man who committed the murder is long

since dead," Damien mused to Michael.

"Probably. I mean, either Celine killed him like the Duke asked that night or the Duke killed him that night like he did when we were there," Michael responded.

"Damn it!" Damien exclaimed, leaping from his seat again. "We can't go to Celine and tell her the Duke had her father killed but we have no proof of anything to back that up."

"Perhaps we should conclude for the evening, gentlemen," Alexander suggested. "Allow us all some time to think."

With reluctance, Damien and Michael agreed. "I guess so," Damien said. "Good night."

Everyone said their goodnights and Michael and Damien retired for the night. Damien spent the better part of the night tossing and turning. They had no way of gaining Celine's trust. They were no closer to solving this puzzle or to returning home.

CHAPTER 20

*D*amien tossed and turned in his bed. They were getting nowhere. They'd just spent a second night in the past and they had no idea why.

Their memories were returning, but the process was slow and painstaking. Perhaps once they recalled all the details leading up to their trip, they would have a breakthrough. Until then, they were stuck guessing at everything. And upsetting Gray, as usual. Gray, Damien mused. The man stuck in his mind. An idea formed, and a smile crossed his face. He'd run it past Michael in the morning. With his mind settled, he turned over, falling asleep for the rest of the night.

Damien bounded out of bed the next morning. He dressed as fast as he could and made his way to Michael's room. He rapped at the door, hoping Michael was awake.

Michael opened the door, still fastening his shirt. "Good morning."

"Good morning, did I wake you?"

"No, I was up," Michael assured him as Damien entered the room.

"Good. I have an idea, and then I figured we could keep working on our memories."

"Sounds good, what's the idea? Hope we wake up from this nightmare soon?"

Damien chuckled before turning serious. "Haha, no. Last night I was going over everything in my head, over and over. And I was thinking how no matter where we are, Gray seems to hate us."

"Yeah, no kidding. What is that guy's problem?"

"In general, I don't know, but this time I might have an idea."

"Which is?"

Damien grinned at him. "Well, in all the other instances when we've time traveled, it's been to fix something, right?"

"All two times, you mean," Michael countered.

"Whatever. It stands to reason we're supposed to fix something again this time. What if we're supposed to fix the situation between Celine and Gray?"

"Fix it? How? She's married to another man!"

Damien pressed his lips together in a thin line. "That I'm not sure about, but what if Celine sent us back to make sure she meets Gray, falls in love with him and marries him?"

"Okay, well, she sent us to the wrong year because she was supposed to meet Gray in the 1700s. Not in 1812."

Damien considered it. "Yeah, yeah, I agree it's not the best time, but what else could we be here for?"

Michael shrugged. "To make sure she doesn't ruin the world with the Duke?"

Damien made a face at him.

"Okay, okay, your idea makes more sense. But how do we do that?"

Damien puckered his lips as he rubbed his chin. "No idea. I only got as far as an idea of why we're here."

"I guess we'll figure it out as we go."

"Like always," Damien agreed.

"All right. Let's move on to working on those memories," Michael said.

"Okay, where did we leave off?" Damien asked.

"We remembered being at Alexander's a good bit and everyone was concerned about your health."

"Right. My health, my health, why my health?" Damien pondered, pacing the room.

They spent their morning hours before and after breakfast attempting to recall more of the events leading to their trip to 1812. Neither of them could come up with any additional memories. The process became frustrating for them both.

After lunch, Alexander had business to attend to. He asked if they would care to join him for the walk and some fresh air. They agreed it might be best to relax their minds.

* * *

CELINE APPROACHED number four Canterbury Way. She climbed the steps, knocking at the door. She adjusted her cloak and ensured her hair was presentable as she waited. The butler opened the door.

"Mrs. Marcus Northcott to see Mr. Alexander Buckley," she presented herself.

"Mr. Buckley is currently out but should return soon. Would you care to wait, Mrs. Northcott?"

"Yes, thank you." Celine entered the home, following the butler to the sitting room.

"I shall announce you as soon as Mr. Buckley returns," the butler informed her.

"Thank you." Celine perched on the edge of the couch, awaiting Alexander's return.

Moments later, the door to the room opened, and a man walked in. Celine expected Alexander but was surprised to find an unfamiliar face. Celine gazed at him, finding his stormy blue eyes mesmerizing.

"Oh," the man said, speechless for a moment. "Apologies, I didn't realize anyone was in here."

Celine smiled at him as she rose. "No apology is necessary, Mister… Well, it is my turn to apologize, I do not believe we are acquainted."

"No, we have never been introduced. I should have remembered a face as beautiful as yours. Grayson Buckley, at your service."

"You are too forward, Mr. Buckley," Celine replied, extending her hand for him to take. "My husband would not appreciate your brazen sentiments. Mrs. Marcus Northcott."

Gray stopped for a moment, realization dawning on him. "You are Celine Northcott?"

"I am," she answered.

He arched an eyebrow at her, his eyes never leaving hers. "Forgive me, I did not expect you to be so… well, I should hold my tongue before I upset your husband again."

Celine offered him a slight smile. The two held each other's gazes for a moment until the door opened.

"Duchess Northcott, I…" Alexander announced, stepping into the room. He stared at the scene in front of him.

Celine backed a step away from Grayson, averting her eyes from his as she glanced toward the fireplace.

"Oh, excuse me. I did not realize you were not alone."

"I was fortunate to make the acquaintance of your… brother, is it?" Celine asked.

"Cousin," Alexander corrected.

Celine nodded and offered a slight smile. "A pleasure, Mr.

Buckley. Thank you for providing company as I waited for your cousin's return."

"Of course," Grayson answered before leaving the room.

"Allow me to begin anew," Alexander stated. "My sincere apologies for the delay. I had business in town."

"No doubt you are a busy man," Celine answered. "I took a chance to pay you a call regarding your request yesterday."

"How gracious of you," Alexander replied.

"I have spoken with Lady Blackburn, and she was courteous enough to favor my request. I have secured an invitation to Lord Blackburn's ball to be held two days hence." Celine held out an invitation.

Alexander accepted the card from her. "Oh, how wonderful! My cousins will be thrilled to hear the news. We cannot thank you enough for your graciousness to orchestrate the invitation. You are too kind, Duchess."

Celine offered a tight-lipped smile. "Tell me, will your other cousin, Grayson, attend?"

"Oh," Alexander answered, thrown by the question, "I am unsure of his plans."

"I see," Celine replied. "The invitation extends to your family, please see that he is also included."

"I will," Alexander promised. "And thank you for waiting, I hope I did not keep you too long."

"Not at all. I shall see you at the ball, Mr. Buckley."

"Good day, Duchess Northcott."

Celine departed the house, though her thoughts did not. Alexander opened the sitting room doors, finding Michael, Damien, and Gray on the other side.

"We just saw her leave," Damien said. "Well?"

"She acquired the invitation."

"All right! Now all we need is a plan," Damien exclaimed.

"The ball is in two days. We should discuss our approach this evening."

"We haven't had much luck in remembering anything else," Michael admitted.

Gray poured himself a brandy, silent thus far.

"Oh, before we enter any discussions, Gray, Duchess Northcott made a point of extending the invitation to you," Alexander said. "Thank you for keeping her company before I returned."

Michael and Damien glanced at each other.

"An easy task," Gray remarked, staring into space. "She is quite lovely."

Damien raised an eyebrow at Michael.

Alexander gave him an odd look but continued with the conversation. "Well, we need a plan, gentlemen. I suggest we discuss it following dinner."

"Can't plan on an empty stomach!" Damien exclaimed.

The four men dined, then spent the evening in a discussion about how to handle their interactions with Celine at the upcoming ball. By the end of the evening, they were no closer to a plan. They retired for the evening, frustrated.

Before going to bed, Damien did not miss the opportunity to call Michael's attention to Gray's obvious fondness for Celine. It added credibility to his theory that they were meant to restore Gray and Celine's relationship. Damien fell asleep hoping tomorrow brought them more information.

* * *

CELINE RETURNED HOME after her visit at the Buckley residence. She'd expected to find Alexander Buckley at home, pass along the invitation to the ball, and return home without incident. Alexander had not been home and instead, she had met his cousin, Grayson Buckley.

In her position, Celine met many people, but none of them had the effect on her Grayson Buckley did. She recalled his stormy blue eyes. They were piercing, almost as though they saw into her soul.

What was it about the Buckleys that struck her so? First, her odd encounter with the Carlyle brothers. They had also made an impression, albeit of a different kind. Something about them seemed familiar to her.

She tried to shake the feeling from her as she removed her cloak. It would pass, she assured herself. If it did not, she would get to the bottom of it. Her gut reactions were rarely incorrect. If there was more she needed to know, she would find out.

* * *

PRESENT DAY, **Bucksville**

Gray rubbed Celine's shoulders. "Why don't you get some rest, Celine?"

Celine shook her head, her eyes never leaving Damien's limp form. "I can't, Gray."

"He's fine, Celine. You heard Millie, his breathing is normal, pulse is normal."

"But his body temperature is still low."

"It's nothing to be worried about. It's only a tad bit low. Millie didn't think it was an issue," Gray responded.

"Why is it still low? In both of them?" Celine questioned, leaping from the bed and pacing the floor.

"Reaction to the stress, perhaps," Gray suggested.

Celine shook her head. "No. No, that's not it. Something else is wrong, Gray. Something is off."

"There's no evidence of that," Gray answered.

"I sense it."

Gray approached her, wrapping her in his arms. "You're worried, Celine. With cause. Damien's condition is a concern, I agree. But we don't have any evidence that supports it being anything beyond a reaction to the shock wave."

Celine laid her head on Gray's shoulder. "I hope you're right, Gray. I hope you're right."

"I am," he assured her. "Now, why don't you get some rest?"

"I'd like to stay with him," Celine said.

"All right. But try to get some sleep."

"I will. I just want to stay in case anything happens," Celine responded.

"Okay. Good night, Celine. I love you."

"I love you, too, Gray. Good night."

Celine climbed onto the bed next to Damien as Gray left the room. She grabbed Damien's hand. His fingers were cool to the touch, reflecting his lowered body temperature. She squeezed them between her hands, trying to warm him.

"Please be okay, Damien," she whispered before closing her eyes to sleep.

* * *

1812, LONDON

Damien climbed out of bed early the next morning. He found himself unable to sleep again. While he slept better than he did the previous night, he was now wide awake despite the early hour. As he dressed, a light knock sounded at his door. He opened it, finding Michael on the opposite side.

"Couldn't sleep, sorry if I woke you," Michael said, pushing past him into the room.

"I wasn't sleeping either."

"I was up most of the night. And after a night's worth of pondering it, you're right. We have to be back here to do something, and I agree it's to right whatever wrong occurred between Celine and Gray. Something obviously went haywire, and she ended up married to that jerk, Northcott. Now, why Celine sent us back to 1812, I'm not sure, but she must have considered this the best time for us to do whatever it is we're supposed to do."

Damien didn't answer, a slight smile on his face.

"What?" Michael questioned, noticing Damien's expression.

"You're starting to sound like me."

Michael cracked a smile. "You must be rubbing off on me."

"Okay, so we agree on what we need to do, what our goal is," Damien summarized. "Now, we need a plan to do it."

"That's where my similarities to you end," Michael claimed. "I've got nothing on that front."

"Neither do I," Damien admitted. "While I'd feel *way* more comfortable going to this ball with a plan, this might be one of those times where we have to wing it. We might need more experience with new Celine to form a plan."

"Yeah," Michael agreed. "Perhaps that's the issue. I feel so off-kilter with her. In every other instance, we've just been honest with her, kind of told her what facts we had, and she pitched in to help us. This time it's like she's the enemy. We almost can't trust her."

"If she's as close to the Duke as Alexander says, we can't trust her, no. Which is why we have to get her to trust us and distrust him. If we could only find some way to prove the angle with her father's death..." Damien responded, his voice trailing off.

"But how?"

"I'm not sure. It's a dead-end at the moment. I want to use it, but right now we can't."

They paused in their conversation, each considering the

problem. "Okay, let's go back to working on the memory loss," Michael suggested. "Perhaps something will pan out there."

"Okay," Damien agreed. "Let's see. You said everyone was concerned for my health. I've been wracking my brain about this, but I'm not sure. Everyone's concern for me implies it was something beyond a common illness like a cold..."

"COLD! That's it!" Michael exclaimed, cracking his hands together.

"Huh?" Damien responded.

"Shh, wait..." Michael hushed him. His brow furrowed as he recalled it. He let his rambling thoughts spill out of his mouth. "Cold, you were cold... always cold... hypothermic. We had to keep warming you up. Why? You'd be asleep... no passed out, and you'd wake up freezing and sick."

Damien fed off Michael's comments, processing the information to aid in his memory recollection. His brain showed him snippets of memories. He struggled to piece them together. "Okay, stream of consciousness here. I remember bits of pieces of things that fit with what you're telling me. Waking up in the woods sick, near the fireplace at Alexander's and being wrapped in a blanket a lot."

"Yes, right! You were always cold. Why were you always cold?"

Damien considered it a few moments longer. "The place I went was cold. I was going somewhere. Where? Why would I be going somewhere alone? And why was it cold there?"

Michael glanced at him. "You passed out! You'd go there in your mind or something like that. It was weird. It was another place, like not on earth."

"I went to a place not on earth?" Damien questioned.

"Yes. At first you figured it was a dream, because it happened when you fell asleep. Then Millie hypnotized you.

And then you'd just fall over shaking wherever you were, and you'd be in this other realm."

"Yes, yes, that's right. And Celine would be there! She'd talk to me and tell me what was happening, but it was so cold, she'd have to send me back within minutes! I remember!"

Michael snapped his fingers. "Yes! Now, what did she tell you? Do you remember that?"

Damien pondered it longer. "Uh, she was missing. She told me... she told me the Duke had her! And she was getting Celeste changed back from a vampire!"

"She told you she was at the old mill. But we went there, and no one was there. It was some kind of spell!"

Damien's excitement grew and he perched on the edge of his seat. They were close to piecing everything together. "Yes! Then what? How did we find her? We must have found her because she sent us back here right?"

"Yeah... but how?" Michael questioned.

Damien paced the floor of his room. "It's no use, I have no idea!" he exclaimed, throwing his arms in the air in frustration.

"Oh, come on!" Michael responded after another moment of musing. "We're so close!"

"Do we know if Celeste is not a vampire anymore?" Damien asked.

Michael pondered a moment. "I'm not sure."

Damien sighed, scrubbing his face with his hands. "Okay, good stopping point, I guess. It's almost time for breakfast. We can try again later."

They made their way to the dining room, joining Alexander and Gray for breakfast. They discussed any ideas for a plan but informed the Buckleys they may need more time. Gray agreed, suggesting they use the ball to observe and learn rather than enact anything too extravagant.

The idea didn't sit well with Damien. He liked to be prepared, however, he didn't see any other choice. Alexander had business in town, so they spent the day wandering around London. They visited several of the sights, feeling almost like tourists. The distraction provided Damien with much needed stress relief and entertainment.

Michael enjoyed the experience far less than Damien. They returned to the house for dinner, opting to turn in early in the hopes that a good night's rest allowed them to fill in the remaining gaps in their memories. They also wanted to prepare for the upcoming ball tomorrow evening.

* * *

CELINE JOINED Marcus at the breakfast table early. "Good morning, darling," Marcus greeted her, glancing up from his newspaper.

She kissed him on the cheek. "Good morning." She was served her usual breakfast of porridge. "Have you much business to attend to today?"

"A fair amount, but I shouldn't be late."

"We dine with the Richardsons tonight," Celine informed him.

"I haven't forgotten but thank you for the reminder, my dear."

Celine smiled at him. "I hope I shan't make us late. I've my final dress fitting today for the ball tomorrow."

"I'm sure the dressmaker can see you early," Marcus suggested.

"I've tried, but she is completely booked. Surprising at this time of the year."

"Arrive early, dear, she will not turn you away. Not with what I pay her."

Celine smiled at him again.

"Did you secure the invitation for the Buckleys?"

Celine pushed the porridge around in her bowl. "Yes. I called on Lady Blackburn yesterday. She was most gracious in accommodating my request."

"I should think she was. Lord Blackburn owes us several favors."

"I informed Mr. Buckley yesterday. He was quite pleased."

"And now he owes us a favor," Marcus noted.

"I did not realize he had another cousin. Grayson Buckley. Are you acquainted with him?" Celine questioned.

"I've met him once," he responded, never glancing up from his paper. "A useless man if I've ever encountered one."

"He seemed... kind."

"Kind? My dear, there are many virtues in a man to be prized, but kindness is the least among them."

Celine glanced to him before continuing to eat her porridge. "You do not care for my comments. Oh, dear Celine, you are too tenderhearted."

"A quality you do not value."

He stood, folding his paper and setting it on the table. "In you, dear, I treasure every quality. You are not a woman who gives in to foolish notions. But you should rely on my expertise in these matters as your heart sometimes clouds your head. I am off. Enjoy your day, my dear." He kissed her forehead before disappearing from the room.

Celine considered his words. She recalled a time when she had been a foolish romantic. She was a child then. Her father, who raised her alone after her mother's death, had doted on her, allowing her to run free. The result was a carefree young woman with headstrong convictions. Marcus had reigned in her blither nature. And she was all the better for it, she reminded herself.

Still, she mused, as she finished her breakfast, Grayson Buckley awakened sentiments in her she hadn't entertained in a long while. She shook her head, dismissing the notions. Foolish girl, she reflected, you have made your choices. And you have made good, solid choices. Her sister's voice echoed in her head, adding the last line. No one had been more thrilled with her decision to marry Marcus Northcott than her older sister, Celeste. Yes, she reflected, she had made a solid match in Marcus. A match most women could only dream to achieve. Yet she had achieved it. She must suppress these foolish romanticisms and focus on her chosen path.

CHAPTER 21

Celine stared at Millie as she conducted her physical exam of Damien. Another new day and still no changes in his condition. Michael's remained the same as well. Neither showed signs of waking from their coma.

Millie commented that both of their body temperatures remained low, dipping a fraction of a degree lower than yesterday. The change baffled the doctor. She suggested adding an additional blanket. She also proposed adding medical equipment to monitor vital signs and provide nutrients to both patients while their conditions remained unchanged.

The news did not sit well with Celine. She viewed it as a sign that they were worsening rather than improving. While Millie assured her this wasn't the case, she refused to believe it. Millie departed to make the necessary arrangements, leaving Gray and Celine alone with Damien.

Celine stood at the foot of the bed, staring at Damien. "He looks so peaceful," she said, tears rolling down her cheeks.

"Celine," Gray soothed, pulling her into his arms. "Don't cry. Millie said they weren't worse."

"But they aren't better either," Celine lamented.

"They will be."

Celine pressed her palm against her forehead. "You don't know that, Gray. For once, none of us does. I feel so helpless. They are laying there, and we cannot help them, not with medicine, not with our powers. We don't even realize what's causing this!"

"I agree this is frustrating. Alexander has come across nothing in his research to help, either."

Celine sighed as she wandered to the side of the bed, sinking onto it. She rubbed Damien's arm. "I want to help, and I don't know how."

Gray rubbed her shoulders. "Let's let Millie help them. Perhaps we can discover something from her monitoring."

Celine nodded in agreement, hoping the equipment was a blessing rather than a curse. They spent the afternoon assisting Millie in setting up a variety of items designed to monitor their vitals. Celine stared at the monitors set up, all recording different items, beeping and blinking various displays. She watched the heart rate monitor, counting with bated breath until the next beat displayed on the screen.

Millie also recommended monitoring Michael's and Damien's brainwaves. She wanted to log their brain activity to determine if there were any patterns. Celine gazed at the equipment, the various wires and tubes leading from Damien. She shook her head in sadness. "Please come back, Damien, please."

* * *

1812, LONDON

Damien knocked at Michael's door before breakfast. Michael opened it, standing back as he entered the room.

"Ha, I beat you today!"

"Yeah, I actually slept. Did you?"

"I did! I'm shocked. With the ball tonight and no plan, I assumed I'd be up for hours, tossing and turning, but I fell asleep and stayed asleep. Must have been all that fresh air we got yesterday," Damien surmised.

"Mmm, yeah, all the fresh air."

Damien plopped into the armchair. "Yeah, yeah, yeah. I realize you don't like the past."

"Not really, but it was a nice distraction, I'll admit that much."

"Ready for breakfast?" Damien inquired.

"Yeah, then let's try to piece together more of our memories."

"Sounds like a plan!"

They met Gray and Alexander for breakfast. Gray planned to attend the ball with them, and Alexander offered them clothes to borrow. They agreed to attend and observe rather than enact any sort of plan, hoping the night provided them with more information to work with. With their evening plans settled, Michael and Damien withdrew to the sitting room to continue their discussion regarding their memories.

"Okay, how did we find Celine?" Michael questioned as they sat in armchairs near the fireplace.

Damien walked through his memory. "I remember her telling me not to come to the mill until Celeste was cured."

"But we went anyway," Michael answered.

"We did? I don't recall that," Damien argued.

"Yeah, we went with Millie. We were…" Michael stopped dead.

"What?"

"We hid until Gray and Alexander made sure no one was there. But you weren't there!" Michael exclaimed. "Just Millie and I were there."

"That can't be true. Where was I? I wouldn't have missed that!"

"Were you sick again?" Michael mused.

"No!" Damien answered. "No, I wasn't! I was with Celine!"

"What?"

Damien's eyes grew wide. "Yes. When I showered that morning, the Duke somehow let himself into my bathroom and asked if I wanted to see Celine. He said I had to come alone. So, I did. I met him by the cliffs, and he took me to Celine." He paused a moment. "He walked out right through a wall… weird."

"You met with the Duke?" Michael inquired.

"Yeah, I did. What the hell was I thinking?" Damien questioned himself.

"You weren't. That guy is crazy. Like deranged crazy. I can't believe you did that! I'm not that brave."

"Yes, you are," Damien countered. "And you would have done it for Celine."

"I'm glad you regard me so highly," Michael replied. "Okay, so you were with Celine. Yes, that's right, now I remember. We went searching for you."

"Yeah, and you spilled the beans to the Duke in the process. He was there when you came in. And Gray spoke with Celine, told her not to contact me because I was missing."

"Oh, that's not good," Michael answered.

"Nope, it wasn't. This memory is so clear now. No

wonder I repressed it. It gives me the creeps even reflecting on it now. The Duke was furious! He screamed at Celine about betraying him and he grabbed her. I tried to stop him, but he threw me across the room. The next thing I remember is waking up in a cave with Celine."

"Wow, sorry, man. That's crazy," Michael said.

"Anyway, Celeste was there. She said she was going to tell everyone where Celine was so they could rescue us. Did she?"

Damien furrowed his brow, trying to determine what happened next.

"She did," Michael confirmed. "She came to the house. Gray was concerned about me, but I was fine. It was during the day. So, she is cured! Anyway, she told us, and we went to the cave to get you. But the Duke came. Alexander pushed me behind a tree. There was a massive fight. He almost killed Gray."

"Yes, but Celeste somehow dissolved the enchantment surrounding us. And Celine was super mad and came out of the cave like a bat out of hell after the Duke. She told me to run as soon as I could and take you back to the house."

"Yeah, I remember," Michael agreed. "Did we run?"

"Yes, we did," Damien confirmed. "Did we get to the house?"

"I don't remember," Michael confessed. "No, wait. The last thing I recall is turning around. Celine and Marcus both launched some kind of attack at the same time, and this big blue arc exploded from between them. It was coming right for us. That's the last thing I remember."

Damien chewed his lower lip. "Me too. Did it hit us? I seem to remember feeling like I was being electrocuted."

"Yes! I remember that too. Like a bolt of lightning hit me. That's the last I remember."

Damien glanced around. "There must be more, right?

Like we were fine and then Celine sent us back here. We just can't remember."

"Uh…"

"What?"

"Every other day when we've done this, I've realized there was more, but it's just beyond my mind's reach. But today…" Michael's voice trailed off.

"You feel like there's nothing else. There is no hazy memory just beyond your reach."

"Yes, exactly! How did you know?"

"Because I have the same feeling. Which may mean…"

"There is no more," Michael surmised.

They were silent for a moment. "So, if that's true…" Damien began.

"Don't say it."

Damien swallowed hard. "Sorry, but I have to. If that's true… perhaps Celine did not send us back in time."

"I asked you not say it."

"So, in other words, perhaps the blue electric arc sent us back in time, not Celine.

"To a world that's unrecognizable. This can't be true." Michael sank his head into his hands.

Damien pondered a moment. "Did that weird blue arc mess up everything?"

"Maybe we're just dreaming this. Like the arc put us to sleep or something," Michael pondered aloud.

Damien pinched Michael's arm.

"Ouch! What the hell, man?"

"Testing the sleep theory. Not asleep, you wouldn't have felt that," Damien responded.

"Next time, warn me."

"Sorry," Damien apologized. "Okay, so we're not asleep. Perhaps some communal hallucination? Either way, it lends credence to our theory that we need to restore Gray and Celine's relationship."

"I'm not arguing, but how do you figure that?"

"If that arc somehow messed up the world and sent us back in time to a changed world, doesn't it make sense that we need to fix it and then return? Otherwise, we'll just return to an unrecognizable world in our time."

"Good point, okay, I can buy that."

"Okay, cool. So, we go to the ball tonight and start pushing Celine and Gray together."

"Will that actually work?"

Damien shrugged. "Can't hurt. You heard him talk about her yesterday. Sounded like he was quite taken with her."

"Yeah, it did. 'She's lovely,'" Michael imitated.

"Well, she is. You fell for her."

"Point taken. Okay, okay, so we start pushing them together. Even still, this plan could take *months* or longer to work. We can't stay here for months."

"We're going to have to come up with some way to speed up the process. But for now, we should make sure they see each other tonight. Talk a little, that kind of stuff."

"Okay, sounds good. At least we have a partial plan."

"Yeah, I feel better. Also, I feel hungry. It's almost lunch time! Shall we go to the dining room?"

"Yes, I believe we shall, good sir."

Damien stood, bowing to Michael. "After you, my good sir."

Michael stood and bowed to Damien. "No, no! I wouldn't hear of it! After *you*, my good sir."

They turned toward the door leading from the room to find Gray standing in the opening.

He crossed his arms, staring at them. "Lunch is ready... my good sirs," he told them, rolling his eyes at them. He turned and left, mumbling to himself about how strange Michael and Damien were.

Michael and Damien glanced at each other.

"Oops," Damien said to Michael.

"Oh well, he never likes us. Who cares?" Michael responded.

Damien nodded, and they made their way to the dining room for lunch. He spent the afternoon teaching Michael how to play chess in an effort to distract them both and make the time pass faster.

Early evening arrived, and they disbanded to dress for the ball. The experience intrigued Damien who was thrilled to attend an honest-to-goodness ball in London. Michael was, as usual, less thrilled with the idea, stating he preferred to attend a modern-day party. Damien promised to throw him one as soon as they returned to their time.

They paced the sitting room floor in their finery, awaiting Gray and Alexander. They arrived in the foyer, dressed for the ball. Donning their cloaks, they proceeded outside to the waiting carriage. Michael groaned at the sight.

"Oh, great. Another carriage ride," he lamented.

"It'll be better than walking," Damien assured him.

"Uh, I'm not convinced. I'm still not over the last carriage ride."

They climbed in the carriage and traveled to the Blackburn residence. They proceeded inside and were ushered to the ballroom where the master of ceremonies announced them. Several guests had already arrived. They glanced around the room.

"I don't see Celine," Damien remarked, scanning the crowd.

"Nope."

Alexander brought them refreshments. "Gentlemen, some

refreshments. It appears Duchess Northcott has not yet arrived."

"We noticed," Michael said.

"She's here now," Gray commented, gazing at the entry-way. "She looks stunning."

Celine, escorted by Marcus Northcott, stood in the doorway as the master of ceremonies announced them. They proceeded into the room, swamped by several guests as they arrived.

"Wow, they're popular," Damien commented.

"They are a duke and duchess, and he is fourth in line to the throne, is it?" Alexander queried.

"Third, I gather. Philip Winston was third, but he met with an unfortunate accident," Gray responded.

Michael and Damien spent over an hour observing the ball and Celine. She smiled, chatted, danced, and seemed to be the delight of society. She rarely enjoyed a moment alone, making it impossible for them to approach her to discuss anything outside of pleasantries.

Two hours into the ball, Celine approached them. "Mr. Buckley," she said in greeting to Alexander. "I trust you and your cousins are enjoying your experience?"

"Duchess Northcott," he greeted her, bowing. "Yes, they are enjoying their experience immensely. Thank you again for your assistance in procuring an invitation."

Celine turned to Michael and Damien. "And how are you finding your stay in London?"

Damien still had difficulty getting over her accent.

"We are enjoying it thoroughly," Michael answered as Damien lost his ability to speak, marveling at Celine's strange behavior.

She turned to Grayson. "Mr. Buckley. I am pleased that we should meet again."

"As am I," Grayson answered, never taking his eyes from

her. She smiled at him, a genuine smile, it appeared to Damien.

"There you are, darling," Marcus chimed in, joining the group. "Ah, Buckley, enjoying the party?"

"Yes. We were just thanking your gracious wife for securing an invitation for us. May I introduce my cousins, Michael and Damien Carlyle? I believe you have already met Grayson." Alexander motioned toward Michael and Damien.

Marcus nodded his head toward them but did not extend his hand. "A pleasure," he stated, his voice filled with anything but. "If you gentlemen would excuse us. Darling, the Williamsons are asking after you. We should speak with them."

"Of course," Celine responded. "Good evening, gentlemen."

Damien shook his head as she departed. "It's just too weird."

"What?" Gray questioned.

"To them, her behavior is strange," Alexander explained. "They noted a similar scenario after we called on her."

"She acts nothing like the Celine we know," Michael added.

Gray followed her with his eyes. "She is quite lovely."

"Careful, cousin," Alexander warned. "She is a married woman with a powerful husband."

"Not if we can help it," Damien replied.

"What?" Alexander questioned.

"She's not supposed to be married to him! We deem this is what we're here to do. We've been trying to recall for days how we got here and why we're here. And that's what we've come up with. We believe we're supposed to right the course of history. Get Celine away from that maniac and with Gray, like she's supposed to be."

"You two are mad!" Alexander answered. "I think we'd better be going."

"No way, uh-uh," Damien argued. "I'm not going anywhere. Not until we do what we've set out to do." He turned to Gray. "Ask her to dance."

"What?" Gray responded. "I couldn't possibly."

"I agree. It calls too much attention," Alexander agreed.

"Fine. I'll do it then," Damien said. "We've got to make friends with her somehow!" He strode to Celine.

Alexander, Michael, and Gray watched in astonishment as he approached her.

Damien bowed and addressed Celine, "Duchess Northcott, might I have the pleasure of a dance? As a thank you for the invitation."

Celine glanced at him. A confused expression passed over her face before she gave a slight smile and offered her hand. He led her to the dance floor. She curtsied to him, and he bowed to her. They began to waltz. Damien had limited knowledge of the dance but tried his best to pass himself off as an expert. He cringed as he stepped on her toes time and time again.

"This is quite an interesting thank you, Mr. Carlyle."

"Sorry," he mumbled.

"You really are quite terrible at this," Celine answered, laughing. He twirled her before they curtsied to each other. "Do they not dance in America?"

"It's very different," Damien assured her.

"I'm not surprised," she responded as they finished their dance. They applauded. She thanked Damien for the dance, and he assured her the pleasure was all his. They left the dance floor with Damien returning to Michael, Gray, and Alexander and Celine returning to Marcus.

"What was all that about?" Marcus inquired as she returned.

"A thank you for the invitation."

"I'm surprised your toes survived his thank you."

"He is quite clumsy, although charming in an odd sort of way," Celine responded.

"Charming? The champagne must have gone to your head, my dear. Now, might you care for a dance with a real man?" He extended his hand to her.

She laughed, accepting his invitation, and allowing him to lead her to the dance floor.

* * *

"ARE YOU CRAZY?" Michael asked when Damien returned.

"No. At least I'm trying something!" Damien answered.

"Don't look here. I'm not dancing with her, no way," Michael responded with a shake of his head.

"That was quite a bold move," Alexander agreed.

"Plus, you're a terrible dancer," Gray added.

"Yes, I know. So do her toes. It would have been better had you asked her," Damien answered.

Gray rolled his eyes. "Perhaps later. She's dancing with her husband now."

The foursome continued to observe the party as it unfolded. Eventually, Gray found the opportunity to invite Celine for a dance. The two floated around the dance floor. Celine wore a wide grin for the entire dance. She laughed and appeared much more like the carefree Celine Michael and Damien were familiar with.

As they danced, Marcus approached Michael, Damien, and Alexander. "Mister," he paused, "Carlyle, was it?" he asked, addressing Damien.

Damien cleared his throat, swallowing hard. The Duke was as unnerving in this time as he was in any other. "Yes, Damien Carlyle. That's correct."

"What an interesting dance technique you possess."

"I'm a little rusty," Damien admitted. "But I wanted to thank her for arranging our invitation."

"What business did you say you're in?"

"Ship-building," Damien replied, recalling this was the business of the Buckleys.

"Ship-building, of course. Perhaps we shall run into one another in our business dealings."

"Perhaps," Damien answered, wishing the conversation would end.

"I'd like to get better acquainted, particularly given your obvious interest in my wife." The music ended, and the dancers applauded. With that, Marcus stalked away to retrieve Celine from the dance floor.

"Oh, man, now you made him mad," Michael lamented, pulling at his collar. "What were you thinking pulling a stunt like that?"

"Yes, I agree," Alexander echoed as Gray rejoined them. "You're all over his... what was it you said? Radar?"

"Yeah, yeah. I realize that. But I had to do something. We can't just stand here while history goes haywire and do nothing!"

"I judge it is time we leave," Alexander suggested.

"No, we can't leave now. We must stay and determine if we can learn anything to help us!" Damien insisted.

"This is quite unwise," Alexander warned.

"I'm inclined to agree. But I wouldn't mind staying," he said as his eyes followed Celine around the room.

"You are all daft," Alexander declared.

As the party continued, Michael and Damien noticed Stefano slip in through a side door.

"Look!" Damien exclaimed, nodding his head toward the man.

"Yeah, I see him. What's he doing here?" Michael inquired.

Stefano threaded through the guests, approaching Marcus. He touched his elbow, whispering a few words to him. Marcus nodded and answered him. He approached Celine, who was speaking with Lady Blackburn and her daughter. He spoke a few words to the group, leading Celine away. They talked for a few moments before Celine nodded. He kissed her cheek before leaving her.

The group watched Marcus depart with Stefano in tow. " Where's he going?" Damien questioned.

"Urgent business?" Michael suggested.

"Is it normal for someone to leave their wife at a party?" Damien asked Alexander.

"Certainly, he's left his driver to return Duchess North-cott home," Alexander assured him.

They spent another forty-five minutes monitoring Celine's activity. She spoke with several more people before returning to speak with Lady Blackburn.

"It appears she's leaving," Alexander informed them. "She's thanking Lady Blackburn for the evening, most likely. We should also depart."

"Wait, wait, wait," Damien responded. "This is the perfect time to talk to her."

Alexander's eyes widened. "Talk to her?"

"Yes. Her husband is nowhere to be found. We can corner her alone and talk to her!"

"Corner her? Damien, I must put a stop to this madness!" Alexander responded. "I insist we depart."

Damien ignored him. "There she goes," he said to Michael. "Now's our chance."

"Yep, let's go," Michael agreed.

"Gentlemen!" Alexander began as Michael and Damien

followed Celine out of the ballroom. He groaned as he raced to catch up to them. Gray followed him.

They all caught up with Celine as she stood fastening her cape near the front door, waiting for her carriage.

"Celine!" Damien called to her. "We must speak to you. Alone." He grasped her wrist, dragging her to a nearby unoccupied sitting room.

CHAPTER 22

eline stumbled back a step as Damien let go of her elbow after shoving her into a nearby sitting room. "Mr. Carlyle! What is the meaning of this?"

"Sorry, Celine. But we have to speak with you," Damien insisted.

"My apologies, Duchess. My cousin may have imbibed too many cocktails," Alexander said in an attempt to smooth things over.

Damien waved his hand in the air. "No. No, I'm not drunk. We have to talk. About your life."

"I'm baffled, Mr. Carlyle. I do not understand the meaning of your statements."

"Something happened, Celine. Something went wrong. It's hard to explain this but, you're not supposed to be married to Marcus Northcott," Damien explained.

"I beg your pardon!" Celine spat.

"He's right, Celine," Michael chimed in. "The night you promised yourself to him, when you became what you are, it wasn't supposed to happen that way."

Celine's face was a mask of confusion and shock.

"We were there that night, Celine, we realize what happened," Damien said.

"You most certainly were not," Celine answered.

"We were supposed to be!" Damien insisted. "Something went haywire. But you weren't supposed to marry him! We were supposed to be there to help you. To stop you from joining his… cult."

Celine sighed, setting her jaw. "Gentlemen, I have little idea as to what you are referring to. I believe you to be quite mad and I plan to inform my husband of this… outburst."

"Celine, please listen," Damien begged her.

"I will do nothing of the sort." She twisted to face Alexander. "Mr. Buckley, I am shocked you are party to this! And you, Mr. Buckley," she added, twisting to Grayson.

"That night, you found out your father was dead. You wept over his dead body. And Marcus informed you he would be your new family. He asked you to kill the man who killed your father. To bring him to justice. It all happened in a cave near your sister's house in Martinique."

"You do not know of what you speak!"

"Are we wrong?" Damien questioned.

"Quite!" Celine answered, sidestepping to leave.

"Then tell me, what did we get wrong?" Damien questioned, blocking her from leaving the room as she stepped forward.

"I shall not! Stand aside, Mr. Carlyle or I shall scream."

"Just explain how we were wrong, and we'll drop the entire thing. Please."

"I did not kill the man," Celine answered. She struggled for a moment. "I… I assumed I had mortally wounded him, but Marcus assured me he would survive. He asked me to trust him. My husband was correct."

"Wait, wait, wait, he lived? The guy who murdered your father?" Michael inquired.

"Yes, he survived. He's still alive to this day, in fact. I have not committed murder at my husband's behest. Now, as you can see, he holds no malevolent interests."

"Ha!" Damien laughed. "No malevolent interests? Celine, he is the one responsible for your father's death."

"I beg your pardon?!"

Damien raised his eyebrows and nodded. "Yes, Marcus Northcott is responsible for your father's death. He ordered that man to kill the Marquis."

"I have heard enough of this nonsense. I shall listen to no more! My husband is no more responsible for my father's death than you or I. How dare you impugn his reputation! I shall not stand for this, sir!"

"We're telling the truth," Michael informed her. "Believe it or not, we are. We're not doing this to hurt you. We're trying to help you."

"That's right," Damien added. "Stop and consider what we've said for a minute, Celine. You're smart and you're good at reading people. You've got instincts. Use them. Marcus did this to force you to be alone. He promised he'd take care of you, that he'd be your family. He wanted you to feel alone and have no other choice but to turn to him."

"Gentlemen, I have listened to enough. I warn you to keep your distance from this day forward. If you continue to harass me in this manner, I shall have no choice but to convey your slanderous words to my husband. Good night!" She stormed from the room, disappearing through the front door and into her carriage. The carriage pulled away as they watched from the window.

"Well, that was an epic fail," Michael stated.

"That was pure madness, gentlemen," Alexander replied, almost breathless. "If she relays this to Duke Northcott… I do not wish to imagine the repercussions."

"I'm sorry, Alexander," Damien apologized. "But we had to do something. I saw an opportunity, and I took it."

"Your so-called opportunity may cost us our business if not our lives," Alexander protested. "Now that you've made us look like fools and ruined us socially, I suggest we leave before you do any more damage. Unless, of course, you'd like to burn the house down before we depart for good measure."

Damien opened his mouth to respond but couldn't find any words to address the situation. He nodded, a sheepish expression on his face. They climbed into their carriage when it pulled up and returned to the Buckley house.

When they arrived home, Damien attempted to apologize again. "I'm sorry, Alexander. I just…" His voice trailed off as he searched for more words.

"She's never behaved like this before," Michael continued. "Every other time, we've just been honest with her, and she's understood and helped us."

"Yeah," Damien added, picking up on Michael's assessment. "To the point of telling her we were from the future. She just accepted it and jumped right in to help us. I never expected her to behave this way."

Alexander did not respond right away. "It is finished. I hope to salvage the situation… somehow. Please, next time, discuss these things before you accost the Duchess."

Michael and Damien nodded then excused themselves, unable to make any further amends with Alexander and Gray. Neither of them could sleep, instead commiserating in Damien's room.

"Well, we really messed this up," Michael remarked as he entered Damien's room in his nightclothes, borrowed from Alexander.

"In more than one way," Damien agreed.

"How could this happen? Did that one electric arc really screw up history this bad?"

Damien rubbed his face. "I don't know. Perhaps the blue arc was some fluke, and we aren't meant to change anything. Maybe we're just stuck here."

"No, nope. Not going to accept that."

"We may have no choice."

Michael shook his head as he paced. "I am *not* living in an era without bathrooms. We have to get back home!"

"Don't worry, we may not live long here."

"Why?"

"Celine hates us. She's probably telling the Duke everything we said about him right now. And then he'll kill us."

"What a mess," Michael groaned, defeated. He sank into the armchair in Damien's room.

"I feel really bad about Alexander. The Duke thinks we're cousins. He'll destroy Alexander and Gray right along with us."

"Yeah, we really didn't think this one through at all," Michael admitted.

"It was my fault," Damien answered. "I couldn't just do nothing and wait and see how things played out. I never imagined she'd be so… loyal to that creep."

"I guess she's had years of practice. It's been over twenty years since that night."

"Damn, what a fool I was," Damien lamented.

"Don't beat yourself up. I didn't stop you. I considered it a good idea, too."

They sat in silence for twenty minutes before Michael suggested they try to sleep. Damien agreed, although he was sure he wouldn't manage to sleep. They would reconvene in the morning to attempt to salvage the situation.

* * *

Celine glanced out of the window as she pulled away from the Blackburn manor. The conversation she experienced within the walls replayed in her mind. It troubled her. It was, of course, nonsense, she assured herself. She shut her eyes for a moment, trying to block her musings.

She found herself unable to stop dwelling on the subject. The younger Mr. Carlyle's face burned through her memory. His eyes were so honest. His impassioned speech seemed candid. Did he honestly believe what he said?

Celine replayed the events of her sixteenth birthday in her mind. She recalled as though it were yesterday her father's body flung in front of her, cold and stiff. Tears formed in her eyes. She held them back. She recalled Marcus pulling her away from her father's body and wiping her tears. She recalled his promise. He pledged to protect her, provide for her, become her family. He vowed to give her anything her heart desired. She refused to give in at first. Only after hours had she weakened.

Distraught and alone, she trusted him and allowed him to guide her hand in stabbing her father's murderer. Celine gasped as thick red blood poured from his chest. Marcus assured her the wound was not fatal, but Celine swore the man breathed his last, raspy breath. After a few moments spent with the body, Marcus stood, extending his hand toward the dead man.

To Celine's surprise, the man rose, appearing healed. She advocated he be turned over to the authorities, but Marcus disagreed, telling her the man may prove useful to them.

"You must trust me, Celine," he said. "From this day forward, you must trust me. You are mine eternally."

Celine agreed with his decision, assuming him to be much more experienced in these matters.

The memory faded from Celine's mind. She considered the information provided by the Carlyles. Was Marcus responsible for the entire scenario? Had he orchestrated her father's death to trap her into marriage?

Damien's first words echoed in her mind. "We were there, we were supposed to be there. We were supposed to help you."

What did they mean?

The carriage pulled to a stop outside her home. She waited for the footman to assist her into the house. Her maid readied her for bed before retiring herself. Celine stared in the mirror, unable to dismiss the conversation with the Carlyles.

As she brushed her hair, a knock sounded at her door. "Come in."

Marcus entered her room. "Still awake?"

"I was about to retire."

"My apologies for departing early from the party. Something came up that required my immediate attention."

"There is no need for an apology, husband," Celine responded.

"All the same, I prefer to voice it. I trust there were no further... incidents with the Buckleys or their cousins, the Carlyles?"

"No," Celine lied. "I departed without speaking to them."

"I am glad they did not trouble you further, my dear."

"'Tis no trouble," Celine answered.

"I'm not sure your toes would agree," Marcus replied. "Well, doubtless, you are tired. I shall leave you to sleep." He kissed her forehead and departed from the room.

"Good night," she replied as he left.

Celine climbed into bed, relaxing back into the pillows behind her. She hadn't told her husband about her strange encounter with the Carlyles. Why, she wondered? The question plagued her until she drifted off to sleep.

* * *

Present day, Bucksville

Celine raced down the hall, bursting into the dining room. "Something is happening, please come," she said to Millie.

Millie leapt from her seat, following Celine upstairs to the bedrooms. The various monitoring equipment showed a variety of activity. Damien's heart rate increased, along with his breathing. His blood pressure was spiking. His brain showed high levels of activity.

"Damien?" Millie inquired. "Can you hear us? Damien?"

Damien did not respond.

"I'd like to check Michael, just a moment." Millie disappeared from the room, returning in minutes. "He is the same. Elevated heart rate, breathing and blood pressure with high levels of brain activity."

"What does it mean, Millie?" Gray questioned.

"They're experiencing something. A dream possibly," she suggested.

"At the exact same time?" Celine queried.

"That is odd, I agree. Even if this is an effect from the shock wave, their bodies would respond and recuperate differently. It's almost as though they are responding to a stimulus. Yet there is no stimulus in common. No similar lights, sounds, voices. They aren't even in the same room."

"Is there anything we can do to soothe them?"

"Continue to stay with them, talk to them," Millie suggested. "I'd like to monitor them and note when this activity stops."

"I will bring the rest of your dinner to you," Alexander offered.

"Thank you. I'd prefer to stay near them in case anything changes."

"Should we be concerned?" Celine asked.

"Not at this time. However, the elevated heart rate could lead to something more serious. I prefer to take no chances."

Celine nodded in agreement. Gray placed his arm around her shoulders, steadying her as she gazed at Damien's limp form, covered in two blankets. *What is happening, Damien,* she wondered?

* * *

1812, LONDON

Alexander departed from the house early the next morning, prior to breakfast. The scene the previous evening with Duchess Northcott had the potential to bring serious repercussions. If Duchess Northcott told her husband about the incident, he would exact revenge. Alexander hoped Marcus's urgent business that drew him from the party lasted well into the evening, and Celine hadn't the chance to speak with him about it yet.

This still allowed her the opportunity to discuss the subject over breakfast. He hoped she didn't. He planned to call on her early and determine if there was any way to salvage the situation and avoid a confrontation with Duke Northcott. He would appeal to her good nature, throw himself on her mercy. With luck, he would convince her to forget the incident and make no mention of it to her husband.

He stationed himself down the street from the Northcott residence. Nervous energy filled him as he watched the house. By mid-morning, Duke Northcott emerged, strolling down the street. Alexander allowed him to pass before he hurried to the residence.

Knocking at the door, he waited for a response. The butler answered. "Yes?"

"Mr. Alexander Buckley to see Duchess Northcott," Alexander presented himself.

"At this hour? The Duchess is still abed."

"Please tell her I am here. It is quite urgent," Alexander insisted.

"You should return at a decent hour with your business, sir," the butler answered, swinging the door closed.

Alexander stopped him. "Please, sir, I would prefer that you announce me now. The business cannot wait. I believe the Duchess will appreciate your service in this matter."

The butler considered it a moment, then widened the door's opening. "Please come in, Mr. Buckley." He led Alexander to the sitting room and requested he wait.

A tense few minutes passed as Alexander waited. After a time, he wondered if she would refuse to see him. If so, should he attempt a second visit? As he pondered his options, the door across the room opened. The Duchess strode in, still in her dressing gown. Alexander leapt to his feet.

"Mr. Buckley, I am surprised you would dare set foot in this house after the incident last night," she said, stopping across the room from him.

"Duchess Northcott," he greeted her, bowing, "it is that specific incident that propelled me to call upon you at this hour."

"Do you wish to continue to defame my husband's name?"

"No," Alexander admitted. "I wish to beg your pardon for my cousins' impropriety. I humbly throw myself on your mercy. I'm sorry to say my cousins may have enjoyed too much in the way of spirits last night. They spoke out of turn. I wish to apologize on their behalf and hope we may consider the incident concluded. In particular, I hoped to request your discretion, particularly where your husband is concerned."

Celine smirked, arching an eyebrow. "In other words, Mr. Buckley, you wish to learn if I have already discussed the matter with Duke Northcott."

"I'll confess that was one of my goals in speaking with you, yes," Alexander admitted, licking his lips.

"My husband can be a harsh and unforgiving man," Celine responded.

Alexander nodded, fearing the worst.

"But he knows nothing of the incident."

Relief coursed through Alexander. A chance still remained for him to salvage the situation. He had only to convince Duchess Northcott to continue her silence on the subject.

"Do you plan to inform him?" he inquired.

"You have no right to stand in my home and ask me these questions, Mr. Buckley. But in answer, no, I do not."

Alexander breathed a sigh of relief. "Might we then consider the matter closed?" he questioned, hoping to be finished with the discussion soon.

"No, Mr. Buckley, we may not," Celine answered.

A lump formed in Alexander's throat and his stomach turned over. He was glad he had chosen not to eat breakfast this morning, fearing he may not be able to keep it down.

CHAPTER 23

Celine made her way to the couch, perching on the edge. Alexander remained standing.

"Please, Mr. Buckley, be seated."

Alexander seated himself across from the duchess, unable to speak. He assumed she would lecture him on the incident, give him a tongue lashing before allowing him to leave. At least this was his sincere hope over something worse.

"In truth, Mr. Buckley, I am unable to forget the incident," she began. "It has disturbed me to my core."

"I understand, Duchess Northcott, I offer my most heartfelt apologies…"

Celine held up her hand, cutting him off. "I do not wish to entertain your heartfelt apologies, Mr. Buckley. I wish only to gain the truth."

The words left Alexander speechless for a moment. What truth did she wish to gain?

"I'm not sure I understand," Alexander responded.

"Your cousins accused my husband of a grave crime. There is a truth to the matter. I wish to learn it. I also desire your cousins be present when I do, so that, if they are being dishonest, they might know it."

Her words stunned Alexander. The duchess hoped to learn the truth about Michael and Damien's story concerning Duke Northcott's involvement in her father's death. Did she suspect it may be true? Or did she prefer to prove them wrong? If the latter, for what reason? What did she gain by it?

"I judge your cousin, Damien, spoke in earnest last night when he told his story. Perhaps he is mad and does not realize the error of his ways. If so, he must be shown the error."

"Quite right," Alexander agreed.

"On the other hand, perhaps he is correct. In which case, I should prefer to learn the truth about my husband."

Alexander wondered if he may be imagining the conversation. Was Duchess Northcott admitting suspicion of her husband? Were Michael and Damien correct in their assessment that her marriage was a mistake? "I shall ensure my cousins are available to you when you need them."

"I shall request their presence tonight at midnight. I require your assistance as well. We shall meet at The White Horse pub. Are you familiar with it?"

"Yes," Alexander said, still parsing through his shock. "I am surprised, Duchess Northcott, you are familiar with it."

"I am not as naïve as you imagine. I am well-versed in many things. Give me some credit, Mr. Buckley. Now, are we agreed?"

"Forgive me, Duchess Northcott, but meeting at The White Horse at such an hour is unsafe for you."

Celine let her icy blue eyes settle on him. "I am capable of taking care of myself, Mr. Buckley. Now, are we agreed?"

"And what of your husband? How will you explain your midnight roamings to him?"

"My husband will be none the wiser to our clandestine meeting. I shall see to it that he is unaware of my absence."

"I must admit, Duchess Northcott, I am stunned. But we are agreed. I shall see you at midnight to proceed with whatever plan you deem best."

Celine stood, offering him the slightest of smiles. He leapt to his feet.

"I'm glad we are agreed. Good day, Mr. Buckley."

She strode from the room, leaving him alone.

"Good day, Duchess Northcott," he called after her. It took all his strength not to collapse onto her couch in astonishment. His weak knees carried him out of the house and away from the Northcott residence.

He pondered the conversation his entire walk home. He continued to question whether or not it occurred or if he had merely dreamt it. He had traveled to speak with Duchess Northcott, expecting to be berated at the very least, or faced with the news that her husband sought vengeance over the matter. Instead, she had assured him of her husband's continued ignorance on the subject and proceeded to make plans to determine the legitimacy of the wild story Damien and Michael conveyed to her at the party.

He reached his home, climbing the steps and entering the foyer just before lunch. He removed his overcoat and joined Michael, Damien, and Gray in the dining room.

"Alexander, sorry we missed you this morning," Damien began. "We wanted to apologize again and see if there was anything we could do to rectify the situation."

"Yeah," Michael chimed in. "We feel terrible about it."

"Actually," Gray voiced, "I have already made arrangements for us to leave and travel back to the States. The Duke's reach is far, but it gives us some time to plan. Perhaps if we are not immediately available, tempers will cool before he deals with us."

Alexander seated himself across from Damien and next to Gray. He shook his head, still finding it hard to fathom what he was about to impart to them. "It seems that won't be necessary, Gray." He directed his next statement at Michael and Damien. "There is something you can do."

"Anything, name it," Damien responded.

"Won't be necessary?" Gray questioned. "Have you also gone mad? Surely Duke Northcott has learned of the accusations made against him last evening. He has a clear reputation as a cruel and unforgiving man. We shall be ruined if not disposed of."

Alexander shook his head. "He hasn't learned of the situation."

"You're sure?" Gray queried.

"Quite," Alexander assured him.

Gray narrowed his eyes. "How are you sure?"

"I have been to visit Duchess Northcott this morning. I paid her an early morning call, hoping to prevent her from speaking to her husband."

"My God, you *are* mad," Gray interjected.

"She has not informed her husband of the situation," Alexander told them.

"I find that hard to fathom," Gray responded.

"Instead, she has asked for my help in ascertaining the truth of the situation."

Gray stared at him, his eyes wide. "You're joking."

"I am not," Alexander answered, shaking his head, still finding the situation incredulous himself. "Although, I understand your bewilderment. I was party to the conversation and still find it difficult to believe."

"Tell us what happened!" Damien insisted. "It's a good sign she didn't tell the Duke, and that she wants to learn the truth!"

"As I said, I paid an early morning call to the Duchess. I

threw myself upon her mercy and begged her forgiveness for the entire incident," Alexander explained. "She informed me that she had kept the matter secret from her husband and planned to continue to do so."

"That's great!" Michael said. "We're in the clear!"

"I assumed so, however, she confided that the incident disturbed her. Nevertheless, your conviction as to the truthfulness of the matter struck her. She judged you to be earnest in what you told her. She feels compelled to determine if your story is true."

"Now, that's the Celine we know!" Damien exclaimed, high-fiving Michael.

"She asked us to meet her at The White Horse pub at midnight. She prefers you to be present when she verifies the factual nature of the story so that if you are found in error, you might realize it."

"Please tell me you did not agree to meet her," Gray queried.

"I did. I'd rather that than have her discuss the matter with Duke Northcott," Alexander countered.

Gray sprung from his seat, leaving his half-eaten lunch behind. He paced the floor. "What if it's a trap?"

"Celine wouldn't do that!" Damien argued.

"You miscalculated how Duchess Northcott would react last evening. You can't be sure," Gray countered.

"If it was a trap, to what end?" Alexander asked.

"To our end," Gray answered. "Her husband will finish us."

"Duke Northcott would not require nor use his wife's assistance to lure us into a trap," Alexander surmised.

"I'm with Damien, I vote we meet her," Michael replied.

"How sure are you gentlemen about your story?" Alexander queried.

"Very sure," Damien assured him. "It was the Duke who ordered her father killed. I'd bet my life on it."

"You already have," Gray informed him.

They finished their lunch, discussing arrangements for their midnight jaunt. With any luck, Celine would learn the truth about her husband and trust them. Damien and Michael spent the afternoon and evening filled with nervous energy, awaiting their excursion. Damien spent much of the time pacing the floors, anxiety, and anticipation building.

As the midnight hour approached, the four men prepared themselves for the trip. Gray elected to join despite his suspicion of a setup. They left the house, traveling on foot to The White Horse pub, located in a less-than-desirable area of town. They milled around outside the pub, hoping the sketchy characters that loitered near the entrance kept their distance.

At the stroke of midnight, a hooded, cloaked figure approached them. "Mr. Buckley, thank you for joining me," Celine greeted them. "We shall now get to the root of this issue. I shall prefer to remain anonymous as we enter the pub for obvious reasons."

"Yes, of course," Alexander answered.

"Shall we?" she replied.

"Just a moment," Gray interjected. "What is your plan?"

"It shall be revealed as necessary. We shall begin by entering the pub. If I am not mistaken, the man who murdered my father should be inside. I assume you both should recognize him if you should see him?" Celine asked of Michael and Damien.

"Yes. We would recognize him," Damien responded, hoping it was true.

"Point him out when you spy him," she replied, pulling on the pub door. She entered the pub, her hood still covering her. They followed her into the pub.

Loud laughter and muddled conversations abounded as they entered. Michael and Damien scanned the crowd. Damien's pulse quickened as he worried about recognizing the man again. They had been in a cave lit only by candlelight. Suppose they could not distinguish his features. His certainty of moments ago began to fade.

"Do you see him?" Celine shouted over the din.

Damien shook his head, panic building in him as he glanced over the various faces. "Wait, there!" he pointed toward a man against the right wall.

"Yes," Michael confirmed. "That's him."

"Indeed, it is," Celine confirmed. She passed a few coins to Alexander. "Tell the barkeep you require use of his storeroom and that we shall not like to be disturbed for the course of the next hour. Bring the man with you."

Celine stalked across the room to a door in the back, disappearing through it.

Alexander raised his eyebrows at Gray. "You heard the lady," Gray responded. "You talk to the barkeep. I'll retrieve him."

Michael and Damien followed Gray, who requested a few moments of the man's time. He revealed a few coins, assuring the man it would be worth his while. They met Alexander in the middle of the bar. He secured use of the backroom from the barkeep. They proceeded through the door Celine disappeared through moments ago, finding a hallway. A small room located on the left held barrels. They assumed this was the storeroom, ushering the man inside. Celine stood in the back corner of the room; her hood pushed back. She removed her gloves, setting them aside.

The man spotted her and tried to run from the room. Gray and Alexander reached for him, but Celine stretched her hand in front of her, drawing him back like a magnet draws metal. She released him into a chair placed in the middle of the room. Shackles closed automatically around his feet and hands.

Damien gulped. This version of Celine took no prisoners. A sudden wave of uneasiness crept over him. If they were incorrect, she would turn her obvious displeasure to them next. He glanced to Michael, whose forehead glistened with beads of sweat. Michael made a face at him and Damien mirrored his expression. Both of them realized if this gamble did not pay off, they were in serious trouble.

Celine removed a glowing vial of liquid from her cloak.

"What is that?" Damien inquired.

"A simple yet effective truth serum," Celine answered him. "Once he drinks this, he will have no choice but to confide in us the truth about anything we ask."

"What if it doesn't work?" Damien questioned further.

"It will work."

"But how…"

"Mr. Carlyle," Celine interrupted, cutting Damien off. "I am not an amateur. I do not appreciate your doubt concerning my ability to obtain the truth from a simple criminal."

Damien gulped. "Sorry. It's just really important."

"Is it? It is my husband that has been accused. Do you imagine it is of little importance to me that I should be so cavalier as to use a questionable method?"

"No," he squeaked out. "Sorry."

Celine sighed. "Let us proceed. Gentlemen, tilt his head back so I may pour the liquid into his mouth."

Alexander and Gray obliged her, holding the man's head back while Celine emptied the vial's contents into his mouth. They shoved his mouth shut, holding his nose until he swallowed.

"The concoction should take a few moments to take effect," Celine indicated.

"Going to tell your husband about this, missus!" the man threatened as he coughed, choking on the liquid forced into him.

Damien glanced to Celine, wide-eyed at the man's admission. Celine rolled her eyes at him, raising her eyebrow. "Never fear, he will not convey any part of this incident to my husband nor anyone else. Now, Mr. Ward, shall we begin?" Celine placed herself in front of the man.

"I ain't answering no questions," he spat at her. "I'll tell the gov'ner, I will. Tell him his old lady was asking me questions in the middle of the night."

"Spare me your threats, Mr. Ward. Now, you shall answer my questions."

"HELP! HELP!" the man screamed at the top of his lungs.

Celine shook her head, annoyed with him. "Your efforts are futile. No one can hear your screams, Mr. Ward. First question: Were you on the island of Martinique on the twenty-eighth of July 1786?"

"Aye," the man answered. "I were there."

"Did you on that evening kill the Marquis Gaspard Devereaux on his way to board his ship to return to France?"

"Aye," the man said, his eyes glassy and unable to focus. "Squealed like a pig, he did."

Celine closed her eyes for a moment, inhaling and setting her jaw. Anger coursed through her. Yet she restrained herself, pressing on with her questioning. "Why did you kill him?"

"To rob him."

"Who ordered you to do this?" she questioned.

"No one, missus."

Damien's heart sank at the man's answer. They had miscalculated. Celine's father had been killed in a simple robbery in this chain of events. He stared at the floor, awaiting the wrath of Celine Northcott to be turned onto them.

Celine continued; her comments still directed toward the man. "Did someone order you to kill the Marquis Devereaux and claim the motivation was robbery?"

"I killed him and robbed him for a few coins," the man repeated.

Celine fumed, her jaw tight. "I do not wish to hear your concocted story. I want the truth. Did someone order you to kill the Marquis Devereaux and claim the motivation was robbery? Search the depths of your feeble mind and answer me."

The man remained silent.

"Tell me, Mr. Ward. I insist you tell me. Did someone order you to kill the Marquis Devereaux and claim your motivation was robbery?"

The man's mouth opened and closed, but no sounds came out. "Answer me, Mr. Ward. Who is responsible?"

"I can't," the man moaned.

Celine grasped his face, squishing his lips between her thumb and fingers. "You can and you must. You are compelled to tell me. Who is responsible? Who gave the order for you to kill Marquis Devereaux?"

Damien glanced to Michael. His eyes were wide as he watched the scene unfold in front of him.

"He did," the man gasped out.

"Say his name. Who?" she barked at him.

The man swallowed hard. "I can't, missus, don't make me."

"WHO?" her shrill voice inquired.

Damien held his breath as he awaited the name of the offending party.

CHAPTER 24

"Marcus Northcott," the man whimpered.

Celine trembled with anger. "Say it again."

"Marcus Northcott," he repeated.

She stood, crossing her arms, staring into space, considering her next move.

"Thank you, Mr. Ward. And now you shall discuss this incident no further." Celine waved a hand over his throat before snapping her fingers. The shackles fell open, and the man stood, trembling. "Go."

"Wait!" Damien exclaimed. "He could go out and tell anyone what we did!"

Celine raised her eyebrow at him. "Ask him to describe the incident to you."

Damien, wide-eyed, glanced between her and the others.

"Did you tell Duchess Northcott about why you killed her father?" Michael asked.

The man opened his mouth to answer, but no sound emerged.

Celine gave them a curt smile. "I assure you, he's quite

mute. Now go, Mr. Ward, before I change my mind to a more permanent punishment."

The man raced from the room.

Celine stalked to the back, retrieving her gloves. She pulled her hood over her. "Gentlemen, our business is concluded here," she stated, pulling her gloves on. "We have established the validity of your claims."

"Celine," Damien said, approaching her and placing a hand on her arm. "I'm sorry."

"I've no need for your apologies, Mr. Carlyle," Celine responded. "What I require is the information you have to share. It is obvious you have knowledge of many things concerning my life. I must learn what you know." She turned to Alexander. "You shall call upon me tomorrow, Mr. Buckley. You will offer an invitation to your country home in gratitude for the invitation I provided to Lord Blackburn's ball. I shall accept and travel to stay there in two days, where we may discuss the matter freely. Are we clear?"

Alexander glanced to the others. "Uh, yes, Duchess Northcott," he stammered, amazed at the turn of events.

"If we are to work together, please, call me Celine," she stated.

"What about the Duke?" Damien asked.

"That is my affair, Mr. Carlyle."

"Call me Damien, please," Damien replied.

"Damien," she said, nodding with a tight-lipped smile.

"I shall expect you tomorrow afternoon, Mr. Buckley." Celine stepped toward the exit.

"Wait, Celine," Gray responded. "Perhaps I should walk you to your residence. This part of town can be dangerous."

"Thank you, Mr. Buckley. However, I do not require your protection. I am capable of defending myself."

"Call me Gray, please," he replied. "For companionship, then."

"I'm afraid I wouldn't make for a very good companion at this moment, Gray," Celine admitted.

"That does not put me off," Gray answered.

"Then you are welcome to join me," Celine responded. "Gentlemen, good night," she said to the others before stalking from the room. Gray followed her.

Michael, Damien, and Alexander glanced at each other for a moment.

"I suppose we should return home," Alexander suggested when he gained his voice.

Damien and Michael nodded their agreement. They left the pub, beginning their walk home.

A few minutes into their walk, Damien spoke. "Okay, wow! Since no one else wants to say it, I'll say it."

"Ah, yeah!" Michael agreed. "For a second there, I assumed we were done. When he kept saying 'I robbed him' and wouldn't admit it."

"Then all of a sudden he just names him. Marcus Northcott did it. I was sweating bullets before that, too," Damien admitted.

"Gentlemen, I must admit, I continue to be shocked at the events unfolding," Alexander responded.

"At least it worked out," Damien replied. "I'm glad for that. We felt awful about what happened last night." Damien stopped walking. "If we had cost you your business or worse, I couldn't have lived with myself."

"I appreciate your sentiments, Damien," Alexander answered. "Come along, we have much to discuss. I'd like to learn everything you know about Celine. We must be prepared for her arrival at the country estate. I shouldn't like any more surprises."

Damien and Michael agreed, promising to review all their information the next morning before Alexander called on

Celine. When they arrived home, they went straight to bed, exhausted from the draining experience.

* * *

PRESENT DAY, **Bucksville**

Celine laid awake in the darkened room. The glow from the medical equipment monitoring Damien's vital signs provided enough light for her to make out Damien's features. She stared at the monitor, counting the seconds until the next spike appeared, marking his heartbeat. She held her breath between beats, afraid the next one wouldn't appear. His chest rose and fell in rhythm.

She held his hand in hers. Cold to the touch, it reflected the drop in his body temperature. Try as she might, Celine could not manage to warm it. They had added extra blankets to the bed, tried hot water bottles, built fires in the room's fireplace, but nothing raised his or Michael's body temperature. In fact, it had dropped further since the initial drop Millie noted.

As midnight approached, the activity on the monitor changed. Damien's heart rate raced, spikes appearing on the monitor closer together than before. His chest rose and fell in rapid succession as his breathing increased. Celine glanced to the monitor representing Damien's brain activity. It showed an increase in activity.

Celine leapt from his bed, racing to Michael's room. She glanced at his monitors. They told a similar story, increased breathing and heart rate along with brain activity.

"What is it, Celine?" Gray asked as she raced in the room.

"The monitors," she answered, pointing at them. "Damien's are doing the same. I'll wake Millie."

"No, you stay with Damien. I'll wake her," Gray offered.

"Thanks, Gray," Celine answered, squeezing his hand as he exited the room.

Celine returned to Damien's room. She stared at the monitors, wondering what story they were trying to tell. Millie rushed into the room moments later. She glanced at the monitors. "And Michael is experiencing a similar phenomenon?"

"Yes," Celine answered.

"Just a moment, I want to see his stats," Millie answered, excusing herself.

She returned moments later. She noted a few things on her chart, then checked a few other vitals. She wrote a few more observations, then rejoined Celine and Gray, who waited at the foot of the bed.

"Well?" Celine asked, clutching Gray's hand that sat on her shoulder.

"I'm afraid the news isn't good," Millie admitted.

"What? Isn't this the same as before? Some sort of stimulus?"

"The symptoms are similar and do correspond with the idea that they are a reaction to some kind of stimulus. However, we haven't identified any stimulus that could be the cause."

"And that's a bad thing?" Celine questioned.

"No, that's not it."

"Then what?" Celine prodded.

"Their body temperature has dropped again. I'm afraid it's becoming serious at this juncture. We haven't had any luck raising their body temperatures and instead, their temperature continues to drop."

"What does that mean, Millie?" Gray asked.

"They will soon begin to turn hypothermic. Without the ability to raise their temperatures, we won't be able to reverse the process."

"What are you saying?" Celine demanded.

"I'm saying that if their temperatures continue to drop unchecked and without our ability to raise them… they will die of hypothermia."

Celine's jaw dropped as a tear rolled down her cheek. "No!" she cried.

Gray squeezed her to him.

"There must be something we can do."

"I'm sorry, Celine," Millie answered. "I'm afraid their bodies are failing. The temperature drop coupled with their other symptoms suggests this is the case. We'll do what we can to keep them comfortable, but you may want to prepare yourself." Silence surrounded them for a few moments. "I'll leave you to process everything and check back later. If there is anything you need, either of you, please ask."

Celine whispered a thank you to Millie, before perching on the edge of the bed next to Damien. The door closed as Millie exited the room.

"Celine," Gray began, putting his hand on her shoulder.

The gesture triggered an emotional response from Celine. She buried her head in her hands, weeping.

"Hey, hey, hey, Celine," Gray whispered, pulling her hands away from her face. "Come on, he's not gone yet."

"Yet," Celine repeated, staring at him. She stood from the bed, pacing the room. "He's dying, Gray. And there's nothing we can do about it. He's just… stuck from whatever that electrical pulse was that Marcus and I generated during our battle. I mean, what…" Her voice trailed off mid-sentence.

"Celine," Gray answered. "It's not your fault it's…" Celine held her hand in the air, stopping him. Her brow furrowed. "What is it?"

"That electrical pulse," Celine began.

"What about it?"

"We're assuming that's what did this to them."

"So?" Gray questioned.

"So, whatever that impulse was it was powerful enough to send Marcus and me to Shadow World."

"Okay?" Gray inquired.

"What if it did something similar to Michael and Damien?"

"Sent them to Shadow World?" Gray queried. "They'd be dead by now, Celine."

Celine shook her head. "No, not Shadow World, somewhere else."

"Why would it send you to Shadow World and them somewhere else? And it didn't affect us at all!"

"The magnitude of the effect must have waned by the time it reached everyone beyond Marcus and me. It was too weak to affect you, Alexander, and Celeste, but Michael and Damien are human. It could have easily been strong enough to have affected them. But by the time it reached them, perhaps it had morphed, and the effect was different. Or the effect was different because they were human. Perhaps both."

"Okay, so what does this tell us? Where could they be?"

Celine stalked around the room, deep in thought. "I've only seen this once before. Marcus and I traveled to Germany before you and I met. A man there told us about Alterra. Given the symptoms, their apparent reactions to stimuli at the same time and the drop in their body temperatures, I'd imagine they are there."

"What is Alterra? I've never heard of it," Gray responded.

"It's a sort of alternate reality. There are myriads of them. Realms where life played out differently. Different choices were made, creating an entirely different world."

"What makes you think they are there?"

"Marcus visited one of these bands while we were in Germany. He experienced the same effects. Obvious signs of reaction to stimulus, decreased body temperature. Of course, it had no effect on him, he is immortal."

"Perhaps it's just an effect from the pulse, Celine. What if you're wrong?"

Celine considered it. "I'm not. What are the chances they experience the same reactions at the same times by chance? They are together, they are experiencing something together."

"So, what does this mean?"

"It means we can save them."

* * *

1812, LONDON

Michael, Damien, Alexander and Gray spent the morning hours discussing information about Celine. Alexander and Gray remained amazed at Michael's and Damien's accounts of the different life Celine led. They were determined to correct the errors that occurred.

Alexander planned to ride to the country estate following his call to Celine to prepare the staff. Michael, Damien, and Gray planned to travel the following day to reach the country estate. Celine would arrive in two days.

Alexander arrived at the Northcott residence and was ushered into the sitting room. He did not wait long for Celine to enter. She offered him tea or brandy. He refused both. Being around her still unsettled him. The strange events of the past few days caused him to view Celine as an enigma. He had witnessed her ferocity when angered, and he had no desire to be on the receiving end of it.

"Please, sit, Mr. Buckley. Are you quite sure I cannot offer you a refreshment? Perhaps some tea?" Celine inquired, perching on the edge of the couch.

280

Alexander attempted to read her controlled demeanor. "Whatever you deem is best, Duchess."

Celine offered the briefest of smiles before ringing a bell. The butler returned. "Tea, please."

"Yes, Duchess Northcott, right away." He departed from the room, returning with a tea tray in a few minutes as Celine and Alexander exchanged pleasantries. Celine poured the tea as he left, offering a cup to Alexander. "I must remind you to call me Celine, Mr. Buckley."

"My apologies, Duch… Celine," he corrected. "And I must invite you to call me Alexander."

Celine poured her own cup of tea, stirring in cream and sugar. She sipped at the cup before setting it on its saucer. "I assume you've made the arrangements?"

"Oh," Alexander replied. "Yes. I've sent word already and plan to ride there after this call to oversee the final arrangements. The staff are very excited to welcome a duchess."

"You needn't make a fuss, Alexander." She sipped her tea. "Your cousins are quite puzzling. Their information is accurate, yet there is no clear way that they obtained it. What can you tell me about them?"

Alexander weighed the amount of information appropriate to tell her. He glanced up from his teacup, finding her crystal blue eyes fixed on him. Her stare made him uncomfortable, and he wondered for a moment if she may be reading his thoughts.

"You may speak freely, Alexander. I do not seek the information to hold over you, only to understand how they might come to possess such knowledge."

Perhaps she could, in fact, read his mind. He decided the best course of action was to tell the truth.

"Then I must confess, Michael and Damien Carlyle are not, in fact, relations of mine. And I must admit to being baffled when they arrived."

"Baffled?"

"Yes. They arrived on my doorstep one evening several days ago, claiming we were acquainted. I had never met them before."

"How is it that they sought you out?"

"As odd as it may sound, they recalled my telling them about the London house while on my uncle's estate in Massachusetts."

"Yet you had never met them in Massachusetts? Or anywhere?"

Alexander sipped at the hot tea. "Correct. When I admitted as much, they told me a fantastical story. Then they asked to see you. They sought your help. But I leave it to them to address this with you."

"What made you believe them?"

"Two things. First, as you noted, they possessed knowledge that they couldn't have obtained. Second, as you also mentioned, their earnestness. It seemed clear they were not attempting to be disingenuous. They deemed what they said to be the truth."

"Hmm," Celine murmured, sipping her tea again. "This should prove to be an interesting visit, Alexander."

Alexander set down his teacup, intending to leave. Before he stood, he asked another question. "Forgive me for asking, Celine, but will your husband travel with you?"

"I expect so. If not with me, within a day of me."

Alexander's stomach turned. He was still unsure of Celine. Her cool confidence made her unreadable. The limited dealings he'd had with her prior to Michael and Damien's arrival gave him the impression they could not be friends. His opinion was changing as he learned more, but he remained uncertain of her. The addition of Marcus Northcott made his skin crawl. Should Celine's attitude somersault, they could find themselves in a terrible predicament.

Celine noticed the apprehension on Alexander's face, reading it easily. She set down her teacup on its saucer. "There is no need for consternation. I am capable of handling my husband. And discussions of this nature are certainly more private on your estate than here."

Alexander offered a tight-lipped smile, unsure of how to respond.

Celine continued, "I am loyal to those friends who prove loyal to me, Alexander. You and your friends have proven more than loyal. Do not fret, no harm will come to you, your family, or friends."

Alexander swallowed hard, trying to dislodge the lump in his throat. "You are most gracious, Celine. However, your husband is a powerful man. I'm sure you understand my concern."

"My husband is a powerful man, but even his power has its limits. I am every bit as powerful as he and trained by him. I know his tricks, his methods. While he is capable of grandstanding and things may prove uncomfortable, no harm will come to you, I assure you. There is no need for apprehension." Celine stared at him a moment. When he did not respond, she added, "If you fear some reconciliation between us, please reassure yourself I am not a woman so easily swayed."

Her forthrightness struck Alexander. He wondered again if she could read his mind. Given her effort to assuage his fears, he stood to depart. "Thank you for your reassurances, Celine. I apologize for my faintheartedness."

Celine stood, offering a fleeting smile. "There is no apology necessary. My husband can drive even the fiercest men to cowardice. However, I find no such weakness in you. You shall prove a staunch ally, Alexander."

"Good day, Celine," he said, bowing to her. "I look forward to your visit with much anticipation."

"I shall see you in two days, Alexander. Safe travels."

He departed from the Northcott residence. His mind swam with deliberations. The events of the past few days were dizzying. While not directly involved in most instances, he had watched Duke Northcott's power grow over the years. Without warning, a visit from the strange and mysterious Carlyles had thrown him into dealings with the Northcotts. In addition, it now appeared Duke Northcott's chokehold on the world may be coming to an abrupt end.

Despite Celine's reassurances, he worried for his family. He was no stranger to the battle between good and evil, but he was familiar with the concept of self-preservation. Some battles were merely beyond his abilities. This may prove to be one of them. Celine was a strong ally, as long as she remained an ally. Her words rang in his head. Could she be trusted? Would the allure of the Duke's power sway her? That remained to be seen.

He hurried home, anxious to get on with his journey. The next two days would prove tedious and be filled with apprehension. He prayed he could trust Celine. Otherwise, he and his family may be doomed.

CHAPTER 25

Marcus entered Celine's bedroom to a flurry of activity. Trunks were strewn about the room, and articles of clothing lay across the bed.

"Celine? What is the meaning of this?" he questioned.

"Alexander Buckley called this afternoon to invite us to stay at his country home. It is meant as a thank you for arranging the invitation for his cousins to Lord Blackburn's ball," she informed him, holding up two shawls, one in each hand. "This one," she said to the maid who hurried to pack it.

"And you accepted?"

"Yes," she answered, glancing at him. "We leave the day after next."

"You did not consider it wise to discuss this with me before accepting the invitation?" Marcus queried, annoyance creeping into his voice.

"No, I did not. He was quite earnest, and I did not see the harm in it. Truthfully, I pitied him and could not find it in my heart to decline."

"I understand this is his second call. He called upon you yesterday as well?"

"Yes," Celine answered without skipping a beat, "he called yesterday to ask if I was keen on the countryside. I told him I find it quite relaxing. He returned this afternoon to extend the invitation."

"Do you not find his sudden interest odd?"

"No, I do not." She glanced to him. "You could use a few days in the country, away from your work. You must make time to relax, Marcus."

"You attempt to draw my attention from the subject at hand and flatter me into agreeing."

"I do not," she answered, returning to her packing. "I am stating a fact. Your machinations are quite taxing, no doubt, dear. If you are unable to depart in two days' time, I shall travel ahead, and you may follow."

"You will do no such thing, Celine!"

"Marcus, I will not argue about this. I have already accepted the invitation."

"Celine..." he protested.

"Marcus, please," she interrupted him. "I do not wish to argue. If you do not find the invitation acceptable, I shall make your excuses for you when I arrive. However, I will carry on with the planned journey. I do not wish to appear rude." The maid approached with a gown. "No, no, Winston, that is most unsuitable. It is a country estate, not Buckingham Palace!" The girl departed with the dress to select something more suitable, murmuring her apologies. "Please remember a warm capelet, there could be snow!" Celine shouted after her.

"I find this most unacceptable, Celine," Marcus said once they were alone.

"Do you, really, husband? I am unsure what you envisage as an appropriate response, however, I suggest you adjust your expectations."

"I will not be spoken to in this manner, Celine," he warned her.

"And I will not be treated as a child. You are displeased, I understand. The invitation is below your normal standard. However, I expect the trip to be most interesting." She approached him, caressing his face with her hand. "Try to see the positive in it, dear."

He sighed. "I shall follow you in three days hence. Please in the future do not make a habit of accepting such invitations without first discussing it with me. Buckley is after something, Celine. I warn you to be wary of him."

"Of course, dear," Celine answered, returning to her packing. "Though I see nothing malevolent in his intentions."

"You are too trusting, Celine. This is why you should consult with me before consenting to requests."

Celine stopped for a moment, turning to face him. "You are quite right, my dear. I am far too trusting. A fact I've grown to learn of late, more and more with each passing day."

He offered her a slight smile before departing from the room. Celine returned to her packing.

* * *

PRESENT DAY, **Bucksville**

"Absolutely not! No way, no how, over my dead body!" Gray shouted.

Celine stood near the fireplace; arms crossed. "We have little choice."

"We'll find another way," Gray argued.

"What way, Gray?" Celine countered.

"I don't care for the idea either. However, Celine makes an excellent point," Alexander interjected. "We have no information about Alterra."

"Then we'll find information. We'll go to Germany if we must. Anything except…"

"We don't have time, Gray," Celine responded. "Damien and Michael are dying. If we waste time searching for information about Alterra and how to retrieve someone from there, they could die."

Gray crossed his arms, staring out the window. "There's got to be another way."

"There isn't," Celine refuted. "Not that we have time for, anyway."

Gray glanced to Alexander and Millie. "You've never come across any information about Alterra?" he questioned Alexander.

"I've never heard the term until today. I've consulted all my references. I've found one obscure reference. But enough knowledge to enter and rescue someone from this realm? No, I have nothing to offer. I'm sorry, Gray. If it helps, I hate this plan as much as you do."

"It doesn't. What about medically? Is there anything we can do to prolong their lives while we search for information?"

Millie shook her head. "I'm sorry, Gray. There is nothing I can do."

"How long do we have?" Gray asked.

"I'm not one hundred percent certain, but I'd say days."

Celine shook her head after Millie delivered the grim news. "They're dying, Gray. We have no choice."

"There must be another choice!" Gray argued, resuming his staring out the window.

"What? Tell me? Because if you can't tell me right now, it's not an option. We can't waste any more time. We don't have the time to waste exploring options! You heard Millie. We have days!"

Gray refused to answer. Celine continued, "When I was

missing, Damien risked his life to save me. I must do the same for him."

"You can't do this, Celine," Gray argued.

"I must!" Celine insisted.

"Do you imagine the plan will work?" Alexander asked.

"Yes," Celine replied.

"We have no assurance this will work. We could end up worse off than we are now," Gray countered.

"I can't live with myself if Damien dies, Gray. Or Michael. We must try. We must take the chance."

"You're playing with fire, Celine."

Celine sighed. "I understand how you feel. But I will not gamble with Damien's life."

"You're already gambling."

"I agree with you, Gray," Alexander interjected. "It is a huge gamble. However, Celine makes a good point. Damien and Michael *will* die if we do nothing."

"I don't propose we do nothing."

"But we don't have time, Gray," Millie replied. "Your plan would be acceptable if those men had weeks or months to live."

"Millie is correct. The amount of time it would take us to track down and assimilate information far outreaches the amount of time they can survive," Alexander assessed.

"Damn it," Gray muttered through clenched teeth.

"For the record, it's not my favorite plan either. But I don't see another choice," Celine stated.

"So, that's it then," Gray grumbled.

"I'm sorry, Gray," Celine responded, staring at him, concern on her face.

"It's okay, Celine. I understand. I realize what we must do. I don't like it. I hate it, in fact, but I accept that it must be done. We're all in agreement then?"

Alexander and Millie nodded.

"Well," Celine answered, taking a deep breath. "then that's it. We're all in agreement. I know what I must do. I must bring back Marcus Northcott."

* * *

1812, LONDON

Michael eyed the carriage outside the house through the window. "How long is this ride again?"

"Better part of the day," Gray answered him.

Michael groaned. Gray glanced to him, then Damien.

"He hates carriage rides," Damien informed Gray.

Gray furrowed his brow in confusion. "Hates carriage rides? They are quite convenient and comfortable. Much more so than riding."

Michael chortled, finding the comment comical. "Are we sure we can't do this here? Celine's already in London!"

"If we want her husband and his associates breathing down our necks the entire time, listening at the doors, questioning our sudden interest in paying her calls or the opposite, then yes!" Gray countered.

Michael glanced out of the window again, watching the last of the trunks being loaded onto the carriage. He groaned as he realized they would soon leave.

The coachmen knocked at the front door, telling Gray everything was prepared. "We are ready," Gray informed them, donning his cloak.

Michael and Damien followed suit and exited the house. Michael scowled at the carriage as they approached.

"Come on, buddy, it won't be that bad. It has to be better than Martinique twenty years ago," Damien said, passing him and climbing into the carriage.

Michael climbed in behind him. "I still fail to understand on the most epic of levels how you enjoy this."

Gray joined them, closing the door behind him. He tapped on the window behind him, and the coachmen cracked his whip, setting the carriage in motion. The carriage lurched forward, bouncing them around as they began their journey down the cobblestone street.

"Nope," Michael said with a shake of his head.

"What?" Damien questioned.

"This is no better than Martinique twenty years ago."

Damien chuckled at him. "Don't worry, buddy. With any luck, this will all be over soon, and we'll be home."

"I will never take my car for granted again," Michael promised, staring out the window as they turned onto another street.

Gray observed the exchange, oblivious to some of what they spoke about. Despite some of their explanations, he failed to understand the full scope of their world. Damien assured him one day he would.

They arrived at the Buckley estate just before dinner. Alexander greeted them as their carriage slowed to a stop.

Damien climbed from the carriage behind Gray and Michael. He glanced up at the house. "Oh, wow!"

"Yeah, weird, right?" Michael said.

"What is?" Alexander inquired.

"It's just like your house in Maine!" Damien replied.

Alexander stared at him, an odd expression on his face. "I have no house in Maine."

Michael and Damien glanced at each other.

"You do where we're from. Well, technically, it's in Massachusetts right now. Maine isn't a state until 1820," Damien responded. "Oh, well, nothing else is the same. Why should that be?"

"Well, shall we? Our meal should almost be prepared," Alexander replied, motioning toward the front door.

"Yes, I'm starving," Damien responded.

"You are in luck," Alexander replied. "There is plenty of food prepared. We'll go straight to the dining room if that's all right."

"Okay by me," Damien responded.

Michael nodded in agreement.

As they walked to the dining room, a path familiar to both Michael and Damien since the route was identical to the one at Alexander's home in Maine, Gray asked Alexander about his conversation with Celine. "How did your conversation with Celine unfold? When will she arrive?"

"She arrives tomorrow. I must warn everyone, she expects Duke Northcott to travel with her."

Shock crossed Gray's face and dismay settled onto the faces of Michael and Damien.

"Are you joking?" Damien asked after a moment.

"I'm afraid not," Alexander said as they sat down for their meal.

"This is unexpected. I thought the point was for her to be unencumbered," Gray replied. "Perhaps we should reconsider."

"I experienced similar misgivings. Michael, Damien," Alexander responded, "does the Celine in your world possess the ability to read minds?"

Michael and Damien glanced at each other.

Damien shook his head. "No. Not that I'm aware of."

"Why?" Michael asked, eyeing the dirty water in his water goblet, then opting to drink the wine instead.

"As I mentioned, I experienced similar reservations after Celine revealed the information about Duke Northcott. She was quick to assure me that she could handle him."

"I'm not concerned about her handling him. I expected to

be able to speak freely, wasn't that the point of this?" Damien asked.

"I imagine we can speak more freely here than in either of our homes in London," Alexander countered.

"You may not be concerned about her handling Duke Northcott, but I am. The man excels in supernatural powers. If he suspects our motivations are to persuade his wife to our side, he will not hesitate to unleash them on us," Gray objected.

"Celine asserted she is equally talent and well-versed in his methods. She also mentioned his limitations. Although I confess, I am aware of none. She assured me we were in no danger."

"No danger?" Gray balked. "Wonderful, as long as he does not convince her to remain loyal to him."

"No way, not Celine," Damien countered. "She'll choose the side of good, not evil."

"She's been married to the man for twenty-six years. Time may mean loyalty runs deeper than we expect."

"But she said…" Damien began.

"It doesn't matter what she said," Gray interrupted him. "She was in shock. When the shock passes, she could easily decide her husband is still worthy of her allegiance."

"What happened to you and your 'she's lovely' bit?" Michael questioned.

"She is," Gray admitted, his voice turning wistful. He quickly strengthened it, adding, "She's also powerful and dangerous. And there is no limit to what Marcus Northcott will do to keep control of his power. And hers."

"Gentlemen, I realize this may not seem like much," Alexander responded. "But she was adamant about her unchanging loyalty to us. She assured me not only would she allow no harm to come to any of us, but that she would not change her mind regarding where her loyalties lie."

"It's not her I'm worried about," Gray confessed. "It's him. Will she have the resilience to resist him?"

"She will," Damien assured them.

"You seem confident," Gray replied.

"We are," Michael answered. "Where we come from, she's done it for centuries."

"Yet this Celine behaves so oddly you barely recognize her, so what assurance do we have?" Gray questioned.

Michael and Damien were silent for a moment. "None, I guess," Damien responded. "But we have to try. And we have to trust Celine. She has never let us down before. Let's hope this time is no different."

"I agree with Damien," Alexander chimed in. "Plus, I'm afraid we haven't much choice. Short of refusing the Duke and Duchess when they arrive, the plan is set in motion."

They finished their meal, making conversation that avoided discussing the upcoming visit. Nervous energy kept everyone awake well into the night. Celine would arrive tomorrow prior to dinner. Damien practiced what he would say to her. He must convince her. The doubts and trepidations expressed over dinner weighed on his mind. What if the new Celine, however she was created, didn't respond like the old Celine? What if she didn't pick good over evil? Would she remain loyal to Marcus Northcott? Were they walking into a trap designed to remove any obstacle from the Northcotts' path? No, he wouldn't believe that, he told himself. They would convince her. They must. Or they were doomed.

CHAPTER 26

The next morning brought a cold, clear day. Michael and Damien spent the latter part of the morning taking in the grounds of the estate. Nervous anticipation for Celine's arrival did not allow them to remain still.

As they trekked around the property, Michael questioned, "Is time standing still?"

"Sure seems like it," Damien responded. "It's been morning forever. Although perhaps that's a good thing."

"Yeah. I'm not thrilled with this plan either at the moment. She's bringing the Duke with her? Why does this seem like a horrible, horrible idea now that it's happening?"

"Because we assumed Celine was coming alone to learn the truth and then..." he paused. "I guess I don't know what I assumed would happen after that. I never thought that far ahead. Gray's right. She's been married to the guy for almost thirty years. Is she just going to leave him?"

"Did people do that in the 1800s?" Michael queried.

"Maybe? I'm not sure," Damien answered.

"Really? A historical fact you don't know?" Michael joked.

Damien shook his head at him. "Very funny. I'm sure they did, actually. Henry the eighth did, multiple times."

Michael scoffed. "How did I know you'd have a historical reference in the end?"

Damien smirked at him. "Because I'm me, that's what I do."

"Anyway, why is she bringing him with her? How did she consider that a good idea?"

"Perhaps she doesn't have a choice," Damien theorized. "It's unusual for a woman to travel to someone's house without her husband, particularly if it's outside of her family."

"So, then what are the chances she's going to leave him, and this all corrects itself? If she's bringing him for appearance's sake, will she really leave him?"

"Perhaps she's still deciding. Perhaps she's as unsure as we are."

"Celine? Unsure?" Michael questioned.

"Well, turn it around and view it from her perspective. And remember, this isn't 'our' Celine," Damien replied. "At sixteen, her sister introduces her to this man. He has her father murdered, shoves his dead body in her face and tells her it'll all be okay if she sticks with him. No one is there to help her. What choice did she have?"

"But she was so spirited when we met her, why did she give in?"

"Yeah, she was," Damien agreed. "But she also had help… from us. Spunk only gets you so far. She may have resisted. With no one there to help her, he may have harassed her for hours or days until she finally gave in. The only reason he didn't have that opportunity the last time was because we were there to help her."

"Okay, good point."

They turned a corner in the garden. "Okay, continuing,

no one helps her, she gets stuck married to this guy. And by the appearance of it, it's a decent marriage in terms of her position. She wants for nothing, she's sought after in society, it is a good match for her. After twenty-some odd years, someone shows up and blows up her world. Tells her the man she's married to is responsible for her father's death. Even if she is questioning everything, she's got to be unsure, perhaps even scared. What will become of her? What if we're lying?"

"Okay, that seems reasonable enough. It's just weird imagining Celine scared and clinging to… that bastard."

"I agree, but we need to be sensitive to her uncertainty. We don't realize what she's been through in this version of events."

Michael nodded in agreement. "So, what do we do?"

"We tell her the truth. All of it. But we highlight the good parts like how strong she is and how much good she's done as the Celine we know."

Michael nodded again. "Right, okay. So, leave out the part about how the Duke made her life miserable for centuries."

"Perhaps not leave it out, but I wouldn't dwell on it. She needs to realize what she's in for, but let's not make it sound so horrible."

"Agreed. Okay, we have our plan. We tell her the truth, sort of," Michael responded.

"And hope it corrects everything and we can go back home to normal Celine."

"Yeah, fingers crossed. This version of Celine is kind of… terrifying."

"Tell me about it. All I could think about when she was doing her thing with that criminal was what she might do to us if it didn't work out the way we thought."

"Yep," Michael agreed. "I do not have any desire to get on this Celine's bad side."

"Me either. So, we tell her the truth… sort of." Damien grinned.

* * *

CELINE'S CARRIAGE pulled up the drive to the Buckley country estate late in the afternoon. She glanced out the window at the modest estate. Marcus would follow her here tomorrow. She hoped to have learned everything she needed to by then. What she learned while here would dictate her next move. In addition, she hoped to learn more about the Carlyles. Who were these strange men and where had they come from? How were they aware of so much about her life? She hoped to have all these questions answered this evening.

The carriage wound to a halt outside the front door. Four men waited to greet her. She waited inside the carriage until the coachmen opened her door, extending his hand to assist her as she exited. She stepped from the carriage, adjusting her dress before greeting her hosts.

"Celine," Alexander greeted her, stepping forward. "Welcome."

"You are alone," Gray noted. "I was under the impression Duke Northcott would travel with you."

"Duke Northcott extends his apologies. He will arrive tomorrow in time for dinner. He had pressing business that did not allow him to leave London just yet," Celine explained.

Damien could have leapt for joy. It was only one night, but still, it was twenty-hour hours that they had alone with Celine to convince her of the mistake she made on her sixteenth birthday.

"Either way, we are pleased to welcome you, Celine," Alexander reiterated.

"I am pleased to be here, Alexander," she answered.

Gray offered her his arm to escort her inside. She accepted, smiling at him. The group made their way inside the house and Alexander led the way to her bedroom. "I hope you will find it suitable," he commented as she entered.

"Most suitable, thank you. If you do not mind, I should like to rest before dinner."

"Of course," Alexander answered.

"I look forward to seeing you at dinner, Celine," Gray told her, closing the door behind him as he and Alexander exited.

They met Michael and Damien in the foyer.

"It appears we are in luck. Celine traveled alone, so we have free access for the time being to discuss her husband with her," Alexander stated.

"Yes, one day is better than none, I guess," Michael agreed.

"I'm still uncomfortable with the idea of that man being in this house," Gray said, crossing his arms.

"With any luck, he won't be here that long," Damien answered.

"You really imagine she will leave him?" Gray questioned.

"I'm not sure, but if she wasn't considering it, why would she have come here?"

No one answered for a moment.

"Perhaps," Gray said, "she merely wants to learn what kind of man she is married to and has no intention of acting on the information."

"To what end?" Damien inquired. "Who would want to know their husband is a complete bastard so they could keep on living with them like nothing happened?"

"Perhaps she'll confront him about it, and they'll have a row and put it behind them," Gray suggested.

"Your husband ordering the death of your father isn't something you have an argument about and then leave behind," Damien argued.

"I agree. Plus, the way she looks at you," Michael said to Gray, "I think we stand a good chance."

"At me? You must be joking," Gray answered.

"Yes, at you," Michael responded. "It's the same look she gives you where we're from."

"And in our reality, she's been married to you for over two centuries," Damien said with a coy expression.

"It's true. The only genuine expression I've witnessed on her face has been when she's near you," Michael added.

Gray considered the information. "It may mean nothing. Perhaps you're reading her wrong."

"I'm not," Michael responded.

Gray opened his mouth to respond, but Damien cut him off. "He's not. He'd know best. Michael and Celine were sort of a couple for a bit."

"I thought you said Celine was married to Gray for over two centuries?" Alexander queried.

"She was, she is," Damien began. "It's complicated. She was Celine and then she wasn't and then she was again. When she wasn't Celine, she and Michael were together, but then when she was Celine again there was no question who she was in love with." Damien glanced to Michael. "Sorry, buddy."

Michael waved his hand at him to dismiss it.

"You're making no sense," Gray responded.

"I told you, it's complicated. Never mind, it's not important. The important part is she is in love with you and has been for centuries. We're sure this Celine is, too. Michael is correct. The most genuine expression I've seen on her face since we've met this Celine is when she looks at you."

"Are you telling me you don't have any feelings toward her at all?" Michael asked Gray.

Gray didn't respond for a moment. "She's a married woman, I hadn't considered it."

"I don't buy that story for a second," Michael answered.

"Yeah, mister 'I'll walk you home for companionship,'" Damien chimed in. "You want us to believe you have no interest in her?"

"She's beautiful, I'll admit it. But she's married."

"And if she weren't?" Alexander inquired.

Gray took a moment before he answered. "She is."

"But if she weren't?"

"If she weren't, I'd have married her in a heartbeat. Is that what you want to hear?"

Michael and Damien glanced to each other, grinning.

"Yep, that's what we wanted to hear," Damien responded.

* * *

As dinner approached, Celine appeared downstairs, dressed in a different gown for the event. They made light conversation over cocktails before entering the dining room. Once they were seated for dinner, Alexander continued his discussion about the estate.

After a brief pause in the conversation, Celine said, "Gentlemen, do you plan to continue discussing trivial pleasantries all evening? My husband will arrive in less than twenty-four hours. I hoped to learn by then what you know and how you came to this knowledge."

The men glanced to one another before Alexander spoke. "My apologies, Celine. I did not care to ruin your meal with such discussions. They must be painful for you to endure."

"Duke Northcott is the source of the pain, not you. Thereby you cannot ruin my meal by speaking the truth."

They were silent another moment until Damien spoke up. "Well, I guess it's our turn then," he said, clearing his throat. Celine rested her crystal blue eyes on him. "Like I said before, we knew about your father because we were with you that night."

"That I cannot understand. No one accompanied me that fateful night."

"It's a long story," Damien responded.

"I have twenty-four hours. Unless the story is longer than that, please explain."

"Well," Damien began, glancing to Michael.

Michael nodded to him.

"We aren't from this time. We're from the future."

"How did you come to be in this time?" Celine inquired.

"We're not sure," Michael answered. "We've traveled through time before. In the other two instances when we time traveled, you sent us back. The first time to help you on your sixteenth birthday and retrieve *The Book of the Dead* and the second time to stop the Duke from stealing a painting that contained a shard of your soul."

Damien picked up where he left off. "This time we have no memory of you sending us back. We think some electrical pulse hit us and sent us back here. But everything here is completely different than it was where we came from. In the future we came from, we're good friends. And you never married the Duke."

"That's right," Michael continued. "On your sixteenth birthday, we were there. We helped you escape from him and took his book to our time where you used it to send him back to Hell."

"But when that shock wave hit us and we woke up here, we found Alexander and he said you were married to the Duke!"

"How did you know to seek out Alexander? How is he connected to this?" She glanced at Alexander. "Are you, too, from the future?"

He shook his head. "No, I am not."

"We're *all* really good friends in the future," Damien said, motioning to encompass all of them. "We knew Alexander from our time."

"How have I survived until your time if I did not surrender to Marcus's demands that night?" Celine asked.

"When you took the book and ran, the man who killed your father chased you. He stabbed you and you almost died. The Duke happened upon you and revived you. You then stabbed him, hence drawing blood during the ceremony, and that turned you into what you are," Damien explained.

"And then?" Celine inquired, her face a mask of confusion.

"We're not one hundred percent sure of what happened after. You sent us back to our time right after that. We left you on the beach in Martinique," Michael described.

"Reluctantly," Damien pointed out.

"Yes, we didn't want to leave you, but you said you couldn't leave, and you'd be okay."

"Anyway, in the years that followed, you were meant to meet and marry… someone else. You'll spend centuries with that person. That's beside the point. The point is, Celine, you were never supposed to marry the Duke. You were never supposed to be on his side. Something is wrong here. And we assume we were sent to this time to fix it."

"We obviously need your help to return to our time, so at the very least, we needed to meet you and get you to agree to help us return to the future," Michael said. "But Damien is correct, this isn't the way things were supposed to happen."

Celine paused for a moment before responding. "Well, I must admit, gentlemen, this is quite incredible. Your claims are almost too fantastic to believe, yet they are grounded in some truth. And I must admit to sensing a strange draw to you."

"When we first arrived here," Damien responded, "we had

no idea how or why we were here. We sought out Alexander because we assumed he could put us in contact with you to go home but… he didn't know us or you."

"And if you send us home now," Michael added, "we'll return to a world unrecognizable to us."

"Right," Damien agreed. "So, we must fix things."

"In other words, you must fix things, as you put it, so you are more comfortable in your world?"

"No!" Damien argued. "We must fix things because this is wrong! What's happening is wrong! You weren't meant to be on the bad side, Celine!"

Celine considered their comments for a moment. "You've given me much to consider," she said at length. She stood from the table.

"Oh, come on, Celine!" Damien exclaimed, also standing. "You can't say that and leave!"

Celine's eyes grew wide. "What would you have me do? What is it you expect of me?"

"I expect you to be the Celine we know," Damien said, approaching her. "I know you're in there. The good Celine, the honest Celine, the Celine who would fight for her friends and her family. I expect you to help us correct what's gone wrong with history, so when we go home, the world is normal again."

"Yet you only share part of your information," Celine responded.

"That's not true!" Michael shouted, leaping from his chair.

"Isn't it? We're all good friends in your time. You leave out details. How did we meet? To whom am I married? These events may not be possible to correct! My life has already hurled me toward the precipice. Decisions aren't easily reversed. Choices may not be able to be undone! Options may not exist to correct the wrongs as you see them. I fail to understand what you propose I do. You have given me no direction toward which you seek me to go. Therefore, I must consider what you've said and guide my own path."

"No, Celine," Damien responded, his voice gentle, taking her hands in his. "Not alone. Together. We're your friends. We care about you, we love you. We want to help."

Michael joined them around the table. "Yes," he said, putting an arm around her shoulders. "We aren't keeping things from you, but we don't know how much to say. We don't know how much we can tell you without impacting the future in some irreparable way. And we don't know your sentiments on the situation. Tell us what you're thinking, what you're feeling. Help us help you."

The four men at the table waited with bated breath for Celine's response.

CHAPTER 27

Celine glanced between the two of them. Damien recognized a glimmer of the Celine he knew in her eyes as she searched their faces. He felt her hands tremble, saw the tears welling in her eyes.

She collapsed into the chair. "I have never felt so alone," Celine choked out, a tear streaming down her cheek.

Gray rushed to offer her a handkerchief.

She accepted it, apologizing. "Forgive me for my outburst."

"There is no apology needed, Celine," Gray assured her.

Damien pulled a chair next to her, sitting down and putting his arm around her. "You're not alone, Celine. We're all here to help you. We don't want you to live this life. We want you to be happy. I want to see you smile again!"

"Am I happy in your world?" she asked, sniffling.

"Very," Damien answered.

Celine pondered a moment. "What must I do?"

Damien took her hands in his. "I think you realize what you must do, Celine."

* * *

PRESENT DAY, BUCKSVILLE

Celine readied herself for her trip, pulling on a heavy cardigan. She planned to check on Damien and Michael before she departed. Gray knocked at the door, entering. She smiled at him without a word.

Gray leaned his side against the far wall, his arms crossed. "I hate this, you know."

She glanced at him again, pulling her hair into a ponytail. "I know and I'm sorry. It's not my idea of a good plan either, but it's all we have."

"It's not your fault. As usual, it's his. At least this time he'll have to clean up his mess."

"It's both of ours, Gray. And neither. Neither of us realized this would happen. Neither of us set out to harm Michael or Damien in this way."

"Ha!" Gray guffawed. "That man sets out to harm anything he comes into contact with. He destroys anything in his general vicinity."

Celine didn't respond, instead, digging through her jewelry box.

"I'm sorry, Celine. I realize you have enough strain on you. I don't mean to make things worse."

"You aren't making anything worse, Gray. But there is nothing to say. I don't disagree with you, but I will not let Damien die. Not if there's a chance I can save him."

"Do you really think you can trust him?"

"No, I don't trust him, but I do trust that he has the knowledge to help us."

"What assurance do you have that he'll help?"

"None, but I convinced him to help Celeste."

"He assumed you would marry him then."

Celine's shoulders sagged. "I must try, Gray. Damien is dying! I cannot live with myself if I let him die without trying everything to help."

"Yes, I understand. I hate it, but I understand. You've always been the braver one of us. For God's sake, though, Celine, be careful."

"I will," Celine agreed. She pulled an item from her jewelry box, wrapped in a velvet bag.

"What's that?" Gray inquired, approaching her.

"An ice crystal. Mined from the ice caves in Shadow World," Celine informed him, removing the round, flat, colorless stone from the velvet bag. The stone emanated a frosty air around it. Gray crinkled his brow as he stared at it. "It's a peace offering for the adjudicator. This is the second time I'll interrupt its repose in Shadow World. I'd rather not be on its bad side."

"Smart. Where did you get a hold of that?"

"From Marcus. Odd that I will use it to free him from there."

Gray shook his head. "I hate to think of that man free. Are you sure you should go alone?"

"Yes," Celine answered. "I'll be fine. It would be best to go alone. We're already disturbing the adjudicator. It would be best for only one of us to do that. And needless to say, the conversation with Marcus will proceed far better without your presence."

"The idea of you having a conversation with that man makes my skin crawl."

"And that is why it will proceed far better without you. You both hate the sight of one another. It will set him off right away if you appear."

"Yes, I realize that," Gray responded. "Don't worry, if he does agree to help, I won't get in his way."

Celine smiled at him. "Thanks, Gray. Okay, I am ready. But first I want to check on Michael and Damien."

Celine and Gray returned to Alexander's and navigated to Michael's room first. She sat on the edge of his bed, reading the monitors around him.

His pulse was steady, his heart rate in normal range. He breathed in rhythm. He seemed the picture of health, if not for his blue lips and ice-cold hands.

They moved to Damien's room. His status matched Michael's. His vitals were within normal range, with the exception of his temperature. His lips were tinged blue and his hands frigid to the touch.

Celine sat next to him for a moment. She slipped her hand under the covers, grasping his freezing hand. It sent a chill through her.

"Hang in there, D. I'm going for help. We're going to bring you home, just hang in there until we do." Celine kissed his forehead, caressing his face with her hand. "Okay. Now, I'm ready."

Gray kissed her forehead. "Hurry back."

"I will."

Celine departed the room, heading back to her own room at Alexander's. She took a deep breath, settling onto the bed. She relaxed her mind, shutting her eyes and the world out. She took slow, rhythmic breaths, concentrating. She slipped into Shadow World while imprisoned by Marcus. She could do it again. She focused her energy, allowing the earthly realm to fall away as she sought the cold and colorless realm of Shadow World.

Within minutes, she navigated to it. She stepped into the grayscale world, pulling her sweater tighter against the chill. She glanced around, listening for any sound in the stillness to locate the adjudicator. After a moment, she heard its shrill call.

Celine navigated toward the sound. She found the adjudicator near an ice cave, gliding through the sky, twirling from front to back, a sign of relaxation for the creatures. She stepped into view. The adjudicator spotted her on its next pass. Its wings fluttered in agitation as it ceased its barrel rolls through the sky.

The adjudicator shot toward the ground like a bullet, sliding to a halt and righting itself just before landing. "What is the meaning of this, Celine Devereaux Buckley?"

Its eyes burned fire red and its wings flapped in agitation.

"Hello," Celine began. "I'm sorry to disturb you… again. But it is urgent." Celine slipped the ice crystal from the velvet bag. "I have brought a peace offering." She offered the crystal to the adjudicator.

Its eyes grew wide, turning from red to white. "Is it…"

"Yes," Celine answered, "an ice crystal. Mined from the caves here. Please take it."

The adjudicator snatched it from her hand with its claw. It rolled the stone in its clawed hand, rubbing it. "Why do you seek me here, Celine Devereaux Buckley?"

"I must request that Marcus Northcott return to the material realm with me. I require his help."

"You've sought me out during my repose to ask me to return Marcus Northcott to earth?"

"Yes," Celine answered. "It is urgent. I require his help, only he possesses the knowledge I need."

"Celine Devereaux Buckley, do you realize what you ask? You yourself landed here after a conflict with Marcus Northcott. To prevent further conflict while I enjoy my repose, I kept him here. Now you seek me to return him?"

"Yes."

"And you use an ice crystal as a bribe?" it asked her, waving the crystal at her, its eyes turning red.

"No, no," Celine corrected. "Not as a bribe, as an apology

for disturbing your repose for a second time. It cannot be avoided, however. It is a matter of life and death, and Marcus is the only one I know who possesses the knowledge to assist me. No matter your decision, you may keep the crystal."

"Has he agreed to assist you?"

"I have not spoken with him yet. If you are not agreeable, it makes no difference if he agrees or not."

The adjudicator considered her statements. "Your request is granted, Celine Devereaux Buckley. He waits in the cabin behind you. Please speak with Marcus Northcott and depart from this realm at once!"

The adjudicator unfurled its wings to fly away, but Celine stopped it. "Just a moment."

It curled its wings against its back.

Celine swallowed hard, realizing her request may ruin the progress she made. Still, she must try for her family's safety. "Might you consider signing his soul to me?"

The adjudicator fluttered its wings, unhappy with the request. "Celine Devereaux Buckley!" it boomed, its eyes fiery red. "What do you mean by this request?"

"Only that you are correct. Our bitter battles have endured for centuries. I fear if he returns to earth unchecked, we may disturb your peaceful repose once again. If I control his soul, there is less chance."

The adjudicator considered her request.

"It is not unreasonable. He has sought to control my soul for centuries," she reminded the adjudicator. "In fact, he holds a soul shard belonging to me right now."

"His soul is not mine to give," the adjudicator countered.

"That is not true," Celine argued. "You are the current holder of his soul. You may return it to his master, to him, or give it to me or anyone you choose. I am asking that you give it to me for your own peace."

The adjudicator considered it. "This is a most unusual request, Celine Devereaux Buckley."

"But not an unfair one. I have no malicious schemes intended, I merely request his assistance and prefer to stave off any battles while you are… unavailable. We may revisit the subject at your convenience. Therefore, the situation I request is only temporary."

The adjudicator mulled her case. "Granted, Celine Devereaux Buckley, as a temporary peace-keeping measure. We will revisit at the end of my repose. I shall place a portal outside the cabin. Leave when you have completed your business."

"Thank you," she stated with a smile.

The adjudicator shot into the sky, leaving Celine on the ground. She turned, finding the cabin the adjudicator mentioned near a grove of trees uphill from her. She drew in a deep breath, preparing herself.

Celine hiked the gentle, sloping hill to the cabin. She stood straighter, squaring her shoulders and taking another deep breath.

She turned the doorknob, pushing through the door. Marcus sat near a roaring fireplace, a book in his hands.

He glanced up as the door opened. An expression of shock covered his face. "Celine?"

"Hello, Marcus," Celine responded.

"I must admit, I am shocked to see you."

"I am shocked to be here, but I had no choice."

"The adjudicator?" he queried.

"No," Celine answered. She paused a moment, swallowing hard. "I need your help, Marcus."

"My help?" Marcus questioned. "Is that what you said?"

Celine sighed, rolling her eyes. "Yes, Marcus. I need your help."

"Oh, forgive me, my dear," Marcus answered, standing

and approaching her. "I presumed I misunderstood. Celine Devereaux, asking for my help? I never imagined I'd see the day."

"Believe me, you were our last choice."

"But I was still your choice." He smirked at her.

Celine allowed him his moment. "So, you'll help me?"

"Why would I? After your most recent betrayal, what would make you assume I would deign to help you with anything?"

"Because it releases you from Shadow World if you do," Celine responded.

"Hmm," Marcus murmured, considering the information. "The question becomes, is my freedom worth the price you ask? Assumedly, I shall be free again anyway once the adjudicator finishes its repose."

"That won't be for months," Celine pointed out. "Plus, there is no guarantee it will return you to earth afterwards."

Marcus raised an eyebrow at her. "What are the circumstances of your request?"

"It's Damien and Michael," Celine responded, her voice wavering at the mention of Damien's name. "That pulse that burst from our battle, the one that sent us here… it's done something to them. From the symptoms, I believe they may be in Alterra."

"What are the symptoms?" Marcus inquired. The barely discernible whimper in her voice as she mentioned Damien's name did not escape him. While she presented a brave front, it was obvious the situation distressed her.

"They experience elevated breathing, heart rate, and brain activity at the same times. And their body temperatures are dropping."

Marcus considered the information. "You may be correct. What do you want from me, Celine?"

"I want you to help me get them back."

"How?"

"You've been there. You understand how to get there and how to get back. I need you to help me get them back."

"It's true. I have visited Alterra," Marcus admitted.

"So, will you help me?"

Celine stared up at him, blinking away tears as she awaited his response. Would he help her? Or would Michael and Damien be sentenced to death?

CHAPTER 28

eline stared at him as he considered her request.

"I cannot fathom Buckley agreeing to this," Marcus answered.

"Gray has agreed. They are dying, Marcus. We have little other choice. I will not let them die."

"So, here you are."

"Yes, here I am. Now, will you help me? Please?" She rested her pleading eyes on him again.

He stared at her teary crystal blue eyes for a moment, then averted his gaze. "I'll need to return to earth. Have you cleared your request with the adjudicator?"

"I have."

Marcus smiled, raising his eyebrows and returning his gaze to her. "My, my, Celine, you really are talented. You have quite a way with that adjudicator."

Celine sighed and flung her arms out. "Well? You've yet to answer me. Will you help me?"

"Oh, I'm sorry, Celine. I was just savoring this moment. The moment Celine has approached me to beg for my help. It really is quite a sensation."

"Yes, Marcus, have your moment. Savor it all you'd like. I am imploring your help. You realize how much Damien in particular means to me. You brought him to me after you imprisoned me because you realized how important he is to me. I would do anything for him, including seek your help. His life is in your hands. What is your decision? Will you help or will you let him die?"

Marcus glanced at her. "All right, Celine. I shall help you. At the very least, it allows me to escape this frigid, desolate place."

Celine breathed a sigh of relief. "Good. Let's go. The adjudicator placed a portal outside of the cabin. I'll return the way I came."

"After you, my dear," Marcus replied.

They left the cabin with Marcus stepping through the portal. After Celine witnessed him depart from the world, she slipped from the realm and back to her own. She opened her eyes, glancing around.

Marcus Northcott stood at the foot of her bed. "Welcome back, Celine."

* * *

1812, Buckley Country Estate

Celine considered their words. She pulled her hands away from Damien's, sitting straighter. "What you ask me to do is difficult, if not impossible."

"We realize it won't be easy. We're not suggesting it will be," Damien responded. "However, living with that man cannot be easy either."

"Especially when it becomes obvious what kind of plans he has," Michael added.

Celine sighed, wiping her face and sniffling. She stared ahead, making eye contact with no one. "I have been aware of his designs for years. Perhaps I am as wicked as he for turning a blind eye toward it for my own comfort."

Everyone assured her she was not.

Damien patted her shoulder. "No, Celine. You did the best you could. He used you, manipulated you. We were there. We know what he said and did to force you into joining him."

"My life has not been difficult. However, it has lacked true happiness and companionship. We are like players on a stage. Well-scripted and choreographed. Each playing our parts with no true emotion."

Damien squeezed her hand. "Your life can be so much more fulfilling, Celine. We promise."

Celine nodded her head, glancing to Damien. She swallowed, composing herself. "I shall write to my sister in the morning. Inform her of the situation and request that I stay with her. My brother-in-law can sort out the legal aspects of the matter."

"No," Michael and Damien answered simultaneously.

Celine's brow furrowed with confusion. "Whatever do you mean?"

"You can't go to Celeste and Teddy," Damien explained. "They're on the Duke's side. They'll tell you to stay with him, try to convince you or worse, force you."

"Surely after I've explained his wicked deeds concerning our father, Celeste will not maintain her loyalty to him."

"She will," Damien informed her. "Trust us, she will. She'll go straight to the Duke. Then you'll be stuck."

Celine shook her head. "Then I've no options. I have nowhere else to go."

"Well…" Damien began.

Gray knelt in front of her, taking her hand. "You'll stay here, Celine. With us."

Celine paused a moment, staring in his stormy blue eyes.

"It is very generous of you. But I cannot accept."

"For what reason?" Gray inquired.

"It will bring too much trouble to you and your family. Not only with Duke Northcott but the general scandal it will cause to your family."

"We'll handle Marcus Northcott. And I'm not worried about scandal," Gray assured her.

"No," Celine responded, pulling her hands from his. "I will not cause this type of scandal for you. I will find another solution."

Gray opened his mouth to speak again. Damien cut him off, speaking first. "You don't have to decide anything right now. It's been a stressful evening. Perhaps you should rest, and we can discuss your options tomorrow."

Celine took the cue. "Yes, I shall rest and hope the dawn brings clarity to me. If you all will excuse me, I shall retire for the evening."

"I'll walk you to your room," Gray offered. He extended his hand to her as he stood. She accepted it, threading her arm through his. Everyone said their good nights and Gray led her from the dining room.

Damien collapsed onto the chair as they departed from the room. "Wow, that was…"

"Stressful," Michael finished.

"Yep."

"I must admit my mind is still reeling," Alexander chimed in.

"That was the most Celine-like I've seen her, though," Damien admitted.

Michael agreed. "That moment, right before she started to cry. Reminded me so much of our Celine."

Damien nodded his head.

"And somewhat like our Celine, she tries to take everything on to herself."

"Yeah," Michael replied. "That's definitely our Celine."

"Well, stubborn or not, at least she's starting to act like she's supposed to. That's a good sign," Damien continued.

"Am I the only one of us concerned about the arrival of Duke Northcott?" Alexander replied as Gray rejoined them in the dining room. "I would have preferred she go to her sister's. The fallout will, no doubt, be immense."

"Celine can handle the Duke," Damien assured them.

"Are we certain of that?" Alexander inquired.

"May I remind you, cousin, it was you assuring us only last night that no harm would come to us."

"That was before you extended our home to her so she could leave her husband. Her very powerful husband."

"If she stays here, she won't let anything happen to you or us," Damien reiterated.

"I'm not sure you understand," Alexander began. "Marcus Northcott has extensive experience in his dealings. Not to mention a good bit of raw talent. He can destroy us without thinking about it."

"We understand. And like we said, Celine will not let that happen."

"I'm not sure she will be able to prevent it," Alexander replied.

"Oh, she can prevent it, all right," Damien answered. "The Celine we know has battled with the Duke for centuries. He's never gotten the best of her. He's made things uncomfortable, but she's never allowed him to destroy anyone close to her."

"We must help her," Gray added.

Alexander sighed. "All right, all right. I shall remind myself of my own advice as of last evening and draw upon your confidence in Celine as we move forward."

"Don't worry, Alexander," Damien responded, standing from his seat, "this is moving in the right direction."

* * *

PRESENT DAY, BUCKSVILLE

Celine sat up, wiping the blood from her nose with the handkerchief Marcus offered her. "Does that happen often?" he inquired.

"No, only when I'm in Shadow World for an extended period of time. Or using most of my energy to keep Damien alive when he's there."

"You should rest, Celine," Marcus suggested.

"We don't have time for rest. Come on," she responded, standing from the bed.

"Just a moment," Marcus interjected, grasping the handkerchief from her hand and wiping a smudge of blood from her face.

Gray opened the door, peering in. He frowned at the scene, stalking into the room. "I thought I heard voices."

"How is Damien?" Celine asked, pushing past Marcus toward Gray.

"No change."

"We're going straight there," she answered, avoiding any conversation between the two men. "Come on," she urged Marcus.

Marcus stalked past Gray, a smirk on his face. "You look a little worse for wear, Buckley. I didn't damage anything vital, did I?"

Gray frowned at him, following him out the door. "Oh, I'm perfectly fine, no thanks to you."

They proceeded down the hall to Damien's room. Millie waited in the room, noting several things on Damien's chart. She raised her eyebrow as Marcus entered the room.

"Hi, Millie," Celine greeted her. "Gray said there's no change?"

"No, none, which is a good thing at this point. There is no sign of further deterioration in their symptoms."

"Thanks," Celine responded as Marcus approached Damien.

He glanced at him, touching his skin with the back of his hand. Celine studied him as he glanced at the monitors.

"They seem to experience intermittent responses to stimuli at various times," Celine mentioned.

"Both of them at the same time?" Marcus inquired.

"Yes. Both of them at the same time," Celine answered.

"Where is the other?" he asked.

"Michael is in the next room," Celine responded, pointing to the wall behind her. They departed Damien's room and went to Michael's. After a moment, Celine said to Marcus, "Well?"

"Well, I'd say you have assessed the situation correctly," Marcus responded.

"So, they're in Alterra?" Gray questioned.

"It seems likely, yes," Marcus answered.

"Can you get them back?" Celine inquired.

"It may not be easy, but yes, I believe I can," Marcus replied.

Celine breathed a sigh of relief. "How soon can you retrieve them?"

Marcus considered it. "That will depend."

"On what?" Gray barked. "Can you help or not?"

"Gray, please," Celine hissed through clenched teeth.

Marcus narrowed his eyes at the man, sighing. "On many things. First, we must determine what Alterra they are in. There are many that exist, you realize. Once we have established that, we will need to find our way to them. And only then can we bring them back."

"So, you have no idea if you can do it or not," Gray surmised.

"What do you need from us?" Celine asked, ignoring Gray's comment.

"I will require several things, most of all your cooperation," Marcus answered, shooting a glance to Gray.

"You have it. Just, please, find them and bring them back before it's too late," Celine replied.

Marcus stared at Gray, his eyebrows raised. Celine tapped him on the chest with the back of her hand, shooting him a look.

He rolled his eyes. "Fine, fine, whatever you say. But I don't trust you and I'll be keeping my eye on your every move."

"A wise idea. Perhaps you'll learn something, Buckley," Marcus shot back.

"Only if I wanted to learn how to be a..."

"Enough! Both of you," Celine interrupted. "The priority is rescuing Damien and Michael before their bodies succumb to the pressures of being in Alterra. I'm not going to listen to the two of you bicker at each other. Let's just do what needs to be done."

"I quite agree, Celine," Marcus answered. "I shall prepare a list of the elements I will need. Perhaps Buckley will be kind enough to retrieve them for me."

Gray shut his eyes, gathering his strength for a moment. "I would be more than happy to," he muttered through clenched teeth.

"Thank you, Gray," Celine said, squeezing his arm. "I'll get you some paper and a pen."

"I'll come with you," Marcus suggested.

"Let's all go," Gray recommended.

They proceeded to the sitting room downstairs, meeting Alexander who waited there.

"Oh, good, another Buckley," Marcus said in greeting.

"Welcome back, Celine. I'm glad to see you were...

successful," Alexander said, shooting Celine a glance.

Celine returned the expression, hinting to him the situation was no more comfortable for her.

Gray poured himself a drink as Celine retrieved the writing instruments for Marcus.

Alexander joined Gray at the drink cart. "Sounds like everything is going well thus far," he said, his voice thick with sarcasm.

"That man is insufferable, and he's even more so now that Celine's asked for his help," Gray answered, staring at Marcus across the room. The man relaxed in one of the leather armchairs as though nothing was amiss in the world.

"I can't imagine any of this is easy for Celine," Alexander mentioned.

"No. I'm afraid my inability to control my animosity toward him is making it worse for her. I refuse to leave her alone with him, but the mere sight of him sets me off."

"I understand, cousin. If you should need a break, let me know. I'd be happy to monitor him for you."

"Thanks. I'll let you know," Gray answered, stalking over to where Celine sat in another armchair near Marcus. He placed his hand on her shoulder, squeezing it. She glanced up at him, grabbing his hand in hers. "You okay? You want a drink?"

"I'm fine," she answered, offering a slight smile.

Marcus glanced up from his work, narrowing his eyes at the scene. He sighed, returning to his writing. Tearing the sheet from the notepad, he held it out. "Here you are."

Gray didn't move.

"Well, chop, chop, Buckley, the faster I get everything I need the faster I can begin work."

Gray closed his eyes a moment, setting his jaw and sighing before he snatched the paper from Marcus's hand. He skimmed the list. "You really need ALL of this?"

"No, I wrote it for my own pleasure," Marcus responded. "Do I look like a man who would waste my own time?"

Celine stood and offered Gray a tight-lipped smile. "Please, Gray, just get everything on the list."

He glanced at Celine, then the list. "Stay with Alexander while I'm gone," Gray said, kissing her on the forehead.

Celine nodded as Gray departed, leaving them alone. She blew out a long breath. "I think I'll go sit with Damien."

"I'll accompany you," Alexander offered.

"Thanks. Help yourself if you want a drink," she offered to Marcus before they left the room.

"Don't worry about me," Marcus called after them. "I'll be just fine."

* * *

1812, BUCKLEY COUNTRY ESTATE

Celine awoke early the next morning. She had slept little, obsessing over her alternatives, the few available. Her new friends informed her Celeste was not an option. With both her parents deceased and no other family to speak of, she had few other options.

Friends tended to be nonexistent in these times. She had nowhere to turn. Gray's offer was her only option at the moment. Yet, she couldn't accept it. She couldn't leave her husband, bringing his wrath on her and whoever helped her. In addition, the scandal it would bring upon their home could bring them to ruin.

She rose from her bed, peering out of the window at the cold, crisp morning. She dressed for the day, leaving her bedroom before breakfast and pulling on a cloak before exiting through the front door, hoping a walk might clear her head.

Celine strolled down the walk leading around the house. Before she turned the corner, someone called her name. She glanced behind her, spotting Gray hurrying down the path.

"Celine, good morning," he greeted her, closing the gap between them.

"Good morning, Gray," she answered.

"Running away?" he inquired. "I wouldn't blame you if you were."

"No," she responded. "Merely hoping a stroll in the crisp morning air might bring clarity to my mind."

"Your mind remains troubled by the conversation from last evening?" Gray asked as they continued around the corner.

"My mind remains troubled by the realization of what I must do, coupled with the lack of options by which I might achieve it."

"What options have you identified?"

"They are few," Celine admitted.

"You do not wish to share them? You were quick to criticize the Carlyles for withholding information."

"You are quick with your tongue, sir," Celine said with a laugh. "You do not allow me to evade your question."

"No, I do not. Because I fear you have identified no options but are too polite to admit it."

"You are quite right," Celine admitted. "I have no family to speak of, no home to seek shelter in. I could, perhaps, stay at one of our other estates until tempers have cooled. However, that may prove problematic."

"You could accept our offer and stay here."

"I couldn't possibly," Celine responded.

"Why? Because it appears improper?"

"That is but one of the many reasons."

"Then allow us to dismiss that reason," Gray replied, stopping along the path to face Celine. "Marry me, Celine."

CHAPTER 29

$\mathcal{C}$eline stared up at his stormy blue eyes. "You must be mad. I am a married woman."

"You are a woman about to leave her husband from a marriage she never should have entered."

"I cannot ask you to give up your life to rescue me from my poor choices," Celine contended.

"You aren't asking me, I am offering."

"I do not believe you realize the full scope of what you offer."

"Don't I?" Gray replied.

"No," Celine answered. "The start to our marriage would not be easy. Beside Duke Northcott's anger, there will be much gossip surrounding it. Your reputation may suffer greatly."

Gray chuckled, flicking his gaze over the gardens. "I don't care much about my reputation, particularly in this country. We shall leave and return to my home in Massachusetts. The scandal will not follow to those shores."

Celine gazed at him a moment, processing the information. "However, your regret may follow."

"My regret?"

"Yes. You make a magnanimous offer, yet you may find the result of my acceptance more tedious than you desired after a time."

"My dear Celine, I doubt I could find marriage to you tedious. I have loved you from the moment I laid eyes on you."

Celine smiled at him.

"And now have I laid all your fears to rest, dear lady?"

"You have made a compelling case," Celine admitted.

"And you have, as you pointed out, no better options. Yet you still hold reluctance. I should be offended."

"There is not much reluctance on my part," Celine declared. "It seems rather odd to accept a marriage proposal when one is still married, however."

"But you will?"

She smiled at him again. "Yes, I will. I know not why I act so frivolously yet I will admit when near you I experience emotions I have never experienced."

Gray returned her smile. "How fortunate I am at this turn of events."

"I am glad you find it so. I express a similar sentiment. I must confess, despite knowing you very little, my heart feels freer with you than I've ever experienced with Marcus."

They walked further along the path, enjoying the crisp morning air. "Are you apprehensive to tell him the news?"

Celine shook her head. "No, although I do imagine he will take it quite badly."

"When will you tell him?" Gray inquired.

"I shan't tell him until we've returned home. There is no need to create a scene here."

Gray ceased walking, shaking his head. "You'll do no such thing."

"You object? Surely you consider it best done privately to minimize the damage and your family's involvement."

"I do not want you alone when you tell him," Gray countered. "You need support. I will not chance him harming you."

"He will blame you, all of you."

They began walking again. "Celine, I will not allow you to return to his house to do this alone."

"Allow me?" Celine questioned, glancing at him with wide eyes.

"As your future husband, you should humor me and follow my advice," he said with a chuckle.

Celine found his laughter contagious. "I shall take the matter under consideration, future husband."

"Shall we return to the house? I don't want you to catch a chill."

"Yes. I do not wish to be late for breakfast either."

"If it is agreeable to you, I shall announce our plans to everyone."

"I hope they are not shocked," Celine replied.

"I doubt it. The Carlyles may even expect it."

"Expect it?" Celine questioned as they approached the house.

"Yes," Gray replied. "When they arrived at our London house searching for you, they told Alexander we were married."

* * *

PRESENT DAY, **Bucksville**

The door to Damien's room opened and Marcus strolled in, followed by Gray.

"Did you get everything?" Celine asked from her position on Damien's bed.

"Surprisingly, he did," Marcus replied.

Gray rolled his eyes at Marcus.

"So, you can begin?" Celine asked, approaching him as he laid his materials on a nearby dresser.

"Yes," Marcus responded.

"How long will this take?"

"Patience, my dear Celine, patience. We must first determine which Alterra they are visiting."

"How?"

"First, I shall need a drop of blood," Marcus answered, approaching Damien and pricking his finger with a needle. He let a drop of blood fall into a glass tube from the materials Gray brought. "Now, we'll mix it with a few of the other items and note its reaction. Come closer, Celine, you always enjoyed learning."

Gray rolled his eyes, shooting a glance at Alexander who shook his head.

"The lighter the color, the closer they are to our current world," Marcus pointed out. "And notice how his blood splits into smaller particles. It will help us navigate to the correct iteration."

"Can you tell where they are?" Celine asked.

"More or less," Marcus replied. "However, this is quite interesting."

"What is?"

"The blood particles exhibit tiny spikes. Notice how they distort along their edges."

"I see it," Celine answered. "What does it mean?"

"It indicates they have not only traveled laterally to another time band but that they also traveled backward in time."

Celine furrowed her brow, contemplating the information. "Did they travel back when the pulse hit them or after, I wonder? Is it still possible to follow them?"

"Yes, it is. Albeit, it will be more taxing than a lateral journey. We should verify that the other one has traveled in the same way."

"Oh," Celine responded, realization dawning on her, "I assumed they had, or at least I hoped they were together."

"It is likely, however, we should still ensure that is the case. It is also good practice for you, my dear."

"I'll retrieve a drop of Michael's blood," Celine answered, taking a vial from Marcus and departing from the room.

"I don't know how much more of this I can stand," Gray whispered to Alexander.

Marcus stared at them. "What's the matter, Buckley? Concerned after I rescue her precious Damien, she will be so grateful she may run straight into my arms and forget you entirely?"

Gray closed his eyes, channeling his inner fury to avoid throttling the man. "No. I'm concerned after this she won't be able to get away from you fast enough."

"Oh, I wouldn't be concerned about that," Marcus answered. "She will, no doubt, feel an enormous amount of gratitude. I can't imagine you're all that memorable. Besides, she already fled from you once."

Gray barred himself from leaping across the room at Marcus as Celine returned with the blood vial.

"Perfect, my dear, and now the other ingredients," Marcus instructed.

"I swear I'm going to find a way to kill that man," Gray hissed to Alexander.

"Just don't do it before he's retrieved Damien and Michael," Alexander warned.

"Well done, my dear," Marcus congratulated Celine across the room. Her blood sample from Michael pointed to the same Alterra location as Damien's. "Now, I must prepare to travel to the location."

"What must we do to prepare? I will go with you," Celine said.

"No," Gray barked from across the room.

"For once, I agree with Buckley," Marcus replied. "That is unwise. It may be dangerous."

"I don't agree with either of you," Celine argued.

"Too bad, you're overruled," Gray answered.

"No, not too bad. You don't suppose Michael and Damien will just go willingly with Marcus when he arrives there, do you?"

"He convinced Damien to go with him once before, I'm sure he can do it again," Gray answered.

"This time it means Damien's life if he can't, Gray. I'm not taking the chance."

"I wouldn't care to take a chance with your life, either, Celine," Marcus interjected.

"Oh, please. After the centuries of fighting between us *now* you're concerned about my well-being? Honestly, Marcus." She rolled her eyes at him.

"Celine, I have always been concerned about your well-being. This is not a journey to be taken lightly. But it would expedite the process if you were there to convince them to come back."

"Thank you," Celine answered. She turned to Gray. "I can't leave it up to chance."

"I'll go instead," Gray replied.

"That is a disaster waiting to happen and you know it. You'll be so busy sniping at each other, you'll lose focus on the task at hand. And besides, Michael and Damien are not much fonder of you than they are of him." Celine thumbed toward Marcus.

"I could do it," Alexander offered.

"I am not sure this is an improvement over sending Gray, other than Damien may trust you more. I don't see the issue here. I am the best person to go."

"I don't trust him," Gray snapped, pointing to Marcus.

"I would never allow anything to happen to Celine," Marcus replied.

"That doesn't guarantee you'll return her to us," Gray retorted.

"Perhaps we all should go," Alexander suggested.

Marcus raised an eyebrow. "To be quite frank, gentlemen, I don't imagine either of you possess the capacity to endure the journey. Celine easily does as do I. Now, shall we prepare, Celine?"

Celine nodded.

"Give us a moment," Gray said, pulling Celine aside. He lowered his voice. "I don't like this, Celine."

"I realize that Gray, but there is not much to be done. I will be careful, I promise."

"I don't trust him."

"Neither do I, but we need him. I'm not going into this inexperienced. I will keep my wits about me."

Gray sighed as he grasped her hands. "Please, please, be careful, Celine."

"I will be. With any luck this will all be over soon," Celine answered, kissing Gray. "Okay. I'm ready," she said to Marcus.

"Good, then we shall begin."

* * *

1812, BUCKLEY COUNTRY ESTATE

Celine waited outside in the cold afternoon air as the carriage trundled up the gravel drive. Gray and Alexander waited with her. The carriage slowed to a stop outside the front door. The coachman leapt to the ground, opening the door. Marcus emerged from the carriage, a dour expression on his face.

"Duke Northcott," Alexander began, bowing, "welcome to our humble estate."

"Indeed, it is humbler than I first imagined."

There was an awkward pause before Celine spoke. "It is quite charming, actually."

Marcus offered her a brief smile. "You do tend to find the optimistic view in most things."

"Please, come in," Alexander motioned toward the door.

"Thank you. I should like to be shown to my room. I have many items to attend to."

"Of course, Duke," Alexander responded. "Right this way."

"Celine, if you wouldn't mind accompanying me. There is a matter I would like to discuss with you."

"Certainly," Celine agreed, following them to the bedroom suite assigned to Marcus and Celine.

Alexander left them, closing the door to the bedroom.

"I hope your journey was pleasant," Celine commented as the door closed.

"Most tedious, my dear."

"I am sorry you did not find it more relaxing," Celine responded.

Marcus removed his jacket, loosening his collar. "I do not find this visit, in general, relaxing, dear. Which is why we shall return home tomorrow."

Celine swallowed hard, unhappy with the news. "They expect us to stay on until Sunday."

"Impossible. I have already accepted an invitation for dinner the evening after next with the Westbrooks. We return home tomorrow."

"You must send my sincerest regrets to the Westbrooks."

"I shall do no such thing, Celine. You will return home with me tomorrow."

Celine sidestepped the order. "You are tired. Let us discuss it later."

"Celine, I will not argue about this. I have already given in to your whim for this ridiculous visit. I shall dine with your interesting new friends. But that is where this shall end. You will return home with me tomorrow and that is final."

Celine bit her tongue, not yet wishing to begin the argument regarding her inability to return home. She didn't understand why she put it off. She possessed no desire to remain married to Marcus. She hadn't wanted to marry him in the first place. Only after hours of torture, her own desperation drove her to it. Wasn't now as good a time as any to inform Marcus she would no longer remain married to him? Perhaps it was best to wait until after dinner, when all that would remain was a night's sleep prior to his departure. Yes, Celine resolved, after dinner she would inform him before they retired.

Celine spent the hour before dinner fussing with her clothing and hair. It distracted her from the task that lay ahead. She did not experience second thoughts or harbor any fear regarding her decision. However, she preferred to complete the task, finish the argument, and move on with her life.

Much to her surprise, after she accepted Gray's marriage proposal, he informed her the Carlyles assumed they were already married when they arrived. She wondered for a brief moment if this was the source of Gray's proposal, but he was quick to cast aside any doubts in her mind. It added to her sense of belonging with him.

They made their announcement at breakfast, telling Alexander and the Carlyles that they planned to marry once any formalities were completed to end her ties with Marcus. She recalled the moment, allowing her sense of joy to wash over her again.

Everyone expressed happiness regarding the decision. This was her destiny, not the life she had been living. She would be free and happy now. She allowed her mind to focus on that rather than dwell on the nastiness in her immediate future. She would get through it, she promised herself. She spent twenty-six years with Marcus. Twenty-six years he had spent lying to her, manipulating her. It would end tonight.

At dinner, conversation was stilted. Marcus's presence and sour disposition toward the Buckleys put a general damper on any conversations. Celine was relieved when the meal ended, and they shared an after-dinner drink in the sitting room. She nursed her sherry, preparing herself for the inevitable confrontation with Marcus.

After one brandy, Marcus suggested they go to bed. "We will retire for the evening. Celine and I must leave early tomorrow morning to return to London."

"Tomorrow morning?" Damien inquired. "Aren't you staying until Sunday?"

"That is impossible, Mr. Carlyle. We have urgent business in London and must cut our visit short. Come, Celine."

"No," Gray interjected, "I believe you are mistaken."

"Excuse me, Buckley?" Marcus responded.

Celine stood, placing herself between them. "Let us speak in private, Marcus."

"No," Gray argued again. "There is no need to speak in private. In fact, it is best not to."

"What is the meaning of this, Celine?" Marcus inquired.

Celine swallowed hard. She took a deep, steadying breath. "I will not return to London with you tomorrow, Marcus."

"Celine, we have been through this. You will not stay on until Sunday. I have already made my decision, and it is final."

Celine shook her head. "No, Marcus. I will not return tomorrow or Sunday or ever."

Marcus glanced around the room, then back to Celine. A laugh escaped his mouth. "Whatever are you talking about, Celine?"

"I am leaving you, Marcus. Our marriage is ended."

Marcus's face changed in an instant. "You must be out of your mind, Celine. Have your new friends put you up to this? Have you gone mad?"

"No, Marcus, I have not," Celine assured him. "No one has put me up to anything. I am quite in my right mind. Perhaps more in my right mind than I have been in twenty-six years."

Marcus chuckled again. "Well, then I am sorry, my dear, however, I simply will not allow it. You shall return with me tomorrow to London. We shall then engage in a lengthy discussion regarding our marriage and your attitudes toward it. Now, come along." He grasped her arm, pulling her toward the door.

She tugged back, trying to escape his grip. Gray, Alexander, Michael, and Damien rushed after her. Gray pushed between her and Marcus, and Celine freed herself from his grasp.

"Do not make this harder than it needs to be," Celine advised.

"Harder than it needs to be?" Marcus questioned. "I will make it impossible, my dear. I will never allow you to betray me in this manner."

"To betray you?" Celine queried, annoyance creeping into her voice. "I have not betrayed you, Marcus. It is you who have betrayed me for years."

"How dare you, Celine?" he barked at her.

"No, Marcus, how dare you?" she answered, heat entering her voice. "My eyes have been opened to the depths of your betrayal all those years ago. It is *you* who is responsible for my father's death. I have learned the truth and come to understand how you have manipulated me. I shall tolerate it no longer. We are finished."

Surprise crossed Marcus's face before he returned it to stone. "You are mistaken."

"Do not continue to lie to me," she shot back. "I am not mistaken."

"I did what needed to be done, Celine. Responsible or not, it is water under the bridge. I am your husband. It is too late for second thoughts."

"No, Marcus, you are not. You are nothing to me anymore."

"Do not say anything further, Celine. You may voice something you will regret."

"I regret nothing except the last twenty-six years of my life."

Fury shown on Marcus's face. "I warn you, Celine, I shall not tolerate much more of this."

"And I shall tolerate no more of you. I suggest you leave at once," Celine proposed.

He set his jaw, staring at her. "You shall tolerate no more? You shall tolerate no more??? I am struggling to hold my patience with you, Celine, but I shall give you one more opportunity. Leave with me now and I shall be generous enough to spare your friends any consequences."

Michael, Damien, Alexander, and Gray gathered around her. Celine stood straighter, pushing her shoulders back and raising her chin. "No."

Marcus frowned at her. "Celine, you are acting like a child. Consider what you are saying. Your reputation shall be ruined!"

"Yours will fare no better, Marcus. Particularly if the circumstances of my father's death come to light. And unable to control even your own wife. Imagine the rumors. The difference is you will care, I shall not."

"We'll see how much you care when every door in London in closed to you!"

"I shall survive."

"Will you? I have spent years providing a life others can only imagine, I have provided everything for you, anything you wished, anything you desired. I have remained loyal to you always. I will not allow you to betray me in this way."

"You have no choice. I have turned a blind eye to your evil deeds for far too long. I shall do so no longer. Our relationship is ended tonight."

Marcus exhaled forcibly, setting his jaw. "Fine. But realize you are responsible for any harm that befalls them."

He raised his hand, readying to strike.

CHAPTER 30

*C*eline flung her hand out, stinging Marcus with a fireball before he could strike.

"Leave, Marcus. I shall allow no harm to come to any of them."

Marcus tried again, but Celine fired another fireball at him, followed by two more. Alexander and Gray readied to defend her.

Marcus paused for a moment. He sniffed, smirking at them. "All right, Celine. I shall go. You have me at a momentary disadvantage. But know this. This conversation is not finished. I shall never allow you to leave me, not truly. You shall not always retain the upper hand. It shall not last. You have won the battle. You will not win the war. I will never let you rest. I shall follow you always and everywhere."

He stepped back toward the doorway. "Prepare, Celine. Gather your strength. You shall need it when I bring the forces of Hell upon you and your new compatriots."

He turned on his heel, thundering down the hall. The floors shook as he stormed away, porcelain vases, mirrors and glass pieces shattered as he passed them.

Celine closed her eyes for a moment as the sounds faded down the hall. "I'm sorry."

"There is nothing to be sorry for," Gray informed her. "And now we are rid of him."

"He shall return as promised," Celine responded. "He will not let this rest."

"Which is why we shall travel to London tomorrow morning and board a ship to America. The further we are from him, the better. Allow his temper to cool whilst he is impeded from contacting you."

Celine gazed at him. "Yes. That is best, I agree."

"Early tomorrow morning?" Damien asked.

"Yes," Gray answered. "I sent a man this morning after Celine accepted my proposal to make travel arrangements for us to leave immediately."

Michael and Damien glanced at each other.

"What about us?" Michael asked.

"Yes," Damien added. "Not to be a pain, but we need to return to our time before you go."

Celine nodded with a tight-lipped smile. "Of course. I shall send you tonight."

Damien wrinkled his nose. "Gee, I kind of hoped to see you get married this time."

"Sorry to disappoint, but it's best for you to go now. With Duke Northcott's ire raised, it isn't safe for you here," Gray responded.

"Gray is correct," Celine added. She approached them, taking one of each of their hands into hers. "Before you go, I must thank you both. Without your bravery and forthrightness, I should never have learned the truth."

Damien squeezed her hand, smiling at her. "You're welcome. I'm glad you're away from the Duke. He is a horrible man. You deserve much better."

Michael squeezed her hand as well. "You're welcome,

Celine. See you in a couple of centuries."

Gray extended his hand to shake each of theirs. "Thank you, gentlemen."

Alexander did the same. "What a strange journey it has been, Damien and Michael. But I am better for having met you. Safe travels."

Everyone said their final goodbyes before Celine readied them to travel. "Now, if you'll concentrate on your time period, I shall open the portal."

Celine shut her eyes, stretching her arms in front of her. The familiar twinkling appeared in front of Michael and Damien and a black opening grew from a pinpoint to a gaping hole, covering the wall in front of them. Wind whipped through the room as the portal to their time opened. Once it was fully open, Michael and Damien glanced at each other before stepping through it.

After a few steps, Damien stumbled, struggling but remaining upright. He glanced down, blinking his eyes a few times to adjust to the new scenery. He'd tripped over a stone projecting from the ground. He glanced around, seeing trees and hearing the sound of the ocean nearby.

Michael clapped him on the back, pointing toward an object to their left. "We made it."

Damien followed his finger, finding the Buckley house in its path. Light shone from the windows, keeping the darkness at bay.

* * *

PRESENT DAY, BUCKSVILLE, ALTERRA

Damien breathed a sigh of relief. "Whew. I am so glad to be home."

"Me too. I can't wait to get out of these clothes."

"Yeah, and into my bed. My real bed."

"Race you?" Michael asked.

"Aw, come on," Damien complained. "I'm never going to win."

"With an attitude like that, you won't. Come on!"

Michael sprinted in front of him. Damien grumbled but raced behind him, trying to catch up. Michael's head start proved too much for him, and Michael made it to the house first. The two men burst through the front door, laughing over their so-called race.

Celine crossed the foyer, a book in her hand. "Michael? Damien?" she asked in a crisp British accent.

"Celine?" Damien asked, sobering quickly and approaching her. Michael followed.

"It is you!" she exclaimed, placing her book on the entryway table and throwing her arms around them. "I didn't imagine I would ever see you again! Why, you appear just as I remember you!"

Michael and Damien glanced at each other, speechless.

"Well," Damien eventually croaked out, "we just left you. The night you told the Duke that you were leaving, we've just come from then."

"And you came here. This is your time?"

"Y-Y-Yeah," Damien stumbled. "Don't you remember?"

"Remember?" Celine questioned, her brow furrowing in confusion.

"Yeah. You remember us, right?" Michael inquired.

"Of course, I do!" Celine answered. "You are responsible for liberating me from my marriage to Marcus. And, of course, allowing me to find true happiness with Gray. How could I forget you?"

"Is that all you remember about us?" Damien probed.

Celine pondered a moment. "I recall that you are a

terrible dancer at the waltz, Damien Carlyle." She grinned, sticking her tongue out at him.

Damien's eyes went wide, and he glanced at Michael. Michael swallowed hard. "Celine, do you have any more recent memories of us?"

"No?" Celine responded in a questioning manner.

"Do you recall using the name Josie at any point?" Damien inquired.

"Josie? No. I have never used that name."

Gray appeared across the room. He hurried toward them. "Michael and Damien Carlyle! What a surprise!"

"Yes," Celine agreed. "They have traveled here using the time portal I opened the night I left Marcus. I had no idea they were traveling here. But we are so glad you did! I hope you'll stay with us. Oh, we should phone Alexander. He'd love to see you if he can get a flight from London before you leave."

"London? Stay?" Damien questioned, his mind whirling. "I... I... I..." Damien stammered, scratching his head as he searched for an answer. The room began to spin, and he found it difficult to concentrate. The world began to melt away, and he slid to the floor.

"Damien!" Celine shouted as Michael reached for him, grabbing him before he hit the floor. "He's passed out! Quickly, Gray, help Michael take him to one of the bedrooms upstairs."

Gray grabbed Damien's arm, swinging it over his shoulder as Michael did the same. Together they carried him up the stairs, laying him on the bed in one of the rooms. Celine took his hand in hers, perching on the edge of the bed.

"Damien? Damien," she whispered to him.

Within moments, he groaned, moving his head back and

forth. His eyes fluttered open, and he glanced around. Celine smiled at him.

"Oh, Celine. Whew! I had the worst dream. It was so weird," he muttered.

"There, there, it's over now. Just rest," Celine answered.

Damien's eyes went wide, and he scooted up the bed, sitting straighter. "No. No! You're still British Celine. This can't be!"

"British Celine?" Celine asked, her brow creasing.

"He means your accent," Michael explained.

"I've had my accent for several years. My French accent waned years after marrying Marcus. I'm afraid this one never did, despite the time I've spent with Gray."

Gray smiled at her, grabbing her hand. "I wouldn't have it any other way."

"Right," Damien answered, swallowing hard.

"Are you quite sure you're all right?" Celine asked.

"Ah, yep. Sorry, time traveling can be…"

"Taxing, I realize," Celine responded. "And, without a doubt, you'll stay with us tonight. After your episode, I should prefer it. Michael, we'll have the room next door made up for you if that's suitable."

"Definitely, and thanks," Michael answered.

"I'll see to it now," Celine replied. "Is there anything else you may need?"

"Change of clothes, maybe?" Michael asked. "Sorry for the inconvenience, we came straight here and…"

"Think nothing of it. I'll drop some things off as soon as I've seen to the room."

"That should be it," Michael answered. "Then I think just a good night's sleep is in order."

Celine smiled at them both. "I can imagine!" S
he and Gray exited the room, pulling the door shut behind them.

Damien slouched back on the bed, covering his face in his hands. "I can't believe this," he said, pulling his hands away from his face.

"Me either," Michael responded, shaking his head, his hands on his hips.

"She doesn't know us other than our 1812 experience! Nothing is fixed, nothing is the same!"

"Nope. It's a completely different history."

"No kidding," Damien responded. "I expected to return home and have everything back to normal. She's even still got that weird accent!"

"I wouldn't care about the accent if only she'd have known us. I mean, she was never Josie! She never met us, she's not your cousin."

"No. And that's super concerning. I assumed we'd come back, she'd be back to our Celine because she became Josie, met us, sent us back to help her and the timeline would be corrected."

"Yeah, I figured the same. I was blown away when she didn't."

"I guess those twenty-six years made so much of a difference she never asked to be Josie?" Damien pondered aloud.

"Or the adjudicator thing said no this time?" Michael conjectured.

There was a knock at the door. Celine poked her head inside. "Just me. Here are night clothes and a change of clothes. Is there anything else? Perhaps something to eat?"

"No, no, we're all good," Michael responded. "Just going to change and turn in."

"Well, your bedroom, as I mentioned, is right next door. Either exit to the hall and turn right to the next door or pass through the bathroom there." She smiled at them. "Good night to you both, sleep well. I'll see you in the morning. I hope you feel better, Damien."

"Thanks, good night, Celine," Damien answered.

Michael nodded. "Good night," he said.

Celine nodded, leaving the room and pulling the door shut.

"Ugh," Damien groaned. "What are we supposed to do now? We obviously don't live here. Do we just go home and try to pick up whatever lives we're supposed to have? Or do we stay here? Or?"

"I don't know, man, I don't know," Michael responded.

* * *

PRESENT DAY, **Bucksville, Original Timeline**

Marcus stirred the concoction, peering at it through the clear beaker. He poured it into two glasses set in front of him. Handing one to Celine, he said, "Here you are, darling. I will warn you, it is a bit vile tasting.

Celine accepted the glass.

"Wait," Gray interjected. "What's that for?"

"To prepare our bodies to jump to Alterra. This should prevent most of the adverse effects. Cheers, Celine." He clinked his glass against Celine's, downing his. "Satisfied? I would not poison myself."

Celine swallowed the liquid in the glass, almost gagging. "Ugh," she moaned, shuddering.

"Celine, are you all right?" Gray asked.

Marcus smirked at her. "I warned you."

"It was still worse than I expected. I'm glad that's over. Now what?"

"Now, you should rest. The journey ahead will prove taxing."

"I don't need rest. Let's just proceed with the next step."

"The concoction will take time to work. Go rest. I will

prepare the next steps and we'll be ready to move on when you return."

"Come on, Celine," Gray instructed. "Let's go."

Gray guided her to their bedroom. "Now, lay down and get some rest."

Celine grabbed Gray's hand. "Stay with me."

Gray sat on the edge of the bed next to her.

"I'm sorry this is so hard on you, Gray."

Gray shook his head, shushing her. "Shh, Celine. I'm more worried about you. I'm fine."

Celine shook her head, disagreeing. "No, I…"

"Celine," Gray interrupted. "I am fine. Stop worrying. I can handle this. I'm more worried about you. The trip to Alterra is enough but to have to go with that man… well, I worry for you."

"I'll be okay," Celine promised. "I just want Damien and Michael home. The sooner the better."

"Well, the sooner you get some rest, the sooner they'll be home. Now, close your eyes."

"Wake me up in an hour. Promise?"

"I promise," Gray said, kissing her hand.

Celine closed her eyes, squeezing Gray's hand. She wasn't sure she could sleep, but she would try. Sleeping would pass the time faster at least, she figured.

The next thing she realized, she was being shaken awake.

"Celine," Gray whispered. "Celine, wake up."

Celine opened her eyes, finding Gray hovering above her.

"Hey, sleepy head, time to get up."

"What time is it?"

"Almost eight."

"Eight? You were supposed to wake me an hour ago!" Celine sat up, swinging her legs over the side of the bed.

"You needed the rest."

Celine pulled her hair into a ponytail, standing. "Hopefully, Marcus is ready."

"I'm not sure I can say I hope for that," Gray responded. "But I suppose the sooner you go, the sooner you'll be back."

Celine giggled, grabbing his hand and pulling him out the door. "Yep. Now, come on. Let's go."

They pushed through the door to Damien's room. Marcus tinkered with a few items on the dresser. "Ah, Celine. I hope you were able to rest."

"I was. I overslept, I'm sorry. Are we ready?"

"Not a problem, my dear. I've just finished preparations. We are ready," Marcus informed her.

Celine nodded. "All right, I suppose we should proceed."

"Be careful, Celine, please," Gray implored her. "I love you."

"I will." She embraced him. "I love you."

"See you soon, Celine," Alexander said. "Be careful."

"Thanks," Celine answered, hugging Alexander. "I will."

"All right," she said, turning to Marcus. "Just tell me what to do."

CHAPTER 31

Celine stared up at his dark eyes as she awaited her instructions to enter Alterra.

"Have a seat here," Marcus told her, pulling a chair away from a table set up in the room. He handed a vial of red liquid to Gray. "If anything should happen, pull Celine's hand from mine and give this to her. It will reverse any negative effects she may experience and wake her from the trance."

Celine watched the exchange. "Why is there only one?"

"I am a pragmatist, my dear. I have no illusions that should anything happen, either of the Buckleys would save me. Now, I shall sit here." He pulled a chair next to hers. "Give me your hand. It should not be hard for us to make a connection, given our shared blood. Close your eyes and relax. You'll feel me pull you toward Alterra. Just follow."

Celine nodded, she placed her hand in his and he closed his hand around hers. Celine closed her eyes, taking deep breaths. She felt Marcus's flesh against her and concentrated on their connection. Within seconds, the sounds of the room faded away, replaced by silence and blackness.

Celine stood unmoving for a moment until she felt a tugging on her arm.

"Celine," Marcus called, his voice echoing into the darkness.

She opened her eyes.

"This way, my dear."

She grasped his hand tighter, following him through the blackness. Celine shuddered as a chill went through her. "It's cold here," Celine said, rubbing her arms.

Marcus pulled her closer. "Yes, we shan't be here long with any luck."

"What is this place?" Celine asked as they walked through the blackness. No features stood out, it appeared as though they walked through an endless dark hall. No sounds echoed, only silence.

"It is an in-between, a conduit between worlds."

"How do you know where to go?" she asked.

"I'm following the trail Damien and Michael left behind. Look," he pointed to a specific area in the blackness.

"I don't see anything," she replied.

"Look closer, Celine. Pay careful attention."

She studied the area he referenced. Tiny blue flecks glistened upon closer inspection. "I see it! How did they find their way through here?"

"They didn't," Marcus informed her. "This is a residue left from the pulse that pushed them through here."

"Oh," Celine answered. Celine pondered for a moment. "How would we have navigated if this wasn't here?"

"I brought the vial of Damien's blood," he answered, removing it from his pocket with his free hand. "Notice how the blood particles are beginning to reformulate into the single blood cell. The closer we are to the Alterra band, the closer to a single normal blood droplet these will be."

Celine stared at the vial, noticing the blood particles, once distended and spiked, returning to a single blood droplet. "We're getting closer."

"Their path along with this blood will lead us to where they arrived. Then we must find them within the Alterra world. You were right to come along. You'll have the best idea where they may be."

Celine nodded, and they continued through the black forest of nothingness. She kept a tight hold of Marcus's hand.

"I'm surprised Grayson allowed you to come, though."

Celine scoffed, side-eyeing him. "Allowed me to come?"

"He treats you like a child, Celine."

Celine rolled her eyes. "He does not. And I suppose even if he did, it's preferable to being treated like a prisoner."

"Touché," Marcus answered. "However…"

"Let's not discuss it," Celine interrupted.

"Have it your way. We seem to be approaching the end of their trail, we should arrive soon. I'll warn you, entering the Alterra world may be a bit painful."

"As long as we find Michael and Damien, I don't care."

"Here," Marcus said, pointing to a shimmer appearing in front of them. He removed the vial of Damien's blood from his pocket. The particles were nearly formed into a complete droplet. "This is the edge of the world they are in. Now we must pass through. You first, I shall follow. Whatever you do, do not stop, continue forward until you are in the Alterra world. Do you understand?"

Celine nodded. "Yes. I understand."

"All right, Celine. Walk straight through," he said, turning her toward the rainbow shimmer.

Celine took a deep breath, exhaling through her mouth. "Okay. See you on the other side."

He nodded. She stepped forward, walking into the dancing colors. As she began to pass through the glistening rainbow barrier, her skin began to crawl. As she entered it fully, it felt as though needles raked across her body. Each movement required great exertion. Within moments, the sensation began to wane, replaced again with the crawling skin sensation. As she approached the other side of the barrier, even this waned, leaving her skin pocked with only goosebumps.

She emerged in an alleyway near a broader street. Daylight waned as twilight approached. She glanced around, searching for a clue to her location. Her clothing was from another era. She placed it in the early nineteenth century.

Within moments, Marcus arrived next to her. She breathed a slight sigh of relief. "You know, this might be the first time I've ever been happy to see you."

"Wonders never cease, I suppose," he answered. "Have you identified where we are? Or when?"

"Judging from the clothes I'm wearing, which I have no idea how I got, I'd say early 1800s. Location is London," she answered, pointing to Buckingham Palace.

"Ah, so it is," Marcus agreed. "Any idea where Michael and Damien may be in nineteenth century London?"

Celine considered the question, shaking her head. She pondered a few moments, then replied, "Damien is good friends with Alexander. Perhaps they've discussed the London house. If so, Damien may have gone there to seek help."

"Let us try there first, then," Marcus agreed.

Celine glanced at him. "Perhaps I should go alone."

"No," Marcus argued. "I will not allow you to wander around this world alone. You've no idea the circumstances that exist. Alexander may not be your friend here."

"Wow! You won't allow me? And you say Gray treats me like a child."

"That is completely different. Now, do you know the way?"

"It's been a while, but I should be able to find it."

Celine set off toward the Buckleys' London house. After twenty minutes of walking, she approached the correct street. "Yes, this is right… I think. It should be near the end of the street. Number four."

They continued down the street, stopping outside of the number four house. Celine took a deep breath, lifting her skirts and climbing the stairs. "I hope they still own it in this time band," she commented, knocking on the door.

Within moments, a tall butler opened it. He gaped at them a moment before Celine spoke. "Alexander Buckley, please."

Without a word, the man motioned for them to enter, his eyes still wide. "If you'll wait here," he managed, showing them to the sitting room. He disappeared, closing the doors behind them.

Celine sat on the couch. "That seemed an odd reaction."

It did not take long before the doors burst open again. Alexander rushed into the room. "Celine?" he gasped, his eyes wide. His coloring turned ghost white as he glanced at Marcus. He swallowed hard, wishing in an instant he had left with Gray this morning.

Celine stood from the couch. "Oh, Alexander, thank goodness you recognize me."

He continued to stare at her, confusion and trepidation on this face. He shook his head. "No, it can't be. This is impossible. You can't be here. And with him?"

Celine furrowed her brow. "Please, Alex, let me explain," she stated, in an attempt to calm him. "This may be difficult to understand but…"

"Wait," he interrupted her, shaking his head, "your accent…"

Celine glanced around, attempting to understand. "What about it?"

"It's… American." Realization began to dawn on his face as the pieces fell into place. "You must be…"

Celine stared at him as he paused.

"You must be the Celine Michael and Damien talked about, but… how? Are you from another time?"

Celine took a deep breath, preparing to explain. "Yes and no. We," she said, motioning to encompass Marcus, "are from another time band altogether, an Alterra to this world. I realize this may not make sense to you but…"

"Oh, no, no," Alexander answered, collapsing into an armchair, "it makes a great deal of sense. More than you realize. An alternate time band, yes." Alexander stared into space, contemplating it.

"You mentioned a Michael and Damien," Celine responded. "Are they here?"

"No. You, rather, the Celine from this time band sent them back to their own time last night."

"Their own time? As in the future?"

"Yes. They said they came from the future. They told quite a fantastical tale about a Celine who had been married to my cousin, Grayson, since the 1700s. I thought them mad at first, but they insisted. You must be the Celine they spoke of."

Celine nodded. "Yes, I believe so. We've come in search of them."

"But…" Alexander began, glancing between Celine and Marcus, "the story Michael and Damien told me… Forgive me, my mind cannot encompass this."

Celine sat on the couch. "In our time band, Michael and Damien are good friends of mine."

"But you are married to my cousin, Grayson Buckley, are you not?"

"Yes, that's correct."

"Yet you travel here with Duke Northcott. Michael and

Damien were adamant that he was the source of your troubles."

Marcus rolled his eyes at the statement.

"In fact, when they learned of your situation here, they seemed to believe it was their duty to correct history. Of course, they believed this to be their time band and that some strange electrical pulse altered history."

"I see," Celine answered. "They did not understand they were visiting a different time band. They were unaware that they had traveled both backwards in time and laterally to a new time band."

"No, none of us realized," Alexander replied, color returning to his face. "How fascinating. Events in your time band seemed quite different to ours."

"Yes, it appears they are," Celine agreed. "You said Michael and Damien were sent to the future last night?"

Alexander nodded. "Yes. Our Celine opened a portal for them."

Celine sighed. They had come to the correct time band, but missed them by less than a full day. They would need to discuss a plan to get to them somehow. "Thank you, Alexander. We should leave." Celine stood from the couch.

"Just a moment," Marcus interjected. "You said events here were quite different. What was Celine's situation that Michael and Damien set out to correct?"

Alexander paused, glancing between the two of them. "They were quite disturbed to learn that you were not married to Grayson, and instead..." He paused. "You were married to Duke Northcott."

"And did they succeed in 'correcting' the matter?" Marcus pressed.

Celine shot him a glance.

"Well, yes. I just put you... our Celine on a ship bound for America with Grayson."

Marcus closed his eyes for a moment. "I see. Well, I suppose we should depart as Celine suggested."

"Yes, thank you. You've been a great help," Celine assured Alexander.

Alexander stood. "There is no need to leave. If you require any assistance, please stay."

Celine understood his impulse and smiled at him. "No, we must find Damien and Michael, but thank you."

"Are you sure? You're certain you're safe?"

"Yes, I'm sure. I am safe. But Michael and Damien, wherever they are now, must be alarmed realizing their plan may not have achieved what they intended. We must find them and take them home."

"Good luck, Celine. I hope you find them."

"Thank you," Celine answered, squeezing his hands. She stepped away to exit the room with Marcus following her.

"Oh, Celine," Alexander said before she left. "Say 'hello' to my counterpart in your time. I understand we are good friends."

Celine smiled at him. "I will do that for you."

They departed from the Buckley residence, making their way down the street.

"Your meddling friends have ruined another time band for me, I see," Marcus complained.

"Oh, stop, Marcus," Celine groaned. "Complaining is not your style. Focus. We need to figure out how to get to Damien and Michael! If they are in the future here, how can we get to them?"

"It's not an issue, Celine. We shall simply go forward in time."

"Simply go forward in time?" Celine questioned, grinding to a halt on the sidewalk.

"Yes, Celine. Have you forgotten I am capable of opening

time portals and traveling through them? I shall open a time portal. You will go through it, and I will follow. Simple."

A smile crept over Celine's face. "That's right. Your newfound ability can be put to good use this time."

"I found it a good use the last time I exercised the ability."

Celine rolled her eyes. "Stop making jokes. Come on, let's get on with this."

"I wasn't joking. Do you suppose they traveled to the Buckley estate in our time?"

"Yes," Celine answered. "They most likely assumed once they 'fixed' the past, everything would return to normal in the future. I'll bet they were distraught once they arrived there. Events were likely quite different due to the aberrations already existing in this time band."

"How unfortunate for them," Marcus replied, rolling his eyes while he guided her to a deserted alleyway.

"They must be so scared. We must get there," Celine urged.

"Yes, Celine, we will get there. Just a moment," Marcus tempered. "Are you always this impatient?"

"I'm afraid so," Celine confessed. "Lucky you missed out on it, huh? Now enough small talk, let's go."

"All right, all right," Marcus answered. "When it opens, go through, do not wait for me."

Celine nodded.

Marcus stretched his arms out in front of him, closing his eyes. Celine waited for the characteristic sparkle to appear in front of her. The wind picked up, and the sparkle turned to a small black hole. The hole grew in size until it was large enough for her to step through. She wasted no time in entering the portal, taking a few steps until she stepped into a recognizable spot.

She glanced behind her. The portal remained open.

Within moments, Marcus stepped through and the portal snapped shut behind him.

"Okay, let's go to the house," Celine insisted, beginning to walk toward the path.

"Aren't you going to tell me how happy you are to see me?" Marcus questioned.

"Don't push your luck. Come on."

They traipsed through the woods toward the house. As the house came into view, Celine commented, "Perhaps we shouldn't use the front entrance. Even at this hour, we may run into someone."

"A wise idea," Marcus responded. "I have no desire to run into any more Buckleys on this trip. It's enough to anticipate dealing with them when we return."

They approached the house, easing open a side door. Celine peeked inside. "Coast is clear, come on!"

They hurried down the hall to a back stairway. "If I know me, I put them in the same rooms they have in our time band."

Celine led them through the halls to the rooms she guessed were Michael's and Damien's. She approached Damien's door. Celine turned the handle inch by inch, easing the door open. She peered into the darkness. A figure lay in bed. She crossed her fingers, hoping it was Damien.

Tiptoeing into the room, she peered closer at the figure in the bed. A grin came over her face. Damien lay asleep on his side. She glanced at Marcus, nodding her head as he slid the door shut.

"D," Celine whispered, reaching out to touch his shoulder. "D, wake up!"

Celine shook him again.

"Huh, what?" Damien asked, sleep still in his voice. He opened his eyes, blinking a few times in the darkness.

"D, it's me," Celine whispered. She flipped on the light on

the night table, perching on the edge of the bed. Marcus approached from across the room.

Damien blinked against the light, covering his eyes for a moment. "Wow, that light is bright." After a moment, he lowered his arm. His eyes grew wide, and he leaned away from Celine, climbing out of bed and backing away. "No. No! It can't be. Celine, no!"

CHAPTER 32

PRESENT DAY, BUCKSVILLE, ALTERRA

"D, wait," Celine said, springing to her feet. "Just a second."

Michael burst through the bathroom door moments later. "Damien, what's going on?" He glanced at the two new people in the room. "Oh, no. Wait, this can't be. How is this happening? Are things just randomly getting worse?"

"Michael!" Celine exclaimed. "Now, wait just a minute, both of you. You're jumping to the wrong conclusion. I can explain."

Damien stared at Celine, cocking his head. "Wait," he said. He glanced to Michael then back to Celine. "Wait, your accent. It's gone."

Celine nodded. "Yes. D, it's me! It's the real Celine from your time."

"Huh?" Michael queried. "Why are you dressed like that?"

"You are not in your own time. You're in an alternate time

band," Marcus explained. "The pulse wave that struck you sent you to an alternate world. We followed you to it but arrived where you did in the 1800s."

Damien and Michael shared a glance, unsure whether or not to believe Marcus.

"He's telling the truth," Celine replied. "You're in a place called Alterra. We've come to take you home."

"We? What kind of world are we going back to?" Damien cried.

"Yeah, this one was bad enough, but you and him working together seems way worse," Michael agreed.

Marcus rolled his eyes.

"The one you are used to," Celine answered, "Your bodies are still there. But they are dying. We came to retrieve you. We must take you back across the in-between to our world to revive you. To save you."

Michael approached Damien, standing next to him. "Yeah, I'm not buying it. A world where you're working with him? Why?"

"Your family always exhibits such deep depths of gratitude, Celine," Marcus commented.

Celine shot him a glance. "Marcus was the only one I knew who had experience traveling to Alterra. I asked him for help."

"You asked *him* for help?" Damien questioned, his arms flailing toward Marcus.

"You are dying, D. Millie can't help you. No one can help. Marcus was the only one who could help me save you."

Damien eyed them, suspicion filling him. "It's me, D. Ask me anything!"

"How did we meet?" Michael fired at her.

"I ran into you when I was Josie at a coffee shop, The Burnt Bean, on Third Street. Right down from your office. I literally ran into you, spilled my coffee all over you. You told me I could make it up to you by going to dinner with you."

Michael and Damien glanced at each other. "When did you marry Gray?" Damien inquired.

"1789," Celine answered.

"What's your mom's name? Your adopted mom, my aunt?" Damien questioned.

"Monica," Celine responded.

Damien glanced to Michael, nodding his head. "It's her."

Celine breathed a sigh of relief. Now they could begin the journey home. The nightmare was coming to a close. Soon, Damien would be safe back in their world. She opened her mouth to speak, but a knock sounded at the door.

"Damien?" a familiar voice with a British accent called through the door. "May I come in?"

"Shoot!" Damien exclaimed. "It's the other Celine! Should she see you?"

"Probably not," Marcus admitted.

"She definitely shouldn't see him," Michael added, pointing to Marcus.

"Ah," Damien glanced around before suggesting, "hide in the bathroom, I guess?"

"Okay," Celine answered, retreating with Marcus to the bathroom and pulling the door almost closed. She left a slit open to peer through.

* * *

PRESENT DAY, Bucksville, Original Timeline

Gray paced the floor, glancing at Celine's limp form in the chair. Her hand clutched Marcus's hand. Alexander sat in the armchair across the room. Millie flitted in and out, checking vital signs on everyone in Alterra.

"Any change?" Gray inquired as she did her latest check of Damien's vitals.

"None. Which is a good thing. They are no worse."

"I hope Celine finds him in time," Gray commented. "She will never forgive herself if he dies."

In an instant, the monitors in the room indicated abnormal activity. Gray stopped pacing, staring at them then Millie. "What is it? What's happening?"

"A stimulus, it seems," Millie replied. "Breathing, heart rate, brain activity are all elevated. I'll confirm it with Michael." She disappeared from the room, when she returned, Gray hovered over Celine. "Michael is the same. What are you doing, Gray?"

Gray held the red vial in his hand. "Something is wrong."

"Wait, cousin," Alexander answered, standing and approaching Gray. "Look, Northcott is experiencing the same."

Millie checked both Celine and Marcus. "They are exhibiting similar symptoms to Damien and Michael. Elevated heart rate and breathing."

"Perhaps they've found one another," Alexander suggested.

"I hope so," Gray responded. "I cannot wait for this to be over."

* * *

PRESENT DAY, BUCKSVILLE, ALTERRA

"Curious?" Marcus inquired, glancing down at Celine as they hid behind the bathroom door.

"A little," she answered, shrugging.

"Come in!" Damien called.

Celine peered through the crack in the door as a figure

entered the room. She recognized herself, although it was bizarre to see herself in the third person.

"Is everything all right?" the other Celine asked. "I heard shouting."

Damien nodded. "Yep," he answered, his voice an octave higher than normal. "Just fine. Just a bad dream. Really bad dream, terrible, the kind that you wake up screaming from. Well, you know that because you heard it, so, we're all good here. Everything is all good."

"Wow," Celine whispered to Marcus. "Good thing she doesn't know him better. She'd be able to tell he was lying in a heartbeat."

"He is rather bad at it, isn't he?"

Celine glanced at him. "Some people have trouble being evil and dishonest."

He made a face at her, and they returned their attention to the events in the bedroom.

"Oh, I'm sorry to hear that. No doubt what you've been through has been traumatic. It isn't any wonder that you'd have nightmares."

"Everything all right in here?" Gray asked, entering the room.

Marcus grumbled, hidden behind the door. Celine rolled her eyes at him.

"Damien had a nightmare," Celine informed him.

"I'm okay now. Michael and I were just chatting for a few minutes before I went back to sleep."

Celine smiled at him. "Good night, then. I hope you sleep well."

"Thanks, good night."

They all said their goodnights and Celine and Gray left the room.

Celine eased the door open, glancing around to ensure the coast was clear before hurrying into the room. "Okay. Let's get going. We don't have any time to waste!"

Celine reached for Damien's hand, but he pulled back.

"Wait, wait," he protested.

"What?" she questioned.

"I feel bad. Like we should leave a note or something for this Celine."

"All right," Celine agreed, "but hurry."

Damien grabbed a piece of paper from the side table in the room and a pen. He spoke aloud as he wrote. "Dear Celine," he said as he scrawled it on the paper. He stopped dead. "Wait, now what? Do I just say 'turns out we aren't from this time band, we went home?'"

"Put 'We learned we're from another time band and the electric pulse sent us here by accident. We're returning home tonight. Sorry we didn't get to say goodbye, we'll never forget you.' Then sign our names," Michael said.

"Oh, yeah, that's good." Damien scrawled it on the paper then signed their names, leaving the note on his pillow. "Okay, that should do it. Okay, ready. Now what?"

Celine stared at Marcus.

"We must find an exit location. There should be one near, they exist everywhere. Come along, we should try the cave near the beach," Marcus said.

"Okay," Celine answered. She grabbed Damien's hand, pulling him along.

"Wait, wait, wait," Damien protested.

"Now what?" Celine queried.

"Just… follow him?" he questioned, motioning toward Marcus.

"Yes, follow him. Do what he says. He's the only one who knows how to do this."

Damien frowned, but acquiesced. "Okay," he mumbled, a hint of uncertainty in his voice.

Marcus raised his eyebrows. "We could always leave you here."

"No one is leaving anyone here," Celine retorted.

"Yeah, just because we don't like you doesn't mean we don't want to go home. This is just a new sensation for us. You know, trusting you with anything," Damien protested.

Marcus clenched his jaw and shook his head. "It is little wonder why I abhor doing good. I receive nothing but grief for it."

Celine sighed and shook her head. "Oh, Marcus. You'll survive. Now, let's go."

Together, they crept through the halls and out of the house. They navigated to the beach cave.

As they entered, Celine asked, "What are we looking for?"

"An etching, small and subtle. Something like this," he answered, drawing in the sand with a stick.

"And you're sure it's here?" Michael asked, studying the walls.

"No, I'm not certain it's here. I have never been to this Alterra. How would I know where one is located? I suggested this spot since they tend to be near natural structures like this."

"Let's just spread out and search," Celine suggested. After thirty minutes they came up empty.

"It's not here, now what?" Michael demanded of Marcus.

"We search somewhere else."

"And what if it's not there either?" Michael questioned. "Perhaps we continue to try sites until our bodies wither away in the real world?"

"I could kill you here first. It would be much faster," Marcus suggested.

"Probably your plan all along!" Damien exclaimed. "You're really something, you know!"

"Will you all please stop bickering? No one is killing

anyone anywhere in any world. We will find the exit portal location. Let's just move to another location as quickly as possible," Celine suggested. "Perhaps the cave that leads to the beach."

"Fine," Marcus and Michael agreed simultaneously.

"I don't trust him," Damien confided to Celine as they walked to the other cave.

"I know, D. I get it, but we don't have much choice. Marcus is the only one who had any knowledge of Alterra and how to move between the worlds."

"I don't like this at all," Damien added.

"I wasn't thrilled with asking for his help either, but I couldn't let you die. There was no way either of you would have found your way back alone. We had no choice."

"I can't believe Gray agreed to this," Damien said.

"He's no happier than you or Michael. But, again, we had little choice."

They arrived at the cave leading to the beach, ending their conversation. After a thorough search of it, they found nothing. Discouragement filled Celine. She plopped on a large rock as they exited the cave to the beach.

"Now what?" Michael asked.

"Wait," Celine answered, narrowing her eyes as her hand rubbed the cold, wet stone's side. "In our world, there is an etching on the large rock just up the beach. Perhaps that is it!"

"Worth a look," Damien agreed.

They traveled up the beach toward the large stone. Celine circled it before she found what she sought. "There!" she called, pointing. "That's it, right?"

"Indeed. Of course, it would be here," Marcus grumbled.

The etched stone lay at the spot from which Celine returned him to the underworld, following her retrieval of his book.

"Let's dwell on the unfortunate placement another time, Marcus. How do we exit this world?"

"I must open a portal. Once I have, we shall enter it and traverse the in-between back to our world. We left a trail coming here, we'll follow it back."

"Okay," Celine answered, nodding. "Open it."

"Patience, Celine. This is intricate work," Marcus responded.

Celine held up her arms, signaling surrender. Marcus sighed and began his work. He removed chalk from his pocket, tracing the etching in the stone. He ground the rest up and blew it toward the cliff wall at the rear of the beach. It settled over an invisible portal, marking the edges. Marcus stretched his hand out toward the chalk-rimmed portal. He twisted his wrist, grasping and rolling away the invisible barrier closing the portal.

"It is open. Time to go, Celine," Marcus said. He grabbed her hand, tugging her toward the portal.

Celine grasped Damien's hand, pulling him as he grabbed Michael's arm, dragging him with them. They entered the portal, passing from Alterra to the in-between. Blackness surrounded them as the portal closed behind them. Damien shivered as the coldness struck them.

Celine kept a firm grasp on his hand. "Don't let go of my hand, D. And don't let go of Michael."

Damien nodded, tightening his grip on Celine's hand and Michael's arm.

"How far do we have to go?" Damien asked, still shivering.

Michael trembled against the cold as well.

"It didn't take us too long," Celine assured them. "Stay strong, it's almost over."

Marcus continued to navigate them through the blackness. Celine noted the tiny traces of their last trip through the in-between that he followed. After twenty minutes, they approached a shimmering rainbow. Celine figured it was their own time band, given that their trail ended.

"This is it," Marcus confirmed. "As you realize, this will not be comfortable. You may want to warn your friends."

Celine nodded and turned to them. "Okay, this is our time band. We just need to pass through the kaleidoscope and back into our time band. It's not an easy transition through. It will be painful. Whatever you do, do not stop walking until you are through."

Michael and Damien nodded.

"You two go first. We'll come behind you."

Damien shook his head. "No. We're not leaving you here with him. No way."

"Damien, please. We can't go together. You must go first. I won't leave you here."

"Celine, no! He could… abscond with you to another time band and we'll never find you."

Marcus rolled his eyes. "I am not going to abscond with anyone."

"See!" Celine said.

"See what? He's a serial liar. Who just kidnapped you, I might add," Damien countered.

"Even if he did, he gave Gray a concoction to pull me back if anything happens. So, even if that happens, you could get me back!"

"Yeah right, like I believe that," Michael said. "He probably gave Gray something to make sure you disappear forever."

Celine sighed, frustrated. "Even if any of this is the case, it is still safer for me to go last. I can come back from an Alterra realm on my own. You cannot."

Damien and Michael glanced at each other.

"Don't even start. No more arguing. You'll go through the portal first, and that is final."

"But…" Damien began.

"No! No buts." She turned them toward the rainbow wall. "Go!"

Michael and Damien glanced at each other. "Rock, paper, scissors?" Damien asked.

"Sure," Michael answered. "Loser goes through first." They extended their arms, pumping them three times before revealing their choice.

Marcus stared at them, a bizarre expression on his face. "What in the world are they doing?"

"Playing 'Rock, paper, scissors' to figure out who will go first and who will go last." She glanced at him. He continued to wear the confused expression as he stared at them. "It's a game. Like flipping a coin."

"Aw, come on!" Damien exclaimed after losing, his scissors broken by Michael's rock.

"Good luck, buddy," Michael answered, clapping him on his back. "See you on the flip side."

Damien nodded to him. "See you in the real world." He turned to Celine, "See you in a minute, right?"

Celine nodded to him. "See you soon, D."

Damien turned toward the shimmering rainbow barrier. He took a deep breath, swallowing hard. He lifted his foot, taking his first step toward his world.

CHAPTER 33

illie leapt from her seat across the room.

"What's wrong?" Gray questioned.

"Something is happening," Millie answered. She raced to the monitors near Damien, reading them. "His heart rate is spiking as though he's experiencing severe pain. But his temperature has raised slightly."

Moments later, Alexander entered. "Millie, something is happening with Michael."

"Is it his heart rate?"

"Yes," Alexander confirmed. "It's spiking."

"So is Damien's. Let me check Michael's temperature." Millie disappeared from the room with Alexander. She returned moments later.

"Well?" Gray asked.

"Michael's temperature is rising, too."

"What does that mean?" Gray asked.

"Could they be returning?" Alexander suggested.

"What about Celine and Marcus?" Gray questioned.

Millie checked their vitals. "No change in either of them."

"Something's wrong," Gray replied.

"We don't know that," Alexander answered. "She would have sent Michael and Damien first. She'd never have left either of them with Marcus."

"No, she wouldn't," Gray agreed, tightening his grip on the red vial. "Even if it meant her own demise, she wouldn't have." He glanced at the vial.

Alexander noticed his gaze. "Don't, Gray. We don't possess any information about the contents of that vial, nor can we trust it does what Northcott says it does. Give her time."

Gray shook his head, disagreeing, but relented. "Fine, but if there is even the slightest indication that she is in distress, no one will stop me from using this."

Gray paced the room while Millie kept a close watch on the monitors, scurrying between both rooms to continue to monitor both men. Within fifteen minutes, nothing had changed except the temperatures of Michael and Damien, both continuing to rise.

Gray rested his eyes on Celine, still motionless in her chair. She showed no signs of return, no increased heart rate or rising temperature. His fingers tightened on the vial containing the red liquid.

Twenty more minutes passed. The tension in the room grew thick. Finally, Damien began to groan.

"Damien?" Gray questioned, racing to his bedside. "Damien, can you hear us?"

"Easy, Gray," Millie cautioned. "He is becoming more responsive. I'd say he's returning to us but let his body do it on its own time."

Gray glanced across the room. "What about Celine? There's no change in her. Something is wrong. She can't still be there. There's no reason for her to be. She should be returning, too."

"I'm beginning to agree that something is off," Alexander chimed in. "Michael's condition changed moments after Damien's. If it indicates their return, most likely, Celine followed after them, or should have. But, perhaps, we are misinterpreting the situation."

Gray stared at the red vial in his hand. "I have to use it."

"Gray, no. What if they are not returning? If you pull Celine back before she's achieved her goal of rescuing Damien and Michael, it could be disastrous!" Alexander cautioned.

"Both Michael and Damien appear to be improving. It stands to reason they are returning. Then, Celine should be, too. She's not because something is wrong."

"Gray, we have no clue either of those are the case. Nor do we have any idea what's in that vial!" Alexander warned.

Gray weighed the options. "We may have no choice. If we allow Celine to slip away, we may lose her for good. And if she disappears, we've doomed Michael and Damien, as well." He uncorked the top, approaching Celine.

"Gray, wait," Alexander advised, barring Gray from accessing Celine's limp form. "What if it doesn't draw her back?"

Gray glanced between Alexander and Celine. "What's the difference? She's not coming back now as it is." He pushed past Alexander's arm. He yanked Celine's hand from Marcus's, tilted her head back and poured the red liquid down her throat.

Alexander approached, and they waited with bated breath for her to recover.

Across the room, Damien groaned again, thrashing his head back and forth on the pillow. Without warning, Celine gasped, shooting upright in her seat. Her eyes opened, and she choked to catch her breath.

"Celine!" Gray shouted, racing to her side. "Celine, are you alright?" He cupped her face in his hands, staring into her eyes.

Celine caught her breath. "Yes. I'm fine. Damien?"

"Not awake yet, but he has been becoming more responsive," Millie reported. "And his body temperature is rising, as is Michael's."

"He should have been back before me," Celine answered, her brow furrowing with concern. She leapt from the chair, rushing to his side. She took his hand in hers. "D? D, come back!"

Marcus gasped, awakening a moment later. He glanced around the room as he caught his breath. "Isn't anyone going to welcome me back?"

"No," Gray answered, grabbing him by the collar. "I had to give Celine the red vial to revive her, and neither Damien nor Michael are back yet. What have you done? What the hell are you trying to pull, Northcott?"

Marcus pushed Gray away, slamming him against the far wall. "I have done nothing. The red vial worked as intended, did it not? I have no idea why the others haven't awoken."

Gray leapt to his feet, ready to attack. "Tell me why you and Celine remained unresponsive when Michael and Damien were already in the process of returning?"

"Stop it!" Celine shouted.

"Yes, please stop," Mille answered. "This may be for the best."

"For the best?" Celine queried.

"Yes. Their temperatures are rising, but their heart rates are high, and they are still below their normal body temperature. This may be their bodies' way of protecting them. Like a coma. They may only awaken once their bodies have normalized."

Celine nodded as she bit her lower lip.

Gray straightened his blazer, shooting a menacing glance at Marcus as he approached Celine, placing his hands on her shoulders. "Let's hope Millie is correct." He turned to Marcus. "Your work is finished here. You should leave."

"I'd prefer to stay to see my work through until the end," Marcus countered.

Gray began to answer, but Celine responded first. "Let him stay. In case we need him," she murmured, her eyes remaining fixed on Damien.

Marcus stalked to the armchair, taking a seat as he smirked at Gray.

Celine squeezed Damien's hand. "Come on, D," she whispered to him. "Wake up."

They spent another twenty minutes on edge before Damien began to groan.

Celine gasped, inching closer to him. "D? Damien?"

He continued to moan, moving his head back and forth on the pillow. Within a few moments, he opened his eyes.

"Damien?" Celine questioned. "Can you hear me?"

He glanced around the room, focusing on Celine.

"Hey," he breathed, his voice soft and shaky.

"Hey," Celine answered, a smile crossing her face as tears formed in her eyes.

"I had the weirdest dream," Damien muttered.

"I'll bet you did," Celine answered.

Damien shivered under his blanket. "Is it cold in here or is it me?"

"It's you," Celine assured him. "Your body temperature dropped. We'll get you another blanket."

Alexander burst through the door. "Michael is awake."

"I'll go to him," Millie answered, following Alexander to Michael's room.

"Michael?" Damien questioned, trying to sit up.

"It's all right, D," Celine assured him. "Rest. It's fine. You need to recuperate."

"But…" Damien argued, glancing around. His eyes grew wide. He gasped, stuttering and pointing toward Marcus. "Ah… Ah… Ah… bad guy… him… Duke… there…"

Marcus rolled his eyes at him.

"Yes, D. We know he's there. It's all right. Don't panic."

"But… but…" Damien stammered.

"D, it's fine. He's here because he helped us. You and Michael were trapped in Alterra, an alternate reality. We needed to retrieve you from there. Marcus helped us."

"Helped? Him?" Damien exclaimed.

"Yes, Marcus helped us," Celine responded. "Relax, D. Everything is all right."

Damien glanced around, staring at Marcus for a while, a frown on his face. "Everything is all right? You sure? Like everything is normal, right? You married Gray in the 1700s and you were Josie and everything, right?"

Celine smiled, patting his hand. "Yes. Yes, you're back in normal time. I married Gray after you helped me that night in Martinique. I was Josie, you're my cousin. My adopted mom's name is Monica. Convinced?"

Damien laid his head back on the pillow. "Just making sure." He shot a glance toward Marcus.

"Do you mind if I go check on Michael for a moment?"

"No. In fact, I'd prefer you did then let me know how he is."

"Okay," Celine agreed, kissing his forehead. "Be right back."

Celine exited the room, heading next door to Michael's room. Alexander greeted her as she entered.

"Hey," she said to Michael. "How are you feeling?"

"A little fuzzy. Like I was dreaming. Something tells me from everyone's reaction, I wasn't just experiencing a long nap with a creepy nightmare."

Celine shook her head. "No such luck, sorry."

Michael stared at the ceiling for a moment. "How's Damien? Were we really in another time band?"

"Yep," Celine assured him. "That pulse sent both you and Damien all the way to Alterra, an alternate time band. Damien's doing okay, he's awake and recovering."

"Wow," Michael replied, shaking his head in disbelief. "I'm glad we're back. I hated it there."

Celine chuckled. "Things were very different, huh?"

"Very," Michael assured her. "I'm glad to be home."

Celine squeezed his hand "And we're glad to have you back."

They sat for another moment before Celine excused herself to return to Damien's room.

"Hey, tell him I said hi."

"Will do," Celine promised as she returned to Damien's room.

"Well?" Damien inquired as she entered the room.

"He's okay," Celine answered, climbing onto the bed with Damien and covering him with another blanket. "He was concerned about you. He has a hazy memory, too."

"Yeah, about that," Damien responded. "It's coming back to me. It wasn't a dream, was it?"

"No," she responded with a shake of her head. "Sorry, D. That was all real."

"And it was some kind of alternate reality?"

Celine nodded her head. "Yes. It was a different time band, one where things happened differently than they did here. Different choices were made, different events were set in motion."

Damien nodded as he spoke. "You aren't kidding."

"Do you remember everything that happened?" Celine asked.

Damien nodded and glanced at her. "Yeah, yep."

"We don't have to talk about it," Celine assured him.

"It's okay. I just… it was really weird. You were so weird, nothing like you. I'm so glad to be home and back with the real you," he replied, reaching out to embrace her.

Celine pulled him into her arms, hugging him tight. "It's okay, D. You're home now."

They sat for a few more minutes together, Celine held Damien's hand.

"Well, it appears all is well," Gray said. "Which means you can leave." He pointed to Marcus.

Marcus stood with a sigh. "Why, thank you, Marcus, for saving the lives of my loved ones. I am so grateful for your help."

Celine kissed Damien's cheek and climbed off the bed. "I'll be right back, D. Try to get some rest."

She walked toward Marcus. "Come on. I'll walk you out."

She squeezed Gray's arm. "Stay with Damien, please."

"Celine…" Gray began.

"Gray, please," she answered.

He kissed her forehead, shooting a glare at Marcus. "All right. Don't be too long."

"I won't be," she promised.

Celine and Marcus slipped from the room, navigating through the halls and downstairs to the foyer.

"Well, I suppose I am once again persona non grata in these halls now that my services are no longer required," Marcus mentioned as they approached the door.

Celine gazed at him. "Thank you, Marcus."

He glanced to her. "I'll never understand what it is you see in these individuals, Celine. They are most irritating."

She took his hand. "I mean it. Thank you. You saved their lives. And that means a lot to me. I appreciate your help. I will never forget it."

He didn't speak for a moment. "Well, it did remove me from that dreadful Shadow World, so I suppose it was to my advantage. Looks like I am free to roam the Earth again."

Celine held back rolling her eyes at his response. "I suppose this is as good a time as any to tell you."

"To tell me what?" Marcus inquired.

"You aren't exactly free."

He furrowed his brow, turning to face her. "What do you mean?"

"When I spoke with the adjudicator and it agreed to allow you to return to Earth…" Celine paused.

"Yes?" Marcus prompted.

"It gave me the marker for your soul." Celine held up the black stone representing her possession of his soul.

"It *what*?" Marcus exclaimed, reaching for the stone. "Give it to me!"

Celine pulled it back. "No, Marcus. While I appreciate what you've done, I must do everything I can to protect my family. Especially after your performance in the in-between. That includes keeping control of your soul for as long as I can."

Marcus set his jaw. "This is unwise, Celine."

"We'll revisit it when the adjudicator returns, until then, it's mine."

He huffed at her. "We'll see about that, Celine." He turned on his heel, exiting the house with a slam of the door.

Celine sighed, watching him disappear down the path. She shook her head, climbing the stairs.

She pushed into Damien's room.

"Is he gone?" Gray asked the moment she entered the room.

"Yes, he's gone."

"For now," Gray griped. "I'm sure he'll be back to cause trouble."

Celine climbed onto Damien's bed, taking his hand in hers again. "Well, perhaps not."

"You give him too much credit, Celine. The man is a menace."

"That might be, but there is something I didn't tell you before that might hold him off for just a little bit."

"What's that?" Gray asked.

"Yeah, what is it?" Damien inquired, interested in the conversation.

"When I freed him from Shadow World, I convinced the adjudicator to give me control of his soul."

Gray's eyes went wide. "You got it to do what? You're kidding?"

Celine brandished the black soul chip. "Nope."

Gray hurried to her side, kissing her. "Celine, you're a genius."

She grinned at him. "He was not happy when he found out."

"You told him?" Gray inquired.

"I did. I warned him to keep his cool and not to do anything destructive."

"So, this means you..." Damien began, unsure where to go.

"Have some control over him. Not lots of control but enough to barter with if need be," Celine responded.

"That's perfect, Celine. It buys us some time."

"Buys us some time?" Damien asked.

"Yes," Gray answered. "It buys us some time to figure out what we're going to do about getting rid of Marcus Northcott."

Celine laid on the bed, monitoring Damien's vital signs. Hours after he'd awoken, returned from Alterra, she still counted his heartbeats and tracked his chest rising and falling. Asleep on his back, she feared him slipping back into another realm, although she realized this was an impossibility.

She slipped her hand around his, squeezing it tight. It was warm to the touch, a sign he remained in this reality. As she scrutinized his vitals, her mind drifted to her encounter with Marcus in the in-between, following Michael and Damien's departure through the shimmering rainbow that marked the edge of their world.

She had stepped forward to return to their reality when he grabbed her arm, dragging her away from the barrier.

"Celine, wait," he uttered, pulling her further.

She wiggled her arm, trying to free herself. "Marcus! What are you doing?"

"Stopping you from making the biggest mistake of your life," he countered.

"What? Are you crazy?"

"No. Celine, you must not return to that world." He reached for her, trying to grab hold of her arm again.

She evaded his grasp and shook her head at him. "What? Of course, I need to return. What are you saying?"

"Celine, I cannot allow you to do this," Marcus answered.

"Gray was right," Celine cried. "I can't trust you! You never stop. Never stop trying to seize any opportunity to get the upper hand! No, Marcus, I will to return to my world. You cannot stop me, and you'd be unwise to begin a battle in the in-between. Too much can go wrong."

"Celine, I'm warning you…" he began.

She stepped past him toward the rainbow barrier, then halted as a shiver passed over her. She swallowed, recovering from the tremor that wracked her body.

"Damn it," Marcus swore behind her. "I knew I shouldn't have given Buckley that concoction to restore you."

She glanced to him as her body was pulled toward the world's edge.

"Oh, Marcus." She shook her head at him, disappointed.

* * *

CELINE'S MIND replayed the conversation over in her head. She chose not to share it with Gray yet. Her reasoning was twofold. First, she did not want to worry him, and second, she hoped to learn something from her musings about it.

Something was different, odd about it. While Marcus always considered her decision to spend her life with the Buckleys a mistake, this exchange was different. There was something more to his statements, something portentous. His tone and demeanor were uncharacteristic of his typical behavior. He seemed perturbed, bothered.

In addition, the red vial he provided Gray did exactly what he disclosed it would, returned her to this world. If he planned to abduct her from the in-between, he'd never have left that ace with Gray. Something didn't make sense about the conversation, Celine reflected, as she studied it. If impeding her return was not his plan, why did he attempt it? Marcus rarely reacted impulsively. What was he hoping to achieve?

Celine found no answers, despite searching the farthest reaches of her mind. As she turned back toward Damien, focusing on the rise and fall of his chest again, one question burned through her mind. *What was the meaning of Marcus' ominous warning?*

Continue the series with *Trouble*, Book 4 in the Shadow Slayers Series.

A NOTE FROM THE AUTHOR

Dear Reader,

Thank you for reading this book! *Gone* was written during the height of the pandemic in 28 days. The story flowed onto the page while we were in lockdown.

I hope you enjoyed reading this book as much as I did writing it! If you loved it, please consider leaving a review and help get the book into the hands of other interested readers.

Shadow Slayers Book 4, *Trouble*, is now available! Keep reading for a sneak peak of *Trouble*!

If you'd like to stay up to date with all my news, be the first to find out about new releases first, sales and get free offers, join the Nellie H. Steele's Mystery Readers' Group! Or sign up for my newsletter now!

All the best, Nellie

TROUBLE SYNOPSIS

A poisoned rose. Life-altering secrets. Can the Slayers overcome insurmountable odds?

Nearly two months after Celine returned from Alterra, carrying with her the ominous warning from archnemesis Marcus Northcott, she is still trying to determine why returning to her world is the "biggest mistake of her life." Living through the most peaceful time she's ever known, Celine struggles to find the meaning behind the threat.

That is until her life turns upside-down. An unforeseen visit from her adopted mother sends her life and the lives of those around her spiraling. As they struggle to hide the truth, Celine begins to experience strange symptoms. Headaches, numb, tingly hands and time losses plague her.

The Slayers search for the cause, but what they find may spell more trouble than they can handle. Will the source of Celine's odd ailment bring about the end for at least one of the Slayers? Will Celine's efforts only end in disastrous effects for her family? If it does, will she be able to undo the wrong she unknowingly caused and restore balance to the already fragile world?

Find out in the fourth installment of the Shadow Slayers supernatural suspense series!

Click here and grab your copy today!

TROUBLE EXCERPT

$\mathcal{C}$eline strolled along the path that clung to the cliff's edge as she approached the seaside house. She stared at it, hovering on the edge of the woods that sheltered her from its sight. She'd visited Marcus shortly after her return from Alterra. She'd demanded to know the meaning of his warning. He'd denied there was any, claiming he only attempted to persuade her to his side as he'd done time and time again throughout the centuries.

Celine did not believe him. But in the days immediately following the revelation that she held his soul marker, she didn't expect him to be forthcoming. Perhaps time had cooled his temper. She would soon find out.

Celine stalked toward the house and climbed the steps leading to the covered porch. She pounded against the door until a dark-skinned man opened it. "Hello, Miss Celine," he said in his South African accent.

"I need to see him," Celine answered.

Dembe, Marcus's manservant and ally, motioned for her to enter the foyer. "He is in the sitting room, Miss Celine."

"Thank you, Dembe," Celine answered with a nod before she proceeded through the open archway.

"Ah, Celine," Marcus said from the armchair across the room. "Back again?"

Celine set her jaw as she eyed him.

"I don't suppose you've come to return my soul marker, by any chance?" he continued before sipping his brandy.

She narrowed her eyes. "No, Marcus."

"Hmm," Marcus mumbled as he swallowed the amber liquid before standing to retrieve another glass. "Too bad. Though one can always hope. Brandy, dear?"

"No, Marcus, I am not here for a drink or a pleasant chat."

Marcus twisted to offer her a smirk. "Another pity, though I cannot say I expected one."

"You know why I'm here."

He replaced the stopper on the glass decanter and took another sip of brandy. "No doubt to accuse me of something."

"You say that as though you're innocent."

He shrugged as he settled back in his chair. "If the shoe fits, as they say."

Celine narrowed her eyes further. "The shoe isn't even your style, Marcus, let alone size."

He rolled his eyes at her. "If you've come for another argument, I decline to participate. Celine, I have had quite enough of this."

"You're just miffed because I still hold your soul marker," she said with a sly smile.

He frowned at her. "What is it you want, Celine?"

"To know why you insisted it was a mistake for me to return to this time band."

"I've already told you though you refuse to listen."

"Yes, yes, I know your story. It was merely a ploy to throw

me off balance. A carefully crafted move in yet another attempt to best me."

Marcus bowed his head to her. "My dear, you have answered your own question."

"I don't believe you," Celine snapped.

"Why? Surely those dimwitted companions you cling to so vehemently concur."

"It's what I think that matters," Celine answered as she stalked to the window. She crossed her arms and stared at the darkening skies.

"Ohhhh," Marcus sang. "I didn't realize you hadn't told them. What an interesting development."

"I didn't say that," Celine said as she spun to face him.

He smirked at her. "You didn't have to, my dear."

Celine set her jaw. "Perhaps you were bluffing. Nothing more than a desperate attempt to win a losing battle."

Marcus offered her an unimpressed glance but gave nothing more away. "Only time will tell, dear Celine."

"So far time has suggested nothing portentous."

"Then why return to question me?"

Celine set her jaw, glowering at him.

"And why have you not confided in your beloved Grayson? Or dear Damien? Or even faithful Alexander? Oh, Celine, it appears your dark side is showing."

WANT TO READ MORE? Find out if Celine determined the meaning of Marcus's warning in *Trouble*! Click here to read!

OTHER SERIES BY NELLIE H. STEELE

Cozy Mystery Series

Cate Kensie Mysteries
Lily & Cassie by the Sea Mysteries
Pearl Party Mysteries
Middle Age is Murder Cozy Mysteries

Supernatural Suspense/Urban Fantasy

Shadow Slayers Stories
Duchess of Blackmoore Mysteries

Adventure

Maggie Edwards Adventures
Clif & Ri on the Sea

www.ingramcontent.com/pod-product-compliance
Lightning Source LLC
Chambersburg PA
CBHW070236200726
48293CB00005B/1641